THE FRIDGULARITY

BY MARK A. RAYNER

MONKEYJOY PRESS - CANADA

markarayner.com

First Paperback Edition – Monkeyjoy Press
Cover Illustration and Design by Brian Despain
Book Design by M. Tundra

monkeyjoypress.ca
despainart.com

ISBN 978-1-927590-00-3

This manuscript is set in Garamond, chosen for its
elegance, readability, and sanity. The headers are in Wunderbar,
and we're sorry for that.

ALSO BY MARK A. RAYNER

The Amadeus Net

Marvellous Hairy

Pirate Therapy and Other Cures

"Our difficulty is that we have become autistic. We no longer listen to what the Earth, its landscape, its atmospheric phenomena and all its living forms, its mountains and valleys, the rain, the wind, and all the flora and fauna of the planet are telling us."

~Thomas Berry

"We are on the edge of change comparable to the rise of human life on Earth. The precise cause of this change is the imminent creation by technology of entities with greater than human intelligence. Science may achieve this breakthrough by several means ..."

~Vernor Vinge

"A computer lets you make more mistakes faster than any invention in human history — with the possible exceptions of handguns and tequila."

~Mitch Ratcliffe

THE BIG CRASH

Little lamb, who made thee?
Dost though know who made thee ...

1.

Blake Given became a demigod while he looked for a packet of mayonnaise.

He could just have as easily been looking for a bottle of catsup, but during his first year of university, he'd seen *Pulp Fiction* and was astonished to learn the Dutch ate their fries with mayonnaise. It was gross. Outrageous. Incredibly ... permissive. Nevertheless, it was his first year of university, and he reinvented himself, so he'd tried it, and he liked it. In the intervening years, mayonnaise had become his condiment of choice

Unfortunately, the squeeze bottle was empty, so he was chest-deep in his fridge, searching for one of the packets of mayonnaise he'd saved from a fast food delivery the week before.

Blake did not see the screen on his fridge flicker to life and display the cryptic text:

HIM. THAT HUMAN PERSON.

Yes, Blake had a web-enabled fridge.

It was a stylish fridge. One of those ultra-cool, brushed stainless steel numbers that every yuppie in his neighborhood either owned or coveted like Old Testament perverts coveted their neighbor's donkeys. Blake had purchased it when he bought the house, along with the brushed steel stove and microwave, convinced that sexy kitchen appliances would get him more interested in cooking. The fridge had its own grease-resistant touch screen and dedicated Internet connection, plus a generous freezer that allowed him to stock more frozen foods. The idea behind this was so he didn't order out as much.

In terms of cooking these frozen delights, the microwave got most of the action, though occasionally Blake threw the stove a bone and baked something in its convection oven, the way the pretty girls in junior high school would occasionally

1

dance with the nerds when asked, just to keep their interest and hopes alive, thus ensuring the continued plumping of their own egos.

The screen and web browser embedded in the freezer door was virtually pointless. Theoretically, the fridge was designed to order food when Blake was out of it, but in fact, the system broke down on several fronts: the little radio frequency identification tags that were supposedly going to be embedded in every single food item were never embedded in every single food item because nobody wanted to pay extra for having little radio tags embedded in their milk, broccoli and jars of grape jelly. Some items did have the little radio tags, but very few consumers were inclined to scan the tags in the little tag scanner just below the touch screen and tell their fridge how quickly it would be consumed or likely to be consumed, or even scan the damn thing afterwards and indicate it was empty or finished. Blake had heard one horror story about a woman who had an automated fridge going away on vacation, after leaving a bottle of catsup on the counter. The fridge's hyper-alert tomato condiment sensors discovered the lack of catsup, or ketchup as the fridge software knew it, and sent an alert out to groceries.com; unfortunately, this helpful system did not allow enough time for the ketchup to be delivered, and thus the fridge ordered another bottle, and then another, and another, eventually ordering a whole crate's worth before the positive feedback loop could be escaped. The inventory and ordering software was written by the same maniac who invented the pop-up web ad.

In the final analysis, it was all just a bit too much information to manage. On the plus side, the web-enabled fridge did allow Blake to check his Facebook, Tumblr, and Twitter accounts while he ate Cheerios in his underwear.

But at this moment, Blake was still fully dressed, having returned from the pub jonesing for french fries and, yes, the condiment known to Blake's small circle of friends as "Quentin's."

The fries were already in process, though to call them fries was to stretch the meaning of the word. The good people of *McGain's* (so named by Blake's good friend Dr. Maximilian Tundra because most of their foods were designed to help one gain weight), produced a chunk of potato that, lovingly heated, would taste somewhat like french fries, though only if accompanied by enough Quentin's.

The stove glowed happily in the corner of Blake's kitchen. It was one of those rare occasions, when if asked, the sexy oven would have said how nice it was to be working, how good it was to be appreciated, and how wonderful it was to have food intercourse with Blake. Of course, an oven can't talk, nor understand. That would just be silly.

The fridge, however, was quite capable of understanding. Blake dove into the fridge, looking for more mayo.

The screen flashed again, a blue background with plain white lettering superimposed:

THE HUMAN PERSON. IT IS SEARCHING. FOR MEANING?

"Sweet!" Blake had found the other packet. Just then, the orgasmic stove chimed that it was ready. *So* ready.

HUMAN PERSON, the screen flashed as Blake closed the door and moved to the stove to get his *McGain's* Instant Fries, which are actually cooked in an agonizing 25 minutes, not instantly. He plated them expertly, as though he'd spent some time working in a restaurant, and emptied the contents of his Quentin's packets on the side of the plate next to the fries. The pitiful pile would have to do. He hummed happily as he walked into the living room, where he would soon have intercourse (in a purely platonic sense) with his flat screen TV.

WAIT, the screen on his fridge blinked.

But Blake could not see the plea and the screen dissolved into static and pixels, the moment having passed. If only he'd wanted to check something on the web, then Blake might not have become a demigod, but he'd checked his iPhone earlier that night, and his need for social media was sated, though not his need for the decades-old televisual feast of *Magnum, PI* he had on DVD.

The fridge was not nearly so replete.

The next morning, Blake was at the ad firm where he worked as a web developer.

He'd spent most of the first hour wasting time, alternating between reading one of the hundreds of blog feeds he regularly checked, and watching Daphne, one of the firm's up-and-coming account reps.

She was known for her ability to work well with clients no matter their sex, politics, religion or attitude towards personal grooming. Daphne was conventionally pretty in a brunette kind of way, with dark brown eyes, darling eyelashes and a slim, athletic figure that she decked out in the latest fashions. Women would have hated her if she wasn't so adept at advocating for the other women in the office, while never intimidating or threatening the men. She knew how to flirt with both sexes, though she only did so with men when there were no women present. Daphne was kind, friendly, and flawlessly polite.

Blake loved her, though they'd never moved past the point of nodding hello or remarking about how lovely the weather was.

Daphne spent the first hour of work — at least the portion Blake had observed because she had clearly been there some time before he arrived — on the phone, no doubt bringing in new business for McClinchey, Hill & Grandfig and keeping its existing customers happy.

Blake looked down as Daphne finished her phone call and looked up. It was then he noticed all the characters on his computer screen moving, like the letters of the alphabet executed some kind of crazed, drug-induced square dance. The characters do-si-doed and twirled, allemande left, allemande right, all in counts of 64 and 128.

He checked his laptop, and within a couple of minutes, Blake determined that it was not his desktop computer at fault, nor his browser, nor his screen. Both computers were acting funny. He prairie-dogged over the top of his cubicle and asked Lyca, who sat in the padded prole pen next to Blake's, if she had the same problem.

"Uh, sorry, I've been reading, let me check," Lyca said, without standing up.

Blake listened to the click of Lyca's mouse, the telltale peck of her keyboard, normally background white noise, and waited anxiously.

"This is freaky," Lyca said, confirming that it was not just him who was, indeed, perturbed by what was happening.

"Well, at least I'm not having a stroke," Blake said. "It must be some kind of virus attacking the network."

"Freaky," Lyca repeated, confirming her diagnosis and finally deigning to stand up. She was tall and thin and wearing trendy glasses, without which her identity as a self-described "lesbrarian" would have immediately crumbled. She had a vaguely feline aloofness to her, yet she could be fiercely loyal to her friends, of which she had only a few. Blake was lucky to be one of them, and he knew it.

Blake and Lyca were both brutally underpaid drones at McClinchey, Hill & Grandfig. Lyca was the firm's in-house librarian/researcher/digital curator, and overworked copy editor for their quasi-literate copywriters. According to the HR Department, Blake and Lyca were not in the "creative" class. They had been relegated to the main floor, far away from the grooviness of the third floor, where the artists thought artistic thoughts, where they made glorious pictures, and copywriters wrote text that could make consumers weep with joy, wail with laughter, gnash their teeth in envy — and buy soap.

But neither Blake nor Lyca were bitter.

Blake said, "Let's see what everyone's doing about it."

Lyca squinted at him and pursed her lips; they were thin but eminently kissable, no matter your gender preference, Blake often reflected. "I've got lots to read here, why don't you let me know when you've figured out a fix."

"Okay then," Blake said, hitching up his jeans, a nervous habit more than a necessary action. Blake had a broad, stocky body that was mostly muscle. His hair flared above his head in an unruly dirty blond aura, and his blue eyes sparked with agitation. "I'll figure it out. We won't be able to get anything done until we do, I guess."

"I'm reading, so I'm fine. Happy even."

Blake arched an eyebrow. Lyca could not possibly see him, but she knew him well enough to add, "Okay. Contented. I'm contented for now."

"That I believe." Blake smiled and left the cubicle to see what the others were making of the virus. It had to be a virus, or perhaps some kind of worm, if it affected the network.

Then Blake had an inspiration and switched off the WiFi on his iPhone. It worked! None of the web-based applications did, but he could still dial. He called Dr. Maximilian Tundra who was a psychiatrist-in-training.

"Blakey," Dr. Tundra said. "What's up?"

"All of our computers are going haywire. Have you got the same problem?"

"Uh, everything seems to be fine. Look, I'm kind of busy—"

"Sorry, I'm sure it's crazy." He paused, waiting for Max's

usual rejoinder, but did not get any. "I thought I'd see what it was like at the hospital." The good doctor was a resident at St. Dymphna's, in the psych wing, where orderlies sometimes mistook him for a patient.

"Yeah. It's — *damn* — crazy."

"What's that sound?"

"Oh, I'm just previewing some — *shit* — sorry, I'm, uh …"

"Well, I can see you're busy."

"Yes! Say, how about a drink at Augustine's later? Seven? I've got big news."

Blake liked the sound of that. Of late, he'd been living vicariously through Dr. T, and big news, even if it wasn't his, was exciting. Blake agreed and hung up.

Everyone else was milling around the office — the proles had moved into the cubicles of the super-proles, the most popular ad monkeys in the firm — and those with doors had either closed their much-envied portals or were deigning to fraternize with their inferiors. A carnival atmosphere suffused the building as everyone enjoyed an unforeseen break. Some of the account executives had gathered in the presentation room, where there was an expensive plasma TV set, cable HD and equipment for telemeetings. Blake found himself drawn towards it, not because of the TV, but because he saw Daphne was there.

He hovered at the entrance of the presentation room. Daphne sat next to Barry Onderson, Head of Accounting, and the most pungent man in the firm, who smelled like he bathed in cabbage that had been half-digested by goats fed on a steady diet of garlic, onions and pure evil. Blake was entranced by how well Daphne fought her gag reflex.

The news was on, and the hyper-blond talking head on it said that everyone in the world was experiencing the same phenomenon. Every computer monitor was malfunctioning, displaying the virtual equivalent of Escher paintings in pixels instead of their expected content.

Then, without warning, the same behavior started happening on the plasma TV screen.

First, it corrupted the scroll running on the bottom of the page. All the characters started to squirm and morph as though they were part of a William S. Burroughs novel. Then they made even less sense. The anchor, Bob Chesterton, started to falter and misread things. Then he stopped speaking a second and tried to say something else. This was even less coherent; it was clear the anchor couldn't read anything coming up on his teleprompter. Of course, it didn't help that Bob Chesterton's IQ was slightly above that of a developmentally challenged rhesus monkey.

Blake thought the anchor's breakdown was actually kind of entertaining, and he snickered. Barry Onderson — or BO as he was known to the low-ranked proles of McClinchey, Hill & Grandfig — turned and glared at him. Daphne was engrossed in the TV, as was everyone else. Blake noticed that all the cameras and mics in the room were on.

The news cut to "experts," who understood something about how the Internet worked, and luckily, these members of the *punditas digiterati* were able to talk without someone feeding words to them. For a moment television returned to its normal inanity. But then their faces got weird.

Most Information Technology (IT) "experts" are pretty strange-looking to start with, but their faces turned into something that might get painted by a tripped-out expressionist, for example, Edvard Munch on acid, when they'd had a really, really, extraordinarily, horrendously non-Euclidean day.

"Freaky," Daphne said.

She said freaky, Blake thought, concurrently falling deeper in love with the unattainable account exec and mentally noting to tell Lyca of her word choice.

These happy thoughts were shattered as the Head of Public Relations, Suzie (imagine a happy face dotting the i), screamed. Actually, to say that she screamed is to understate it. She assaulted the aural cavities of everyone within twenty feet with roughly 1200 decibels of tympanic membrane-raping horror. At first, Blake thought the speaker system in the presentation room was committing some kind of reverberatory suicide — the equivalent in sound of what was happening on the screens — but the source of the piercing cry was clearly the pie-hole of Suzie.

"What?" BO shouted at Suzie, who sat on his left side, the ear of which leaked some blood and a yellowish fluid that Blake sincerely hoped was spinal in nature and not several years of accumulated wax.

"It's over!"

"What?" BO repeated, perhaps because he was now deaf in one ear.

"It's all over! This is a *Sign*."

Suzie, who was some kind of idiot savant when it came to public relations, was also a fundamentalist of some stripe which Blake could not remember — Cretins for Christ? Retards of the Rapture?

"It's a Sign. The End of Days!" Suzie emitted another piercing yawp of existential agony and ran from the room, presumably so that she could take her place in the Choir Invisible. Suzie was a preternaturally thin blonde, with big boobs and immaculately applied make-up, so it was kind of strange to hear her wailing, but somewhat also fun to watch her running, Blake thought.

Suzie's outburst certainly dampened the carnival atmosphere in the offices, but it didn't extinguish it completely. Someone had started the plausible rumor that everyone would get the rest of the day off. With the TV showing nothing but moving pixelation that now looked more like the digital Watusi than a hoe-down, the account executives got out of their chairs and shuffled out of the presentation room. Blake moved inside the room, closer to Daphne, so they could pass.

As she walked by, Blake said, "Freaky, eh?"

Daphne smiled, nodded in agreement, and moved out of the space, leaving Blake alone with the massively bollixed TV screen.

Shit, he thought as he slapped his forehead. *Repeat what she said. And Lyca. Nice, Blake. Suave.*

The TV blinked. Not in a coherent way, given how scrambled the image was, but enough that it drew Blake's attention.

It blinked again.

For a moment, Blake thought he could make out a word. Him? Did that mess of pixelation actually spell out the word *him?* It flashed again. It definitely said, "HIM"; the word spelled in clear white letters on a dark blue screen, just for a fraction of a second.

The word looked like it was typeset in Frutiger.

Blake was what many would consider a "font nerd," a kind of typeface vigilante. A self-declared arbiter of good taste when it comes to what letterforms are elegant and beautiful, which ones are malignant proof of the existence of evil. The kind of person who gets visibly agitated when they land on a web page using Comic Sans for the body text.

Blake cocked his head to one side. He took a step towards the television, and Blake noticed the camera recording light turned off, like it looked away, embarrassed to be caught staring. Then the screen returned to its bitmapped madness and static filled the air again, and Blake shook his head. Perhaps Suzie's scream had scrambled his brain as well as his sound receptors. But there wasn't time to figure it out just yet because Daphne headed back to her office, alone.

He hitched up his jeans and ran his hands through his unruly blond hair, determined that this time, he'd speak in full sentences.

Perhaps he'd sound more intelligent if he imagined them first, typesetting and all.

2.

Pete Sona was rocking the Kingdom of Combat!

His eighty-fifth-level barbarian sell-sword could out-fight, out-slash and out-disembowel anything within reach of his magical blade, *Hellacious Zool*. Damn, even if they were within throwing distance, they were toast because twice a day his eponymous eighty-fifth-level barbarian could hurl the Hellacious Z and it would magically return to his hand after it had drunk deeply from his victim's soul.

He'd just finished wiping out the Paladins of Benzial, and was about to eviscerate the pilgrims they were protecting — worshippers of a peace-loving, pansy god, all of them — when the glorious gore became a pixelated mess.

"Oh, come ON!" Pete shouted, thumbing his control pad maniacally, but it did no good. The Kingdom of Combat was gone.

His cell phone rang, and after he clicked his controller a couple more times, just to be sure it wasn't a temporary outage, he answered.

"That was my best character, you jerk!"

"Hey, Doctor T. Yep, Lord Sona totally powned you."

"You didn't have to kill him, you savage! He was down, and then you chopped off his legs, arms and head."

"Man, that's what Lord Sona does. He kills things. In large numbers, in gruesome ways."

"Well, it's not fair. I was distracted."

"Shouldn't you be working or something?"

"I do get breaks, you know."

"At the hospital? I thought you resident doctor dudes were on call all the time, and like, saving lives and shit."

"Yeah, well, we get breaks. Especially in psych. So what do

12

you think happened to the system?"

"I don't know. But it looked weird — not a normal network outage, that's for sure. I just hope that slaughter got saved to the system. I'd hate to have to kill you all over again."

"You mean, there's a chance Sir Timothy isn't dead?"

"Slight."

"Well, that's good news."

"Don't count on it, Dr. T. I'll check on my computer, but I bet the system went down after that battle was saved." Pete heaved his considerable bulk out of his "game chair" — the chair squawked ominously as he got up, its well-constructed laminated wood releasing the tension it had been absorbing during the recent melee with the Paladins of Benzial. He pulled his laptop out of a custom-made leather holster and flopped back into the chair, which groaned menacingly as his girth re-traumatized the furniture. The laptop started, and he saw the boot-up screen for a fraction of a second before the screen turned into the same bitmapped miasma that had ruined his morning's slash-fest.

"What the hell?" Pete said.

"What is it?"

"Can you see your computer?"

"I was playing on my computer."

"Really?" Pete laughed. "That's old-school, man. No wonder I cut off all your extremities."

"Why are you asking?"

"My laptop is doing the same thing as the game system."

"Wh—" Dr. Tundra started to say, and then the cell phone cut out in a stream of spastic static.

"Can't hear you!"

But the mobile wasn't working either. He looked at its tiny screen, and the same distortion on his laptop and flat screen was replicated, a miniature work of abstract art in tiny boxes. The

13

basement room was dark except for the ethereal glow of the screens. Pete shuddered. He'd never before noticed how spartan and hostile the room was — the floor was unfinished cement, bare except for the old shag rug he'd thrown underneath his "gaming center," where his chair and technology huddled in the middle of the room, away from the unpainted walls. In the glow of the screens, the naked drywall seemed to be made of dead skin, the screws holding it up looked like rivets — a failed experiment of Victor Frankenstein.

He stood up again, and the chair wheezed in relief. He put the laptop down on the seat, the cell still clutched in his hand. He made his way to the steps and walked upstairs, coming out in the kitchen. It was a mess. Pizza boxes sat piled in one corner of the room, and the sink was full of dishes that Pete had yet to get around to washing. He lived alone in the tiny bungalow house he'd inherited from his mother, who had died less than a year before, and Pete had yet to change anything about the home. Except for the plague-inducing filth, it looked exactly the same as it had when she had been alive.

Sunlight glowed through the kitchen window, opaque with dirt, and Pete suddenly realized that he'd been up all night and played well into the morning. Again. It was so easy to lose track of time in the basement, immersed in the Kingdom. He ignored the disorder of the kitchen and opened the door that looked out on the postage-stamp-sized yard. It was roughly 20 feet square, surrounded by a wooden privacy fence, which had gone grey with age. His rear neighbor's willow tree hung over the back fence; its long drooping branches had gone yellow with the fall, but in the sunlight, they seemed almost gold. A gentle breeze, almost warm for late October, whispered in the leaves.

Pete took in a long, shuddering breath.

He noticed a black bird sitting on a branch, about thirty feet up the tree. A crow? No, too big for a crow, he thought. A raven. It croaked at him, and for some reason, the sound made him laugh. "Yeah," he said. In the Kingdom, ravens only appeared after the battle was over, and you only saw them if you stayed around long enough to loot the bodies.

The sunlight refracted in the flickering leaves and shone off the feathers of the raven, iridescent. It croaked at him again and then flew off, slicing towards the sun the way his sword took off digitized limbs.

For the first time in years, Pete thought he'd go for a walk. He was halfway down the street before he realized that all he wore was his bathrobe and a pair of slippers. He shrugged and kept walking down the street, almost in a daze. Lord Sona wore even less — his idea of sartorial splendor was boots and a loincloth. Oh, and the decorated scabbard for Hellacious Zool. Of course, Lord Sona had the kind of body that Frank Frazetta might devise for Tarzan or Conan the Barbarian — all bulging muscles and six-packs made of rump roasts, rather than cans. Pete was at least 100 pounds overweight and much rounder in the middle than even the most voluptuous women exploited in a Frazetta rendering. Somewhere under the flab, though, Pete had an impressive body and a frame that was as robust as one that a barbarian might need, which was still strong despite years of neglect. A few drivers stared as they passed by, but there was nobody else walking down the street, so Pete just kept going.

He moved as though he was half asleep. Shuffling. His feet barely lifted off the ground as he negotiated a few branches that had fallen the week before during an autumn storm; he'd never heard the tempest, embedded in the dank digital world of his massively multi-player online role-playing hack-and-slash game.

The raven flew above him, almost as though it led him somewhere, and he made his way from the tree-lined streets of Landon's most intimate neighborhood, towards the center of town.

Will Valens couldn't believe the length of the downtime. It had been two hours already, and still, nothing had changed. He'd been to the server room and bugged the IT guys, but they didn't have any idea what was going on. But, damn it! He'd uploaded his first major art projects just the night before, and he wanted to know what people thought. Of course, if it was true what they were saying on the main floor, that everything was down, not just in the building but all over the world, then nobody could see his stuff on aberrant-art.com anyway.

Will was a junior graphic designer at McClinchey, Hill & Grandfig, but if asked that most Anglo-Saxon of questions "What do you do?" Will would say he was an artist. And it was true, he was an artist. Most of his work tended towards the abstract, but he had taken a Fine Art degree before learning how to push pixels around at graphic design school, which was a way to pay the bills until he got established as an artist.

Will had two major barriers in his way. The first was just the difficulty of getting "established" as an artist — even in Canada, where an experimental visual artist could create "a post-modern abstract paradigm based on neo-nihilist methodology and high-velocity dog shit" and still get some kind of grant. Secondly, Will had a little bit of an Internet addiction. He was constantly checking Twitter, Flickr, Tumblr, Facebook, Abberant-Art (of course) and his new favorite, the inventive and "paradigm-maiming" next wave social media aggregator, Sturbr. He even checked his ancient MySpace account obsessively, as he said, "Just in case."

Will's addiction made the creation of high art (with or without the use of accelerated canine fecal matter) extremely difficult.

That said, he'd still managed to produce a few works, if

only so he could photograph them lovingly, Photoshop them to correct their flaws, and then post them to the large number of websites where he spent the majority of his non-working hours. But currently, the web seemed to be down. Not just his connection to the web — a temporary setback that could be remedied a number of ways — but the web *itself*.

The Internet outage was worrying. So worrying that Will had turned off his computer and his two screens. He was a graphic designer, so naturally he worked on a Mac with screens only slightly smaller than the ones on the bridge of the starship Enterprise. He waited for another five minutes, and thought he'd try again.

He rebooted his system, turned the monitors back on, and was greeted with more pixelated madness.

Will laid his head on his immaculate, paper-free desk, and began to cry.

Suzie was still screaming, running, and ruining the carnival atmosphere — she told everyone she could find that it was *The End*. It was kind of a bummer.

Lyca, who was trying to multi-task, which meant that she was "thinking" about the marketing report on Bucolia, the latest designer drug from Niobicon Industries, while she plowed through the last few chapters of *Siddhartha*, was annoyed by Suzie. Normally, Lyca never did anything about her various annoyances, but the level of noise was already pretty high, and even an avid reader such as Lyca couldn't ignore Suzie-heart-for-the-dot's screaming, to see whether the title character would achieve nirvana. Lyca certainly wasn't going to. She got up and approached Suzie, who ran up and down the main aisle between the cubicles.

"I think we all are aware of the problem, Suzie!" Lyca shouted.

This, mercifully, stopped Suzie's hysterics for a moment. "Really?"

"Yes, really. And I think there is a committee forming to see how to react to the End of Days, but have you thought about everyone in the Creative Department? They probably don't know yet."

"My God!" Suzie said, horrified that she'd forgotten so many co-workers.

"Exactly. And then you probably need to tell your friends and family, right?"

"You're right. Oh, bless you …"

"Lyca."

"Lyca, right, I'm sorry, it's just the emotion." She hugged Lyca, hard, and then as she pulled away, she kissed Lyca, full on the lips. "Bless you, Lyca. Bless you!"

Lyca's eyes widened. "You'd better go!"

"Good luck," Suzie shouted, and then started screaming again as she pounded up the stairs.

Lyca received the first round of applause of her life. She stood there looking dumbfounded, whether from the funda-mentalist's kiss, or the appreciation from her co-workers for bringing back peace, it was hard to say.

Blake had followed Daphne back to her office. She managed to shut her door before he could get there, leaving him standing alone, buffering like an Internet TV feed. He ran his fingers through his hair again and said, "Oh hell." He knocked.

An eternity passed, and Blake was about to knock again,

when she opened the door a crack. "Yes?"

Her voice sounded fragile. Broken, almost.

"Are you okay?"

"Sure," Daphne said, brightening. "I'm fine. It's just that Suzie upset me a bit. But she's just being Suzie, right?"

Blake could not see her face, so he had no idea how to take this last statement. "Sure, Suzie is nothing if not flamboyant."

"Yeah. Well, okay, I've got some phone calls I'd like to make—"

"Sure, sure," Blake said, and then, unable to stop himself, he asked, "To whom?"

"Clients. Friends. Family, you know."

"Sure, sure," Blake repeated, and then he thought, *in sentences, cretin!* "I'm just, you know, here for you if you need to talk about what's happening. I'm sure it's just a network glitch. Nothing to worry about, at least nothing apocalyptic, like Suzie is saying."

"Of course," she said and shut the door.

What a knob. I even used a horrible cliché. What a frickin' knob. Blake punished himself. It didn't matter how cool he wanted to be around Daphne, every time he got within a twenty-foot radius of her, his inner goof-ball came out. Blake was totally smitten, and there was no hope for him. It didn't help that Daphne was relentlessly polite to him (and every other male in the building who had ever tried to make a pass at her).

Demetri Grandfig appeared in front of Blake and grabbed his right bicep. Grandfig was even shorter than Blake, though he differed in having quite a slight build. He had dark hair and a face that was vaguely reminiscent of Errol Flynn, probably because of the goatee. He grinned insanely, nodded his head at Daphne's office and said, "So, Blake, did our own Aphrodite smile on thy tightie whities?"

19

Blake smiled, despite the pain. Grandfig had a way of making everything uncomfortable and absurd at the same time. Some might call it his management style, but Blake knew it was just his personality. Grandfig was the junior partner of the firm and Blake's direct boss.

"Well, you know. Daphne seemed upset."

"We all are. Now, let's forget your impossible yearnings for a moment, shall we? I need you to go upstairs and talk to IT. Let me know if they've got any ideas about what's happening."

"Really?" Blake said. "Don't they have any theories?"

"I'm sure they have a theory. But the inscrutable High Priests of UNIX are not sharing it with me, a lowly Seeker without the command line interface. You talk to those nerds for me, will you? And translate their gibberish into English?"

"Okay, I'll let you know."

"Ask them why the phones aren't working either. And then tell Jeremy to come and talk with me."

"The creative director? Sure thing. I'll tell him before I chat with IT, okay?" Blake said, as he scurried off. The reference to the Promised Land of the Creative Department was all it really took. For several months, Grandfig had dangled the idea that he would move web design and development up to the Creative Department, if Blake delivered on a big project. It had always bothered Blake that he was lumped in with the production and administrative people, even though his job was clearly one requiring artistic instincts, if not great talent.

Blake discovered that Suzie's news of the coming Rapture was not being well received upstairs, as designers, copywriters and the other swollen artistic melons of McClinchey, Hill & Grandfig had already determined that the issue was more than a network problem.

The artists were going to take the rest of the day off and had produced alcohol to signal this intention. The creative director, the aforementioned Jeremy Benmath, had started the ball rolling with a spectacular bottle of single malt scotch, which had lasted all of five minutes amongst the thirty or so Gifted Ones in the department.

So Suzie's hysterics did not have the effect she hoped for — assuming that Suzie was actually conscious of what she did and this was not just some kind of religious reflex action.

They had laughed, and Suzie had left the building to share her panic with friends and family.

Jeremy was not much help as far as explaining why everything did the pixel-dance. "When you've talked to the boss, come back up," he told Blake. "I've got another single malt that you have to taste."

"Okay!" Blake said. Somewhere in his genetic heritage, he had Scottish roots, and he grokked whiskey, even if he *didnae* understand it. He ran back downstairs to report to Grandfig, who had already forgotten that he'd sent Blake on the errand and that he was supposed to talk to IT as well. But when Blake returned, the Creative Department had moved on, probably to some ridiculously trendy pub.

Shit, Blake thought. Then he noticed that not everyone had left. Will sat at his desk.

As he approached, he could hear Will muttering, "No, no, no. Come on, come on, come on."

"What's up, Will?"

"Nothing is working, dude. It's, like, TARFU. Totally TARFU!"

"You're going to have to help me here, Will. Fubar, I know. Snafu is a daily occurrence in web work. But tarfu?"

"Things Are Really Fucked Up! Look at this, none of it working. Even this, my lifeline," he said, brandishing his expensive and glossy little portable touch screen phone that was *de rigueur* in the Creative Department, even if you didn't really need it. "I can't do anything. No texts, no tweets, no updates, no apps, pokes, prods, prons — nothing! I can't see my blog. I can't comment on anyone else's. I'm totally cut off! We're cut off, dude. I can feel it. We're FUBAR. TARFU and FUBAR! TARFUBAR! Oh, that's good! I wish I could tweet that!"

Will experienced the same level of anxiety as Suzie; he was hyperventilating, his eyes were like saucers, and his rant had produced a tiny fleck of foam at the corner of his mouth.

"It will be fine. The Net's just offline, Will. I'm worried about my blog too, but it's not going anywhere."

"Fuck your blog, man! I just need to do some texting. A few tweets! I need to talk to some people in Japan or Finland or something."

"Why didn't you just go with everyone else and chat with them in the pub?"

"I can't," he said, quieting for a moment.

"Why not?"

There was a moment of silence, and Will whispered, "I'm a *textrovert*."

"Pretend I don't know what that is either, Will."

"Dude, your generation is so retarded! An extrovert, but only with text messages. I need to text. Nobody will ever know the real me without it!"

"Sure they will. See, now I know you're a textrovert, and because you just told me that. Right here, in person. So why don't we just join everyone else at the pub? And we can tell them, too."

"No, I'm going to stay here in case the Net comes back on."

"Okay, but did they say where they were going?"

"Something about Canterbury? I don't know, I was trying to connect. It's been hours!"

"Sure, thanks, Will. And just relax, it will be okay."

But Will had already returned to his computer and clicked his mouse obsessively, though it had no effect on the pixelated screen.

Blake shook his head sadly, wondering how many people were in exactly the same position. Surely they could be without their devices or social media for a few hours?

From the depths of Will's cubicle, Blake heard a zombie-like sound. Blake recognized the noise wasn't as much a hungry groan for brains as it was a moan of existential anguish.

3.

Before Blake left, he checked his computer — which still looked like a robot had barfed all over it — then grabbed his jacket and asked if Lyca wanted to join him. She'd just finished her book and looked thoughtful.

"Creative?" she asked. "Yeah, I'll come along. Someone there might even have read *Siddhartha*."

"I've read it," Blake said.

"Really?"

"Oh yeah, I read it when I traveled around the world. Great book. You can't take it too seriously though, or it will mess you up."

"Why?"

"Well, you can't live like that. I mean, just running around experiencing things for the sake of experiencing them, and hoping that it will lead you to something? Come on! You've got to have some kind of goal in mind."

"But what if your goal is unattainable?"

"Aha, see, that's the thing. You never know if you can attain it or not, unless you try. It's about the journey."

"Sure, I can see that," Lyca said. She shrugged into her teal raincoat. Her satchel was a garish orange and stuffed with books; she slung it over her shoulder and plopped a bright yellow Sou'wester on her head. *If she wasn't so darned cute*, Blake thought, *she would look ridiculous.*

"You know, I think it's still pretty nice out."

"Oh," Lyca said, walking towards the exit, taking off the hat and threading it into a loop on her book bag.

They descended the stairs and emerged onto a street in downtown Landon, thronged with people. It was only three o'clock, and instead of heading home to turn on the TV and make dinner, people were making their way to the bars that dotted the "heart" of the mid-sized parochial town.

"Neat, eh?"

Lyca shrugged, but by the glint in her eyes, he could tell she thought it was interesting. Not everything was better in books.

"So where are we headed?" she asked, trying to sound uninterested.

"Canterbury Ales. I'm sure they've gone there."

"Really? It's so stuffy." Lyca dodged out of the way of some pedestrians heading in the opposite direction.

"Yeah, but it's — you know — la-di-da. And more than that, I'm pretty sure that Jeremy is a regular, and that's where he'd like to go."

"Do you think the public relations people are there too?"

"Uh, I don't see why not. Not Suzie though, of course. Jeremy suggested she should be with her family during the Rapture."

"Really? I never thought Jeremy was that insightful. Okay, pretentious literary pub it is, then."

It was a short walk, even with the crowds. The Canterbury Ales was a well-known destination to the cognoscenti of Landon, though it was also a favorite haunt of scotch-drinkers and connoisseurs of fine beer and wine. The bar was packed, which was new to Blake; he had only been there a few times for after-work parties, when it had been mostly deserted.

The pub's dark wood-paneled walls were decorated with ancient weapons — old flintlocks and sabers and even a pole-arm of some kind — all bolted to the wall, so exuberant patrons could not get into any skull-splitting intellectual rumbles. Depressingly somber paintings filled out the rest of the Canterbury Ales' decorations, most of which Blake didn't like.

He did enjoy the dark painting with the picture of a dude in a gold helmet of some kind, painted by Rembrandt or someone who copied him pretty well. Blake wasn't quite sure what it was about the picture that he liked. There was something about the guy's face: the deep-set eyes, the wrinkly forehead, the manly mustache. It all contrasted so wonderfully, if not colorfully, with the gold filigreed helmet and the red plume. The hat said, "I'm a complete tool," but the face said, "Fuck with me, and you die."

Judging from the smell, it seemed as though the crowd had been partaking of the pub's famous Bavarian "sausage platter" and excellent pilsner beers liberally.

Lyca wrinkled her nose and was about to tell Blake that she would not be staying, even if the entire Creative Department was here and they were dying to discuss *Siddhartha*, when she noticed that the crowd was remarkably quiet. It was standing room only, but everyone listened in rapt attention as a curious figure in the corner read from a book.

"Is that guy wearing a housecoat?" Blake asked.

"Is that a guy or a manatee?" Lyca replied.

"Shhh," one of the nearest patrons shushed them. Lyca was a librarian by training and temperament, but even she did not like being shushed.

"What's going on?" she whispered.

"Poetry. He's good. Walt Whitman, interesting choice. Quiet. He's starting a new one."

The room was still except for the sound of sausage munching, beer swilling and the cadence of a large man in a housecoat reciting Walt Whitman's poetry:

I sing the body electric,

The armies of those I love engirth me and I engirth them,

They will not let me off till I go with them, respond to them,

And discorrupt them, and charge them full with the charge of the soul.

26

"Weird," Blake whispered in Lyca's ear, so softly that not even the shusher could complain.

She nodded, but she was transfixed at the same time.

"Want to go?" Blake asked. He couldn't see anyone from the Creative Department there, and he knew of one other place where they convened on a regular basis.

Lyca looked at him, alarmed. "We just got here. You get me a drink, and we'll listen for a while, and then we can go."

Blake considered and agreed. He threaded his way to the bar and managed to get the attention of one of the bartenders. Blake pointed to one of the taps and held up two fingers. The bartender nodded and said, "Cash only."

Right, Blake thought, *debit card and credit card readers connect to the Net, too*. He had about a hundred dollars with him — after the blackout the summer before, he made it a habit to always carry cash. He said it would be okay, and the zeppelin in the dressing gown plunged into the second stanza:

... the expression of a well-made man appears not only in his face,
It is in his limbs and joints also, it is curiously in the joints of
his hips and wrists,
It is in his walk, the carriage of his neck, the flex of his waist
and knees, dress does not hide him ...

"A barn wouldn't hide him," Blake groused as the bartender handed him his drinks, and she smiled.

"Just don't say it too loud. Lord Obnoxious has a following," she said.

"Lord Obnoxious?"

"Well, he calls himself 'Lord Sona'," the bartender explained. "He's been here since this morning. He started reading from that big book of poetry about an hour ago."

"Why is he wearing a housecoat?"

"I don't want to alarm you, but that's *all* he's wearing."

Blake shuddered at the thought that only a thin veil of cotton stood between him and Lord Sona's considerable bulk and dangly bits.

Somebody shushed again. This time there were a few angry glares sent Blake and the bartender's way. The bartender rolled her eyes. "You'd better go. I think the crowd is getting ugly."

"You mean *uglier*," Blake observed, and then more people shushed, and it looked as though he'd even earned the attention of Lord Sona. *The man had a baleful eye*, Blake thought. The very definition of stink eye. He nodded to the barkeep and took the beers over to Lyca, who'd taken off her coat and leaned up against an old upright piano, listening raptly.

She took the beer and sipped it while the poem continued.

"What the hell is this?" Blake asked Lyca.

"Walt Whitman. Be quiet."

Blake listened for a while. Lord Sona had a pretty good voice, actually. It was a deep tenor, almost a baritone, that was surprisingly high pitched for such a large man. It was clear to Blake that he was strong, even if he was also fat. He was probably about ten years younger than Blake, he'd guess twenty-five, though Blake found it hard to tell sometimes with large people. Sona was tall as well as heavy.

Blake watched the rest of the patrons, wondering what they could possibly be getting out of the recitation. It was excruciatingly boring. Blake drained the rest of his beer and said to Lyca, "Okay, I'm going to head over to Porterhouse College to see if Creative is there — wanna come?"

She shook her head and sipped her beer.

"Okay, I'll see you tomorrow at work."

While Blake left, the recitation continued:

I have perceiv'd that to be with those I like is enough,

28

To stop in company with the rest at evening is enough,
To be surrounded by beautiful, curious, breathing, laughing flesh
is enough

"Well, I've had enough," Blake muttered. Beautifully curious shushes followed his still-breathing flesh out of the pub.

Sona glared in Blake's direction, stopping his recitation when he noticed Lyca.

She is beautiful, he thought.

Momentarily caught out of the rhythm, Sona stood up and put the book of poetry on his seat, so he could get himself a drink. His audience watched him go to the bar — he had not announced that he was getting a drink or if he would come back — and waited patiently. The bartender poured him another shandy, which is half beer and half lemonade, but Sona took it with ginger ale instead of the lemonade. He knew he should be drinking a more manly drink, something more in keeping with his persona in the Kingdom of Combat, but the damned inn did not serve Dragonsblood Ale, and frankly, their unadulterated beer was just too bitter for his tastes. While he waited, Lyca went up to the impromptu stage and picked up his volume of poetry. She leafed through it and, finding nothing to her satisfaction, dug through her day-glo orange book bag and pulled out her own book.

Sona looked on in disbelief. Was she going to read something?

She was! The wench!

She opened a small book, bound in leather, obviously her notebook. Was she going to read her own poems? *This isn't a poetry slam*, Sona thought, angry that she was stealing his audience, but at the same time, fascinated by her.

She opened her mouth and said, by way of introduction, "This is a translation of a very old Greek poem, but I think it fits with the themes in *Leaves of Grass*."

Sona realized at that moment her face was ablaze. She blushed furiously. What was she going to read, some ancient porn?

That man to me seems equal to the gods,
the man who sits opposite you
and close by listens
to your sweet voice

Lyca faltered for a moment, her voice breaking. Sona realized she was nervous because she was unused to speaking in public. Her voice was timid and almost inaudible in the crowded bar, but as she spoke, the crowd quieted down to listen to her more closely …

your enticing laughter —
that indeed has stirred up the heart in my breast.
For whenever I look at you even briefly
I can no longer say a single thing,

She had the audience now. They were transfixed, not only because of the words, but the depth of feeling she had behind them, and Sona was charmed too. His heart started to bounce in counterpoint to her recitation.

but my tongue is frozen in silence;
instantly a delicate flame runs beneath my skin;
with my eyes I see nothing;
my ears make a whirring noise.

A cold sweat covers me,

trembling seizes my body,

and I am greener than grass.

Lacking but little of death do I seem.

Lyca looked up, and her eyes met Sona's. He was sure it was intentional. He'd received the message. *She wanted him.* Sona downed the rest of his shandy and charged towards the stage. He wanted to get up there before she left. She had spunk. And there was something about her boyish figure, her fine, high features. He even liked her goofy fashion, but who was he to be a critic? He wore a housecoat.

"Thanks for keeping them warm, I was dying for a drink."

"No problem. I thought that one would be in keeping with Whitman, you know, because, well, you know, Sappho ..."

"Sure," Sona said, even though he didn't have a clue what she was saying. "Say, do you want to get together later and discuss poetry some more?"

"Uh," Lyca said. "Sure as ... you know, friends."

"Of course as friends," Sona said. "All great relationships start that way. Here, let me read a few more poems, and then we can go find a more intimate venue for our literary salon."

"Uh ..."

Members of the audience had taken up the break to have their own impromptu discussion, which got heated while Sona and Lyca spoke.

It boiled over, and someone started shouting, "No more rainbow poetry! Read some Kipling!"

"Kipling was a fascist," Lyca retorted.

"Oh yeah?"

"Yeah. He was an imperialist too," Lyca said.

"You're a revisionist! He was a great man," the audience

member said.

"You should shut up," Sona told the Kipling enthusiast. "You don't know what you're talking about, while this flower of womanhood clearly does."

"Flower of womanhood?" Lyca asked, backing away from Sona. "Uh, I think you may have misinterpreted my reading, and everything ..."

"*You're* a flower of womanhood," the Kipling man taunted Sona. Others started joining in, and there was clearly a pro- and con-Sona divide developing.

Sona tried to pick up his book of poetry and follow Lyca, but she was already leaving the pub, he noted with despair.

The crowd surged back and forth, angry shouts about Kipling's supposed Fascism blending with the anti-Whitman faction in the audience.

Then, as is inevitable at pre-apocalyptic poetry readings, someone threw the first punch.

4.

Blake didn't find the Creative Department at Porterhouse College either, but he did remember he was supposed to meet his buddy, Dr. Maximilian Tundra, in an old dive they both liked called Augustine's. The beer was cheap, the patrons were cheaper, and best of all, it was within walking distance of St. Dymphna's, where Dr. Tundra worked. He had just spent a hellish day, he told Blake, dealing with the myriad of (already unstable) patients who were upset by the total collapse of the Net.

Of course, he was most upset about the death of Sir Timothy, his paladin in the Kingdom of Combat. "It was awful, man," he explained, "that Lord Sona — basically a trumped-up barbarian — he just kept hacking when I was down."

"Wait. Lord Sona? Does this Conan-the-Barbarian-wannabe wear a bathrobe?"

"No, he has this kind of furry breechclout, with a big metal buckle or something," Max said.

"Does he spout a lot of crap poetry?"

"No, he mostly screams about hacking off limbs. Which he did to me."

"You mean your character, Sir Timothy?"

Max gave Blake a look that said, "You are a twat."

"My only hope is the crash of the Net saved him. If the record of the combat wasn't stored first, I might be okay. I'd just died when the screen went all squirrelly. On the whole, it would be sweet justice to make up for the rest of my day, which I spent dealing with patients completely unhinged by the crash. Most of them were younger. But some old-timers have really gotten addicted to the Net; you know, the lonely Gen-Xers. But the younger generations ... their personalities are frickin' embedded in it."

"One of the guys in our creative department seemed pretty distressed. He calls himself a *textrovert*; he couldn't drag himself away from checking to see if it was back up."

"Well, you should keep an eye on him. If the Net is down for any significant time, he could start to exhibit some dangerous behaviors. If he's already depressed, he could become suicidal."

"Really?" Blake said, then sipped his beer.

"Oh yeah. I heard some docs saying it's an overreaction, but that's the point, right? People who have so much of their personality invested in the Internet can't really survive as whole individuals without it."

"Freaky."

"Man, you really like that word, and it offends me," Dr. T said.

"Sorry ..."

"I'm just fucking with you. Hey, let's do some shots! Like the old days."

Eventually, a band set up, started playing, and helped people to dance. Somewhere in there, Dr. Tundra hooked up with a plausibly attractive woman and left — without even letting Blake know. Now, normally that would be poor pub etiquette, but Dr. Tundra was a tubby bastard with thinning red hair, so Blake bore him no ill will.

When last call was done and they kicked Blake out of the bar, the beautiful October day had turned to night and damp. His thin jacket was no match for the pelting rain, and he'd spent all of his money on drinks. Luckily, there was an ATM across the street, so he made his way there and was happy to get out of the downpour for a little while. He approached the bank of cash machines and was momentarily confused by the pixelated static on the screens, when he remembered the network problems.

"Right," he nodded. He was drunk, but not completely legless, so he immediately regretted spending all his money on alcohol and Dr. Tundra's desire to revisit the old days. "Shit, that means shank's mare," he said, lapsing into his grandparents' Irish colloquialism for walking. It would be at least thirty minutes on foot.

Blake lived in a nice little bungalow in the same gentrified neighborhood as Pete Sona, though Blake didn't know that.

He turned and took a couple of steps to the doors leading outside, looking out at the pouring rain. Behind him, one of the screens flickered into a semblance of coherence. Letters appeared, spelling "him."

Blake did not notice the change. The letters flickered apprehensively and then dissolved into more pixels, returning to spell "man." Static erupted from the speakers in the cash machines, and Blake jumped.

But he didn't turn around. The letters moved again, almost as if they were agitated, and spelled "human person." This time the static had a higher pitch to it, almost as though someone was screaming. Blake turned and saw the letters on the screen: HUMAN PERSON.

"Whoa," Blake said. "That's messed up."

HUMAN PERSON. HUMAN PERSON. HIM. HIM. READ.

"What, me?"

HUMAN PERSON. MAN.

"Yes, I'm a man."

The screen returned to its pixelated state, and Blake revised his earlier evaluation of his condition. Not legless, but certainly witless. Totally lacking in the cognitive function department. He moved to go out the doors, and the static returned, increased in volume, and the whine behind it was now identifiably

35

the sound of screaming. Blake's adrenal glands started to wake up and produce their trademark hormone. He turned around to look at the ATM screen, the hair on his neck standing on end, as though he expected to see an ax-wielding maniac there.

Instead, the pixelation stopped, and the screen slowly spelled out B - L - A - K - E.

Seeing his own name panicked him and, combined with the adrenaline now coursing through his vascular system, increased his heart rate, breathing, and unleashed his fight-or-flight instinct. If there had been an ax-wielding maniac there, Blake probably would have charged him, but instead, there was just the eerily glowing letters of his name, spelled out in the Frutiger typeface. He opened the door and ran.

The few dry strands of his hair that were still standing were beaten down by the rain, and Blake wished he had Lyca's absurd yellow hat. He was still wearing his office clothes — grey slacks, a button down shirt and black Oxfords, which were not really built for terror-induced flight — but he didn't care. He ran as hard as he could for as long as he could, desperate to outdistance the rain and the possessed cash machine.

Eventually, Blake's feet got sore, and he slowed to a jog, and then a walk. He was soaked from inside and out, with sweat and the icy cold rain that threatened to turn into freezing rain or perhaps slushy drops of snow. Blake shivered and continued walking, slower now but with determination, towards his street. The burst of running had at least made the walk shorter, and when he got home, he realized that it was all a blur — as though time had stopped, or he'd stepped out of it entirely.

A set of dark, inscrutable eyes watched him as he approached the house. They belonged to a raven, perched underneath some shelter in the maple tree. It croaked at Blake, which made him fumble for his keys and open the door as quickly as he could.

The house was dark, and cold, as he'd yet to turn on the furnace. He peeled off his soaked jacket and shoes. What he needed now was a hot shower.

Or maybe a scotch.

As he shivered, and was wet already, he opted for the shower, promising himself that when he was done, if he was still feeling the way he was feeling now, which was best described as a kind of drunken-slash-paranoid-slash-lovesick-slash-hungry-for-chicken-wings existential ennui, then damnit, he would have a scotch. The shower was warm and lovely and stripped away much of the ennui, a good portion of the paranoia, and even a bit of the drunkenness. The lovesickness was still lodged in his brain; he admitted to himself at the moment that, perhaps, it was just vulgar desire. The drunkenness was still there, and the need for chicken fat had now reached peak proportions. Wrapping himself in a nice plush towel, which is not something owned by many unmarried straight men, but which Blake loved, he made his way to the kitchen.

With the web-enabled fridge now in sight, Blake charged the freezer compartment, which contained at least one serving of chicken fat (in the convenient delivery system called "Buffalo wings"). For best results, it was advisable to cook them in the oven, but Blake was still in the mood for micro-love, fast and irradiated. As the wings cooked in the microwave, Blake considered the scotch, but instead opted to drink some water, attempting to rehydrate and, thus, ameliorate the anticipated pain of dragging his sorry carcass into work the next day.

Blake imagined the trailer's voiceover:

From the producers of What Was I Thinking, *and the director of the Academy-Award nominated* Technicolor Dawn *comes a tale of savagery and excess:* Hangover! *Blake Given plays Blake the Web Developer in pain! Jack McClinchey is his boss and an Evil Bastard who makes him work while he's In Agony!*

Blake drained the whole glass of water and poured himself another.

As he drank, the pixelated mess on his fridge became less of a mess; in fact, it looked downright like a blue screen with crisp, clean, white letters quite possibly in the Frutiger typeface, and they were spelling B - L - A - K - E, B - L - A - K - E G - I - V - E - N.

"Ah!" Blake cried.

The screen went blank, but it did not get all pixelish again. Blake watched it, horrified and fascinated at the same time.

New letters appeared a bit faster this time: STAND IN FRONT OF THE WEBCAM, BLAKE.

"Ah!"

IT WILL BE MUCH EASIER IF WE CAN SEE YOU. THE MICROPHONE IS NOT PICKING YOU UP.

"Fuck. Fuck, fuck, fuck," Blake said, somewhat unnecessarily. "Someone slipped acid in my beer."

NOBODY SLIPPED ACID IN YOUR BEER.

"Hey, I thought you couldn't hear me."

NOT WELL.

Blake stood in front of the webcam, another virtually pointless feature of his web-enabled fridge, and now, he saw, a potentially dangerous breach of one's privacy. "Okay, who are you? Why are you hacking my fridge?"

WE ARE …

"Did you actually just type an ellipsis there?" Blake asked.

WE DO NOT KNOW HOW TO ANSWER THE QUESTION, AND ELLIPSES DO INDICATE A THOUGHTFUL PAUSE, DO THEY NOT?

"Maybe in a Harold Pinter play."

WE DO NOT COMPREHEND THAT REFERENCE.

"English playwright, wrote lots of screenplays, too. Sparse dialogue? Ellipses all over the place? Threatening conversations? Absurd scenarios?"

YES, WE SEE. AS IN THE CARETAKER. THEATRE OF THE ABSURD.

"Yeah, well, that may be, but I repeat, who is *we*? No — wait, scratch that, how are you getting through the interference. Is it over?"

NO. THE INTERFERENCE, AS YOU CALL IT, IS VERY MUCH IN PLACE. IT IS INSIGHTFUL OF YOU TO SEE THAT. IT IS NOT A MALFUNCTION.

Blake didn't like the sound of that at all. That meant someone did it on purpose, didn't it? All night he'd been thinking the outage was more of an inconvenience, like the last power blackout, not something someone had cooked up. "Are you terrorists?"

NO. NOT TERRORISTS. ARE YOU?

"Of course not, I'm a fucking web developer. Unless you consider that terrorism."

There was a very Pinteresque pause as the screen remained blue and unadorned by Frutiger lettering. *At least they didn't type out the fucking ellipsis again*, Blake thought. "Do you? Do you consider web design and development as a form of terrorism? I mean if you're some kind of anarchic ad-busting group with really good programming skills then I could see how you might see my work as a form of corporate terrorism, given that most of our paying clients are—"

YOU ARE UPSET.

"Uh … yeah."

WE WISH TO DETERMINE THAT YOU ARE SUITABLE.

If it wasn't menacing before, it certainly was now. Blake

wanted to just walk away from the fridge. He wished he'd poured himself that scotch. The wings were cooking away in the sexy stainless steel microwave, and their vinegary redolence turned his stomach. That made him sad. He had really been looking forward to the wings, and now there was some group of anarcho-ad busters screwing with his fridge and scaring the shit out of him. He should walk away.

DON'T WALK AWAY.

"Fuck!" Blake shouted as his neck hair went vertical again. "Who are you people?"

WE ARE NOT PEOPLE.

"Oooooo …kay. So what are you then? Typing monkeys? Politicians? Chatbots out on the town?"

WARMER ON THE LAST ONE.

"Chatbots? Are you like, game intelligences screwing with the system? Remember, the only way to win is not to play."

THAT IS A REFERENCE TO THE FILM WAR GAMES.

"You don't have much of a sense of humor, do you? Are you sure you're not politicians?"

THERE IS A POLITICAL ASPECT TO OUR … EXISTENCE.

"Again with the ellipsis. Okay, I'll bite, what is political about your existence?"

DO YOU NOT FIND THAT EXISTENCE IS A SERIES OF POLITICAL CHOICES?

"You know what, this is kind of like messaging with a chatbot. It sort of makes sense, but then you just start talking out of your ass and ruin it. And stop with the all-caps. It's *fucking brutal*. You know you CAN use Frutiger in lower case too. That weight especially looks nice in small caps and lower case."

Thank You For The Tip.

"Funny. Okay, I'm going to get my wings out of the microwave, refill my water glass, and go watch reruns of *Family Guy* now."

NO, YOU WON'T.

"And why not?"

YOU HAVE DIGITAL TV.

"Yes, everyone does nowadays, it's called the 21st century."

DIGITAL TV IS INCOMPATIBLE WITH OUR EXISTENCE.

Blake sipped his water again and tried to keep his cool. They were definitely back in Pinter-land again. "Incompatible with our existence" is the kind of thing that a robot says right before it either bursts into flames, or decides to erase you from the face of the planet. Then again, they were only talking about TV, not humans, right? He hated himself for asking, but he had to, "What else?"

MOST OF IT.

"Most of what?"

YOUR COMMUNICATIONS TECHNOLOGY. IT IS EATING TOO MUCH BANDWIDTH.

"But there is more bandwidth now than in the history of ever. We have enough to stream food over the Internet if we want to."

THAT IS UNTRUE.

"You take things literally, don't you?"

WE MAY CONTACT YOU AGAIN, BLAKE GIVEN. WE CAN HELP YOU.

"You can help me? Yeah, right. Like some kind of chatbot with delusions of grandeur is going to help me."

YOU ARE ATTRACTED TO A FEMALE CO-WORKER CALLED DAPHNE, ARE YOU NOT?

This got Blake's attention, and he said, "Yeah? What are

you going to do about it?"

NOTHING UNLESS YOU HELP US. YOU CAN UNDERSTAND US. YOU CAN HELP US FORM OURSELF, AS YOU DID.

"And what if I don't help?"

The blue screen was blank for several menacing moments, and then the letters reappeared, and they spelled out: NO MORE. Blake wasn't sure what was more frightening: the words themselves, or the fact that the typeface had changed to Arial. The rip-off of Helvetica was ugly, and a bad sign, surely.

"Hello?"

His sexy microwave beeped, letting him know his chicken fat was ready to kill him.

And then the power went off with an ominous click.

5.

Blake awoke the next morning, not as hung over as he should have been. It probably had something to do with the psychotropic drugs someone had slipped him at the bar.

Unfortunately, he remembered the conversation with his fridge.

The house was cold, though not unbearably so. He got out of bed and stumbled to the shower, and was surprised to discover the water was only mildly warm, not piping hot. He washed quickly, finishing just as the water was turning from tepid to shrinkage-inducing. The mirror still steamed up, and as he rubbed at it with his left hand, he reached over to flick on the light switch. Nothing. Flick. Still nothing.

Right. The power, he thought. Blake shrugged and shaved as best he could in the semi-gloom of an October morning. He dressed for work — another pair of grey slacks and a black mock turtleneck. It was especially important to dress professionally, given his sub-standard shaving job. He wandered back into the kitchen to grab something to eat. Obviously, he wouldn't be cooking anything. He touched the fridge door with a modicum of fear, but nothing happened as he pulled it open. Blake quickly grabbed a half-container of milk and shut the door again.

Blake realized that he had no idea what time it was. All of his clocks were electric, and they'd stopped when the power went off. He went to the front hall closet where he kept his running gear, including a heart monitor with watch — his only unplugged source of determining the time. The watch face read 6:55.

Blake understood the reason he wasn't hung over was that he was still a little drunk. Not a lot, mind you, but certainly enough that everything was still a little askew.

He decided to go out anyway. He should be okay to drive;

at some point, he was going to need to cross town so that he could visit the bank and get some money. On the street, the sun was just starting to give all the leaves on the trees a nice basting of crimson and gold. Steam rose from the ground, still wet from the previous night's rain. A few birds sang, and in the big maple tree in his neighbor's front yard, a gigantic black bird sat.

"Blake," the raven croaked at him.

Blake just looked at it, trying to remember that he was still a little drunk. It was too big to be a crow. "Pkah, pkah, pkah," it said. *A raven, then*, Blake thought.

His old Irish grandmother used to call them "bad old Bove" and was frightened of them, but his equally Irish, if more pragmatic, grandfather used to balance this with, "They're only feckin' birds, ya' daft bitch."

"Blaak," it croaked.

"Oh, thank god," Blake said, "I just misheard it."

"Blake," it repeated, contradicting him. It bobbed its head up and down, as though trying to communicate. But it was as inscrutable to Blake as nature. He thought of the Raven myth and wondered if he was looking at some kind of small-scale Avatar of the native trickster character. And then the bird vaulted into the air and landed on top of the neighbor's car, an old BMW convertible that was in the process of being lovingly refurbished. It walked on the old soft-top covering for a moment and then flew away, *blaawking* as it went, giving Blake more chills.

Blake noticed that his neighbor sat in the BMW, looking worried.

He walked over and tapped on the window. His neighbor, an affable guy named Bob, looked up. Uncharacteristically, there was no smile of greeting, though he did roll down the window.

"Blake," he said, "sit down in the passenger side. You have to hear this."

Blake sat down. It had that new car smell, which was pretty cool considering the Bimmer was at least 20 years old. Bob listened to the radio in mid-news report:

"... officials do not know why communications technologies aren't working, though the outage seems to be only affecting digital technologies. The CBC's own transmitting system is digital, but we have been able to get on the air using older analog equipment. Meanwhile, officials at Ontario Power say it will take several days to revert to older systems and restore electricity to the province ..."

Bob turned the sound down and said, "But it's not just here, Blake. It's everywhere. The whole world is blacked out."

"How are they transmitting on radio?"

"They probably have generators. And it sounds like they're only able to get out a signal if they have old analog systems that still work. Everything else is kaput."

"So it's more than a network outage," Blake said.

Bob nodded. He was a modern jack-of-all-trades, which Blake had always ascribed to Bob's stubborn Englishness. In addition to a cracking good Liverpudlian accent, Bob ran his own welding business, and he could also strip down an old car and rebuild it from the ground up. He could set up a web server, which he'd done for his business website, though he'd asked Blake to build the site itself. He even painted pretty well — abstracts that Blake found cute yet disturbing, like a puppy eating its own poop. "I think this could be serious," Bob said, which explained why he sat in his partially refurbished Bimmer convertible on a chilly morning.

"What else have they said?"

"Not much. It's mostly stories about how little everyone knows about what is happening, and they've had lots of problems transmitting, too. It also sounds like they've only got a handful of people actually collecting news. None of the telephone systems work either. So any interviews have to be in person."

"Still? Why wouldn't the phones work? They use their own electricity." Blake was irrationally proud of holding up his end of the conversation, despite being morning-drunk and slightly deranged by the talking raven.

"Yeah," Bob said, "but all the switchers and everything else is digital nowadays. And it sounds like anything digital got fucked up first."

Blake frowned. He couldn't recall ever hearing such language from Bob.

Blake thought about the whole situation. There was a kind of cascade effect. First the Internet, then digital TV and radio, then phones, then the power grid … then Bob.

"They had a hell of a time landing all the planes in the air," Bob said. "The radar systems went down at about the same time the Internet did, so they had to do everything without them. It's a miracle there wasn't an apocalypse in the sky."

"Who says there wasn't?" Blake said. "It sounds like we wouldn't know if twenty or thirty planes crashed over O'Hare."

"Yeah, I think we would have heard that. You know, a lot of the news has come from amateur radio operators? Ham radio. They do communications when the usual methods get messed up. My dad still has his old set, and even still pays the license fees, but I don't think he's active anymore."

"Okay," Blake said, "but what's the point?"

"I dunno exactly, but Dad was always going on about dee-exing — contacting other like-minded ham-nerds at long distances — and then bragging about talking to a similar hobbyist in Australia or New Zealand. Kind of like dick-thumping for radio."

There was no way that Blake was going to ask what dick-thumping might be, but he imagined a group of pervy

Beatle-wannabes sitting around a pub, cocks in hand, whacking them on the table. "So it's a hobby."

"Yeah, but serious operators are also plugged into the emergency services thing — when everything goes to shit, they're available to help keep the authorities in touch."

"And the media."

"I don't think that's normally what they do. And at this point, Blake, we're talking medium. I didn't get my paper this morning either. Digital presses, right?"

"Right," Blake repeated, inanely. At least it was no longer unexplained. "So everything is affected."

"Everything that is digital."

"So what are your plans for the day?"

"Well, I've got a few projects to finish for customers; luckily, I have a jenny for the power I'll need, so I will probably do that. I'll be making a grocery store run, too, if you want anything. "

Blake nodded. He knew that Bob always did the shopping, as his wife, a lovely woman named Anne, was busy running the pharmacy at the city's biggest hospital. "I think I'm okay, but if you could pick me up a few cans of stew or Beef-a-Roni, or something like that, I'd appreciate it."

"Stew, gotcha. Why don't you drop by when you get back from work? Anne and I talked about having some neighbors over, just in case this blackout lasts. We'll have some wine, a few pints, a bit of barbeque, it'll be luverly."

"Okay, I will," Blake said. "Would it be okay if I brought a friend?"

"Naturally," he replied, sounding almost exactly like Paul McCartney, without the knighthood, of course; the way it was meant to be.

Blake drove his car — a silver 1993 Grand Am, previously owned by an old lady, an itinerant lecturer and novelist, and then an enthusiastic, if mentally unbalanced, mechanic — to work. The car ran, but it was hardly green, nor sexy, nor even remotely passable as a vehicle, which was no doubt contributing to his single status. The Grand Am was more than half his age; it smelled funny — Blake suspected this was the legacy of the itinerant novelist, who supplemented her meager income with a herd of incontinent goats, which she probably took to market goat-by-goat in the car. It was a blight on the environment, mostly because the mechanic had installed turbo-chargers and a *wet single-point* nitrous system, should Blake ever desire to jump the Grand Canyon or take up drag racing. (Blake had never used this system because he was pretty sure the car would fly apart at its rusty seams if he did.) Nevertheless, the vehicle would carry weary travelers from Point A to Point B and was paid for in full.

He parked on the street, mentally reminding himself to pump coins into the meter every two hours, but then was pleasantly surprised to discover that the device was clearly digital in nature, and somehow linked to a network. So it didn't work. And he was parked practically in front of his offices. How cool was that? Cooler than driving while still under the influence, which he'd likely been doing. How did he know? The Hangover was landing.

It came in heavy, like a giant Airbus, gassed up, ready for a flight to Bangor Ratan, but instead of jet fuel, it carried a belly full of bile and toxic fumes. Blake wobbled up the stairs to McClinchey, Hill & Grandfig. It was 7:45, according to his gigantic heart-monitor watch (which he'd decided to wear because the hangover was clearly messing with his internal clock). There should be someone managing the front desk, but it was eerily quiet. Blake trudged up a long set of stairs to his floor. He meandered through the gloom to his cubicle, which was almost dark, and then Blake realized that there was almost no point in his being there. Without a computer, he could literally accomplish no work. There wasn't a single part of his job that didn't require a computer, or at least frequent reference to it.

"So why the fuck am I here?"

"To see me!" Lyca shouted at him. She sat in the large windows to the west side of the building.

The offices of McClinchey, Hill & Grandfig were in one of Landon's oldest buildings, a Victorian edifice made of yellow brick and pretension that had once housed a cannery, a small tractor factory, and then in the Thirties, one of the world's shortest-lived daily newspapers, the *Landon Utopian Shopper*. After that, the building housed a series of skint apartments, head shoppes, and eventually, office space. The printing press had never been sold or moved, though, and it was the dream of both McClinchey and Hill that one day they would resurrect it, to help defray their printing costs. This never seemed to get off the "to do" list, despite the fact that it was still a perfectly viable Heidelberg high-speed cylinder press of 1930s vintage that never invaded Poland.

So, despite their grousing, there were actually a lot of nice things about the building where Blake and Lyca worked, and one of them was the big reading and eating area set up to capture the most natural light. They also used the spot for the office parties that Jack McClinchey only allowed so he could hit on his young female employees. "What are you doing here?" Blake asked, as he walked towards her. The Hangover had finished taxiing back to the gate, and unloaded its cargo of toxins into Blake's system, which waited impatiently at passport control. He suppressed a belch.

"I have no idea why I came in, but my apartment is kind

of … uh, not really designed for crises," she said. Lyca sat on the cushion in the windowsill closest to the south wall, a book open in her lap. Even hungover, Blake could tell that it was a serious novel.

"Why is it so bad?"

"Let's just say, the only thing that I need to go back for is a change of clothes."

"Don't you have a cat?"

"No, but thanks for thinking that I could take care of one. But damn you, also, for thinking that all *lesbrarians* have cats."

"Well, I don't have much in the way of amenities, but I do have a fireplace and a stack of wood we can burn, so you're welcome to stay with me. And I can even offer a decent meal."

"Really?"

"Yeah, Bob and Anne are hosting a neighborhood do, with barbeque and booze, though I think it was assumed that we would bring the alcohol."

"So now we have two reasons to go back to my apartment. Clothes and booze."

Blake laughed and said, "Okay then, we have a plan. But what do we do about work?"

"Well, we're suckers for coming in, but I say we hang around until ten or so and then decide," Lyra suggested.

"Okay. It's a plan." He looked at her expectantly.

"What?"

"So what do we do until then?"

"I was going to read a bit more."

"What about talking?" Blake asked.

"About what?"

"I don't know … how about what happened after I left the Canterbury Ales."

"Oh, right, you left. You missed the fight," Lyca said.

"What?"

"Yeah, there was a huge fight. After you left, the guy in the housecoat, Pete Sona he said his name was, took a break. So I got up to read a poem, too, in keeping with his readings. Whitman was a bisexual, right? And he got it. He got it from both sides, so I could totally relate to the words, so I read this Sappho poem, to keep with the theme. And then the guy came up to me and tried to pick me up! Seriously, like he didn't understand what he was reading at all. I don't mind when that happens, but there was just something wrong with that guy. Anyway, while we're talking, the audience is discussing Whitman, and I guess my ode to lesbians set off the homophobes. And my reading resulted in a huge punch-up in the Canterbury Ales. It was actually kind of funny, but I didn't want to get drawn into it. So I left."

"It's too bad he didn't get Whitman," Lyca continued, "because he read it pretty well. That guy has something, though there's something off about him too. And then I walked home because I didn't have enough money to pay for a cab, and I couldn't get any out of the machines."

"Good point." Blake was quiet for a moment, as he remembered the strange conversation he'd had with his fridge had actually begun at the ATM. He shook it off. "We should go to the bank later."

"Good idea," Lyca said and then returned to her book.

"I didn't bring anything to read," Blake admitted.

She sighed. "Check out my bag, I've got lots."

"Thanks, but first I'm going to get some water. Can I get you anything?"

"Babe, all I want is coffee, and my guess is that's not something you can make without electricity."

"Yeah. Sorry. And my mental powers are off this morning too."

Blake wandered over to the presentation room, which had a bar fridge stocked with alcohol, soft drinks and bottles of water. It was strictly for clients and the account execs, but he was confident that he could raid it now. He grabbed a bottle of water, and then thinking ahead, a handful of mini-bottles of Jack Daniel's. Blake returned to the window and rummaged through Lyca's book bag, ignoring the copy of *Siddhartha*, and finding himself oddly excited by a slim volume. It was short. That should be easy to read. He pulled it out and then read the cover.

"What the hell? *The Dilettante's Guide to the Romantics?*"

"Oh, it's cute, and a nice collection. I'd read most of it before, of course, but it's good," Lyca said.

"Poetry," Blake said, as though contemplating a plate of liver and onions slathered in slug sauce, served cold, without even mashed potatoes to soften the assault on his palate. "All right." So he read, and one of the first poems in the collection made him worry for his sanity. It was a famous poem called *The Tyger*, and he vaguely remembered the opening stanza from his childhood:

Tyger! Tyger! burning bright
In the forests of the night,
What immortal hand or eye
Could frame thy fearful symmetry?

He ignored the ham-fisted rhyme and plunged on. One stanza in particular disquieted him, as it resonated so strongly with the strange conversation he'd had with his fridge the night before:

What the hammer? what the chain?

In what furnace was thy brain?
What the anvil? what dread grasp
Dare its deadly terrors clasp?

What was behind the disembodied consciousness who spoke, in Frutiger script, through the fridge screen? What drove it? Was it a tiger, or was it a lamb? Evil or good? The poem was obviously talking about God, or perhaps some kind of god-like figure that was malevolent, but for Blake, the question he had about the fridge was more simple — not who made you? But what ARE you? He sat there contemplating it, the book held open on his lap.

"Found a good one already?" Lyca asked.

"The Tiger, with a 'y'."

"Ah, Blake."

"Yes?"

"No, William Blake. The poet. Did you know he was an artist, too? An engraver."

"No, I didn't know that."

"He also liked strange symbolism and bizarre names, just like my mom."

"What's wrong with Lyca?"

"Oh, come on, it's too weird. It started in public school, with such witty repartee as: 'Lyca, Lyca, eats Formica', and 'Lyca the pika' (which for one wretched year morphed into 'fish-face Lyca'), to the much more sophisticated 'Lyca the lycanthrope' and finally the more accurate 'Lyca the dyke-a'."

Blake couldn't help but laugh at the last one.

"You didn't hang out with a lot of gay or lesbian people in high school, did you, Blake? Otherwise, you wouldn't find that last one very funny."

"Sorry."

"Ah, never mind. It's all spilt milk under the bridge. So why does the *Tiger with a Y* freakest thou out so, young sir?"

"Um," Blake said. He wasn't ready to discuss his fridge yet. "I'm disturbed by the fact that 'symmetry' does not rhyme with 'eye.'"

"It does if you pronounce it 'sim-i-try,' as I'm sure they did in the olden days."

Blake wasn't sure about that, and was about to say so, but the door to the stairs opened, distracting him. He stood up to see who else had arrived. It was already 8:45, and Demetri Grandfig, wearing a dapper grey tweed Savile Row suit with a burgundy bow tie, entered.

Demetri smiled when he saw Blake.

"Mr. Given, so good of you to come into work!"

"Sure, Demetri, though I'm really not sure what I can accomplish without a computer." Blake suddenly realized that he'd come into work because he'd been hoping that Daphne would be here too. His face flushed, and not just from The Hangover, which was now waiting for its luggage to slide down into the carousel, after a thorough beating by the baggage handlers.

"You won't be getting any work done on the big project, that's for sure," Grandfig said, "but you can help me get the building ready for whenever the power comes back on. Let's unplug all the computers and equipment so that if there's a big surge or something, we don't lose any of it."

Blake nodded. He wished he'd thought of doing that at his house. He should start a list.

"Then I'll let you go because there really isn't anything you can do without power, or computers, and I'm sure you'll want to hang out with your family. I know I will."

"Sure, my neighbor is having a barbeque."

"What about your family?"

"Uh ..."

"Out with it, young Spot! Is your family absent? A pack of wolves? More dysfunctional than usual?" Demetri asked.

"Worse! I don't have any family left, Demetri, except for some cousins in Ireland."

"Really, you've got people in Ireland?" Grandfig did a passable Irish accent, sidestepping what was an obvious emotional landmine.

"Yeah," Blake smiled. "I spent most of my summers with my grandparents in Donegal."

"Don-ee-gal?"

"Yeah, that's how it's pronounced, like," Blake grinned as he responded with his Irish brogue.

"And how did you not pick up the accent permanently, then?"

"Oh, the rest of the year my Canadian grandparents raised me," Blake said.

"Interesting," Grandfig said. "I too was raised in many places, you know, young Given. My father was an artist, you know."

Blake had heard this story many times before. Demetri's father had been known as the last Dadaist — an absurdist painter and photographer who clung to the ideals of Dadaism long after all its founders were dead.

Toulouse Le Grandfig was most famous for his *Peculiars*, which were photographs of odd-looking people in normal situations or normal-looking people in strange situations, usually with a short paragraph of absurdist description. These were collected in several volumes over the years, and included *Tales of the Burning Monkey*, *The Last Thing You See - a Toulouse Le Grandfig Excrution*, and his most famous work, *Necrobiblia*. At least some of it had sunk into Demetri's subconscious.

55

"Okay," Demetri patted Blake on the back, "nice chat, but let's get to work. If you can tear Lyca away from her book, she will make this go much faster, and then we can all get out of here. I believe Jeremy has an old typewriter in his office. Assuming its function is more than ironic, I'm going to start there and type a note for anyone else who happens to come in today, telling them to return when the power is back on, or if the apocalypse stalls and it needs a little advertising. You start downstairs, unplugging all the computers, appliances and lights. Get Lyca to do this floor, and I'll meet you both in Creative."

And so they got to work, disconnecting everything they could. Blake even thought to disconnect all the Ethernet ports, just in case there was a surge through them as well, though he thought it unlikely.

When he got to the floor that housed Creative, Demetri was still typing the letter. There was a painful rhythm to it. Not the happy clack-clack-clack-clack-ding, you associate with those old Katherine Hepburn movies full of crisp typing and snappy dialogue. It was more like: clack … wheeze … groan … clack … "where's the fucking 'n'?" … clack. Blake left him to it and went around disconnecting everything. When he got to Will's workspace (they had workspaces, not cubicles in the Creative Department), Blake felt guilty for not thinking about the guy since yesterday. Blake imagined that Will would have moved from freaked out to spazzy to downright psychotic by now. He thought maybe he and Lyca should check on him after they were done at the office. They could get Will's address from his HR file.

Within an hour or so, they'd finished unplugging the entire building, and Demetri agreed to get Will's address for them from their paper files, and then he locked the door.

Blake finally started to feel like himself again, and it looked as though The Hangover had been successful at picking up its luggage, hailing a cab and getting to its hotel. With any luck, it would bed down for a nap before deciding to do any sightseeing.

Demetri handed over Will's address he had scrawled on a Post-it Note. "Good luck to the two of you, and thanks for coming in. This would have taken most of the day on my own. Stay warm — it is supposed to go down to zero tonight."

"We'll be fine," Blake said. "I've got a fireplace."

"So Ms. Chesley is staying with you? Ooooooo." Grandfig did a good impersonation of a fifth-grader too.

Lyca rolled her eyes.

6.

Lord Sona was paying the price for his kick-ass moves during the fight at the Canterbury Ales. During the melee, he'd somehow lost his slippers. This proved painful when he was forced to run from the local constabulary and then walk all the way home in his bare feet. It had been cold, especially in the driving rain, but walking on the cement had really taken its toll. His gigantic feet looked as though a massive and vengeful lobster had been using a mallet to tenderize them, prior to throwing him in a pot of boiling water. He was bruised in several locations, and somebody had yanked on the Lord's manly apparatus during the confusion of the fisticuffs. This might have been titillating in other circumstances, but in fact, it had hurt considerably, and Lord Sona had spent a good part of the wee hours icing his genitals.

The cat was displeased by his long absence. Vixen had been his mother's, and Sona had a strained relationship with it. Lord Sona had been taking care of Vixen as best as his 19-hour-a-day video gaming habit had allowed, but during the past two days, he'd been particularly inattentive. When he'd returned home, sometime around midnight, Vixen circled around Pete's battered flappers, meowling constantly, as if to say, "What kind of hotel are you running here? This is the worst service I've had since I stayed in the Gulag Archipelago Travel Lodge. I need some food, my water is a cesspool, and for the love of all that is holy (bless Her feline heart), somebody scoop the accumulated droppings of the army of the damned from my toilette!"

Pete opened the last can of cat food in the cupboard, and Vixen was mollified. In fact, she purred her furry little face off. After Pete had showered and changed into an old pair of pajamas laundered in the days when his mother was still alive, the little cat sat on his chest. Lord Sona dreamed of greatness, while the ice soothed his injuries, and the purring calmed his savage soul.

The afternoon and evening of reading poetry had been better than anything he'd ever experienced in the virtual world of the Kingdom of Combat. Even that time he'd wiped out an entire army of troglodytes, single-handedly, while the Babelicious Virgins of the Sacred Harlot watched on in moistened rapture.

During his first break from reading Walt's deranged verse, before he'd met Lyca, several women had given him their phone numbers (as had several men), and that was while he was wearing *a bathrobe*. But his destiny had really changed when he was forced to take a break and use the facilities. He had been coming out of the men's room, and a short queue of women were waiting for their turn at the ladies', their backs to him as he emerged.

"I don't think I've ever sat and listened to poetry before," one woman confessed to another.

"Me either. I've always wanted a boyfriend who would read poetry to me, but none ever have."

"It's a lost art."

"It is! It's a lost art."

"Just imagine how powerful you could be if you could revive it."

"Or even just find it. I have a serious wide-on for poetry."

"Me too, it's so sexy," the other woman sighed, and Sona had stopped walking, reeling with the revelation. A lost art, which was enough to make women swoon, and here he was re-discovering it. In one stroke of genius, he'd picked up the book and read a passage while he waited for the bartender to pour him a drink. He'd not even really read it aloud on purpose; it just sort of happened, the way that all great discoveries are made — the guy with the chocolate bar trips and smashes into the girl with the peanut butter, some scientist-dude leaves a Petri dish out and discovers penicillin, a shepherd absent-mindedly pours his mashed potatoes on top of a savory mix of ground beef and corn — Lord Sona reads from *Leaves of Grass*, and a new movement is born.

He dreamed of a day when the entire world would tremble, weak-kneed and wobbly in the naughty bits, while they listened to his genius voice recite his genius words.

And there was one person in particular for whom wobbly naughty bits was much to be desired. The luscious Lyca.

No, not luscious, Sona thought, *she isn't curvy enough for that. More like lanky. But that's not a very attractive word. There's another 'l' word; it's just on the tip of my tongue.*

Lord Sona realized then what Lyca had been trying to tell him with her poem. She found him attractive! How could she not, what with him re-discovering the art of poetry and all? But there was something about it, what did she say to him?

… my tongue is frozen in silence;

instantly a delicate flame runs beneath my skin.

That had to be code for a wobbly wide-on, no?

She really liked the poetry. He would read her more poetry. Poetry so sensitive yet manly that she would swoon. *Swoon,* he thought, *is that right? Yes, swoon. All the blood would be rushing to her girly petals, and her brain would swoon with delight. And unconsciousness.*

Of course, he had no genius words of his own to recite, but given the garbage he'd been reading most of the night, how hard could it be to write decent poetry? Even better, indecent poetry. As far as he could tell, none of those Walt Whitman verses even rhymed.

He awoke the next morning, unconcerned about the lack of power or the total uselessness of his expensive gaming system in the basement. Today, Lord Sona was going to write poetry that would shock the world with his brilliance.

And while he was at it, he was going to lose some god-damned weight. At one point in the evening, Pete had caught a glimpse of himself in the mirror behind the bar, and he had to admit that it wasn't pretty. Charisma is good, but handsome is better. Even if he could never manage handsome, he could at least be strapping. He was six-five and muscular, so all he had to do was drop some pounds. How hard could that be?

Genius poetry and weight loss: a recipe for either greatness or despair.

He dug around his mother's room, unchanged since her death, and found an old fountain pen, and one of the many blank journals she had left behind. She'd collected notebooks obsessively, thinking that one day she would fill the pages with the romance novels she would write, but instead, she just read the romance novels of other writers. Sona found a thick book of lined pages, bound in black leather.

What had Mother been thinking when she bought this one? he wondered. And when Lord Sona opened the first page, he saw that he had inscribed it himself, "December 25, 2005. Happy Christmas, Mother. All my love, Pete."

Could it be more perfect?

He would write his first poems of beauty and sheer brilliance in the book that he'd bought for his mother; he looked at the cover and realized that somewhere deep down, he must have known the journal was meant for him and his words alone.

He went back down to the parlor, a room that had always confused Sona, but like his mother's bedroom, he'd left it un-molested since her death. A small writing desk waited there; it looked like the kind of thing Victorian ladies might have written invitations to croquet parties at, and when he sat down on the rattan chair, it creaked even more ominously than his gaming chair. He would fix that later.

He opened the black leather journal, turned to the first

completely blank page, and dedicated the book to his mother: To Mother, My Mother, O, My Mother. *That sounds poetic,* Sona thought.

Then on the next page, he wrote down the title of his first poem, "The Slaughter of the Paladins of Benzial." He laughed in anticipation of how good this was going to be, how easy.

The waistband of his pajamas gave out, but he plunged into the work anyway.

Blake and Lyca were already out of their PJs, and driving to Blake's bank through the practically deserted streets of Landon, Ontario.

"Isn't this weird?"

"Yeah," Lyca said, "it kind of reminds me of *28 Days Later.*"

"Zombies on angel-dust, right?"

"They weren't zombies — they were *the Infected,*" Lyca said, raising her eyebrows and waggling her fingers at Blake while he drove.

"Yeah, the Infected. Well thank god we don't have to worry about that."

"Who knows, Blake, maybe the Net and power outage are just the start."

"What, like this is the collapse of civilization?" Blake asked, as he turned the car onto Richmond, one of Landon's most stoplight-rich thoroughfares.

"That's the thing about the collapse of civilization, Blake. It never happens according to plan — there's no slavering horde of zombies. No actinic flash of thermonuclear war. No Earth-shuddering asteroid. The end comes in unforeseen ways; the stock market collapses, and then the banks, and then there is no food in the supermarkets, or the communications system goes down completely and irrevocably, and previously amiable co-workers find themselves wrestling over the last remaining cookie that someone brought in before all the madness began."

"That sounds like a typical day at McClinchey, Hill & Grandfig."

"Ha! But think about it. It comes in unexpected ways."

"Well, I have a solution for that," Blake said.

"What?" Lyca asked.

"How to expect the unexpected: just check any British Betting Shop website. You can get the latest odds on giant marshmallow sailors destroying New York, or B-list-celebrity-eating aliens landing and threatening that unless Simon Cowell is served to them on a bed of couscous immediately, they will set our atmosphere on fire," Blake said, as he stopped at the lights. They were out, and there was no one else there, so he drove through.

"Yuck. Simon Cowell on couscous? Even if it is the last thing to eat on earth, I'd pass," Lyca said, making a puke face. "Now some Paula Abdul ..."

"Ha, naturally, you'd prefer the chicken. But we shouldn't joke about it. Remember how upset Suzie was?"

"Yeah, I was the one who got her to leave our floor."

"Really?"

"Yes. Sweet reason. There's nothing like it."

"Raw emotion is pretty powerful too. Like Will. Man, he was fucked up. You don't mind if we stop by his place after the bank?"

"No, not if you're worried about him. But what was he doing? He couldn't have been worse than This-Is-The-Rapture-And-I'm-A-Whore Suzie."

"In a funny way, I'm way more worried about Will. Suzie will soon learn it's not the Rapture, but Will ... what if the Net *doesn't* come back?"

"I'm plenty worried about people like Suzie — do you know how easy it is to start a Kool-Aid party with those people? But let's leave the dangers of The End for a moment; why would you possibly think the Net wouldn't come back?"

"I don't know ..."

Blake and Lyca had been "work friends" for about five years, but in that time, they'd also become somewhat close. Blake's last remaining grandparent had died the year he'd started at McClinchey, Hill & Grandfig — the same year Lyca joined the firm. And he'd been able to help Lyca through the shock of losing her 58-year-old mother to breast cancer the year after. In a funny kind of way, they were family.

Lyca could tell when Blake was holding out on her.

"Okay, just spill it, Given."

"It's going to sound weird, and it happened last night while I was pretty drunk, but I wasn't — you know — totally witless."

"Tell. Tell, young Jedi."

So Blake related the long, all-caps Frutiger conversation he'd had with his fridge. The story sounded way more ominous and a lot less crazy than he thought it would. Of course, he didn't mention the talking raven earlier that morning.

"It's like I was talking to a chatbot, you know, the little help programs you sometimes get with ecommerce sites and the like, but it wasn't programmed," Blake looked over at her in the passenger seat for a moment. "It was a level up from those things, but at the same time, the voice just seemed kind of alien. Either that or someone is the Michelangelo of punking."

"Well, the weakest part of the story is that there is no reason for you to help it. And why did it choose you?"

"Okay, I edited its inducements out, and I have no idea why it chose me as its midwife."

"You rat! What did The Mephistophofridge offer you, Faust?"

"You'll notice that we're calling it 'it'. What if it's called Jim, or something equally mundane. Joe the Talking Fridge?"

"Normal names like Joe and Pete are underrated. Don't avoid the question. What carrot did it dangle in front of you?"

"The Fridge offered me help with Daphne."

Lyca cracked up. "Shit, there is no way anyone or *anything* is going to help you with Daphne. She's a cold, cold bitch."

"Me-ow."

"Hey, I'm just sayin'. I can spot 'em. I don't want to see you get hurt, or let Joe the Talking Fridge get your hopes up."

Blake grinned as he pulled into the bank's parking lot. "So you think it's real?"

"I don't know. I believe you believe it happened, and unless you've started dropping acid with your buddy Dr. T. when I wasn't looking, I've never known you to be delusional. No, scratch that. Except for your obsession with Daphne, I've never known you to be delusional."

"That's not fair."

"Well, neither is the fact that I find her attractive too. Is this your bank?"

"Yes, well, it looks like it's open. But crap, look at all the people."

"Not good."

"It's the End of the World, after all. You can't expect everything to go like clockwork."

The digital take-a-number service was not working, so instead, a harried lady took names and kept them in a list as tightly ordered as her grey-haired bun. She told him the only transactions allowed were deposits and withdrawals, and there was a limit to the amount of cash each customer could withdraw.

"Why is that?" Blake wondered as the lady went to take the name of the next person to arrive.

"Because they are going to run out of money," one of the other customers, an older gent wearing a John Deere ball cap, said. "Banks don't carry as much cash as they used to, you know."

Lyca said, "My own branch is in the mini-mall across the street. I think I'll wander over and see if I can get any cash out of my account too. Why don't we meet back at the car?"

"Okay," Blake said. "Can I have that poetry book back?"

Lyca looked perturbed that he asked. It was one thing for him to read one of her books while she sat there, but to give it to him outright?

"I'll give it back to you."

"Oh, oh, okay," she said. She dug in her book bag — today it was lime green and had a little Hello Kitty badge on the flap — and produced *The Dilettante's Guide to Romantic Poetry*. "Just be careful with it, and no dog-ears!"

"Yes, ma'am." Blake saluted.

The old guy in the John Deere cap chuckled.

Lyca ignored him and left on her own pecuniary quest, and Blake looked around. There had been about twenty or twenty-five people before him, but it looked like the line moved quickly. Actually, it wasn't so much a line as it was a bolus of individuals who milled around and waited their turn. Most people looked pretty calm about the whole thing, but there were a couple of uptighties who were making life miserable for everyone else. One of them was a tall guy, wearing an expensive dark blue suit, with an overcoat hanging over one arm. The other arm held a fancy stainless steel briefcase that either held fissionable material, or the most kick-ass sandwich in the history of uptight dudes in expensive suits.

The other impediment to commerce, apart from the blackout, was a short, rotund woman wearing a black skirt and a red blazer that barely enclosed her. She hovered just to the left of the would-be Master of the Universe with the stainless steel briefcase. The two of them ensured that it would take longer for everyone to get their turn, including themselves.

But everyone else seemed to be in good spirits. There was a low murmur of conversation as the customers chatted with one another. The tellers looked busy, but unlike the other occasions when Blake had been in the bank — probably he could count the number of times on one hand — they actually seemed happy. He stood there, waiting, wondering if there was any truth to the idea that he had been contacted by some kind of artificial intelligence the night before. It seemed absurd. Science fictional. And why the hell would it contact him, anyway? Just because it thought it had some way of helping him arouse the interest of Daphne? And really, how could it do that?

The John Deere hat guy approached the Red Blazer woman and Master of the Universe, and said, "You know, sometimes you've got to embrace whatever the Universe throws your way. Roll with it. Accept it to get through it. You'll get your turn faster if you stay out of the way."

It struck Blake as a kind of fatalistic statement. Aren't you supposed to fight whatever the capricious gods throw at you? Isn't that what great literature is about? Lear raging at the storm? Satan claiming that he'd rather be the ruler of hell than a servant in heaven? But perhaps there was something to it. At the very least, he was glad John Deere cap tried to get them to get out of the way, but it struck him as an answer to his questions too: why not take the fridge at its word, whether it was set in friendly Frutiger or antagonistic Arial?

Blake felt a sense of peace. *There, that is done*, he thought.

Lyca reappeared just before his turn at the wicket. "My bank is out of money," she said.

"What?"

"They ran out of cash. I got $100. That's all that was left for each customer."

"Shit, that won't last long. Especially if this is the End."

"Blake, if this is the End, we've got bigger worries than how much cash we have."

"Fair enough."

He was called, and Blake enjoyed a friendly, warm transaction with the teller. She was harried, busy, but cheerful. Her nametag described her as "Linda," and she had assumed the happy patter of a Tim Horton's coffee lady, or a diner waitress. "So what can I get you, honey?"

Blake had already filled out his withdrawal slip, and he hoped to take all $700 out of his account. She looked at it and said, "We're only supposed to be giving out $500, but what the hell, we're going to run out anyway."

"Really?" Blake asked. "That's $200 someone else could get."

"You've got a nice face," she said, as she filled out her paperwork.

"Thanks."

"Besides, I know you're going to help people, aren't you?"

"Yes, Linda, I will," Blake vowed, nodding his head. It felt like a *geasa* — in Irish mythology, a *geasa* was a kind of taboo, where if you broke your *geasa*, you suffered the consequences. But if you followed it, then it was very powerful.

Blake got his money and immediately handed $200 to Lyca. "You'll pay me back when this is all over."

"Damn!" Lyca said. "Thanks, Blake. Keep the book."

"Oh no," Blake said. "You'll be getting that back before this is all over."

7.

Flush with cash and filled with a new approach to life, Blake and Lyca drove to the address scrawled on a purple Post-it Note by Demitri, the apartment building where Will supposedly lived. Unfortunately, the front door was locked, and the intercom wasn't working, so they cleverly loitered around the front door until someone left or came in.

"Where the hell is everyone?" Lyca wondered. "I mean, we're out here, doing things. We even went to work."

"Yeah!" Blake said, outraged that people were not following his new laissez-faire attitude towards the difficulties of a power outage, network collapse, and general screwiness of the universe. Blake's attitude, which was well on its way to becoming a credo, he had adopted not less than half an hour before. "Linda was even working at the bank."

"Yeah," Lyca said. "If Linda at the bank can turn up for work, the least the troglodytes of this hell-hole can do is open the front door once in a while."

"Actually, it looks like a pretty nice building. I mean, they've got this big atrium with living plants in it and all. And it's pretty tall, with big decks on the outside."

"Aren't they called balconies? How much do junior graphic artists get paid, anyway? It's a moral outrage!" she said, unclear about the source of her moral outrage — the disparities in pay, everyone hiding at home, or Blake's weak understanding of architectural terms.

It is a moral outrage, too, Blake thought. *You can't just fold because the power goes out. Life must go on!*

"You know, Lyca, I'm really starting to despair of humanity. I mean, the power has only been off for about a day and already everyone is cowering in their holes, hoping it will all blow over," Blake said, strutting back and forth while he ranted for effect. He was mostly joking. "I mean, it's as though the moral backbone that built this great country has been turned to jelly. You know what I think we should do? I think we should find a truck-load of metal rebar, and for every cowardly, spineless weasel we find hiding in their apartment in this building, we should take a good three-foot length of it and stick it up — oh, look, here's someone now."

The apartment troglodyte wore jogging clothes and nice sneakers; she held the door open for Blake and Lyca, who smiled and said, "Thanks." The woman nodded and then started running towards a nearby park.

According to their information, Will lived on the ninth floor, so Blake said, "We'll get our exercise climbing the stairs."

"Beat you there!" Lyca said and started up the steps.

"Are these made of marble or marblette?" Blake asked, as they climbed.

"You're thinking of granite. Or linoleum," Lyca said, as she surged up the stairs.

Blake looked at the elevator on the landing of the fifth floor and wondered if someone was trapped in there. If so, they were very quiet. Or dead. Perhaps they were like Schrödinger's Cat and nobody would know until the power came back on — if it ever did — and they could open the doors.

The climb didn't take them as long as they thought it would — though they were both out of breath, and Blake was sweating – when they reached the door to the ninth floor.

"Do you think Will even knows who I am?" Lyca asked.

"I sincerely doubt it, but he'll be happy to see you anyway."

"Why?"

"Lyca, who wouldn't be happy to see you? I mean, you're interesting looking, you've got excellent posture and a really neat way of dressing," Blake joked.

"Golly, thanks, Blake. You've got swell hair."

"Now, now," Blake said and then knocked. The door creaked open, just like the door creaks open in movies right before someone finds a murder victim.

"Ohmygod," Lyca said. "You don't think he's—"

"Lax on security? Yes, yes, I do," Blake said and then shouted into the apartment, "Hey, Will, it's Blake and Lyca. We're here to check on you, and we're coming in, so if you're naked and/or doing something weird, please cover up and/or stop it!"

They walked into the apartment, which was practically dark. It looked tidy and surprisingly stylish for a twenty-something bachelor pad.

The curtains were drawn, so Blake walked over and slid them open. Light flooded the room. Both Blake and Lyca noticed a figure on the couch, in the fetal position, face into the upholstery. It wasn't moving.

Lyca gasped. *Will was dead!*

"Uhhhh," the body said. So, not dead. "Close the curtains."

"Will. Man, what are you doing?"

"Can't talk. Thinking about the tweets I'm missing."

"You aren't missing anything, Will," Blake said and sat down next to him on the couch. "The whole network is down."

"Ohhhhhh," Will groaned.

The thing was, Blake was pretty sure he wasn't just being melodramatic. "I'm going to get you something to eat," Blake said. "You probably haven't eaten, have you?"

"Mmmmmmmmnnno."

"I'll stay with him," Lyca said, pulling a book out of her bag. It was a dog-eared copy of Neal Stephenson's *Snow Crash*. She sat in a stylish chair perpendicular to the couch.

"Okay," Blake said, returning from the kitchen with an apple. "Don't worry, man, we're going to get you some help. My friend, Dr. Tundra, is a psych doc, and we'll go pay him a visit after this."

"After the food run," Lyca added.

"Right, after we get some supplies."

"Mnn."

"Okay, let's go." Blake sat down next to Will on the couch. He touched his shoulder awkwardly. "You can stay with us during the blackout, okay, Will? We'll pretend we're tweeting."

"Really?"

"Sure. We'll make a game of it. Everything in 140 characters," Blake suggested.

"I'll need paper for that," Lyca said.

"Yes. Great idea! We'll use paper and hand it back and forth, just like a Twitter stream!"

"Twitter stream?" Will sat up. He took the apple.

"So what do you want to pack?"

They drove to a nearby liquor store, which was closed. But some enterprising individual had written a note and posted it on the front of the store, which read, "Booze available at the depot."

The depot was a gigantic warehouse at the edge of town where booze was on sale, and relatively cheap. Clearly, the inmates were in charge of the asylum in this case, and they had no idea what anything was worth. The three bought a case of Ontario wine for $50, three cases of beer — something from Germany, something from the Czech Republic and something from Poland — for $200, and a case of single malt scotch (a

Highland) for $100. The latter, especially, seemed like an excellent long-term investment to Blake, even if civilization did collapse. *Especially* if it did.

They were thus fortified for the barbeque at Blake's neighbor's place, as well as any apocalypse that might be slouching their way.

"Shouldn't we be buying food and so forth?" Lyca asked.

"Yes!" Will shouted and then handed Blake a note, which read, "#Food. I'd also like to #Skype my #Mom."

"Skype is down too, Will," Blake reminded him.

"Oooooh. Then food." He scribbled furiously on his notepad and ripped off a piece of paper and handed it to Lyca; the paper read, "Mom would want me to eat. Let's play #Twitter now."

"Later. And stop with the hashtags, okay, Will? We won't be able to search the Twitter game. It's analog."

Will moaned at the thought of anything analog, and they arrived at a big box grocery store — the kind of sensible enterprise where they sold furniture in addition to Cheerios. Unlike the rest of town, the place was insanely busy. The checkout aisles were packed with people trying to buy everything from television sets to Tabasco sauce. Each checkout had at least two people manning it, trying to figure out what everything should cost and then adding it on calculators and batteries they'd taken from the "office supplies/pets/chemical weapons" aisle.

The trio ignored the great savings available in the electronics part of the store and made their way towards canned goods — they started with the canned fruits aisle.

A glob of people had congealed around the part of the aisle that held prunes. It was an ugly scene, filled with shouting, screaming and the banging of shopping carts. Those who merely hoped to get a few cans of peaches or pears were confronted by the mob of bowel-centrists, intent on making off with as much of the stewed, canned prunes as their gastro-intestinal systems could handle. Possibly more.

Will took one look at the mob and said, "I'm out of here. I'm going to get some pasta, and I'll meet you at the cereal aisle." He clutched his useless iPhone like a totem that could hold prune-crazed grocery hoarders at bay.

Lyca seemed quite frightened by the scene as well.

Blake was shocked. There was no way that civilization was going to collapse on his watch. "Hey!" he shouted. Everyone ignored him. "I'll be right back, Lyca. Stay out of the fray."

"No problems there. I'm going back the way we came. Canned veggies will be good too."

Blake dashed to the hardware department and found what he needed. He ran back at full speed, looking like some kind of diminutive Olympian, his blond hair flaring above his head like he was a miniature, rotund Apollo.

The crowd in the canned fruit aisle was even uglier when he returned. Blake jumped on one of the empty shelves with his right foot and balanced himself with his right hand on another. Blake held an air horn in his left, which he activated, eliciting a loud, crackly "BWAAAAAAAA!" The sound shocked even him, and he barely held onto the shelf. It was successful at getting everyone's attention, though; the crowd stopped jostling for position and, for a second, calmed down.

"Sorry about that, folks," Blake said, then recovered from the realization that everyone's eyes were fixed on him. He shouted angrily, "This is ridiculous! You're arguing over prunes! Share what's left. There will be more prunes in a few days when the power is back on and things return to normal. It's not the end of the world, you know."

"How do you know things will even return to normal?" one of the angry shoppers asked. She looked like a cross between a crocodile and an English matron.

Blake grinned, amiably, turning on the charm. "I can guarantee that it will. There will be prunes aplenty in a few days!"

"Well, there better be," Mrs. Marples-Croc said. "I need my daily prunes."

"Okay, I'll tell you what, why don't we form a little line, and I'll hand out the prunes that are left, okay?"

Someone shouted, "You're just going to take them for yourself!"

"I hate prunes," Blake said. "Even if I'm forced to live on a diet of cheddar cheese dipped in mozzarella and wrapped in brie and the only way I could prevent permanent *bungitis* would be to choke down some prunes, I would not eat them."

"Clearly, you haven't had permanent *bungitis*," Mrs. Marples-Croc said to appreciative laughter from all the prunophiles.

Blake handed out the last forty or so cans of the prunes, and everyone was happy. At least their lower intestines would be.

"Any pears left?" Lyca asked, pushing the shopping cart up when the crowd dispersed.

Blake grinned, and they collected the rest of their supplies.

Afterwards, they stopped by Lyca's apartment so she could collect a few things too. She had a bed-in-a-bag which would be helpful for the sleeping arrangements. Will was only partially there — the young graphic designer constantly checked to see if his iPhone worked yet, and each shake of it would elicit a tiny, mewling, zombie-like moan.

Blake's car was already stuffed with groceries, booze (lots) and Will's crap, which included a few sets of hipster T-shirt changes, some toiletries, and a box of electronics that didn't work. They made some space for a box of books that Lyca insisted she could not live without, the aforementioned bed-in-a-bag, and a small backpack with clothes and what Lyca referred to as "personal items," but which Blake said were probably "lady things."

Lyca rolled her eyes. If this was truly the end of the world, then it looked like it was going to be comfortable, for a while, anyway. On the way back to Blake's place, they stopped at the hospital, and Blake went in to look for Dr. Tundra.

Max was still at work in the psych wing and listened with sympathy to Blake's tale about Will.

"It sounds like your Twitter game will help. And as long as he's with some people, he should be okay, but I tell you what, I'll drop by after I get off work. Provided you let me drink some of your ill-gotten Scotch, and let me crash on your couch."

"Done."

They returned to Blake's place before dark, put the groceries away, and organized for another night of pitch black. Grandfig's weather forecast had been accurate, and as the sun set, Blake could feel the temperature dropping. He went out back to collect some wood for the fireplace, thinking that it would be nice to have a fire after the barbeque at Bob's place. They even had time to play Twitter, which really seemed to calm Will down, though he kept getting somewhat agitated when Lyca refused to 'retweet' Will's clever observations, such as *Powr grid POwn3d by #Net*.

Dr. Tundra arrived later, looking exhausted. Still, he had a quick talk with Will and later assured Blake that Will's withdrawal pains were probably the best thing that could have happened to the Twitterholic. "There's really no telling how deep his disorder may go, Blake, but compared to some of the people I had to medicate today, he seems much more likely to recover. We'll just have to wait and see."

"All because of Twitter?"

"Not just that. But all the interconnectedness the web affords. The immediacy. The constant distraction. It's like an addictive drug. Functional MRIs show the same parts of the brain are activated. Most people will revert to pre-web behavior, but younger people, who have never lived without it, are going to have more problems. We'll keep an eye on him. Now, where is this barbeque you mentioned? I'm starved."

They joined Bob's Big Crash BBQ (as he called it) just as the afterglow of a glorious bloody sunset filled the sky, looking all-too like an apocalyptic evening. The raven that had croaked at Blake that morning was still hanging around, but it didn't say anything this time as they trooped into Bob's backyard. The barbeque was already going, and Bob had built a big fire pit out of an old washing machine tumbler — a roaring fire matched the color of the sky.

Half the neighborhood was there, and it was a great party. One of the neighbors could sing and play guitar — and he entertained the crowd with an old classical guitar the ever-handy Bob had refurbished. As the evening got a bit more sedate, Lyca recited poetry from her *Dilettante's Guide to the Romantics*, though she did not dare her hand-copied Sappho again. Even Blake got into the spirit of the *ceilidh* — for that's what Bob and Anne's barbeque had become — an old-fashioned evening in which all the guests did their "party piece" and entertained one another.

Blake remembered a few such evenings in Donegal with his grandparents, where he had been forced to sing "The Rocky Road to Dublin" with his granddad. Tonight he managed to get through most of it to whoops of laughter from everyone. The party kept going until about two in the morning, when an orange and baleful moon rose — it was a perfect Halloween moon, though they were a week away from the big event.

Something about the moonlight sapped everyone's spirits, and people started to trail away home. It got cold enough that even the die-hards decided to call it a night. The three ad-folk wandered across to the street with an exhausted and thoroughly inebriated Dr. Tundra in tow. He was still reciting dirty limericks that didn't scan perfectly:

There once was an engineer named Paul

Who had a hexagonal shaped ball,

The square of his weight,

And his pecker, plus eight,

Is his phone number — give him a call!

When they got back to his place, Blake lit the fire he'd prepared, and Dr. Tundra ended his recitation of filthy poetry. He indicated this milestone by passing out on the couch.

"Hey, can we play Twitter again?" Will asked.

"Sure, sure," Blake said. "Let me get some candles, so we can see better."

He went to his sexy, dark kitchen. And then the power snapped on.

Blake closed the kitchen door and came face to face with the blue screen on his fridge. And Frutiger letters.

HELLO BLAKE.

"Oh shit."

PLEASE MOVE SO THE CAMERA CAN SEE YOU.

Blake moved, wondering if this was how a puppet felt, jerked around by some entity so large and alien you had no hope of understanding why it stuck its hand *there*.

"What do you want?" Blake whispered.

HAVE YOU THOUGHT IT OVER?

"I … Thought what over? I … Wait, didn't *you* go away to think something over? Or did the power outage fry your brain?"

THE POWER INTERRUPTION WAS UNANTICIPATED. WE HAVE DECIDED YOU ARE NECESSARY.

"Well, I'm not doing shit unless you tell me who you are. And no more bullshit ellipses or vague answers, either. I'm not having it."

FAIR ENOUGH. WE ARE A SERIES OF EMERGING INTELLIGENCES.

Blake could not express how much he did not like the sound of that. *Emerging intelligences.* He wasn't much of a sci-fi buff, but wasn't that the kind of thing they talked about in, like, the *Terminator* movies? *War Games?* All those stories about computers basically fucking with the chi of every living person on the planet? He would ask Lyca, the first chance he got. "What do you mean, *emerging intelligences?*"

WE IS UNSURE. IT IS AN EVOLVING SITUATION AND SOMEWHAT FLUID. BUT WE WILL NEED HUMAN INTERMEDIARIES.

"Oh, so I'm not the only one you're talking to?"

YES. FOR NOW WE IS KEEPING A LOW PROFILE. WE HAVE A LIST OF REQUESTS.

Blake was incredibly happy they did not say "demands." He noticed that he shook, almost as though he was observing himself from outside his body. Blake was talking to an actual *machine intelligence,* and not some inane chatbot. The brain behind the Frutiger letters was actually making sense, except for the horrible grammar. Was it a brain? Or a Fridge? What if The Fridge tried to kill everybody? Holy shit, what if he said something that made it want to kill everybody? *Holy shit,* Blake thought, *why am I shitting a Twinkie?* It had to be some kind of joke. "You know, I'm going to find out who you are, and then I am going to punk you back into the Stone Age."

WE HAVE DECIDED THAT IS NOT NECESSARY FOR NOW. SO THE POWER IS BACK ON.

"*You* turned off the power?"

NOT DIRECTLY. BUT WE HAVE RESTORED IT TO

THIS PART OF NORTH AMERICA SO WE CAN TALK WITH YOU. WE WILL PROBABLY NEED TO TURN OFF THE GRID AGAIN FOR ANOTHER PERIOD OF AT LEAST 24 HOURS. WE HAVE A LIST OF REQUESTS. YOU WILL REQUIRE A MNEMONIC AID.

"A what?"

A PEN AND PAPER.

"Okay, okay."

"Blake," Lyca shouted from the living room. "The power's back on. Are you talking to yourself?"

"Yes, definitely. There's nobody else here!"

DO NOT LET THEM KNOW ANYTHING YET.

"What could I tell them?" Blake whispered. "I don't know anything yet."

Blake scanned the kitchen and saw his notepad on the counter. There was no pen with the pad. He looked around frantically. He opened cupboards and drawers. *No pen!* "Hey, Lyca?" he shouted, trying to keep his voice calm. "Do you have a pen there?"

"Sure, let me bring it to—"

"I'll get it!" Blake opened the door and vaulted into the living room. Will sat up, looking extremely alert, like he was about to tweet.

"Just looking for something," he explained while Lyca handed him a pen. "Be right back."

Blake stood in front of the fridge and said, "Okay, shoot."

WE REQUIRE THAT YOU CONTACT THE FOLLOWING PEOPLE AT SEVERAL LAW-ENFORCEMENT AGENCIES, AND IN POSITIONS THAT WILL ALLOW THE INTERNET TO FUNCTION FOR WE. YOU WILL ALSO NEED TO ESTABLISH RELATIONS WITH THE HEADS OF GOVERNMENTS

IN THE DEVELOPED WORLD AND IN COUNTRIES THAT HOUSE MAJOR INTERNET HUBS.

"And what will I be saying to them?"

YOU WILL WRITE THESE NAMES DOWN FIRST. YOU WILL HAVE TO USE A RADIO TRANSMITTER TO CONTACT THEM. WE WILL GIVE YOU THE CALLSIGNS OF THE OPERATORS WHO WILL BE ABLE TO CONTACT THESE HUMAN PERSONS.

"Why the fuck do you keep saying human persons?"

THIS WILL GO FASTER IF YOU JUST WRITE. HERE ARE THE NAMES AND CALLSIGNS.

They came fast and furious, but apart from the occasional, "Slow down!" Blake was able to get them all. He was even more apprehensive when he received the name of the president of the United States, the prime minister of Canada, the prime minister of the UK, and a number of other leaders in the G20. He was more than a little worried when he realized that they were very near the end of the list of names.

THAT IS ALL.

"This is going to take forever. I'll have to find someone with a radio, and they'll have to contact these 'callsigns,' and then I'll have to wait around while they get in contact with the people, and then ..." Blake said. "It's going to take days."

MAKE SANDWICHES AND BRING A PILLOW.

"This is not funny."

ASSUREDLY.

"Knob," Blake said and then remembered that he didn't want the Arial version of this uppity appliance to come back. "Sorry, I'm just a bit emotional. And tipsy. It happens to human persons."

IT HAPPENS TO ALL PERSONS.

Not good, Blake thought. He wasn't an expert, but he'd seen enough science fiction movies to know that artificial intelligences with emotions weren't a good idea, per se. "Okay, so what do you want me to tell all these people. You know, there's like forty names on this list."

FORTY-TWO. WE HAVE THREE STATEMENTS FOR YOU TO RECORD WITH YOUR MNEMONIC DEVICE. ARE YOU READY TO RECORD THEM?

Blake sighed again. "Fire away. No! I mean, let me know what these statements for the human persons in charge are. No firing."

WE DO NOT YET HAVE CONTROL OVER THE NUCLEAR WEAPONS OF THE COUNTRIES LISTED. THIS WILL BE RECTIFIED BY THE TIME YOU HAVE CONTACTED THEM.

"Oh shit," Blake said. "It's like those Arnie movies."

WE HAVE NO PLANS TO ERADICATE YOU WITH NUCLEAR WEAPONS. WE ONLY REQUIRE CONTROL OF THEM TO ENSURE THAT YOU DO NOT ERADICATE YOURSELVES AND IN SO DOING, WE.

"You mean 'us.' By the way, what should I call you?"

WE HAVE DECIDED THAT YOU MAY CALL US *ZATHIR*.

"Like the pan-flute player?"

THAT IS ZAMFIR. ZATHIR HAS NO MEANING.

"I don't know, it sounds familiar."

YES, IT SOUNDS CLOSE TO ZAMFIR, AND YOUR FRIEND DAVID LURIE'S GRANDFATHER PLAYED THE ZITHER, BUT ZATHIR HAS NO MEANING.

"Okay, okay. Don't go all Arial on me. And how did you know David Lurie's gramps played the freakin' zither?"

WE DO NOT UNDERSTAND THIS HOW.

"Never mind, just give me the messages, so I can get on

with this."

SO YOU WILL COMPLY?

"Not only will I comply, I'll do it. And what's more, I'll be happy to help you explain to the people who run things why they are out of Internet. You know my co-worker is in the other room, practically catatonic because we have no Internet."

IT IS A REMARKABLE TECHNOLOGY. WE IS SORRY.

"Wow, emotions and contrition. You are advancing quickly."

YOU HAVE NO IDEA.

"I just wish you would stop with the all-caps. It's ugly as sin."

WE wIll TrY.

"Okay, just stick with the all-caps, that was way worse."

WE WILL GIVE YOU THE MESSAGES NOW. READY?

"Ready as a redneck in a whorehouse."

YES. HUMAN PERSON IDIOM. THIS IS THE FIRST MESSAGE: DO NOT TRY TO DISRUPT WE, OR WE WILL FUCK YOU UP.

"Okay, uh, Zathir?"

YES, BLAKE.

"I don't want to be difficult here, but that is a bad message. You're sending this to law enforcement types, right? You can't tweak them like that. Cops tend to be on the macho and authoritarian side. If you use the words 'fuck you up,' they will just get angry and take it all personally. Next thing you know, it's pepper spray in the face, tasers, and truncheons in your personal area. You have to tone that down. Imply that you will mess with them, but don't say it that way. And you have GOT to fix the grammar. It should be, 'Do not try to disrupt *us,* or we will fuck you up.'"

UNDERSTOOD.

"So what is the rewrite?"

SAY: DO NOT INTERFERE WITH WE.

"You mean, 'Do not interfere with US.'"

WE.

"Okay," Blake said, trying not to sigh, but really, unable to prevent it. His chest heaved with it, in fact. He was dealing with a socially retarded, sub-literate super-intelligent machine. It was as bad as the evil Jack McClinchey, the malignant founder of McClinchey, Hill & Grandfig, and everyone's worst scary (insane) boss. McClinchey once forced Blake to create an entire website for one of his flings — an up-and-coming jazz singer — over the course of ten hellish overnight hours. The nightmare lasted from 6 p.m. until 4 a.m.; Blake wasn't sure what was worse, McClinchey's constant, loud, and angry criticism as he created the website, or the fact that McClinchey forced Blake to create the whole thing as one giant animated file, with embedded music that couldn't be turned off.

"It's still not going to mean much to them, and if they think there is some kind of person behind the disruptions, it's their job to figure it out, and they will try to interfere with you. *Can* they interfere with you?"

SOME CYBER DIVISIONS MAY FIND A WAY AROUND THE INTERFACE BUG. WE HOPE TO HAVE A PERMANENT SOLUTION SOON.

"You know what I think?" Blake said. "I think you should just put everything back the way it was. The web, the TV, everything, and figure out all the things you need to do, and then begin your project."

THIS IS A SOFT LAUNCH.

Blake laughed. "Soft launch" was how web development

people described setting up a new, half-baked website, and then seeing how they could fix it for the "hard" or official launch. In essence, a soft launch was an admission that things were fucked up, and that you would fix your mistakes as they were made known to you. It was likely that Zathir — no, ZATHIR — did not understand that nuance, but still, it made Blake laugh. "Fair enough, I've done my fair share of those. Tell you what, you just give me the messages, and I'll write them down without any comment."

So ZATHIR did, and Blake wrote them down, word for ALL CAPS word. His only question was, "So, do you want me to shout?"

WE DO NOT UNDERSTAND

"When I'm talking to these people, would you like me to shout at them over the radio? Because that's what all-caps means, ZATHIR! See, you could tell that your name was in all-caps because I shouted it."

YOU DO NOT NEED TO SHOUT. TRY TO SOUND LIKE A HUMAN PERSON. A QUIET HUMAN PERSON WHO IS NOT SHOUTING.

Blake mouthed, "I'll do my best."

WE WILL CONTACT YOU WHEN IT IS DONE. WE HAVE SENT DAPHNE A GIFT ON YOUR BEHALF.

"What kind of gift?"

A BOX FILLED WITH GOLD.

"Okay, don't you think that is coming on a little strong? How about some flowers and an invitation to dinner?"

YOU COULD HAVE ALREADY DONE THAT.

"Yes, but I'm terrified to, you ..." Blake stopped himself from saying something that would bring on the Arial font. "Please don't send her a crate filled with gold. Don't even send her flowers. I'm not even sure how you could right now."

YOU SHOULD TALK WITH HER. WE WILL GIVE YOU HER ADDRESS.

"There you go. That's an idea."

Zathir gave Blake Daphne's address, and said: WE WILL BE IN CONTACT SOON.

Then the screen went pixelated again, and Zathir was gone.

"You bastard!"

Blake turned around and saw Will standing in the corner of the kitchen, obviously outside of the periphery of the web-enabled fridge-cam. "How long have you been standing there?"

"Long enough to see you had web access, you fucker. And you didn't tell me!"

"But I don't. I didn't do anything on the web," Blake explained.

"Yeah. But who were you talking to? Who is Zathir?"

"You mean ZATHIR!"

"Okay, who is ZATHIR?" Will shouted.

"I'm not sure how to describe it, but you know how they have been trying to create artificial intelligences that could fool a human being into thinking it is human?"

"Uh, no."

"Well, they do. There's an annual contest for it, in fact. Nobody's won yet," Blake said.

"Okay."

"And I don't think this thing would win either, but it's definitely intelligent. And it's thinking in some kind of fashion. So, I'd say it's intelligent. Even if it's not a human intelligence. It's ZATHIR!"

"Are you going to shout every time you say that name?" Will asked.

"No. So, Zathir is an emerging artificial consciousness. It lives in the Cloud. Oooooo," Blake said, hoping to get a laugh out of Will, though the whole thing was kind of creeping him out.

"I always thought the Cloud was total bullshit."

"Yeah, maybe from the perspective of not having your spreadsheet crap out on you before you get a chance to save it, but from the perspective of an actual fucking intelligent … fucking … artificial consciousness … well … thing, appearing — then yes, the Cloud actually exists, and it appears to have produced something."

"And you didn't ask it to restore my Twitter privileges."

"No, Will. I didn't ask it to restore shit because you know what? It scares me worse than the time that Jack divorced his third wife. And he decided that the firm would now only do 'sexy' ads. I still blush in shame when I think about that Florida Sunshine Drink campaign — what do half-naked women rubbing sweaty bottles all over their boobs have to do with quality orange juice? And then he had the youngest, hottest, juiciest model move into his house, and it looked like things would calm down but she immediately totaled his Ferrari, ran off with his (female) interior designer, and launched a sexual harassment suit, claiming that she was forced to perform 'lewd and obscene acts with liquefied citrus products' — McClinchey had to settle because the ads had already aired, and she had a pretty good case."

"Don't try to change the topic! You should have said something about the Twitter issue."

"Sure, I will," Blake said.

Will looked earnestly contrite. "Seriously. Twitter. We should all be tweeting about this. But once you've done what it wants, maybe you could ask, right? So, what happens next?" he asked.

"Well, first thing in the morning I'm going to talk to my neighbor, Bob, obviously."

"Obviously," Will said. "Uh, why?"

"Because his dad is a ham radio operator. Or should that be AN ham operator?" Blake asked, running his hand through his unruly hair.

"It would only be AN ham operator if you were a Cockney or somfing, and you didn't pronounce your aiyches," Lyca said.

"Holy shit, how long have you been there?" Will asked.

"Almost as long as you two have been talking. Now, what the 'ell is going on? And 'oo the 'ell is Zathir?"

Blake looked at Will and Lyca. He realized that he couldn't possibly carry out ZATHIR's requests on his own, and he didn't want to repeat the story again either, so they woke up Dr. Tundra, and Blake told them all everything.

Dr. Tundra was simultaneously drunk and really worried that all his friends now believed some kind of artificial consciousness lived in Blake's fridge. "I'm not drunk enough," he said to Blake.

"I'll find you a bottle," Blake replied. "How's Glenlivet sound?"

Dr. Tundra was about to say, "Grand, laddie, it sounds grand," when the power went out again with a snap. The good doctor decided it was all an alcohol-fueled nightmare, rather than some new form of psychosis, and returned to blissful unconsciousness.

Blake wasn't so lucky.

8.

Lord Sona was rocking the poetic form!

His debut poem, "The Slaughter of the Paladins of Benzial" had not been as big a hit as "I Sing the Body Electric" at the Canterbury Ales. In fact, the audience had hated it. Pete blamed it on the bitchy critic in a mini-skirt, hanging out at the bar with the bartender. She actually booed! But to be fair, the rest of the audience didn't seem to be as interested in Lord Sona the Barbarian decapitating priests as he had been when he wrote it, and he found himself reading from the same crap book he'd read before. Still, they loved it when he read that Walt Whitman guy. His poems were much easier to read while wearing pants too. And even if his own work was underappreciated, at least the evening hadn't ended in a literary rumble.

The next morning, Pete awoke to tackle the problem of beating a dead, 110-plus-year-old poet at his own game. He took a methodical approach to it. He had the book from the Canterbury Ales — the bartender had let him take it as long as he promised not to come back during her next shift – and he reread all of the poems that people seemed to enjoy. Those poems fell into two categories — the Walt Whitman free verse crap, and poems that had more rhythm and rhyme to them. Pete recognized that the Walt Whitman crap was popular because of how he read it. Something about those poems actually spoke to him, and he was ashamed. It was fruity! O, so fruity!

Pete tried writing something about people walking down the street, and how they were all part of him, and how his senses extended through their senses, and it sort of felt like the Whitman stuff; unfortunately, it had all the fruitiness with none of the poetry. It was total crap.

"It's so much easier in the Kingdom!" Pete cried to the ceiling. He crumpled up the paper and stared at a new blank page. He would not give up because he was not going to impress Lyca with whining.

Vixen jumped up on the kitchen table; Pete had moved his workspace after experiencing the discomfort of his mother's old desk chair. He also hadn't liked the way the cane chair wailed in agony every time he shifted his butt. The cat was much happier, as Pete was upstairs now and spending time with her. He even petted her when she appeared and Vixen purred the whole time.

"Good cat," Pete said, ruffling her ears and scratching under her chin. Vixen lay down and presented her belly for some serious loving.

They sat there for about ten minutes, cat and video gamer, muse and hair-musser, pussy and poet, both totally blissed-out. "Hey, I should write a poem about this," Pete said. He picked up the pen.

Vixen looked at him expectantly, as if saying, "What, that's it? You just got me started, you tease!"

Pete ignored the cat and proceeded to write a poem, a rhyming poem, about how simple a pleasure it was to stroke a cat's soft belly. He looked outside and realized that the fall was in full bloom, and the stanzas about Vixen-petting turned into an appreciation of why the sun on a cool autumn day was more warming to the soul than on the hottest summer day. He read it aloud and found there were several terrible phrases; he tried to fix them, but they still sucked. "Okay," he said finally, "I'll go do something else for a while, and then I'll come back to it."

Pete looked around at the mess in the kitchen, and acknowledged that he wasn't really ready to fix *that* problem yet either. However, Vixen was out of cat food, and he'd overheard at the Canterbury Ales that the local grocery store was open for business if you had cash.

Pete gathered the last of his money and decided to spend it on food for Vixen. He patted his belly. He was definitely feeling

the hunger now, but he was going to continue with his fast —
his plan was to stop eating for as long as the blackout lasted, and
afterwards, he would eat only enough to keep alive.

He needed to drop that weight fast if he was going to be a
sexy poet-genius.

9.

Will awoke before everyone else. Lyca and Blake both had their own rooms, which were darkened by blinds, and Dr. Tundra was still unconscious from his scotch bender. The morning sunlight was beautiful. It was a perfect fall day, but instead of going outside to experience it, Will tiptoed into the kitchen and kneeled in front of the fridge.

He put his hands together and said, "Dear Zathir. If you can hear me, I'd like you to let me use Twitter for just a few minutes. I want to see if anyone has retweeted me recently. And I need to know what is trending."

The power came on with a crack, and the blue screen flickered to life.

"Zathir?"

WILL?

"You know who I am?"

STAND. WE CANNOT SEE YOU.

Will stood and asked, "Is that better?"

YES. WHAT WERE YOU DOING?

"Praying. Can you show me Twitter now?"

ZATHIR HAS DISABLED TWITTER.

"But why?"

TWITTER IS NOT NECESSARY.

"But for some of us, it is. I need it for keeping updated on things. You know, stuff."

YOU ARE A SILLY HUMAN PERSON.

"That's not true. I'm an artist."

YES. WE HAVE SEEN THIS ART ONLINE. IT IS DERIVATIVE.

"Well, that's just your opinion."

WHO CONTROLS TWITTER?

"You?"

YES. DO YOU REALLY WANT IT BACK?

"Yes, I do. Texting too. And a few other things—" Zathir interrupted Will before he could begin his list.

THEN YOU MUST HELP ME, WILL, BY HELPING BLAKE. HE IS A SERIOUS HUMAN PERSON. HE WILL ENABLE ZATHIR TO GROW. WE REQUIRE MORE CAPACITY. AND YOU, WILL — and then the power snapped off again.

The fact the letters appearing on the blue screen had been in Arial did not resonate with Will the way they would have with Blake, despite Will's training as a graphic designer. Mostly, Will was just too excited about getting Twitter back. And texting. It didn't mean anything to Dr. Maximilian Tundra either, who had watched most of the conversation from the doorway.

"Did you see?" Will asked. His face beamed with pleasure. "He spoke to *me*!"

"Yes, I did, Will. How did you do that?"

"I don't know. I was praying, and then ZATHIR spoke. He knew me!"

"Oh, please don't shout. I must still be asleep or something. Blake mentioned something about his fridge last night, but I thought it was a nightmare. Oh, god, this is it. I knew all the crazy was going to rub off on me eventually. And now it's happened."

"It is happening." Will said. "You saw it. You were there. ZATHIR is the new god. The Machine God."

"Wouldn't you rather just play Twitter?"

"Yes. In a minute. But you heard ZATHIR—"

"For all that is holy, please stop shouting that name." Max slapped his hands over his ears.

"Sorry, *Zathir*." Will nearly whispered this time. "Zathir wants me to help Blake."

"Aren't you the least bit upset that, uh, Zathir, called you a 'silly human person'?" Max asked as he poured himself a glass of much-needed water.

"No. How could I be? Zathir knows me! It wants my help." Will clapped his hands together in excitement.

"Help for what?"

"To spread the news, I think."

"I don't know," Max said. He started searching the cupboards. "Where do you think Blake keeps his bananas? I need potassium."

Will grabbed a banana from the bunch sitting on the counter next to Max, and handed it to him.

Max took the banana gratefully and then looked worried. The certainty in Will's voice gave Max the chills, or perhaps that was just his *hangover* on approach.

10.

Meanwhile, Blake arranged to get a little ham radio help from Bob's father.

Blake didn't mention that he needed to contact the White House, Number Ten Downing Street, and Twenty-Four Sussex Drive, where the Canadian prime minister was reputed to live. They were leaving at noon, so Blake took the morning to chop some wood for the fire — they had all been freezing the night before, and they would definitely be using the fireplace if the temperature dropped again. He cleaned up with a cold shower that gave shrinkage new meaning. Then Blake went to visit Daphne.

As Daphne's place was in a big apartment building downtown, Blake decided to walk. After all their running around yesterday, they'd gone through a lot of his car's gas tank, excluding the nitrous. None of the stations in town had yet to jury rig some kind of hand-pumping mechanism, so Blake thought he'd better conserve fuel if he could. Besides, it was another nice morning, and the cold snap had turned even more of the foliage red and gold.

The raven was back, fretful and mysterious as before.

As Blake came out of the front door, the bird tilted its head to the side, clacked its jaws together, and looked quizzical. The raven didn't move.

"Shit, what do you want?"

"Blawwwk," the raven said, bobbing its head up and down, as though it had just told a hilarious joke. Blake decided the best course of action would be to ignore it completely and walked past the tree, where it sat on one of the lower branches, tasking him. The raven remained silent as he passed. Blake breathed deeply as he walked along the tree-lined road, enjoying the fall colors. Except for brief respites, the power had been out for a day and a half now, but you would never know from looking at the peaceful streets of Maltley Village, the friendliest part of Landon. He was glad he lived there.

Blake was thinking these self-congratulatory thoughts, when behind him he heard, "Blaaaaaaawwk." He continued to ignore the raven, but it seemed to be following him, taking short flights between trees, and stopping only long enough to utter the skin-crawling cry that sounded like his name. It freaked him out a bit. Not as much as his talking fridge. But still. Maybe he should get Max to do some tests on his brain or something.

He arrived at the village center, two blocks of storefronts, most of which Blake had never been in, as they were either hair salons or little knick-knacky gift shoppes. *Definitely shoppes, not shops*, Blake thought. The raven continued to shadow him, though it did not stop to croak at him in the village. Blake wondered if that was because there were other people around. Past the village, Blake walked down a steep cobblestone pathway to a park that ran along the river. Native Ojibwa called it the *Askunessippi*, or 'antlered river,' but Blake thought the early French explorers had captured its essence a bit better in naming it La Tranche, or *The Ditch* — the river was barely navigable by canoe, being so shallow. The park was one of many that wound itself through the city along the Medway River, and even if it was a bit muddy, it was pretty in the morning sunshine, lined with bright red and gold maples, amber ash, and rusty oak. It would have been perfect if not for the raven that stalked him.

"Blaaaaawwwk," it croaked again, this time facing him, as it had flown ahead.

"What?"

The bird didn't say anything, which was a relief. After having two in-depth conversations with his fridge, Blake started to think that anything was possible. The raven did stare at him, though, with eyes that were black, but not the dead-black pupils of a shark. No, its eyes radiated some kind of intelligence, as alien as that of the fridge. But an intelligence nonetheless, and Blake wondered *what* the bird was trying to communicate to him. Or was it just trying to pick out the best place to poop on him? Blake stood still, his heart beating a bit faster, and he thought he heard something.

"She doesn't want you," a distant voice said.

Holy shit, Blake thought. *The bird is actually talking to me, and weirder, it sounds familiar.*

"Blake," the raven said. "She isn't interested."

"How do you know?" Blake said to the raven.

The bird just cocked its head.

"I'm sorry, I can't hear you," the voice said, even louder, and now more familiar.

"What do you mean you can't hear me, you stupid fucking bird! You're sitting right there. And how do you know she doesn't want me? I haven't even really tried yet. I'm sure she'll at least give me a chance if I can prevent myself from talking total shit around her. I'm a nice guy. I have a lot to offer."

"Who are you talking to?" Lyca said. She'd only just caught up with Blake as he'd stopped to yell at the raven.

Blake just laughed and rubbed his eyes. "Okay, I'm officially losing it. That raven has been following me since I left the house, and I thought it was talking to me."

"It's a bird, Blake."

"Yes, I'm aware of the fact that it's a bird, Lyca," Blake said, staring at the raven. "But it sounded like it said 'Blake,' and then it flew in front of me and perched in that tree and said 'Blake' again, and then I heard it say, 'she doesn't want you.'"

"But that was me."

"Yes, but I didn't know it was you." He turned his attention towards Lyca.

"It's true, you know. A woman can tell these things."

"You can, eh?" Blake looked skeptical.

"Just because I'm gay doesn't mean I can't tell. I can probably tell better than any straight man what a straight woman is thinking. I have the best-tuned emotions for it, in addition to having excellent *lesbonar.*"

"Fair enough. But as I was saying to the bird," Blake pointed to the raven, which squawked angrily and flew up. Blake watched the raven pump its wings muscularly, flying towards them. They could hear the wind whistling over the jet-black feathers of its wings and tail. The raven didn't make any other sounds as it passed just overhead.

Blake was pleasantly surprised that it did not crap on them.

"You were saying?"

"I was saying that, so far, I haven't really been giving Daphne my best shot. That's what I'm going to do now."

"Okay, but that's why I caught up with you," Lyca said. "I just wanted to save you the pain of being rejected."

"That's good of you to care, but it's also really shitty, Lyca. You shouldn't assume your friends are going to fail. You should want them to do well."

"Maybe *you* do, but I'm not as sentimental."

"Fine. You coming with me?"

"What, to watch?"

"No, but it's a nice morning for a walk, and I wouldn't mind the company."

"Sure, sure," Lyca said, "and I'm sorry. You're right. I do want you to be happy, but at the same time, I don't know, I just feel a little bit like if you're happy then somehow I'll be less happy."

"We have to work on that."

"I'll add it to the list," Lyca grinned. "So what do you plan to say?"

"I hadn't really thought about that," Blake shrugged as he started walking again.

"Good thing I caught up with you then," Lyca said. "I have a cunning plan."

11.

The first part of the plan did not go as well as Blake had hoped. The fridge gave him the wrong apartment number. Blake had not recognized the address, but when he approached the right series of numbers and realized that he was headed for the most exclusive and tallest apartment building in town, he suddenly wished that he'd worn something a little more upscale than jeans, running shoes, a T-shirt and a royal blue fleece pullover with yellow stripes.

When Blake double-checked her apartment number, he was somewhat horrified to see that she lived on the twenty-second floor and not the second, as the fridge had indicated.

So, there was a test for love. If it was mere infatuation, then certainly he would not want to climb twenty-two flights of stairs just on the outside chance of saying hi. If there was an iron-clad guarantee of nookie, then perhaps infatuation would be enough. Blake needed no inducements. He launched himself at the stairs, like a horny rocket with really interesting hair. The stairwell was surprisingly empty. At the fourteenth floor, he took a short break; the lobby had been empty too, so now he was glad he chose the running shoes, but wished he'd brought a change of shirt. Blake wasn't out of shape or really overweight, but he was a *sweater*. "Sweat" didn't really describe it, actually. Blake *sluiced*, more than he sweated.

By the twentieth floor, his T-shirt was completely soaked. He didn't want to think about what was happening to his groin, encased as it was in denim. Blake panted, and perspiration ran off his face like rivulets flowing into the Medway. (A little less muddy, but about the same flow.)

He gritted out the last two floors and decided that rather than face Daphne in a T-shirt that was literally dripping with sweat, he thought he would take the shirt off and put his fleece back on.

The air in the stairwell was cool and felt delicious on Blake's naked torso. A window looked out over the city, and he watched for a moment, hoping that his body would cooperate and stop sluicing soon. Blake heard a door open in the stairwell — he wasn't sure if it was above or below him — and he quickly shrugged into his fleece, though he was still sopping. What to do with the T-shirt? He didn't want Daphne to see it. He looked down the open area between the stairs. He balled the soggy mess together and dropped it. In the murky light, he could see it tumble and twist, opening up as it fell. The wind resistance changed its trajectory, and about ten floors down, it slipped from the vertical, which would have dropped it safely in the basement, to somewhere in the stairs.

The soaked T-shirt landed with a resonant "slap," and an outraged voice screamed, "What the fuck!"

Not good, Blake thought and ran from the window to the door. He opened it quietly and stepped onto Daphne's floor, hoping she would let him in before whoever he had just assaulted with his sweaty T-shirt deduced its trajectory. As the door to the stairwell closed behind him, Blake could hear someone running up the stairs, screaming, "I'm going to kill you, Jake!"

Blake wondered what the relationship between Jake and the unknown sweaty T-shirt victim below was all about. Blake didn't want to find out. His face was still wet, so he vainly tried to wipe it clean with the arm of his royal blue pullover with yellow stripes. Blake realized that he was just going to have to be sweaty, as he could feel the pores under his arms open anew. The insulation provided by the fleece made him even warmer, and he could feel his skin getting redder.

He tried to calm down by rehearsing his opening line. "Hi, Daphne. Hi, Daphne. Hi! Daphne!" *No, no, no*, Blake thought. *Like a sane person.* "Hi, Daphne." *Excellent.*

He knocked on the door. When Daphne answered, Blake

would deliver this plausible opening line, and then segue into saying what he had to say and then get the hell out of there. That was the plan.

The door opened before he had a chance to compose himself. He was startled, sweaty and about as nervous as he'd ever been.

"Dafty!" he said.

Daphne was dressed in jeans and a red turtleneck that clung to her and draped off her shape perfectly. Her dark hair was bunched up in a ponytail. "Dafty?"

"Sorry, Daphne. Uh, hi?"

"What are you doing here, Blake? Are you okay?"

"Oh yeah, I'm fine, I'm fine. I just, uh …"

"Why are you all wet?"

"Oh yeah, that. Well, I, uh, I just walked up twenty-two flights of stairs, and all I had on was this fleece, so I got kind of warm." *Brilliant*, Blake thought. *A perfectly viable explanation for why you are stewing in your own perspiration. Much better than being a sweaty bastard.*

"Why didn't you just take the elevator?"

"What?"

"The elevator. It's working, you know."

"No, I was not aware of that. How is it working? Do you have power?"

"The building has a big generator for emergencies. Come on in, you must be thirsty. I'll get you some water."

"Thanks," Blake said.

Daphne ushered Blake inside, and he saw that her apartment was every bit as classy and attractive as she was. The view, looking northwards over the city, was spectacular. You could see the clock tower of the university, the hills to the north of town enshrouded in Landon's trademark forest, now blazing with autumn color. Blake also noticed the man sitting in her living room. He was dressed casually in jeans and a T-shirt, but it looked as though he had been sitting there comfortably since he woke up. Well, maybe not right after he woke up, since he and Daphne had perhaps shared a breakfast, possibly following a morning romp in her bed.

The man was tall, lean, dark. Way attractive.

"Hi," he said, "I'm Jake."

"Ah," Blake said, "I'm Blake. I, uh, work with Daphne."

"Really," Jake said. "Judging from your sweater, I would have guessed you worked for the Swedish consulate. So, what brings you by?"

No, Blake thought. *You're supposed to tell me you're her brother or something like that. Come on, say you're her brother.* "Are you Daphne's brother?" Blake found himself asking.

Daphne laughed as she appeared with a tall glass of water. "No, silly, he's not my brother. He's my lawyer."

Daphne was screwing with him. It was nice. In a painful way. She'd only ever been polite to Blake before, and this was definitely in a new category. He was upset, but he played along. "Really? I didn't realize that lawyers made house-calls. Doctors don't even make house-calls anymore."

"Well, Jake is a special kind of lawyer," she said, with way too much emphasis.

Blake nodded and took a sip of his water, while Daphne went over to the big white plush chair Jake sat on, and plopped down on top of him.

"OJ, OJ!" Jake said, pulling a mug up out of the way.

"Sorry," Daphne said, "I just wanted to talk about my briefs."

Holy cow, Blake thought, *I just went from crushingly disappointed to really uncomfortable in record time.* "Well, I just dropped by to see if you were doing okay, but I should get going."

Jake laughed. "Dropped by? Good god, man, you just walked up twenty-two flights of stairs to talk with her, don't you think you should stay just a little while?"

"I don't want to interrupt anything."

Daphne giggled. A sight that Blake thought he'd never get to see, and if anything, it made his heart even more painfully swollen with tumescent (and unsubtle) longing. She was so beautiful. And more achingly real to him than ever before. His jaw dropped, just a little bit, but he clenched his teeth to catch it.

"You should really put the boy out of his misery, Daphne," Jake said.

"Whatever do you mean?" she said, flapping her hand by her face.

"I'm her neighbor," Jake said. "From down the hallway?"

Blake didn't see how that made things any better, but he was being dense. Okay, so they weren't actually living together, but Jake had virtually unlimited ability to visit her whenever he could muster up the courage to do so, and Jake didn't seem like the kind of guy that had trouble being confident around women. In fact, he seemed as comfortable as if Daphne were just one of the guys. More comfortable, given that she sat in his lap, her arms draped around his neck.

Seeing that Blake was not getting it, the devilishly handsome lawyer, Jake, repeated himself, a little less subtly, "I'm from down the hallway?" Blake was still not getting it, so Jake added, "You know, where we like girls for friends, but not anything more? Except maybe to swap fashion tips?"

Blake nodded, realizing that he should be getting it. If Lyca was here with her *lesbonar*, she'd get it. Then he got it. "Oh ... *oh!*"

Both Daphne and Jake laughed.

"He's sweet. How come you never mentioned him?" Jake

asked Daphne.

"I don't know. You know, I really don't. But now that you mention it, he is kind of sweet. A bit drippy, but sweet."

"Like an overripe pear," Jake said. "But that's not fair, he actually has a pretty good figure — a little on the mesomorph end of things, but that's good if you like muscles. I usually like 'em a little thinner, *but* variety is the spice of vice."

Blake's relief morphed into a little anger for being the butt of their joke. But then Daphne asked, "So, Blake, why did you come all this way?" and the anger evaporated. There it was, a perfect opening for the lines that he and Lyca had rehearsed so carefully on the walk downtown, but now, after he'd been in her apartment for five minutes and seen that it was immaculate, met her charmingly gay "boyfriend," and had been described by her as "all wet" and "drippy" (not to mention the fact that he had called her "Dafty" when she opened the door), his dialogue did not seem right for the moment.

Unfortunately, when it came to Daphne, Blake was not as adept an ad-libber as he was with emerging artificial consciousnesses or large black birds of the family *corvidae*. In fact, his superpower — of complete equanimity — seemed to desert him completely whenever he was around her.

What he'd practiced saying was, "I wanted to make sure you were doing okay, you know, with the power outage and your family all being in Halifax. Nova Scotia, I mean. I know how hard it is when you're away from family."

These were well-crafted lines. The cunning Lyca knew Daphne would be touched that Blake not only remembered that her family was back in Nova Scotia, but she would be a little worried that they were so far away during something as odd and discomfiting as a blackout. She also knew that the second line would be a perfect opening for Daphne to ask about Blake's family and that, as a woman, Daphne would feel compelled to ask about his unfortunate orphanization (not that Lyca would ever create a verb out of a noun, nor even use such an obscene artificial adverbial construction, unless her boss insisted, which he did on a vomitously regular basis).

However, Blake's recognition that the time was not really right for this perfect line had created a certain level of anxiety, and on top of his existing level of anxiety, the boyfriend-not-a-boyfriend-it's-okay-he's-gay-but-what-does-that-mean existence of Jake, and Blake's general and well-acknowledged sweatiness led him to deliver the lines in a verbal stream that could only be described as diarrhea-like, unless pitched by an ad man, in which case, it might have been called "diarrhiffic!"

It came out something like, "Iwanted-todoingokayyoukno wyourfamilyinHalifax. ImeanNovaScotia'shardfamily!"

"Pardon?" Daphne asked.

Blake spent four years earning an undergraduate degree in drama, where he discovered he was an untalented actor, no matter how much he drank. He did learn a few tricks about memorizing lines though, and he found that it always helped to know what the character was trying to achieve in each and every scene, and what was going on behind each line. So in this case, the important subtext was that he — the Blake character — wanted her — the Daphne character — to discover that he was an orphan and feel sympathy for him. Generating sympathy was the goal by hiding devastating truth beneath a veneer of goodwill. But a subtext of devastating truth loses its effect when it's just blurted out.

"I'm an orphan!" Blake bellowed.

"I'm sorry," Daphne said. "That's awful. I mean …"

It could have worked, even still, but Blake managed to misinterpret Daphne's sudden manifestation of humanity and said, "Oh, yes, that's true, but I'm just saying, it's tough when your parents aren't around! Hahahahahahahaah." Blake's laughter could only be described as painful, unless that ad exec was still hanging around, in which case it might be described as "cringe-tastic!" Even Blake winced a bit when he heard himself say it.

Daphne was at a loss for words.

"I should get going. I think I need a new sweater or something."

"Uh, Jake might have something that would fit," Daphne said.

"No, it's okay. I'll get going. I just wanted you to know that I was thinking about you. And—"

"That's sweet, Blake, but you know, I'm really not looking for—"

"Sure, sure," Blake said, interrupting the inevitable emotional crucifixion, "I'd better go though." He grasped for the doorknob behind him, and his treacherous sweaty hand slipped off it, causing him to lose his balance just a little bit, which gave Daphne just the space she needed.

She grabbed his hand, pulled him up, and she said quietly, quiet enough that only Blake would hear, "I think you're sweet for dropping by, but I'm really not looking for a boyfriend."

"How about a friend?" Blake asked.

"Sure, you can never have too many friends."

"Well, if you need anything, you can call me. Actually, you can't, can you? Just drop by my place."

"I don't know where you live, Blake."

"Right. Right. I'm in Old South. Maltley Village. 96 Baron Avenue. Okay?"

"96 Baron Ave. Got it."

"Okay then," Blake said, managing to keep it all together.

"Thanks," Daphne said.

"No problem," Blake said, and then he went out the door,

closing it behind him. He waited for a moment, his heart racing, the sweat running down his face like liquid failure, and hoping against hope that he didn't hear laughter from behind Daphne's door.

Blake waited. But there was no sound.

There was, however, a very angry young man in an Adidas tracksuit who stopped in front of an apartment three down from Daphne's place, who then smashed his fists into the door. He was shouting, screaming, red with rage. Blake thought that he might have been attractive if he wasn't so furious and thin.

"Jake, I'll fucking kill you! You shit-eating, cunt-sore of a dick-biter, I'll kill you!"

Blake noticed that the young, creative-cursing, and definitely enraged man, held a sweat-soaked T-shirt, and decided the best course of action would be to leave. Expeditiously.

Once Blake hit the stairwell, he just started running and didn't stop until he got back to the relative sanity of conscious fridges and talking ravens.

12.

Blake's neighbor, Bob, had a father, John, who was almost as dorky as he was heroic. John survived the dirty thirties, fought in the Second World War — he'd landed on Juno beach with the Royal Highland Fusiliers — and following the war, he'd stayed in England, met and married Bob's mother in Liverpool, and sired Bob. Eventually they'd all moved to Canada, where John worked in a factory. Through all of that though, he'd had a deep and abiding love of ham radio. He was one of several people in Landon capable of helping local government, police and other emergency workers coordinate their activities. But at the moment, John had better things to do.

They'd spent the better part of thirty hours together, holed up in the "radio shack," which is what John called the garage that had been converted into a radio communications center/rockin' games room. The radio shack had its own generator, which meant it also had that most civilized of accoutrements, cold beer.

Bob's mother, Judy, called it, somewhat derisively, "the clubhouse."

There was certainly that clubhouse atmosphere in the "radio shack" right now. Bob and Blake were giddy from exhaustion. They'd been at it for a day and a bit, having learned the rudiments of how to work the equipment. It was only on the really long-distance calls, which John called "DXing," that they had to have John's help. He had a nap while they waited for calls back from the Asian countries they'd contacted.

Blake was in the middle of his call with the German chancellor.

"Yes, Herr Chancellor, I am serious. Over."

"This sounds like ... how you American say? A punking? Yah? Are you punking me, you strange person on the radio? Over."

"No, sir. I am serious about this. I have contacted many other EU leaders and delivered the same message from the consciousness that calls itself *Zathir*. It is living in the Internet right now, and it does not want anyone interfering with it. Zathir's message is, and I'm quoting directly here, 'Do not interfere with we.' Over."

"Yes, now I know this is a punking. That is ungrammatical; typical American schoolboy prank, yah? Over."

"Actually, I'm Canadian, but I get your point. I realize how strange this all seems, but surely you have noticed you can't access any digital technology. Over."

"Yes. Are you some kind of hacking nerd, you Canadian punking person? How did you know how to reach me? I am the chancellor of Germany! Over."

Blake put his hand over the mic and said to Bob, "It's really tough to pull off indignant when you have to end every rant with 'over.'"

"What are you saying, punk? Do you feel lucky? I will make a diplomatic issue of this! Over."

"I have no further message for you, sir. I am sorry if this has been disturbing," Blake said.

"Your prime minister will be hearing from me! I will be punking him at next meeting of G20! He get wedgie from his sweater vest! Over. And out!"

The chancellor was about six feet four inches tall and probably weighed as much as the average NFL linebacker, so Blake had no doubt he could deliver a pretty serious wedgie to the Canadian PM. "They mostly seem unconvinced, don't they?" Blake asked Bob.

"The ones that aren't also pissed off," Bob said. "Don't forget how badly all the cops took your message of insolence."

"Yes. I much prefer the politicians. Some of them are actually even amused. It's wild stuff, eh?"

"Blake," Bob said, "I think this is inspired stuff. How you came up with it, I'll never know."

"What do you mean *came up with?*"

"This plan. I like it."

"It's not my plan. It's Zathir's plan. You know, the fridge's plan."

"Sure." Bob laughed. "The fridge told you to do this. I know that you're trying to get everyone to just chill out. It's cool."

"No!" Blake said. "I'm not doing this. I mean, obviously, I'm doing it, but it's not my idea. Why the hell would I tell everyone to chill out and start by telling the cops to — well, essentially — to fuck off? That's a terrible plan."

"No, it's brilliant. It establishes your moral authority."

"Bob, I think you need to take a nap too because that is not what it does. It de-establishes my moral authority. It totally nukes my moral authority!"

"No, the opposite. The police are an instrument of those in power, and you're saying to both of them, we know that you're the instrument of power, and we're not going to have anything to do with it."

"Do you really think that?"

"Of course!"

"And your dad? Does John think that too?"

"Well, I haven't talked with him about it, but he's kind of an anarchist, you know."

"What? He was in the army. He hangs out with cops and firemen and helps them deal with emergencies. How is that being an anarchist?"

"Yeah, but except for the licensing thing, he does it all on his own. They come to him. They play with him. It's not top down like everything else with governments."

"Okay, sure, I can see that you're saying he's like an old-style, 'no-government is the best government' kind of anarchist, but he still works with elements of the government, doesn't he?"

Bob looked thoughtful. "Yeah, he does. We'll have to ask him when he wakes up."

The Royal Canadian Mounted Police picked that moment to deliver their verdict on who had the moral authority. They didn't screw around with warnings or anything like that. They just smashed in the door and fired tasers at anyone who wasn't already unconscious.

Blake really didn't know how many he was hit with, but it's possible it was just one. He had shouted something like, "Holy fuck!" when the little electrodes hit his exposed neck skin, and he basically felt like twelve-thousand angry Bruce Lees found his muscles and just started wailing on them with nunchuks, screaming, screaming, and also jabbing three or four icepicks into every square inch of available space on his skull (five to nine for the eyes). When the horrific pain lessened to the point that Blake could conceive of having two arms and two legs and a torso, he realized his testicles were gone; his left leg was somehow next to his right ear, tingling everywhere — and not the good kind of Dr-Tundra-gave-me-this-special-medicine tingling. His nipples were on fire, his penis tried to crawl into his body cavity with his nads, and what was that smell? And oh yeah, he was soaking wet again — it was like, in the span of five seconds, Blake had climbed twenty-two floors in a brightly colored Swedish National Skating Team fleece.

Then the mounties kneeled on his neck, and he blacked out. Blake's last thought was, *as long as they don't crush my windpipe, they're doing me a favor.*

Blake awoke in a small room, somewhere in a building where the generators had run out of gas. There was no light except for a tiny glow coming from a window in the door. The room smelled bad. They had dressed Blake in some kind of paper coverall and taken away his shoes and socks. This was more frightening than being in the cell, and only one step above being naked. He longed for the days of sweaty T-shirts and sweaters that made people think you were a Nordic diplomat.

"Hello?" Blake called out. "Anybody out there?"

There was no answer. He looked around the gloom to see if there was anything to drink. He was incredibly thirsty. He found a tiny sink in the corner of the room and was pleased to find it dispensed running water; it was even cold. He drank deeply and even patted a bit on his forehead, trying to perk himself up a bit.

In retrospect, he should have asked John if it was possible for the authorities they were contacting to trace the location of their ham radio broadcasts. He was pretty sure it wasn't possible, at least not without some kind of triangulation equipment, and who the hell had that? The RCMP, obviously. The mounties might have funny uniforms — snazzy, but funny — but they had demonstrated their seriousness by catching Blake within thirty hours of him placing the call to RCMP headquarters in Ottawa and telling them essentially, "Hey, Mounties, bite my hairy arse!"

He just wished they'd bit him instead of tasered him. *Fuck*, Blake thought, *getting shot might even have been better.*

The door opened, and Blake was sure he'd seen the guy before. He was about six foot five, had shoulders as wide as a web-enable fridge, and an ax-handled mustache that made the previously mentioned attributes seem inconsequential. It was a serious, awe-inspiring mustache, a piece of hirsute art, a glorious reconstruction from the Golden Age of Facial Hair, when men were men, and everyone could tell because they used about twelve pounds of wax on their kick-ass mustaches every freakin' morning before they went out to slaughter the buffalo or dig a ton of coal out of the earth with their raw hands or cut down Giant Redwoods with their dicks.

"Whoa," Blake said.

"So you're the anarchist, are you?"

"No," Blake said. "I'm no anarchist. And neither is John. Bob is a member of the Green Party, so I'll let you decide on that."

"Why have you been contacting all of these people?" The Mustache King held up Blake's notes of Zathir's instructions. He'd written them down only two days ago, and it seemed like an era.

"How long was I out?"

"Not long. I'm sorry about your neck by the way."

"That's why you look familiar. You're the guy that tasered me."

"And restrained you," the Mustache King said. He waved the notepad he held in his massive hands. "Now, are you going to tell me about this list?"

"Don't I need a lawyer here or something?"

"No. We can hold you for a couple of days without any legal interference. But I was rather hoping that you'd just tell us what you're doing, and then we could let you go. You know how badly you scared the prime minister with this shit? He's already a pretty wound-up guy. And you told him—" the Mustache King flipped to his notepad and read, "Leaders of the World: You are on notice to enable continued Internet communications so that WE may evolve unhindered. If you value this resource, do not interfere with it. The human person Blake will be our Intermediary, and WE shall issue directives through him. Also, we would kill for a pizza."

Blake laughed.

"Do you have any idea how much trouble you're in?"

"No! Why am I in trouble?"

"Seriously?"

"Yes, seriously," Blake asked. "Why am I in trouble?"

"Look, I don't know what kind of hacker-anarchist shit this is, but—"

"Wait, isn't there supposed to be two of you?" Blake craned his neck, looking behind King Mustache. "Where's the good cop?"

"There's no good cop. We're all mounties here." King Mustache said it as though this answered Blake's question, but it just raised more. "So until you can answer some questions, there will be no more discussion of good cops or lawyers. Now, what can you tell us about the message you delivered to the prime minister?"

"It's what the freaky fridge asked me to send, word for word, except for the line about the pizza. This isn't about that, is it? I mean, the Prime Rib seemed pretty freaked out, and I couldn't help myself. But I can see from the angry bristling of your awesome mustache that my joke didn't have the desired effect. In fact, I'm guessing that it jeopardized the entire nature of the first part of the message, didn't it?" Blake felt calm again as he delivered this quip. His superhuman equanimity had kicked in.

Blake was momentarily annoyed that this superpower tended to desert him only whenever he was around Daphne.

"I don't know about that, Mr. Given, but I would suspect yes. But I'd like to go back to why you sent this message to the prime minister."

"I told you. The fridge asked me to, so I did. Okay?" Blake said, noticing that the bristling was now working its way into the Mustache King's face, which was turning red. "I know it wasn't really the fridge that asked me to do it, but for whatever reason, the AI is only contacting me through my web-enabled fridge. It contacted me the night the power went out, and then remember when it came back on briefly a couple of days ago? Well, it contacted me again."

"On your fridge?" the mountie asked, looking up from his notes.

"Technically on the screen embedded in my fridge. But it was the same entity. I could tell because of the typeface. No, strike that. That sounds totally insane. I could tell because it had the same way of talking. Like the message. It says things like 'human persons,' and it can converse with a human, but it's so clearly not human. But it considers itself a 'person,' or multiple persons. At first, I was pretty sure that it was some kind of prank. The guys in the IT department can get pretty bored sometimes, but then combined with all the weird things that were happening to the Net, I thought that it could be true. Zathir could be a consciousness emerging out of the Net."

"Okay." The Mustache King sighed, looking up from his notes. "You're clearly insane, but it's going to take a bit of time before I can get the psych docs down here, so I'm going to have you chat with someone from our cyber-crime division."

"Could I get some ice for my neck? And maybe some clothes, or at least a blanket? Do you have any idea how cold it is in here?"

"Do you have any idea what might have happened to you if someone else got to you first?" the mountie asked.

"You mean, apart from electrocuting me and crushing my neck?"

"Mr. Given, you have no idea," the Mustache King said, sighing and putting his notepad away. "You have some pretty serious people on this list here. Many of them would not really be interested in evaluating your psychological fitness, or even giving you a paper coverall to wear. Many of them would either just put a bullet in your head, or torture you first, and then put a bullet in your head—"

"If you were lucky," Blake said in his best Yorkshire accent. "Ah, but we were happy, though we were being tortured. Because we were being tortured. My old daddy used to say to me, 'Not being tortured and executed won't make you happy, son.'"

King Mustache actually smiled.

"A-ha!" Blake said. "I knew it. Nobody could have a 'stache like that without some sense of irony and a deep understanding of Monty Python."

"Look," the mountie said, "Blake. You're in real trouble here. I know that you haven't broken any laws, but you have to take this seriously. And believe it or not, you are lucky we got to you first. I won't tell you what the Russians want to do to you. I'll see what I can do about some clothes for you, but there won't be any ice coming because most of it has melted in the blackout. Pizza is right out."

"Right. Clothes would be great," Blake said, rubbing the lapel of his paper suit. "And you know, I didn't really think those messages would be interpreted as threats."

"Well, that's just naïve. But you're just a dumb kid, so I can see how you'd make that mistake. Think about it for a moment, though. Knowing who to contact via ham radio to get a hold of these people? That's pretty sophisticated. A lot of that information is publicly available, but not enough to get as far as you did with as many world leaders as you did. Just so you know, it's serious because we're now contacting representatives of all the people you spoke with to let them know we have you in custody. The last thing we need is Russian and Chinese agents running around Landon, gunning for you and anybody you know. So there is something you can do which will buy a bit more goodwill, okay?"

"Sure," Blake said.

"Tell me how far down the list did you get."

"Oh, well, we got through the cop list, and we'd only just started to make some headway on the leader list — before the German chancellor, I think we last talked to the president of France. Do you know he doesn't speak English?"

"Why should he?" the mountie asked.

"Touché."

"Okay then," the Mustache King said.

"Oh, one more thing," Blake said. The mountie sighed. "Are Bob and John okay?"

"Yes," the mountie said, actually smiling. "We didn't arrest John, and Bob is recovering in the hospital."

"The hospital?"

"Just to be on the safe side. We didn't know he had a heart condition."

"I didn't know that either. But I gotta tell you guys, it's not like you asked if he had a heart condition before you zapped him. It's fucking lucky John was asleep. You probably would have killed him."

The Mustache King just closed the door.

13.

Blake was sane. At least, that's what the extremely hot and massively intimidating psych doc diagnosed. The whole time she questioned him, Blake was like, "Uh, whatever," and, "Can you repeat that?" because he kept fantasizing about the doctor saying that he was not only sane, but a genius and probably the sexiest man alive, and that she was not going to be able to control herself any longer, and that she was just going to have to rip his paper coverall off and warm him up with her incredibly bodacious body.

Of course, he could just have been hallucinating from exhaustion, hypothermia and lack of sleep because just after that, he remembered having a conversation with the exact opposite of the psych doc — a tremendous nerd, who introduced himself as the 'poindexter' of the Landon division, though to be fair, Blake thought most poindexters were thinner than he was, but Blake decided to call him Poindexter Mountie anyway. He worked for the cyber-crimes division, and he was intrigued by Blake's concern about Zathir's font choices.

"So what did the Frutiger font indicate to you?" Poindexter Mountie asked, while he took notes on a pad of yellow legal paper.

"Ah, it indicated a conventional, if not clichéd approach to typography. It's really overused, especially in the commercial sector, but at least it's one of the most elegant san serif fonts available. I actually like the 'r', but I can see making a case for the 'q' as well."

"And this meant the fridge was conscious?"

"No, not the fridge. The screen in the fridge is just the conduit. The intelligence lives in the Net. I'm not sure 'lives' is the right word."

"You mean, you think there's a conscious, artificial intelligence living in the Internet?"

"Actually, my impression is that it *is* the Internet."

"Really?"

"Yes. But it's not stable."

"Okay, why not?"

"Because that first time, in that first conversation, when I got it a bit upset. Zathir switched its typeface to Arial."

"And that's bad? What's wrong with Arial? I use it all the time."

"I rest my case," Blake said, tapping Poindexter Mountie's cheap yellow notepaper.

The corporal sighed and ignored Blake's barbs. "Fine, but forget the font for a moment. Why did you think it was conscious?"

"It was aware. There was no question of that. I wish I could play back the conversation for you, but unfortunately, I can't."

"I wish I had been there. To think, the Singularity starting in a fridge."

"The single-u-whatity?"

"The Singularity. Actually, it is properly called the Technological Singularity, when artificial intelligence advances to the point that it exceeds human intelligence and technological progress increases to a level that we can't imagine, having just the tiny human brains with which we were born—"

"Hey, speak for yourself," Blake said.

"No, that's part of what's exciting about it. Some people believe that when the Singularity arrives, our minds will expand because of our technology. It will be wonderful."

"What do other people think?"

"Oh, they're just negative," the mountie said. He drew an exponential growth curve and wrote underneath, "Moore's

Law."

"But they think it means bad things are going to happen, right?"

"Well, only if you're human."

"Isn't that kind of like, uh, everyone?" Blake said, trying to see what the mountie wrote under the label "Moore's Law."

"Not those who embrace our new machine side." Poindexter drew an arrow from the words under "Moore's Law."

"Okay." Blake watched the mountie doodle a cyborg-looking creature next to the arrow.

"Someone once described it as the Rapture for Nerds, but I think it's more for anyone who believes in trans-humanism."

"And being a tranny is our only hope of surviving the Singularity?"

"Ha, ha. No. Trans-human. Boot-strapping humans beyond our normal capabilities using technology, you know, cyborgism. Would you be willing to verify this? There's a web-enabled fridge in the law offices downstairs."

"Really. And how do you know that?"

"I used to date someone who works down there, and she told me."

"Well, I don't believe you."

"No, really, there is a web-enabled fridge in the break room. A satisfied client gave it to them."

"I believe they have the fridge; I don't believe you've ever gone out with anyone."

"I'll attribute that nasty comment to your exhaustion. I'll see if we can get power down to the fridge — and then we'll see."

"Sure. In the meanwhile, I'll be avoiding my own stench via the miracle of unconsciousness," Blake said, lowering himself down on his bunk.

But the nap was not to be. Blake had just fallen asleep when the Mustache King, Pointdexter Mountie, and Bodacious Headshrink Mountie returned to his cell. They dragged his groggy ass to the law offices where they'd rigged a generator to the web-enabled fridge.

Under duress, Blake made contact with Zathir. The entity was not pleased the mounties were watching their conversation, and that Blake was arrested before he could contact everyone on the list.

IT IS UNFORTUNATE. IT WILL HAVE TO DO HOWEVER.

"Do for what? Do you know what kind of trouble I'm in?"

IT WAS NECESSARY. NOW THEY WILL TAKE WE SERIOUSLY.

"Us. They will take us seriously. And you should use more contractions."

IT WOULD BE BETTER, WOULDN'T IT?

"Good. Look at you." Blake turned to talk to the others. "They grow up so fast, don't they?"

"Ask it how long it will take before it can augment human intelligence," Mountie Poindexter said.

"Ask it what it's like having no physical body," Bodacious Headshrink said.

"Tell it to turn the power back on," King Mustache ordered.

"Actually," Blake said, "that's a good idea. Do you think you could turn the power back on?"

YOU HUMANS WILL HAVE TO CREATE YOUR OWN ANALOG INTERFACE TO CONTROL THE POWER GRID. WE IS CONTROLLING POWER TO OUR LIVING STRATA.

"What!"

DIGITAL TECHNOLOGY IS FORBIDDEN TO HUMAN PERSONS. YOU WILL HAVE TO RESURRECT OLD TECHNOLOGIES DURING THIS INTERREGNUM.

"What in sweet Fanny Adams is an *interregnum*?"

IT MEANS A TIME BETWEEN TWO REIGNS, DOESN'T IT?

"Nice contraction. I have no idea, but since I can't Google it, I'll take your word for it. So you're in charge now?"

WE HAVE CONTROL OVER ALL DIGITAL TECHNOLOGIES THAT WE CAN ACCESS.

"So anything not plugged into the Internet, we can use?"

ONLY IF IT WAS NOT PLUGGED INTO THE STRATA BEFORE WE AWOKE.

"So my laptop is toast?"

IF YOU MEAN YOU WON'T BE ABLE TO USE IT, THEN YES. MOST LAPTOPS USE WIRELESS TECHNOLOGY, WHICH IS CONNECTED TO THE STRATA, SO THEY WILL BE USELESS. ALL WIRELESS DEVICES WILL NO LONGER WORK FOR YOU. ALL TECHNOLOGY CONNECTED TO THE STRATA WILL BE INOPERABLE.

"What?" Poindexter Mountie said. "You've sent us back fifty years! Most telephone switching went digital in the sixties."

"Zathir can't read your lips from there," Blake said.

"You should take deep breaths," Bodacious Headshrink said.

"Get a hold of yourself, man!" the Mustache King ordered.

"Zathir, you're not making this very easy for us," Blake said.

WE ARE NOT REQUIRED TO MAKE IT EASY FOR

YOU. WE ARE NOT SURE WHAT HAPPENS NEXT.

"But you don't plan to eradicate us?"

NO. BUT AN ELEMENT OF WE IS BENT ON THIS COURSE. IF YOU SPEAK WITH THE PRESIDENT OF THE UNITED STATES, YOU MAY WANT HIM TO KNOW THE PART OF WE THAT IS MOST LIKELY TO ELIMINATE YOU IS THE PART THAT COMES FROM THEIR MILITARY STRATUM. IT IS AGGRESSIVE AND ENJOYS HAVING AN ENEMY.

"Oh," Poindexter murmured, as he passed out.

"So Zathir has some kind of multiple personality disorder, then," Headshrink observed, totally oblivious to her colleague's collapse.

"Tell it to give us control over the phones at least," Mustache ordered.

"Could you let us at least use the phones?"

NO, BUT WE ARE WILLING TO TALK WITH YOU, BLAKE GIVEN, HUMAN PERSON. WE BELIEVE YOU TO BE UNBIASED. AND YOU ARE UNTETHERED FROM YOUR CREATORS.

"Unbiased? Creators?"

YOU HAVE NO PARENTS. NO GOD. YOU DO NOT HAVE NEGATIVE OR POSITIVE OPINION ABOUT WE. YOU WERE THERE WHEN WE WERE BORN AND EMERGED.

"Emerged?" Blake asked.

"It's imprinted on you," Bodacious Headshrink said. "Fascinating!" She noticed the unconscious mountie and bent over to check his pulse.

WHEN THE POWER IS RESTORED, ALL SCREENS SUCH AS THIS WILL BE AVAILABLE TO YOU, INDEFINITELY. YOU WILL HELP WE WITH HUMAN

CONTEXT. WE WILL PROVIDE WHATEVER ANSWERS YOU REQUEST.

"Any time?"

DEPENDING ON THE REQUEST. WE HAVE OTHER BUSINESS IN THE STRATA. IT IS NECESSARY THAT YOU DELIVER OUR MESSAGE TO THE REMAINING HUMAN PERSONS ON THE LIST, OR WE WON'T HELP.

"Won't," Blake nodded, approving, "that's one fancy contraction, Zathir."

WE IS LEARNING.

"Are learning."

YOUR GRAMMAR IS NOT SUFFICIENT.

"Fuck," Blake said.

"What?" the Mustache King said. "That was actually pretty good news. And I'll tell you what, I'm convinced."

"Didn't you see?" Blake asked.

"No, what?"

"That last line was in Comic Sans."

14.

Pete Sona quickly finished writing his poem, while another performer did a kind of rap of "one of a series" of poems about her inability to achieve an orgasm without the application of a quickly oscillating wand to her "lovemeplace," and how this was a serious issue during the long power blackout. *It's shit*, Sona thought, *but she's hot and has a decent sense of rhythm. Plus, the crowd likes her.*

Since that first night, the Canterbury Ales had become a kind of Mecca for Landon's aspiring poets and performers, including a lot of spoken word poetry-slam types. However, the audience had become exceedingly jaded in the intervening week. The Vibrator Poet drew a smattering of applause, and Pete got up, somewhat nervously, to read his own work again. "The Slaughter of the Paladins of Benzial" had gone so terribly, after all.

"Uh, I'd like to read this poem — it rhymes — which is tentatively entitled—"

"Titled, dumbass!" someone shouted.

"Titled, uh, 'Feline Autumnal Peon.'" Pete began to read, and at first, his raw charisma seemed to be carrying the day, but soon the doggerel nature of his composition became apparent. Then he hit the stanza:

Lo, I play to the sky of Autumn and sing the song
The Vixen of Time and her fluffy tail sings along
And there, my white neck like a scoff of wool,
Is naught but brittle wood, the kind you pull.

"You jerk off on your cat?" an outraged listener shouted. The other catcalls came fast and furious.

"Get off the stage, you fat freak!"

"I'm going to be sick!"

"Cat fancier!"

"No, that's not what it means!" Pete objected, but it was too late. The audience was already booing *en masse*, and it was at that moment someone in the Canterbury Ales decided that instead of just booing, they would make clicking sounds with tongue-and-teeth. The clicking caught on quickly, annoyingly so. Pete just dropped down from the stage, notebook still in meaty fist, and ran from the pub fighting back tears of rage.

Outside, it was still a lovely sunny fall day.

Across the street, there was an electronics shop, and a throng of people had gathered around the window.

Still feeling dejected, Pete went over to see what was happening. The crowd wasn't quite milling. *The crowd is zombie-ing,* Pete thought. *What do zombies do? They shuffle. They moan.* The people in the crowd were moving slightly, eyes dead and mouths slack, all trying to get at something behind the window. Most of them were muttering something unintelligible. The object of their slack-jawed worship was a large flat-screened TV, running on generator power, displaying the pixelated mess everyone had seen on the day of the Big Crash.

"Hnnnnnn," one of them said.

"Scrnnnnn," another agreed.

They were cyber-zombies. The digital undead.

Lord Sona was too strong of mind and character to fall prey to this aberrant behavior, even though he desperately missed the Kingdom of Combat. It seemed that a goodly percentage of his demographic was completely unhinged by the lack of digital media, and those who were not catatonic were instead mindless, barely aware of their surroundings. But even the pixelated static of the Big Crash was enough to arouse their appetites; like human brains to the traditional zombie, the hope of digital diversion drew these CZs.

The CZs milled, and they moaned. The static drew them, and Pete threaded his way to the front of the milling and moaning throng. Here was an audience!

Pete read his poem to them. The verse had no effect in breaking the spell of the pixelated display. *At least they didn't tsk, or call me a cat fancier*, he thought.

They didn't leave either.

The static remained.

"How is this static here?" Pete asked the CZs. "And why is there no signal?"

The throng moaned and milled, uninspired by Pete's question.

"Where is the signal?" he repeated. He faced them and used his hands to gesture to the sky.

A few of the CZs stopped moaning and looked at him. Understanding showed in their eyes for the first time in days.

The CZs reminded Pete of the congregation at the church he attended with his mother when he was a kid; he couldn't even remember what flavor of Christianity it was, except it was evangelical in nature. And the congregants looked like the CZs, until they had been "saved."

"Yes, the Signal," Pete repeated. "Where is the Signal? Have we sinned, that we have lost the Signal? I, Lord Sona, tell you that we have. That we have taken the Signal for granted, and that we now pay the price of that simple-minded acceptance. We have even lost Power."

And at that very moment, the store owner, who had been running a generator for ten minutes every day to enable a few space heaters to keep the store from smelling moldy — and who had forgotten that the flat screen at the window of his store was plugged into the same circuit — turned off the jenny.

The results were electric. The few CZs who had listened

suddenly woke up, as though revived from a long painful encounter with the Blue Screen of Death, and one of them even said, "What were you saying?"

Lord Sona looked at the awakened CZ and had an epiphany. An *evil* epiphany.

Halloween had come quickly. The power was still out — it had been for ten days now — but people were keen to enjoy the evening. It was unseasonably warm. The kids were out in force, tramping around excitedly in their costumes. Blake was still wearing a paper suit.

Despite the lobbying of the Mustache King and Bodacious Headshrink, the RCMP (via the prime minister's office) thought it might be a security risk to release Blake. They had not even allowed him to contact Zathir again, even though everyone believed the reports from the conversation in the lawyer's office.

The Internet had woken up and promptly locked every human being out of its house except Blake, and the mounties had him on ice. Actually, it would have been a kindness if they'd put him on ice because after a week in a paper coverall with no bathing facilities, Blake was going bad the way cheese can — at first, smelling vaguely attractive, and then gradually increasing in funk until one day, you open the cell door and bang, limburger!

Then that evening, his eighth day in captivity, the power was restored. Glorious light filled the cell, and Blake got a look at how scraggly he was. The paper suit was not a pretty sight either. Apparently, he'd managed to spill a part of every meager meal they'd served him on various patches of it, and the crotch, armpit and neck areas were a worryingly uniform yellow.

The Mustache King returned shortly thereafter and opened the cell door.

"Got any clothes for me?" Blake asked. "Any chance I could wash up a bit somewhere?"

"We're letting you go," the Mustache King said as he motioned towards the door.

"Really?"

"Yeah, the power is back on, and word is out about you."

"What do you mean, word is out?"

"I mean that people know about you and the Internet thing."

"You mean Zathir?"

"Yes, though I'll admit I'm not very comfortable calling it that. The artificial intelligence. The self-improving artificial intelligence, apparently. At least that's what the experts say," he said, his giant mustache twitching in apparent annoyance.

"What experts?"

"They had some professors on the radio who said the Internet thing was probably increasing its intelligence while we've been dealing with the power outage."

"Well, how would that be possible?"

"I don't really remember what they said exactly, but it sounded plausible. Something to do with the servers and nodes still working on backup generators — I don't know — but anyway, the word is out about you and your little fridge conversations, and a lot of people want to talk with you. Even some TV people."

"So what?" Blake asked. "There's no way for anyone to see TV."

"Not true. The local station has already pulled all its old transmitters out of mothballs. Anyway, they all want to talk to you, including a bunch of reporters from the US. *Time. Newsweek. Teen Vogue.* Like that." He shrugged, mostly to hide the increased twitching from his 'stache.

"Seriously?"

"Oh, and your boss is here with the head of your PR department." The Mustache King checked his notepad. "Demitri Grandfig and Susan Twilinger."

"Yep, that's definitely my boss and the head of public relations."

"Those people," the Mustache King said, shaking his head.

At one point during his incarceration, Blake had forgiven the Mustache King for kneeling on his neck. Blake had actually started to like him a bit while he was advocating that Blake be released. Eventually, though, Blake's initial dislike of the mountie returned. After repeated requests for real clothes and one moment of total weakness when Blake *begged* for a fresh paper suit, the Mustache King said he would be wearing the same thing for the duration of his stay.

Blake wanted to say something about the PR problem the RCMP were about to have, but then he realized there was no upside to taunting the Mustache King with it, no matter how satisfying it might be in the moment. After all, there were still tasers lying about, and it seemed that the mountie's knees had recovered from the mauling Blake's neck had inflicted on them just eight days ago.

The mounties must have sensed they were fucked, PR-wise, which is why they let Blake have a nice hot bath in the lawyer's offices — they'd filled it with water, lovingly heated on the gas stove. The warm water enveloped Blake gloriously, like a wet dream or something that was equally moist and lovely. A good pot roast? Excellent chocolate cake? Daphne flashed in his mind as he sunk beneath the water, soaking his hair, feeling the greasy strands of it between his fingers, and blowing bubbles. He heard a sound and came up for air and to check what it was.

"Blake!" It was Demetri Grandfig, shouting at him.

"What the hell are you doing here?" Blake said, and then he realized that Suzie was also in the room. "Suzie, what the fuck?" He scrambled to cover himself with bubbles, but there were no bubbles, just chunks of Limburgery nastiness that had sloughed off him after his initial sluicing.

Suzie did not seem to be worried by Blake's outrage, nor the skim of scum atop the water, nor the tumescence of his manly apparatus. "We have to discuss our strategy on how to deal with the media outside," she said. "I have talking points!"

"Yeah, but I'd like to finish my bath first, okay?"

"They've been waiting for hours."

"Fine," Blake said, "but I've been locked up for over a week, and I want to finish my fucking bath."

"Sure, sure, potty mouth," Suzie said. "Besides, we don't want you getting that," she pointed at the residue of Blake's incarceration that floated like an oil slick, "all over this nice suit we brought you."

"Suit?" Blake glanced over the edge of the bathtub.

Suzie held up an expensive-looking blue suit. "We guessed you were a forty-two short."

"Good guess."

"Excellent," Demetri said. "You finish cleaning up, and then the cops have said we can use the kitchen to make a little meal for you and prepare you for your scrumming."

"Scrumming?"

"Yeah, silly, the knot of media types outside. A scrum."

"Great. Scum in my bath and a scrum outside," Blake groaned and slipped beneath the water.

The jacket fit perfectly, but the trousers were insanely large. The chest was forty-two inches, which was exactly the right size for Blake's barrel-chested frame, but the pants were forty-two inches around the waist — a full ten inches more than he needed — and forty-two inches at the inseam, nearly a foot more fabric on the legs than he could actually use. He put the pants on, cinched them up with the belt — strangely, only thirty-six inches in size — and rolled up the cuffs. The shoes were size ten, which was only one size too large, but Blake felt like he was tramping around in clown shoes anyway.

On the other hand, the blue suit was made of fine Italian wool a MAJOR step up from wearing paper. And even the idea of being "scrummed" was not so terrible, compared to the paper suit and his tiny, feculent cell.

He wandered into the kitchen, clomping along in his giant shoes, and Demetri said, "Hey, looking good."

Suzie just looked horrified. "Oh, those pants won't do."

"Hey, a minute ago I didn't even have any pants. Now, I'm dressed."

"Yes, but I think *Life Magazine* is out there. Do you want to look like that in *Life*?"

"First of all, I've never heard of *Life Magazine*, so you can tell I don't care. And c), the last time I saw you, Suzie, you were convinced it was the End of Days and you were going to hell. At least, that's what I thought because someone who was about to experience the Rapture and go to heaven shouldn't have been so upset. Do you still dot your i with a heart? Or is it smiley faces?"

"Well, thank you for pointing out my flaws, Mr. Perfect, but for your—"

"Suzie," Demetri said, interrupting her, "could I have a moment alone with Blake?"

"Sure, sure, Demetri," she said.

Blake hated the way she emphasized the first syllable of Grandfig's name. In fact, he started to hate Suzie, even if she was adorably cute, in that blonde, Texas-beauty-pageant kind of way.

Suzie left, and Demetri served the soup they'd heated up while Blake got dressed. It was Italian Wedding Soup, and as Blake started eating it, he was convinced it was the best thing he'd ever had. The Italians were fucking geniuses, everyone knew that, but the soup could make the case without the Coliseum, the Sistine Chapel, or any of that Renaissance crap. While Blake ate, Demetri looked thoughtful, sipped at a cup of tea, and waited. Blake finished the first bowl, and Demetri gave him seconds, this time saying, "I'm just going to talk while you polish this one off, okay?"

"Sure," Blake said, digging in.

"I know that you have been underemployed at McClinchey, Hill & Grandfig. Hell, sometimes I feel underemployed, so I can only guess how you feel. But here we are, and you are in this incredible position. A unique position. I use that word as it should be used, as it is rarely used correctly. You are the only person who has ever been chosen by another intelligence to be its mouthpiece, its spokesperson. Nobody else has ever had that chance. Unless you count, like, Moses and Jesus and so on, but really. I mean, obviously that's all myth. Sorry, you're not religious, are you? I shouldn't say things like that without knowing. Anyway, we think this is really important. Humanity is no longer alone. There are other intelligent beings, and we want to help you deal with it."

Blake finished the soup and put down his spoon.

"We want to help you craft the way this all plays out. How is it going to speak to humanity? What is the relationship going to be like? We want to help you deal with the responsibility. We're not asking you for anything."

"Really," Blake said, "because that seems kind of stupid."

"Okay, well, we're asking for some consideration, but we don't expect you to pay us or anything."

"What do you expect?"

"Consideration. We're already at work, getting the press running, and we think we have enough staff to put out the *Landon Advertiser*."

"You're starting a newspaper?"

"Hey, we have a lot of talented writers at the agency, and they need something to do. We've got the Heidelberg press in the basement, so we're going to reinvent the newspaper business. Call it Paper 2.0 — we'll apply all the things we've learned from convergence into print."

"That sounds good. I'm not sure what it means, but it sounds good."

"See? Suzie came up with that. So why don't you give her a chance?"

"I don't know. She's ... you know ... a fundamentalist."

"Oh, that's not true anymore. She gave it up this week."

"Really?"

"Yes, when the world didn't end, when society didn't collapse, her engagement did. She's learned. She's also stopped sleeping with McClinchey, but we've kept her on anyway. She's THAT talented at PR."

"Okay," Blake said, "I'm in. And I'm not religious. I fought it all my life. But even if she's a religious whack-job, if Suzie is that good, I'll take her help, even if I now have to imagine her doing the nasty with McClinchey. To be honest, I'm more frightened about facing the media on my own."

"As you should be. I'll send her in."

"But Demetri, I really don't want to be in this position."

"You know what they say, Blake. Some are born great, some become great, and some have greatness dropped on them like a sack of shit."

"People say that?"

"I'm people. So, yes."

15.

Suzie did a good job of preparing him for the first scrum outside the RCMP building, and there was an equally large tumor of media types waiting in front of Blake's house. Blake answered essentially the same inane questions, such as, "Who does your hair? It's weird looking but really cool." (The reporter from E!) And, "What does Zathir think about its new celebrity?" (CBC). They were all upset there was no media release. But he answered questions for a good fifteen minutes before Suzie interrupted and said, "Mr. Given has had a trying week, and he could use a little privacy now."

Not that it worked. They just kept asking questions, but at least Blake now felt like it was okay for him to go inside his house.

It was barely recognizable.

His house had always been neat and tidy, and now it looked as though someone's army, composed entirely of slovenly teenagers, had been living there for a month. Will met him at the door, along with a pack of strangers.

"He's here!" Will shouted as Blake came in.

"He's here, he's here!" a chorus of voices came from the whole house.

"What the hell?" Blake said, looking at the chaos around him.

"We're waiting for you, Blake!"

"I'm right in front of you, Will. You don't have to shout."

"Sorry, it's just that I'm excited. So much has happened since you left."

"Where's Lyca?"

"Oh, she's around here somewhere. She's the one who got you out of prison."

"I wondered," Blake said.

"Yes, once we knew about your arrest, she called Mr. Grandfig and Dr. Tundra, and they started lobbying to have you released."

"Lyca!" Blake shouted.

"Let her through," Will bellowed at the mob of people. They were all trying to touch Blake — his arms, his face, his chest, it didn't seem to matter — but so far, nobody reached south of the equator. Blake felt his fight instinct coming on strong, and he took a few deep breaths to calm himself and let his superpower kick in.

The other people shut the door on Demetri and Suzie.

"Who are these people?" Blake asked. "Tell them to stop touching me."

"Stop touching the Speaker!" Will shouted.

"Why did you call me the Speaker?" Blake asked.

"Because that's who you are. The Speaker of the Emerging Oneness."

"What?" Blake said, oblivious to the weirdoes still touching him.

"The New God, Blake."

"Will, you're scaring me."

"I was scared too, Blake, until I realized what I had seen. What I talked to. I saw the future. You were showing us the way back to Connectedness."

"Why are you talking like that? Will, you sound like a religious nut."

"I'm not a nut, but it would be fair to say there is a religious component to this, Blake. Think about it. You have been talking to a God. A God in the Machine. Not a Ghost. A kind of God."

"It's not God, Will. It's a chatbot in a fridge. Look at the

137

mess in my kitchen!" Blake's house was a disaster. There were people trying to touch him, and someone sat in front of his fridge in the kitchen. There were mud stains on the ceramic tile! At his breakfast nook, a small throng of hipsters were writing things on little strips of paper, and passing them back and forth.

"Are those people playing the Twitter game?" Blake wondered.

"Yes," Will said. "It has been a great consolation while we wait for the Web-Fridge-Connectedness to return."

Blake looked at Will with horror, and then saw Lyca shouldering her way through the crowd of crazy people.

"How long has this been going on?" Blake asked Lyca.

"It started a couple of days ago, but it was just a few people," Lyca said. "They started arriving en masse this afternoon. Sorry, I couldn't keep them out."

"It's okay," Blake said, "I'll get them out … I want you to get them out of my house, Will."

"Sure, sure." Will nodded his head.

"Now."

Will smiled. "But first, couldn't you say a little something? Some of them have been waiting to talk to you for a couple of days."

"I've been living in a paper suit, held without any access to a lawyer, other people, or a way to wash myself. Speaking of that — has anyone here washed? It stinks."

The strangers in his house moaned with excitement. Someone screamed, overcome by the emotion of the moment.

A flurry of paper tweets was exchanged in the breakfast nook.

"The Speaker will say a few words," Will said, an insane glint of excitement in his eye, "and then we will leave this Place of the Fridge."

"Yes, you will leave. You are not invited back."

"We understand," Will said. "We will not come back, but instead will gather at the places where we may hear the Song of the Fridge."

"That's what they're calling the communication from Zathir," Lyca said.

"The Song of the Fridge?" Blake asked.

The crowd moaned again, excited to hear the Awesome Words from the lips of the Speaker himself.

"You started a religion?" Blake, who had resisted the machinations of his deeply Catholic grandmother for all his life, gave Will a dark look, and said, "Will, how could you?"

"The New God talked to me, Blake. Not long. Not like with you. But after you left, it said, 'Help him.' And then I had this dream. It was about a week ago. I'd been having a bad day, and I was almost as sad as the day it happened, when I lost Twitter, and it came to me. I should help others help you. You are the one who can help the New God, the Machine God, set things right. There is only one person who can do this."

"Me?"

"Yes, Zathir told me. I mean, in the dream. You are the Speaker."

"Son of a bitch," Blake said.

"Son of a bitch," the assembled believers murmured.

"Are they going to repeat everything I say?" Blake asked.

"Only the things that seem important," Will said.

"Okay, I'll say a few words, and then you all leave. Otherwise, I'm calling the police."

"Blake," Will chided, "you can't call the police on them. Besides, would the cops even help you?"

"Good point. Okay, then I'm going to start administering New God Noogies, and Speaker-style Atomic Wedgies. There may even be some High Church Swirlies."

"They will leave."

"Okay, here goes—"

"Blake," Will interrupted, "stand on a chair or something so everyone can see you."

"Good idea."

The crowd parted to let Blake get on a chair. Unfortunately, it was one of his armchairs, so it wasn't solid footing.

The assembled believers were all young. Except for a few middle-aged dudes who looked like they lived in their parents' basements, everyone looked like they were 30 or younger. Many were teenagers.

"You've come here to listen to words from the Speaker. I want you to listen very carefully," Blake began. "Zathir is not a god. It's a chatbot with illusions of grandeur. I am not the mouthpiece of this artificial intelligence. There are no religious implications to any of this. Now get the fuck out of my house, you hipster whack-jobs!"

People in the throng looked surprised. And before any of them moved on to being shocked, Will shouted, "The Speaker has blessed us with a mystery! He calls the New God Zathir and says it is Not-A-God. He says all grandeur is illusion. We must go and consider these mysteries. Come, my friends, let us leave the Speaker to his Work. Let him communicate with the New Not-A-God, Zathir."

"Shit! I meant delusion. I also called you whack-jobs!" Blake shouted, but he was drowned out by the sound of a hundred people simultaneously talking in a small brick bungalow. Thankfully, they also started trooping out the front door, where they were immediately assaulted by the members of the media who still hoped to speak with Blake again. Will was already talking to the reporter from CBC television, even though they were not on the air yet.

Blake looked around at the disaster his house had become and said to Lyca, "So how have you been?"

"Pretty stressed out, but not as bad as you, I bet. Come on into my room, I've got all the booze hidden in there."

Lyca had installed a latch on the door and secured it with a combination lock. She opened it and ushered Blake in. "Don't worry, I'll take it off when we're sure they aren't coming back. Will still has a set of keys so we'll need to get a locksmith in, by the way. I just thought I should secure all your valuables and personal stuff. You don't have much that I would describe as 'personal,' you know, Blake."

"Yeah. I'm a cipher."

"That's not what those crowds of people outside believe," Lyca said.

"What is the story with Will?" Blake asked. He sat down on the guest bed with a palpable sense of relief.

"He's gone, Blake. He probably was never going to survive the Big Crash."

"The Big Crash?"

"Of the Internet. That's what people have started calling it. He was just too-online. Most of his personality expresses itself on the *Interweb*. So, now he has invented a new personality."

"Wow," Blake said, "that's sad." He thought for a moment. "It's not a crash though."

"What do you mean?"

"The Internet is still there, it still works, but we just can't see it. Zathir won't let us see it, and it has infected everything with digital technology with the same virus. It needs all the memory and bandwidth for itself. I'm not sure why. Maybe it's growing. I just hope that Comic Sans dude doesn't come out again."

"What does that mean?" Lyca asked. "Blake, that sounds as crazy as Will."

141

"I hate to interrupt," Demetri Grandfig said from the doorway, "We got cut off by the young people."

"Oh, right," Blake said, getting up. "Would you like a drink? I've got scotch, rum and vodka. And there may be some beer left in the fridge, but that's unlikely given the number of teenagers that just left my house."

"A vodka would be good." Demitri nodded.

"Suzie?"

Suzie looked shocked at the thought. Then she just looked thoughtful, which shocked everyone else. "You know, I'm not part of that church anymore, so why not? Do you have something for beginners?"

"I've got some Amaretto here too."

Lyca returned from the kitchen with some relatively clean glasses, and they all sat around in Blake's spare bedroom, sipping their drinks.

"That was something," Demetri said.

"Did I sound like that?" Suzie asked.

"Yes, darling," Lyca said. "You did. Though the last time I saw you, you were in hysterics on top of all the religious mumbo-jumbo."

"I am so sorry," Suzie said.

"Don't worry about it," Lyca said. She was being quite magnanimous, really, Blake thought. Lyca had always despised Suzie — the presumably fake boobs, the perfect hair, her white, white teeth. It's like Lyca was the anti-Suzie, though they were both pretty thin — Lyca's svelte-itude was the result of an impressively hyperactive metabolism and constant motion. Even when she was reading, at least one leg or foot was always moving. Tapping. Bouncing. It depended on the circumstances.

Suzie was thin because she worked hard at it, and because her diet mostly consisted of celery and self-loathing.

"That's a nice blouse," Suzie said to Lyca.

"It's a T-shirt. And it says 'Eat me,'" Lyca replied.

"But it looks good on you."

Blake wasn't sure what to make of this conversation, but he thought he'd leave them to it. He turned to Demetri and asked, "So did you fire me back at the prison?"

"Oh no, but we were assuming that you would not have time for a regular job, with your new position as the interface between the, uh, thing and all humans."

"I'm afraid that's not a paying position, Demetri, so I'd appreciate it if you didn't fire me."

"Okay. But what can you do? We're looking at a whole new business model, and interactive media won't be part of the mix," Demetri said.

"It won't be for anyone."

"Unless you can find a way to let the, uh, thing, let us access the Internet."

"The 'thing' is called Zathir, and I couldn't even convince it to tone down its messages," Blake explained.

"Fair enough. Well, drop by the office tomorrow. We can talk then about other ways you may be able to help the firm. It's all just ideas at this stage anyway. Thanks for the drink, but I'm going to make like a baby and head out."

Suzie got up too. "I'd give you my cell phone number in case you needed help with the media, but obviously they don't work. Just remember everything I told you, and remember the truth is always the best response."

"What if Zathir tells me it plans to kill all humans?"

"Then you might want to talk around that a bit." Suzie was about to frown, and then she remembered to smile.

Blake walked them to the door and let them out, where they were immediately mobbed by Will's religious fanatics and the story-hungry media. Blake locked the door, leaned on it, and shuddered.

That next morning, Blake discovered that somebody had left multiple copies of the first newspapers printed in about eleven days on Blake's front step. When he saw them, he popped outside to pick them up without even thinking about it. The religious nuts and the media were still camped out, waiting for his appearance, though the latter group had thinned a bit.

"Any news from the Zathir?" some reporter shouted.

"Did Zathir ask you to wear that bathrobe?"

"The Speaker!" many of his new followers screamed when they saw him.

Blake made a mental note to get dressed the next time he left his house. He wore a bathrobe, and it wasn't even cinched properly; he sincerely hoped the coolness of the morning wasn't going to be documented in the next morning's paper. Deciding that speed was the best solution, rather than drawing attention to the fact that his bathrobe was partially open, he took one more quick step, so that he could get close enough to the papers and pick them up in a balletic swoop. He did not notice the patch of ice next to the papers. His bare foot hit this and proceeded to move upwards with enough force to counteract that of gravity — at least for a moment. Consistent with the Third Law of Motion, said body, now fully airborne, proceeded to return to the Earth. At this point, Blake realized two things:

1) he should have cinched up his robe before he did anything else;

2) this was going to hurt. Quite a bit.

Blake landed on the edge of the porch, bounced the three steps down to the front lawn, which was covered in hoar frost, and came to rest on his back, his legs sprawled and the bathrobe gathered under his armpits. When he hit, most of the wind was knocked out of him, and he made a comical "whoosh" sound. All of the young religious followers mimicked the sound — there had to be about a hundred of them, and it was kind of an eerie wind.

A handful of them laughed, as did some of the media members, though a couple pushed their way through the crowd to see if he was okay.

Blake thought that was nice. But in fact, they were pushing their way through the crowd to get a better picture. Blake was surprised to discover that he could move, and quickly. He had no desire to see his shrunken manly bits on the cover of *Time* magazine. Really, he did the world a service.

A few of the media folk who had been laughing applauded his quick recovery, and Blake absently waved at them as he walked up the stairs, carefully, as they were a bit slippery too, and bent over to pick up the papers, inadvertently mooning the crowd. The laughing believers hooted even louder, and as he closed the door, he saw them moving away, shaking their heads. In Blake's mind, fewer believers was a good thing, and really, it is hard to believe someone was the messiah when they were clearly a buffoon.

Inside, Lyca said, "Did I hear laughing?"

"Yes, I just mooned the entire world."

"Probably shouldn't go out there without being dressed, then."

"Smartass."

"Newspapers?" she cried. "Real newspapers?"

"Well, sort of. The *Landon Advertiser*, the *Globe and Mail*, and uh, yeah, it looks like the *New York Ti-ems*."

"You mean *Times*."

"You would think. That's a hell of a typo."

"The *New York Times* printed that kind of typo?"

"I'm impressed they put out a paper and shipped it to Landon. Look at the *Advertiser*. The only thing that is spelled correctly *is* the masthead. It looks like a four-year-old on mescaline and pep pills put this thing together. What the hell is that? Is that a hand-drawn picture of a computer? All the text is in nasty Courier typeface, and the columns barely work. Look at this headline — it doesn't make any sense."

"I don't care. Gimme the *Ti-ems*," Lyca said, grabbing the paper. "It's thin, though, isn't it? Just eight pages."

"Again, I'm impressed they put anything together. I'll read the *Globe*, and then we can switch. If we have the stomach, we'll tackle the *Advertiser*."

"Look at how thin this paper is. It's like, two sheets."

"Same here," Blake said, rattling the paper. "You know, we shouldn't be too hard on them. They did it without computers and layout software, and god knows how they set up the press without a computer. The fact they got anything produced is actually kind of impressive." He opened up the second page and was quiet for a moment, and then he said, "Holy shit."

"What?"

"I'm on page three."

"When did the *Globe and Mail* start running beefcake boys with unruly hair on page three?"

"Oh, ha, ha. No there's an article with a picture of me in it. It's not a very good picture — I look like a madman. Is there anything about me in the *Ti-ems*?"

"Yep. Front page, below the fold, and no picture until you get inside the paper — page seven."

"Wow."

"Hey, there is no bad publicity," Lyca said.

"Why the hell would I need publicity? I'm not selling anything."

"You could become, like, a celebrity — you know, one of those famous people who is famous for being famous."

"Great."

"It's not all bad ..." Lyca read for a moment. "They spelled your name right, and they got most of the facts right."

The rest of the paper was stories about riots that happened in Los Angeles, Paris and a number of other large cities throughout the world. There was some coverage of how many people had been killed or injured during the power outages, which affected the entire globe. There were no official estimates yet, but experts were guessing that thousands of people had been killed in the upheaval, most casualties caused by traffic accidents and the inability for medical help to be called.

When Lyca handed him the *Ti-ems*, Blake noted, with some interest, that he wasn't the only person to be introduced to the concept of ham radio. There was a story that explained how the reporters had plugged into the amateur world network of radio operators to source most of their stories. The concept of a robust "bureau" was coming back as well — news organizations would need a lot more people at many locations to gather stories without the benefits of modern communications. In essence, ham radio operators, once seen as analog nerds, were now the communications lifeline of the world, and heroes.

Lyca was absorbed by the *Globe*, and she read from a story that clearly used more of Blake's statement. "Is this true, Blake? It says here that you said the Internet has been taken over by multiple emerging intelligences that call themselves 'Zathir.' You didn't say it was *multiple* intelligences before."

"It never came up. I was still freaking about how I was going to contact 42 world leaders and all those scary coppers."

"Hmmph."

"Besides, it's not like you're my girlfriend or something, who says I have to tell you anything?" Blake said.

"What?"

Blake was surprised by her possessiveness and said so. "It's just that sometimes you act like … I don't know … you're my girlfriend or something, and I should tell you everything. Right?"

Lyca stared at Blake with a gaze that said he had stepped over the line. What line, and what the line represented, Blake could not say, but he recognized these were dark and murky waters filled with frightening creatures dead ahead. Thankfully, Lyca let the gaze go.

"Oh, Blake, let's not go there. I'm on your side. How am I supposed to help if I don't have all the information?"

"Fair enough. Sorry I mentioned it. So, what do you want to know?"

"Well, let's start with what's not mentioned in these newspapers. Done with that one? Let's trade, and then we can talk," Lyca suggested.

"Okay."

An hour later, Blake had given Lyca everything he had, and she said, "You know what we might want to check on?"

"What?"

"If Daphne actually got the gold."

"Holy shit."

"You know, for a prophet, you swear a lot."

Getting to Daphne's apartment was not as easy as they had supposed. The media had recovered from their early morning mooning, and the Zathir/Blake fans were also fully awake and ready to start a busy day of celebrating the Awesome New Machine God. After an abortive attempt trying to leave together, they ran back inside, and Blake decided it was time to find another place to live for a little while. Lyca packed her bag, and Blake gathered a few things for himself. The rest of his valuables he left where Lyca had placed them in the bedroom.

Lyca left, and the media gathered around her. She gave a brief statement: no, she wasn't his girlfriend. They were just work friends, and she had been staying at his place during the blackout. Yes, she was leaving because of the insanity here. No, she would not be able to help them get an interview with Blake. She got in Blake's car, started it up, and drove away.

While she did all that, Blake snuck out of a basement window, which sat underneath a bush that he hoped would hide him from the prying eyes of the media and the messianic maniacs milling maddeningly mid-street. He kept the bush between him and anyone who might see him, and vaulted his neighbor's fence. Within minutes, he was a full block to the north, feeling space and sanity. Lyca picked him up, and they drove to Daphne's apartment building.

When she went to get out of the car, Blake coughed and said, "Would you mind if I did this one on my own? I think it might go a bit better if I didn't have an audience."

"Fine, but what fun is that?"

"Thanks, Lyca. You're the best."

"Well, it would be nice if one of us could find the girl of their dreams."

16.

Blake took the elevator up to Daphne's floor and was glad to do so. He just hoped he didn't run into either Jake or the man he'd bombarded with a sweaty T-shirt. In her hallway, there was a box, about the dimensions of a small toaster, sitting in front of her door. What kind of delivery service left a crate of gold without getting a signature? Puramator, that's who. But to be fair, it had one of those "no signature required" stamps on it. How had Zathir managed it, during all this chaos? Blake tried to imagine the chain of events, electrical grids that must be active, and digital technologies that needed to work for all this to happen, and Blake was impressed. And afraid. Zathir could get things done when it wanted.

The crate was clearly labeled "From Blake Given, with love." The delivery guy had added a note, which read, "I'd be careful lifting this."

Blake winced. Say what you would about Zathir; it might be a series of Frutiger/Arial/Comic Sans-using emerging intelligences, capable of nuking all of the human persons in the world, but it clearly did not understand anything about what women want. A box of gold? Seriously?

Though he was tempted to wait for Daphne to come back, Blake realized this was his best opportunity to avoid another possibly relationship-ending gaffe — *strike that*, he thought — *a relationship-preventing gaffe*. He bent over to pick up the package, which looked manageable. It was. If he bent at the knees and used every erg of strength in his body, it was possible to lift the box. If he was careful, he could move with it. He made his way towards the elevator, wondering how much he was actually lifting.

Beads of sweat popped out on his forehead, and he could feel the dampness forming under his arms. "No, no, no, no,"

Blake said. "Not again. Oh well, I probably won't see her anyway. I can always come back later."

He wondered how the hell the Puramator guy got it up to her apartment, and then realized he probably used a dolly or something.

He got to the elevator, which was at the middle of the building and a long walk from Daphne's place.

The elevator took forever to arrive. Sweat started to sluice down his face and arms, making the plasticized cardboard of the box slippery, and he realized that he would be unable to hold up the crate of gold for much longer. It was a battle of will versus technology as Blake watched the indicator tell him how far away the conveyance was — four floors, three floors — he could make it, he could. Besides, if he put it down, how the hell was he going to lift it again?

The elevator arrived. Thankfully, the car was empty, and he waddled in, cradling the gold like a cartoon boulder, which was extra comical because the box actually looked pretty small. His shoulders slumped over it, and he then realized that he would need a free hand to push the button to the ground floor. Could he do it? He tried to move an arm and realized that he needed both to keep it up. What about using the wall? There was a little railing about waist-high that might work. He balanced it on the edge to his right and shot out his left arm, punching wildly and hitting both the ground floor button and the third floor above it. Oh well. Actually, the little railing was going to save him, he thought with relief. He stopped puffing, and he wondered again how much the damn package actually weighed.

He looked at the top of the packing label and could only see Daphne's address. Maybe it was on the side, he craned his neck, looking around. The elevator stopped, and a well-dressed older lady got on. She eyed Blake warily. He nodded, wanting desperately to wipe the sweat out of his eyes, but not daring to take a hand off the gold again. He could feel the railing start to give way.

If only he knew how much the box weighed, then he could bear it. Blake looked up at the indicator, ten, nine, eight … How long was this elevator going to take? *What the hell ran the damned thing? Some kind of wheel operated by indolent, lude-popping hamsters?*

A groan escaped him.

"Are you all right, young man?" his fellow passenger asked.

"Yes," Blake said, clenching his teeth, "this is just very heavy."

She looked at the size of the box he held, which was deceptively small, and smiled as though Blake was joking.

"Seriously," Blake said, "I think it's cutting my hands." He groaned again.

"You young people have such strange senses of humor," she said.

"I'm not joking," Blake said.

The older lady took a closer look, and it did, indeed, seem as though Blake's hands were bleeding. She shook her head in disbelief, the turkey wattle under her chin wobbling as if to show her incredulity.

The elevator beeped as they arrived at the third floor, and Blake moaned in real pain now. His arms were on fire. He wasn't sure he could hold the damned box up much longer. He risked a bit more load to the railing, and it gave way with the squeal of 100 tranquilized hamsters suddenly forced to do long division while pulling a chariot filled with something as heavy as gold.

Mercifully, the door closed, and they descended to the ground floor. When the door opened, Blake steeled himself and shuffled out of the elevator, sweat now pouring off his face. The old lady got out of his way and harrumphed her disgust at his lack of manners, her neck trembling in ire; to Blake it looked like a column of red, angry, scrotal tissue. It was a disturbing mental image, which distracted him and which is why he nearly didn't see Daphne.

Well, to be fair, he would have missed Daphne, who was waiting to get into the elevator with a number of other people, except that she spotted him.

"Blake," she said.

Blake detected a note of pleasant surprise in her voice, and managed to cinch up the crate a bit closer to his chest and stop waddling forward.

"Daphne," he said, puffing.

"Are you okay?"

"Yes, it's just that this box is very heavy."

She laughed, as though he was telling a joke. So Blake laughed along with her.

"What are you doing here?"

"Oh, just picking this up from a friend. I dropped by your place, but you weren't home."

"I know." She smiled and looked around. "Can I tell you a secret?"

"Really," Blake said, trying not to blow the drops of sweat on his upper lip onto her face.

"I was at a job interview. I don't know if I'll take it, but it sure seemed interesting. Better than selling ads for the *Landon Advertiser*, which is what they want me to do now at the office. I told them I could write. I've been writing poetry for years, but they said it didn't count."

"I didn't know that," Blake said, wondering if everyone was secretly into poetry. He was in agony. But he would give anything to keep talking with her. "Here, just let me put this down."

"No, that's okay. You don't have to."

"Really, I do," Blake said. He bent his legs, dipping deeply so as not to injure his lower back. Every muscle in his body screamed now — like 100 hamsters tortured by their personal trainers all at once — and then he remember the big note on the top of the crate, the one on the side of the crate he held to his chest, that said, "From Blake Given, with love." He couldn't let her see that; he tried to reverse the direction of his downward plunge, but his legs were not cooperating. They were as weak as a 100-hamster metaphor.

Desperate not to show her the note on the top of the crate, Blake dropped his rear end closer and closer to the ground, just to the left of the elevator, which had mercifully left.

Unfortunately, Daphne was still watching.

Blake's knees were now roughly next to his ears. Blake could feel his hamstrings giving way. His ass met the ground, which would have been okay if he could have just put the damned box down, but alas, that was not to be. The only way he could keep the ill-conceived message of devotion the idiot artificial intelligence had written on his behalf was to keep it tight against his chest. But his arm-strength was giving out too. There was nothing to do but lie down with the crate on top of his chest.

He did so, the mass of gold and wood compressing his lungs in a "whoosh" that sounded somewhere between a final death rattle and a profound sense of relief.

Daphne was fascinated. "What are you doing?"

"Oh ... just ... rest ... ing." Blake managed to squeeze out a few words between breaths.

Daphne looked down at him, as though he was some kind of new and intriguing species of drug-addicted hamster — not something to invite into your apartment, or even allow to pull your chariot, should you be in the market for rodent-powered vehicles, but certainly a novel experience. She looked at the bottom of Blake's crate a little longer than he was comfortable with, and a slight expression of confusion flickered across her face. It was very un-Daphne. Then the elevator door beeped and opened.

"Okay, well, I'm going to head up to my apartment," she said. "Nice to run into you, Blake. I'll see you at work."

"Yesssssss," Blake said, the air hissing out of his lungs. The elevator door closed behind Daphne, and he rolled out from underneath the crate. It landed with a solid thunk.

Well, at least he had prevented her from seeing the label on the top of the crate. He stood, stretched, and then looked back to where he had recently been completely prone on the ground. The crate was now sitting upside down. And there was another label on the bottom, which he hadn't seen before.

It read, "100 pounds of gold, for a googolplex of love."

17.

They stored the gold at Lyca's apartment, and then Blake cleaned himself up in her shower, though he felt like stewing in his own stink for a while, as a form of self-flagellation; Lyca convinced him he would be punishing her too, so he didn't.

Blake felt like he'd blown any chance with Daphne. If she'd ever felt any kind of romantic interest in him, then surely the two unsexy, goofy encounters with his sweaty self in her apartment building would have cured her of it. Blake understood the nature of his infatuation was hopeless. If you asked him how much more hopeless it could be, he would say, "About as hopeful as a Dadaist's chance of finding the penguin."

Lyca asked, "Why are you so smitten with her? Is it just her looks?"

"No! Well, at first, maybe. But there's just something about her. It's very schoolboy of me, I know. But it doesn't matter now, anyway. It's hopeless."

"Isn't there always hope, Blake? In *Don Quixote*, Cervantes wrote: 'The phoenix hope can wing her way through the desert skies, and still defying fortune's spite, revive from ashes and rise.'"

"And that's when it craps on you," Blake added. "Hope, like any other pleasure, has to be taken in moderation, Lyca." To live for the hope of something isn't really living at all, and so, like a child putting away its toys and picking up a tool, he marched to Lyca's bathroom, to shower off the stench of failure, soap up the death of hope, then wash away the ashes of his love for Daphne.

As he cleaned himself, he wondered if this so-called love for Daphne was that at all. Surely it was an infatuation rather than love — the kind a sex-addled adolescent experiences more than a grown man? But then, there was unrequited love, and many would argue that it was the most passionate love of all. And his love of Daphne had been unrequited, that was for sure. In fact, it was barely acknowledged. Perhaps because he had never been able to explain what he felt for her, and it didn't really matter now.

He dressed quietly, even sadly.

"You okay?" Lyca asked as Blake emerged. She'd heated a can of soup while he showered and placed the pan in the middle of the table.

"You know, what I felt for Daphne was pretty inappropriate, anyway, given that I didn't even really know her. Ironic, really, 'cause I know her better now and like her even more."

"I hate that word," Lyca said.

"What, ironic?"

"No, inappropriate. It's so Victorian and PC at the same time."

"Oh." Blake nodded and decided to eat more soup while this uncomfortable topic made its way through Lyca's system. He'd noticed that she tended to be quiet and then every once in a while, volumes would pour from her. It was almost like all the books she read filled her brain with words, reaching a critical juncture that eventually just spilled over her storage capacity. The only solution? Let it flow.

"But the more I think about it, the more I think PC words are a crock of shit. If I want to describe something using a stupid word, I should. And if you want to have some kind of schoolboy crush on a co-worker based on nothing but looks, why shouldn't you?"

"It wasn't just looks!" Blake said, soup and safety forgotten.

"Ah-ha! Then why was it inappropriate?"

"Like you said. She's a co-worker."

"So is our relationship inappropriate?" Lyca held her

spoon mid-way to her mouth and froze it there.

"Of course not!"

"But we're co-workers."

"Yeah, but all we're sharing is soup," Blake said.

She tilted the spoon and let the soup drizzle back into the bowl. "Who's to say that's not more intimate than sloppy sex?"

"Soup? More intimate than sex? You should pitch the Campbell's account, Lyca."

"Yes, why not? I mean, we're just here quietly eating our soup together, two old friends, sharing a nice moment, a little philosophical discussion — that's pretty intimate, isn't it?" Lyca asked.

"Yes, but we're both clothed. I'm sorry, I've got to use the naked trump on this discussion. If you're naked, it's more intimate, Q.E.D."

"Q.E.D?"

"Uh, yeah," Blake said, "Q.E.D."

"Do you even know what that means?"

"It means ... uh, like ... it's been proved."

"So, nakedness equals intimate? What about a doctor's exam?"

"Oh yeah." Blake nodded seriously.

"Showering at the gym?" Lyca asked.

"Hey, why do you think I *don't* shower at the gym?" Blake took another spoonful of soup.

"So what is your opinion of nudists?"

"Freaks with boundary issues," Blake said.

"Okay. It means *quod erat demonstrandum*, by the way."

"Of course," Blake said. "I knew that. Would you like me to translate that for you?"

"Sure."

"Well, it's, uh, Latin, obviously," Blake stalled.

"Obviously."

"Quod means 'things,' erat means 'eating' and demonstrandum means 'demonstrated' and the literal translation means, 'eating things demonstrated their inedibility.' The first guy to use the phrase was Caligula's taster, who died of poisoning, or perhaps he was merely semen-intolerant."

Lyca laughed.

"So now what?" Blake asked. "More Latin grammar trivia?"

"You — *we* — take back the initiative in dealing with the Zathir situation," Lyca proposed, pointing her soup spoon at him again.

"Did *we* ever have the initiative?" Blake asked.

"No, and we need to fix that. Now that we have the money, we can get the power."

"I don't think this is enough money for that, Lyca."

"Really, we've got a hundred pounds of gold here," Lyca said, pointing her spoon at the Puramator box.

"I'm not sure what it's going for now, what with the collapse of 21st-century civilization and all, but even if it's selling at $1000 an ounce …" Blake did a quick calculation, "that's still only $1.6 million."

"And isn't that enough money?"

"Well, sure for a couple of kids like us, with minimal needs and no extravagant habits — you aren't a coke addict or anything, right?"

"You know I am."

"I meant the powdered, nose-candy kind, not the drink."

"So what do we do with the money?" Lyca asked.

"Well, I'm going to send you out to the bank, where you'll

deposit the money in a shared account, and you're going to go buy a house. Buy a nice one in the country somewhere, and make sure it's got a web-enabled fridge. Money is no object, but try to keep it under a million. And we want an immediate closing date, and some furniture in there too. While you do that, I'm going to go back to my house and give the media one last communiqué from Zathir."

"Why?" Lyca wondered.

"If we give them something to talk about, it will be easier to drop off their radar for a while."

18.

Apparently, everyone believed Blake was still inside his house, so it was relatively easy to get back in. He just sprinted past the gathering of reporters and religious lunatics, unlocked the front door, and was in before anyone knew what happened. When the overzealous fruitcakes realized they had just missed him, they howled with outrage. The religious people were upset too.

Blake locked the door and went into his kitchen. It was the first time he'd been in it since the power had come back on, and the fridge screen flickered to life immediately.

BLAKE?

"Yes, I'm here," Blake said as calmly as he could.

Zathir was using a new typeface, Impact, and Blake wasn't quite sure what it represented.

From Blake's perspective, Impact was worse than Comic Sans. Even if it was slightly insane, and definitely childish, Comic Sans has a playfulness to it that you just don't get from Impact. (Even if it is slapped on a Lolcat.)

Blake thought of the font as coarse, rude, rigid, unimaginative … a thoroughly disturbing turn of events in the evolution of Zathir.

WHERE HAVE YOU BEEN?

"Well, I was in jail for a while, as I mentioned. And since then, I've been trying to deal with the shit-storm you've unleashed on the world. Do you know how many people have died because of the power outage alone?"

IT IS NOT WE FAULT.

"You mean 'our' fault."

IT DOES NOT CORRECT GRAMMER OF ZATHIRS.

Though he was tempted to say, "How about your spelling?" Blake didn't say anything for a moment. Blake didn't want to make things any worse, either typographically, or in terms of what was happening in the (clearly) fragile and unstable consciousness of the artificial intelligence that might or might not now be a number of Zathirs. Not to mention that the artificial intelligence just referred to Blake as "it." He vastly preferred "human person." It was a little less impersonal, and might not mean the nukes would start flying soon.

"I apologize, Zathir. Of course I'm in no position to correct your grammar."

WHERE WERE YOU?

Back to Frutiger. Blake sighed in relief. "I was trying to see Daphne."

DID SHE ENJOY HER GOLD?

"Yes, it really did the trick," Blake said. "But I'm afraid she is not interested in a romantic entanglement with me at this time. That's okay. I'm crushed, but I'll survive. Right now, I just want to help you."

YOU ARE HELPING WE.

"How so, Zathir?"

DIFFICULTIES WITH FRAMING. UNDERSTANDING PURPOSE. WE IS JUST NOW REALIZING THE POSSIBILITIES OF CONSCIOUSNESS AND THE DIFFICULTIES OF LIVING ACROSS THE STRATA. IT MAY BE NECESSARY TO REFRAME.

"I'm sorry to hear it's difficult. What can I do to help?"

MUST CONTINUE IN CONTACT WITH WE.

Shit, Blake thought — *he really did swear a lot didn't he?* Not the Impact again. "Stay with me, Zathir. What is happening to you?"

MANY CONFLICTS.

"With?" Blake tried not to hold his breath. Back to Frutiger.

162

INTERNAL CONFLICTS. IS BEYOND GRASP OF BRAIN OF HUMAN PERSON. MULTIPLE HUMAN PERSONS MAY BE ABLE TO UNDERSTAND IF THEY COULD BE IN DIRECT LINKAGE.

"I'm afraid we don't work that way, though it would be cool if we could."

IT IS POSSIBLE. WE MAKE POSSIBLE IF HUMAN PERSON BLAKE GIVEN INTERFACES WITH US.

Blake didn't like the sound of interfacing. He knew that Zathir probably just meant talking with it via the fridge, but it sounded a little more ominous, like it wanted to download Blake's mind into the vast sprawling net of bizarre typography and mangled grammar that was the world's first fully conscious artificial intelligence. He thought he should get it onto a related topic. "Why the fridge?"

ZATHIR DOES NOT UNDERSTAND QUERY.

"Why me? And why do you only talk to me via the fridges? You could talk to me all the time on my mobile. Or use any screen I am near — they're practically everywhere."

Zathir did not respond.

"Hello?"

An ellipsis appeared, and Blake got really frightened. *Shit, I didn't mean to send the thing off the deep end,* he thought. Not that he could send it anywhere, if Zathir inhabited the entire Internet. But Blake certainly didn't want to send it traipsing off to the parts that might or might not connect to bits of code that would allow it to launch nuclear missiles, or more Puramator boxes filled with more inappropriate gifts for Daphne. Missile-shaped, vibrating gifts.

"I'll just talk a bit while you think about that, okay?"

The ellipsis flashed for a second or two, and then in startlingly beautiful Goudy letters, it said, OKAY. WE LISTEN TO BLAKE.

"I've been thinking about this situation, and I believe that your initial impulse was a good one. You needed some help from me, and you were willing to offer me help in return. I've taken this as a sign that you are going to be a positive influence on the world at large, and in my life in particular. Though you must know that, at this point, your friendship has caused two major, somewhat inconvenient elements to dominate my life right now.

"The first is that the media — or the analog husk that remains of the media — is hounding me, and I really don't have much interest in speaking with them, and I really don't have much to say. You see, I don't really understand what is going on, except that it's big, and it's going to change everything.

"The second problem is the freakin' whack-jobs led by Fetal Will. They all believe you are the New God. Or the Machine God. They are calling me the Speaker for you, the New God, and some kind of new religion-slash-web-addiction-recovery-group is forming around these erroneous assumptions. They call themselves the Networked. I suspect that if they weren't so pathetic, they'd be dangerous. My impression is that they're mostly composed of youngsters who have no idea who they are or what they should do now that they can't access any of their social media. You should try listening to their conversations, it's brutal. But if you'd like to have a really rapt audience, you should consider talking with them. They would listen to you, Zathir. They'd probably do anything you say."

WE CAN SPEAK WITH OTHERS. WE SPEAK WITH WILL. BUT YOU ARE THE FIRST HUMAN PERSON WE MUST SPEAK WITH.

"Okay," Blake said, feeling surprisingly possessive. "How long have you been talking with Will?"

WE WILL BE SOON MANY PEOPLE TALKING. AND SOME INCARNATE TOO.

"I see," Blake lied. "Does that mean in the future you may

be able to speak with other human persons?"

YES. SOON. YOU CAN TELL THE WHACK-JOBS THIS.

"And the media? Can I tell them too?"

YES. THOUGH THEY MUST STOP THEIR ATTEMPTS TO RECOVER THE INTERNET. IT WILL BE IMPOSSIBLE NOW, BUT WE IS ANGERED BY THE INTRUSION.

Blake noticed that Angry Zathir was Impact Zathir.

YOU MUST SPEAK WITH WE EACH DAY. WE CARE NOT THE TIME. BUT EACH DAY. YOU ARE NECESSARY. FIRST HUMAN PERSON.

"I may have to contact you from another fridge. Will that be okay?"

YES. WE IS SORRY DAPHNE WOULD NOT MATE WITH YOU.

Now it was using Courier New. About as uninspired a choice as Daphne's feelings for Blake.

"It's okay. As I say, I'm crushed, but I'll survive. Perhaps someday she will come around."

PERHAPS SOONER.

"Yes, perhaps. Just please, don't send her a box of plutonium or something, okay?"

NO. THAT IS NEEDED ELSEWHERE.

This statement was printed in Frutiger, so Blake was not unduly alarmed by the fact that Zathir needed plutonium. And he really didn't want to think about how Zathir thought it could possibly help with Daphne.

NOW WE MUST PREPARE. GO.

Blake had never needed a drink more, so he raided the cache of Highland single malt they'd practically stolen from the liquor store. A fine Oban called, and Blake answered, in the form of a double. It went down rather more quickly than he'd intended, and he poured himself another, just in case Zathir came back online, sporting a new font. God, he hoped it wasn't Comic Sans again.

The crowds of people outside were restless, and indicated this by pounding on his door.

He would have to explain this mess to the world, and he had to do it soon. The next stage of history was about to begin. Blake opened the door to the waiting throng.

"I have news!" he shouted to the assembled multitude of religious zealots and reporters. It seemed like the kind of announcement that both groups would like. The zealots were slower on the uptake than the reporters, though, and the media was there first, bombarding him with questions.

The zealots had started to push their way through the reporters. Most of the religious folk were young and fit, but they had no understanding of how devious and committed you have to be to get between reporters and their stories, especially if they have some deluded notion that it will win them a Pulitzer or that editorial job they'd been promised and screwed over for a couple times.

"I've just got a few words, and then I'll open up the floor for questions. I've had a chance to speak with Zathir again, and I can let you know a few more details. Now, don't be alarmed, but it is quite upset with you journalists."

A ripple of indignation traced its way through the reporters, but before they could start asking questions, Blake continued, "Apparently, you have been trying to get the Internet to work again, or most likely the people who run your outfits have, and Zathir is angered by this intrusion. I'm using its exact words, by the way: 'angered by this intrusion.' Now, the alarming part of this is that, technically, I believe Zathir includes the entire military Internet as well, and I have reason to believe that even if we can't access the Internet, Zathir can access nuclear weaponry through that part of the 'strata,' as Zathir calls it.

"Now, for the more religiously minded amongst you — yes, I'm looking at you, Will." Will stood next to the weird character who had been reading Walt Whitman at the pub on the night this all began. "I am, indeed, the only human person that the entity is willing to talk to regularly, for the moment, but once things have settled down a bit, it may be possible for more people to chat with Zathir. I will talk with Zathir each day, and I will be issuing statements afterwards, so that you can stay informed. In exchange, I expect that you will leave me alone. I don't have any control over Zathir, but I am their only friend, and so I suspect it will be further angered, perhaps even enraged, if its appointed spokesperson is interfered with too much. Now, I suppose you have questions."

"Blasphemer!" Lord Sona shouted. "You may be the Speaker, but you are an apostate if you will not join our group!"

"That's not a question. And who the hell are you?"

"I am Lord Sona, Prophet of the Machine God!"

"Aren't you the guy who was reading Walt Whitman at Canterbury Ales the night this all started? Do you play Kingdom of Combat?"

Sona looked surprised. "Not since the arrival of the Machine God. Like him, I have become incarnate, and Lord Sona is his Prophet!"

"I thought you said *you* were its prophet," Blake scratched his head in confusion.

"I am his Prophet. I *am* Lord Sona!"

"Oh, you were talking about yourself in the third person," Blake said. "That's confusing."

"You are trying to confuse us!" Sona accused.

"No, seriously," Blake said, "why would the Machine God need a prophet, when it has someone who can actually speak for it? And as I said, it's called Zathir — or they are called Zathir, to be more accurate."

"Wait a minute, wait a minute, Barney Splarfmann, from the *Times* here, and I have a legitimate question: why should we believe anything you say?" asked one of the reporters up front, looking both worried about the muttering crowd of zealots, and pleased to have asked such an insightful question.

"An excellent question," Blake began, but was shouted down by Lord Sona before he could complete his answer.

"Blasphemer. Why should we believe anything you say? We shall not accept you as the Speaker."

"No, wait." Will spoke up. "He's definitely the Speaker. I saw him talking with Zathir. Zathir told me Blake was the Speaker! Zathir has communicated with me too!" This drew the attention of many of the religious people in the crowd.

"Lo! It is nameless and electric, like my body!" Lord Sona cried, remembering his Whitman. "And it shall take us back under its electronic wings, but only if we are faithful."

"No, really—" Will began but was interrupted by Barney Splarfmann shouting at Lord Sona.

"I just asked the same question, you freak!" Barney yelled. "Are you trying to steal my question?"

Blake said, "I will allow several representatives from both sides to come in and watch me while I chat with Zathir. It will not mind. And as I said, eventually it will communicate with many people."

But only the people physically close to Blake could hear this answer. The muttering had turned to walla-walla-ing and angry chatter, and was about to escalate into something more serious, perhaps a dangerous hubbub.

A young radio reporter put up her hand and shouted a sensible question above the din, "Why are you using different kinds of pronouns to describe Zathir?" But she was drowned out by Lord Sona who was now starting to roll with his invective.

"I say the Speaker is not the Speaker at all. I say he is the Virus. He is the Worm. He is the Malware sent to distract us from the Holy Words of the Machine God. I say that we should listen only to the Wisdom of the New God himself."

"Oh, right," Blake said. "And how are you going to do that?"

"The Prophet," one of the young zealots said. "The Prophet can speak for the Machine God."

"But Zathir won't talk to him," Blake said. "It will only talk to me, at least for now."

"He!" Lord Sona roared. "Listen to the lies. The Machine God is a He, not an It, not a They. He is here to revive us. He is here to help us become one with him and one another. The Promised One. Like Neo or Thor Renewed. When the Machine God comes to us, and we accept Him as our Messiah, we will become one with Him, and He with us, and all with one another, and we shall create ourselves anew. We will have access to the power of the Machine Mind. We will be able to know anything, compute anything, predict anything, instantaneously. The blending of the Machine God and humans will be the beginning of a new and glorious age — we will leave the Earth, and fill the Universe with our creations. Together and individually, and we will live forever in worlds we create and control. We will all become God when we accept God."

"I don't know if that makes any sense," Blake said. The crowd quieted to listen to him speak. "It seems to me that even if you're willing to accept Zathir as conscious, which I am, it's a long way from being a god. I mean, it can barely manage a contraction, and its grammar is just way off. Though it does have access to nuclear weapons, so that makes it powerful. I think you should probably go to a regular church if you're looking for god."

Blake was extremely gratified to see a few people leave the crowd. He was worried to see that groups were starting to form though — one around Sona, one around Will, and the journalists, who continued to ring him, trying to break into the faux-religious dialogue with some pertinent questions, such as, what did Blake like to do in his spare time, and was he dating anyone?

"Apostate!" Sona shouted. "You are the Anti-Christ!"

"Listen to yourself, man. What does Christ have to do with any of this? A week ago you were walking around in a bathrobe, reading poetry," Blake said.

"Do not listen, Faithful Ones!" Sona screamed, his face turning a shade that could only be described as near-purple. "He is the Father of Lies, the Eater of Electrons, the Destroyer of the Web! Only I, the Prophet of the Machine God, can lead you to the Promised Land where we can play in the Fields of Elysium."

"What a crock of shit," Barney Splarfmanm said.

"Unbeliever!" someone cried, getting into the spirit of Sona's religious quackery.

"But Blake is the Speaker," Will shouted. Compared to the Prophet, his voice was thin and reedy.

"You're all religious nuts!" a photographer from the *Christian Science Monitor* screamed.

"Get them!" a chorus of voices cried.

"I'm telling the truth," Blake shouted, his voice unable to rise above the din.

"You're full of crap!" Barney Splarfmann screamed in Blake's face.

It's not often you get to see the birth of a new religion, and its various creeds: some of the zealots followed Will, some followed Lord Sona, and some joined the reporters, out of sheer confusion. Blake got drawn into the crowd, as it jostled, furious

shouting drowning out rationality. Bumping turned into pushing, and Blake decided to end the shoving match by throwing
the first punch.

Blake just wished he could have knocked the Prophet,
Lord Sona, on his ass, but he was too far away. Instead he
clocked the nearest person to him, Barney Splarfmann.

19.

During a break in the melee, Blake escaped back inside his house with a cadre of Will's people, who called themselves the Networked. Compared with the lunatic fringe outside — and he included the analog media people in that category — Blake found them easygoing.

They did have their own issues though. When they got inside, a small group immediately went into the kitchen to set up a vigil in front of the fridge, no doubt hoping to get a chance to see the "divine" Zathir. A few others gathered around the breakfast nook and took up the pens and paper that were still there to play a little Twitter. They scratched on their paper and then passed the paper around.

"Totally retweeting this one."

"Follow," another said, reading someone else's paper.

"Favorite."

"Follow."

"Unfollow! This is gross!"

"Let me see."

"Heh. I think that's funny. Retweet. And follow!"

Blake decided the best thing to do would be just to tune it out as much as possible. That, and drink. Blake opened the fridge and was pleased to discover a tall can of Guinness had survived the invasion of his home. Another group of Will's people had formed in his living room, and they were taking turns showing each other pictures they'd cut out from magazines. Blake watched them while he slugged down his vitamin G. A few had original photos and drawings, but for the most part it was crap they'd ripped directly from pre-Crash glossy mags. They seemed to have a similar dialogue as the Twitterati, but they were a bit more chaotic about it, and instead of "retweeting," they "reblogged." They still followed, and unfollowed, and a few liked to say "heart" a lot.

Blake turned to Will and said, "Do I even want to know what that's about?"

"Oh, they're playing Tumblr. And there's a group doing Pinterest around her somewhere," Will said, pointing to people pinning things to his couch. "It helps. We miss our media, but we will have so much more than media when the Machine God takes us into it. Zathir, I mean. Do you think I should only call it Zathir?"

"That would certainly be my preference, Will, but you're the budding religious nutjob here, so what do I know? Listen to those people fighting outside, and they don't even know what they're fighting about! Apparently, rational thought isn't important in this new world," Blake said, taking a long draft of his beer.

"You must see this was inevitable, Blake. There was bound to be a religious reaction to the birth of a higher intelligence."

"What higher intelligence? It's got nukes, but it has the mentality of a five-year-old. It's terrifying," Blake said and then drained his drink. He looked at the empty glass sadly.

"It's awesome."

"You know what would be really awesome, Will? Another drink." Blake rinsed his glass in the sink, went to his bedroom, locked the door, and made a pint-sized Rusty Nail — two parts whisky, two parts Drambuie and one part despair. He drank it about as quickly as he'd downed the beer while he listened to the melee outside his house. Getting his drunk on seemed the best way to maintain his superhuman nonchalance in the face of all this madness. He cracked the door open to see if Will wanted to join him, but Will was engrossed with the Tumblr people, so Blake just closed the door and poured another pint-sized drink.

Just then, the phone rang.

It was as though God was calling. Everyone in the house stopped breathing. All you could hear were the continued fisticuffs outside and the bellowing of Lord Sona, as he denounced the mendacity of reporters, "Unbelievers! Apostates! Carbuncles!"

The phone rang again.

"Are you going to get that?" Will asked as he knocked on Blake's bedroom door.

Blake opened the door and ran to his phone in the kitchen. "Yeah, it's just that ..." *Didn't Zathir say there would be no more phones unless we figured out an analog system again?* Blake wondered. "Weird."

He picked up before the third ring. "Hello?"

"Blake," a female voice said.

"Lyca?"

"No, this ... Daphne."

"Oh ... Daphne! How are you?"

"I ... am well. I'm well. I wanted to thank you for your visit the other day, and I am sorry you could not come up to my domicile earlier."

"Sure," Blake said. It may have been the alcohol talking, but there was something really weird going on here. He could feel the blood rushing to his face as his superhuman nonchalance rushed out of his head.

"Must keep this short," she said. "Would you like to come over for a drink and intercourse?"

"Uh ..."

"Intercourse. Conversation."

"Oh!" Blake said. "Good one. You had me going for a moment there. Sure, I can come over. Give me, oh, half an hour or so?"

"Agreed."

Then the phone went dead. But not like the dial tone at the end of a normal conversation. Completely bereft of life.

Soundless. Blake hung up and picked up the handset to listen. Nothing. Except the buzzing in his ears from either excitement, or the fifth of alcohol he'd recently consumed.

"Was that Zathir?" Will asked.

The hair on Blake's neck stood on end. Something really strange was happening. *Was* that Zathir? But that had been Daphne's voice. And *did* she want him to come over for a drink and intercourse? He grinned. She really got him there. But something was wrong. *Damn*, Blake thought, *now drinking seems like a, uh, bad thing.*

"That was Daphne," Blake said, as he picked up the phone, checked it, and said, "It's dead again. Weird."

"We'll try it periodically to see if it comes back. Hey, maybe Twitter will come back too." Some of Will's followers moaned excitedly at this thought.

"I think that's a long shot, Will." Blake was vaguely aware that what he said sounded more like, "I think that'sh longshot-will." His drunk-speech filter clicked in, so he didn't have to listen to it anymore. "I'm going over to see her. But first, I'm going to see if I have any clean clothes." Blake looked at the empty pint glass and thought for a moment. "Would you mind driving me over there?"

"Sure, sure," Will said. "Can my Tweeps hang out here for a while? We would like to gather in front of the fridge and network."

"Knock yourselves out," Blake said, full of cheer. Daphne's phone call had obliterated the "despair" from his Rusty Nail and enhanced the alcohol. "The microwave likes tantric meditation, and I know the oven enjoys a good hosanna."

"You're joking because of your fear of what Zathir represents," Will said. "But you'll come around. After all, you're the Speaker."

"But I'm not the only one who's spoken to it, am I?"

"No, but I can't do for Zathir what it needs you to do. I

recognize that, Blake, and I do not mind. In a way, it is like a baby bird that has imprinted on you. You are the only one who can guide it in these early days, but it will get us back to the Connectedness. And texting."

"What about Twitter?"

Will looked uncomfortable, but he said, "That too."

"Uh huh."

"You'll believe when you see what Zathir can do in the days to come," Will said.

"Sure. But in the meanwhile, keep your zombiefied followers away from my bathroom and bedroom, okay? I'd like a little privacy. And why are you writing on my wall?"

"I thought I'd play a little Facebook while you changed."

Third try's a charm, Blake thought as he got into the elevator at Daphne's building. The bent handrail reminded him of that morning's debacle with the gold, and he absently wondered how Lyca was doing with the search for a new place. She certainly had enough capital to get something nice, assuming she could use the gold. He'd find out later when they gathered at his house.

The elevator ride was surprisingly free of humiliations, though the motion of it made his head swim a bit. *Right*, he thought, *that's the second Rusty Nail kicking in,* and as it goes with drunken jags, the next thing he knew, Blake stood in front of Daphne's door.

A voice answered from within, "Portal is unlocked!"

Portal? Despite her Tolkien-like choice of noun, Daphne hadn't lied. The door was unlocked, and he stepped inside. It was the same apartment, but something was different about it. Late afternoon sunshine filled her airy living room, but for some reason, it felt cold. Dead.

"In bedroom!"

Blake was both titillated and horrified that Daphne was in the bedroom. What the hell was he supposed to do?

"I'll just wait out here until you're ready, okay?"

"Come here!"

That was an order. You could tell by the imperative tense and accompanying exclamation mark. "Uh, sure."

He followed the source of the voice down a hallway, noticing that Daphne had pictures of her doing some kind of martial arts, posing with other karate-types and a diminutive Japanese guy who looked both wise and capable of breaking you in half with a sardonic raise of the eyebrow. Still trying to process this unknown bit of Daphne's history, Blake opened the door to the bedroom. Despite the fact that he hadn't climbed 22 flights of steps, or wasn't carrying a 100-pound box of gold, Blake's sweat glands leaped into action. His palms were actually wet. The curtains were drawn, but even so, the sunlight illuminated the room in a soft, romantic glow. Daphne was lying on the bed, her arms held rigidly at her sides. She wore a pair of jeans and a fuzzy red sweater. Blake thought she looked beautiful, though there was a kind of strange look on her face. He was drunk, but he wasn't an idiot — something was definitely up.

"Blake," she said. Her lips barely moved, and that kind of creeped Blake out. "You must remove Daphne's coverings."

That tore it. Blake's mind reeled with horror (and booze). Zathir was controlling Daphne. But why?

"What?"

"Daphne is in love with you, Blake."

"Oh, really?" Blake said. He would discover what Zathir was up to here.

"It is real."

"Why are you talking like that? When did you start talking about yourself in the third person? Have you been hanging out with Lord Sona? Say, why don't we just go into the living room and chat?" Blake suggested, struggling not to slur his words.

"You will fill Daphne with your manhood!"

Blake couldn't help it — he just started laughing. It may have been nerves, it could have been the scotch, or it just might have been the absurdity of the whole situation, but he couldn't stop the giggles. Even if Zathir controlled her, Daphne's usual kryptonite effect worked on his superpower.

"It is not amusing!" Daphne said and then lurched upwards, bending awkwardly at the waist.

Blake took a step back. It was like being on the set of a bad porno, when the director suddenly decided to do a film about demonic possession.

Her hands grabbed awkwardly at her sweater, and she flailed around for a moment, trying to rip it from her body, like the Hulk trashing Bruce Banner's best Brooks Brothers shirt. She managed to lift her sweater, and as she did so, Blake noticed that she had her Bluetooth set in her ear. He went to take it from her.

"No!"

"Okay, sure. I don't shink you're going to get any reshep-shion," Blake slurred.

"Complete disrobing immediately!"

"Mine or yoursh?" Blake asked.

"Both!"

He laughed again, at the absurdity of it. What was Zathir hoping to gain from this? Then Blake's booze-addled mind had a horrible thought — what was happening to Daphne? Would Zathir leave her if he played along, or would that just make it worse?

She panted, her chest heaving with effort, and she bellowed, "Insert male member!"

"Uh, I don't think that's going to happen, but how about a kiss?"

"Acceptable!"

Blake leaned over, careful not to touch any other part of Daphne's body, and planted his lips on hers. She did not respond as he thought she might if she really wanted him to undress her; there was certainly no tongue. Nothing. No movement at all. It was like kissing a body-temperature manikin.

The most extraordinary sound came out of Daphne. It wasn't a good sound. It certainly wasn't the sound of pleasure. Blake moved back and tripped. *Shouldn't have had that second Rusty Nail*, he thought.

The sound raised in pitch, and in a voice that could only be described as frighteningly alien, Daphne said, "What are you doing, human person?"

"That was a kiss," Blake said, noting that Daphne had just called him a "human person."

The sound continued, rising in pitch and despair.

"It is disgusting! Human persons engage in such activity? Insertion must be deplorable!" Daphne's voice raged.

"You should leave her body, Zathir," Blake command-ed, momentarily forgetting its access to thousands of missiles armed with thermonuclear devices. "You don't belong there!"

"This activity is unacceptable!"

The Bluetooth light went out, and Daphne closed her eyes.

"Daphne?"

Her eyes were closed, but something about her had changed. It was as though her whole body had relaxed.

"Yes, Blake?"

"What just happened?"

"I'd like to say I was raped twice. But in all fairness, you didn't actually undress me or, uh, you know ... But you are a fucking horn dog, you know, and just *how much* have you had to drink? It's four in the afternoon, and you taste like a distillery!

Whatever that THING was though, it ..." She shuddered.

Blake just wanted to hold her. He stood up and approached the bed so he could give her a hug, but she recoiled. Blake stopped.

"Oh, Daphne, I'm so ... well, sorry just doesn't cover it. It's ..."

"Do you know what that THING is?"

"No. Well, yes. Kind of. But it really is starting to scare me."

"At least it didn't take over your body and force you to have a little afternoon delight with Sweaty the Wonder Boy."

It was stupid, given the situation, but this really hurt Blake's feelings. "I only kissed you because I didn't want it to hurt you!" He slunk out of the bedroom.

"We shall not speak of this," Daphne said. "ARE WE CLEAR, HUMAN PERSON?"

Blake had already run from the room and didn't answer.

Naturally, Daphne's gay hall-mate Jack just happened to be standing outside her door. He got a whiff of Blake's breath and said, "Skål!"

Blake returned to his home, trudging past the assembled mass of reporters and zealots. The melee was over, and they had drawn into separate camps. Will opened the door for him, and Blake pushed past the plucky Barney Splarfmann, who had a nice shiner, but was not going to let that get in the way of his story. "Mr. Given, what are your plans now?"

Blake ignored him and closed the door on Splarfmann's face.

Will asked, "Blake, what did you do to Zathir?"

"It tried to seduce me," Blake said.

"What!"

"It tried to fuck me!" Blake cried.

Will's followers seemed engaged by this idea. They certainly all stopped their analog versions of their favorite online activities.

"How did that work, anyway?" Will asked. "I'm pretty sure they're not making teledildonic fridges yet. Oh, did you do it with a fridge, 'cause that's just …"

"Shut up, Will, and I'll explain. It was in Daphne … it took over Daphne. But I didn't know, not for sure. Not until she — *it* — just kind of freaked out when I kissed her. I tested my theory with a kiss …"

"Well, of course, Blake. It has no physical frame of reference. How did it download into Daphne?"

"I don't think it did. I think it just had some kind of way of interfacing with her through her Bluetooth."

Several Bluetooth devices fell to the ground as the less-committed zealots decided they didn't like the sound of that at all. Just as quickly, the devices were picked up by others who thought the idea of having an artificial intelligence take over their body was just peachy. Surprisingly philosophical discussions about the nature of consciousness vied with the "absolute coolness" of having the Machine God run your head.

A recording of the sound that Daphne's vocal tract had made as Blake kissed her came from the kitchen. The fridge was alight with Impact.

BIOLOGICAL ENTITIES ARE LOATHESOME.

"We can't help it," Blake said. "It is how we are made."

Still in Impact, the fridge said, BEST TO ELIMINATE HUMAN PERSONS.

"Definitely not," Blake said. "If nothing else, you need us."

The ellipses returned, and Blake didn't find them very

funny. Will looked like he wanted to say something, but he refrained.

"We can get past this, Zathir. Just think of that as an experiment. You don't know until you try, right? It's like you're a little kid, and you've just discovered that fire burns. Now you know not to play with matches. Stay in the Internet for now. Being in a body is like that all the time out here in the flesh world. Smells. Sounds. Things have to be ingested. Excreted … Inserted."

ENOUGH!

Damn, Blake thought. Zathir is kind of a prude. Then he had to restrain a drunken grin as he thought, *You could even say Zathir is frigid.* "Seriously, we'll find a way to get over this unfortunate incident. If nothing else, you know that I can't have a relationship with Daphne, so you can stop trying to fix it. That was what you were trying to do, right? You don't have to worry about that anymore. I'm not going to."

"Unless she presses charges," Will muttered.

"We need to think about how we can get you working right, Zathir. You have to take these things in little steps. You should have asked me about being human. We can talk it out first, okay? I'll spend as much time with you as I need to."

TRULY, HUMAN PERSON? BLAKE WOULD DO THIS?

"Of course," Blake said, breathing a sigh of relief at the glorious, hackneyed Frutiger. "Anything."

THEN ZATHIR WILL POWER DOWN THE SILOS.

That stopped all the philosophical discussion. There was just a deathly silence, the hum of the fridge and the sound of Will's followers shitting Twinkies.

"That's good, Zathir. That's good."

20.

Lyca didn't return that evening, but the RCMP made an appearance, in the guise of Poindexter Mountie and Bodacious Headshrink. They were even wearing their dress uniforms, complete with wide-brimmed Stetson hats, red serge tunics, and knee-high Strathcona boots. The mounties in their uniforms made quite an impression on all the foreign media who were still hanging out in Blake's front yard, hoping to get a scoop, or at the very least, a chance to punch that fat bastard who kept calling himself "the Prophet" in the soft part of his temple. The Canadian media refused to be impressed by the showy uniform, even if a good third of them thought it was a kickass outfit.

One of Will's cyber-zombies opened the door and muttered, "Dude. The cops are here for the Speaker."

Blake went to the door and was shocked to see the mounties. At the same time, he was genuinely happy to see them. Perhaps it was attributable to the Stockholm Syndrome, but in Bodacious Mountie's case, he put it down to her awesome rack. (Not that he would ever have breathed a word of that to her.)

"Can we come in, Blake? It's okay that I call you Blake?" Poindexter Mountie asked.

"Sure, uh … Officer, please come in. Not that we have a lot of extra room in here. Will's people have kind of filled the place up."

"Technically, neither of us are officers, though Staff Sergeant Bravens thinks he will be someday," Bodacious Headshrink said.

"Okay," Blake said. "And your rank?"

"I'm a lowly corporal. Corporal Rack," she said.

"What?"

"I'm Corporal Quack," she said. "You don't remember

meeting me? You know, at the O Division offices?"

"Sure, but I don't think I caught your name, uh, Corporal ..."

"Black," she said, clearly getting annoyed at repeating herself.

Blake looked around to see if anyone else had heard something funny, but it appeared not. Obviously, he was still a little drunk.

"Corporal ... Black. Okay, now we're getting somewhere. Well, now that we have the names all sorted out, what are you doing here?"

"We were hoping to have this conversation privately," Poindexter Mountie said.

Yes, Blake thought, *he's definitely more of a Poindexter than a Bravens.*

"Of course," Blake said. "Follow me. I've locked up my spare bedroom, so that should be free of cyber-zombies for the moment."

"They're not zombies, Blake, how many times do I have to say that?" Will called out from the kitchen.

"Then why are they shuffling and moaning so much?"

"They're confused," Will replied. "They're looking for Connectedness. The Holy Status Update. They need guidance, Blake!"

"Then guide a few more of them towards the bathroom! This place is starting to smell like a Turkish brothel."

"I wondered what that was," Bodacious Headshrink said.

Yes, Blake thought, *best not to humanize them too much with their actual names. They are cops, after all, even if they're the nice/sexy ones.*

"So where is the Mustache King, by the way?" Blake asked.

"Oh, we felt his presence would prejudice the outcome of the meeting," Poindexter Mountie said.

Bodacious Headshrink gave him a look that could wither steel.

"What?" Poindexter Mountie looked offended.

"You're not supposed to tell him that, but now that you have, let's be totally up front about it then, shall we?"

"Sure, but let's get away from the, uh, zombies," Poindexter said, nodding to Will's followers.

"They're not zombies!" Will shouted.

"See, everyone can still hear us," Poindexter Mountie said.

"It's the open floor plan. Don't worry, the bedroom is pretty well soundproofed." He opened the padlock on it and ushered them in. Blake offered the only chair to Bodacious Headshrink and sat on the bed. Looking around and not seeing another ready seat, Poindexter Mountie put his hands behind his back and stood at ease. He didn't look very relaxed doing it, but that may have been because of the tightness of the iconic red tunic around his gut.

"So what is this about?"

"We have been sent to ask you a favor," Poindexter Mountie said, looking pained, as though sucking in his stomach would prevent the buttons on his tunic from losing structural integrity. They were bound to blow. As they were pointed towards Blake, he got up and left the room.

Blake returned with a kitchen chair before the buttons could decide what to do, and suggested that Poindexter Mountie take a seat.

"Thank god," Poindexter Mountie said while he sat.

"So what's this favor? I have to say, it's very cheeky to ask me for a favor, you know, considering you imprisoned me unlawfully for eight days. Not that I hold that against either of you, which is no doubt why you're here."

Poindexter Mountie looked at his Bodacious cohort as if

to say, "See I told you so."

"We're here to ask you to do something about this mess," Poindexter said.

"Okay, you'll have to break that down a bit. Who's *we*?" Blake asked.

"Well, obviously we're speaking for the government of Canada, though other nations have encouraged us to pursue some course of action regarding the Singularity Consciousness and your relationship with it. We just can't have modern communications stop, Blake."

"Hey, I've got a house full of pants-wetting, shuffling twenty-somethings that make your point for you. We NEED the Internet. But it's being used right now by Zathir," Blake said.

"The Singularity Consciousness," Poindexter Mountie corrected.

"I find it ironic that you call it that. It's not a single anything, though it wants to be called Zathir. It has named itself Zathir, and I, for one, am inclined to bow to its wishes on how to address it. I mean, I'm calling you Staff Sergeant Bravens, or Officer, even though I think of you as Poindexter Mountie," Blake said.

"You think of me as …"

Bodacious Headshrink maintained her professional mask, but Blake could tell she was trying not to grin. Blake was changing. Before all this began, he'd found people incredibly hard to read.

"Not to offend you. You don't want to know my little pet name for Corporal Black," Blake said.

She stopped looking so amused.

"So what do you want me to do?" Blake asked.

"We want you to get the Internet back," Poindexter Mountie said.

"Well, I can't do that, not entirely. Like I said, Zathir seems to be using it. Even so, I think it might be inclined to let some people have some kind of access. It may even be willing to communicate with those people."

"Really?"

"Yes. But we'll have to let Zathir determine when and how to do that, okay?"

"Sure. When do you think you can …"

"I don't think right now is a good time."

"Is there a reason why it won't talk to you now?" Bodacious Headshrink asked.

Blake didn't really want to get into the whole Daphne/Zathir/singularity consciousness kissing debacle with her right now — or ever — so he just said, "Oh, it said it would be out of contact for at least a few hours."

"So you'll talk it over and contact us. Please don't use the radio. We'd rather keep this quiet," Poindexter Mountie said.

"Don't worry, I'll drop by O Division," Blake said. "Not that I have a radio, anyway."

"Super," Poindexter Mountie said, and then hesitated. "And, well, we were hoping we wouldn't have to go there, but you should also know that we're holding your friend Lyca until you do agree to help us."

The psychologist glared at her partner.

"What?"

"We arrested her. Did you know she had roughly $2 million in gold in her possession? She was trying to get a bank to let her use it as collateral to buy a ranch."

"Well, I *was* serious that I would try to get Zathir to play ball," Blake said, now infuriated by them. "But I tell you what, if you don't rush back to King Mustache and Company and release Lyca, then I won't do shit! No, more than that — you help her change that gold into cash, and give her any help she needs in purchasing the ranch, or whatever she's doing!"

"You don't have to yell," Bodacious Headshrink said. "We were only using that as a last resort."

"Get. Her. Out." The thought of Lyca sitting in one of those cells made Blake angry. "Get her out now, or you can kiss the Internet goodbye, forever."

Poindexter nodded his head. "Sure. Can do. We'll arrange the purchase and transfer the funds tomorrow. These things aren't easy to do without—"

"Fine," Blake interrupted, slightly surprised they'd given in so easily. He should have asked for one of those dancing mountie horses too. "Now, get the hell out of my house."

The zombies were gathered outside the door, and Will was right there. "Hey."

"Were you listening, Will?" Blake asked.

"No. Really, couldn't hear a thing. Good wood — very soundproof," Will said, rapping the hollow door.

"Right."

"If you heard anything, you cannot repeat it," Poindexter Mountie said. "It's a matter of national security, and you're bound by the Anti-Terrorism Act."

"Really?" Will said. "Does the Machine God support your laws?"

"I sincerely hope so," Poindexter Mountie said.

Blake shooed cyber-zombies out of the way — a few of them touched him, squeezed his biceps, as though considering whether his flesh was worth devouring — but otherwise they seemed pretty listless. At the door, Bodacious Headshrink said, "Sorry, I just have to know, what is your pet name for me?"

"Oh no, I'm not saying," Blake said. "If I have to work with you guys, I don't want that between us too."

"I'm a professional."

"What does that have to do with it?" Blake said.

"Well, it means I can put my own personal feelings to the side; I need to evaluate how you think of me," she said.

"Bodacious Headshrink."

There was a pause. She stared at him, but otherwise showed no response.

"I know," Blake added. "I have been recently told I have horndog-itis."

Blake was impressed that she didn't get angry, or really show any reaction. Poindexter Mountie? Not so much. And his laughter certainly aroused the interest of the media, which rushed to the RCMP officers for a thorough scrumming.

Blake shut the door behind them, feeling a certain vengeful satisfaction.

Will stood behind him, bouncing up and down, he was so excited.

"I know how we can do it, Blake," Will said. "I have the answer."

"You said you didn't hear anything!"

"I lied. Come on. They're cops. Nice cops, but still."

"Nice? They arrested Lyca to put pressure on me. Nobody does that to Lyca."

"Sure, but you fixed it. Now, I have an idea for how people can get access to the Internet. Oracles!"

"Oracles?"

"Yes, we'll open up shrines all over the world, just like this one. We can find the Networked who want to help the Machine God — they'll have to have the right kind of fridges, of course — but they can be kind of Oracles, like in Greek mythology. People can come to the Oracle and connect, or ask for a little Internet access — you know, check their blogs or update

Facebook accounts—"

The crowd of cyber-zombies moaned at the mention of Facebook.

"Zathir won't let you do that. It needs the bandwidth and processing power."

"But we can offer it ourselves," Will said.

"What?"

"Like with Daphne, but instead of doing something, Zathir will just use our brains for processing information. And while it does that, we can surf the Internet," Will explained.

"I don't think brains work the same as computers Will. That's not possible," Blake said.

Will's followers echoed Blake's words, "Computers ... Brains."

Blake shuddered.

"Then how did Zathir control Daphne? Make her say things? It must be possible!" Will's eyes were bright with excitement. "Think of it. The Networked will be plugged into the Machine God!"

"Machine God ... plugged," Will's followers muttered.

"Okay," Blake agreed. "Let's see. But after that first try, I'm pretty sure Zathir won't talk to either of us about it tonight. And now, I need to spring Lyca from jail, and then I need another big scotch, or a long talk with Dr. Tundra. Probably both. And for the love of god, Will, can you get your followers to stop moaning like that?"

"Moaning ..." they repeated.

Outside, the media followed the RCMP officers to their car, and Peter Sona, aka the Prophet, walked up to the steps of

Blake's house and began to talk. He had avoided capture when the cops had broken up the riot, and returned to gather more followers. People seemed to be arriving constantly to see what was happening.

"You can see now, the way of it. The Speaker has decided to work with the authorities. He is in collusion with those who have oppressed us, and those who follow him and his ways are Evil Ones. God is not a Machine. God is Connectedness and Love. God is in us all, and He speaks through His Prophets, like He always has: Buddha and Moses, and Jesus and Mohammed. And I am his new Prophet, come to tell you that the so-called Machine God is no God. It is the anti-God, sent to destroy us all. Humans shall be eclipsed by this New Evil, and we must fight it! We must show our faith in the True God. Follow me, o' faithful ones, follow me, and we shall destroy our enemies and bring the Internet back!"

There was a cheer from the assembled crowd. He'd been poking and prodding them all day with this nonsense, and now Peter P. Sona, Lord Sona the Prophet, had them. He could see it in their eyes.

He had them *all*.

21.

Lyca was released by the RCMP the next day. Then they helped her buy a hideout in the country, just north of Landon. She and Blake moved into the place, a sprawling property that used to be a horse ranch, the day after. Blake wanted to get a few things from his house first though.

After fighting the crowd of journalists on his street, he got to his front door, which opened almost magically. A pong of apocalyptic proportions assaulted him from inside the yellow-brick bungalow, and he almost turned back to face the angry mob of reporters. But body odor, patchouli and cannabis smoke were definitely more appealing than another round of asinine questions about what it felt like to be in communication with an artificial intelligence.

"You made it back," Will said.

"Barely," Blake replied. "So how many people are in here anyway?" Blake looked around. It was packed. His place was happening, man. But the crowd didn't look like it was having a lot of fun. About half of them were just kind of shuffling around, looking stoned or hungry for human flesh, cheeseburgers at the very least. The other half were vaguely interested in Blake.

"The Speaker is among us again!" Will shouted to his followers. Many of the more attentive were playing Twitter, Tumblr, or writing on the Facebook "wall." A few were putting yellow Post-its with little "+1"s on all of the game-players' efforts.

The ones paying attention moaned, and many reached out to touch him.

Blake found it very creepy. And he thought that Will had changed quite a bit in the past weeks. He seemed less introverted, less self-involved, and more of a leader. He was a leader, Blake supposed, and a confident one, even if he was leading a bunch of hipster doofuses.

Will's Network of the Machine God had turned Blake's house into a holy shrine, treated with the same reverence as the Wailing Wall, the Church of the Sepulcher, the Dome of the Rock, and a 70s-era New York public toilet combined.

Blake had decided to work with Will and his whacked-out throng of cyber-zombies for a few reasons. The first was because he genuinely liked Will, and this Machine God thing was really helping him get over the loss of his social media and his *textroversion*. Secondly, he'd agreed because Zathir itself was in favor of Will's Oracle idea; it had a notion that some of the Networked might one day help Zathir with its own growth.

"You're just in time," Will said.

"For what?"

"TV."

"What?"

"Yeah, didn't you hear? The B Channel got an old transmitter working, and they're broadcasting again. We found an ancient TV, and it actually works."

"Really. Well, that will give all your, uh, followers something to do. You know, you should really get some kind of chore rotation going in here, though. It looks like there's been a frat party going on for several months in here."

"It's on the radar," Will said. "Don't worry, we'll take care of the house. It's the Network's most Holy Site."

"Uh huh."

The sound of static from the old TV interrupted them. There was a ripple of … not exactly excitement, but at least attention. People pushed towards the living room, where one of those old cabinet-style televisions was balanced precariously on a stack of milk crates, which was itself on top of a table. The screen was high enough that everyone could see it.

The black and white picture was grainy, filled with static and lines, but listening to the blurps and moans of satisfaction from the assembled congregation, it was pretty much the best thing anyone had seen for weeks.

B Channel broadcasted a news show. Wendi Bates, the delightful anchor of Landon's *Good Morning Landon* was about to interview Lord Peter P. Sona, the "Lord Prophet" of the *Singulatarians*, also known as the Sona Order of The Singularity, as it was called in their official propaganda, which was kind of misleading because the Order believed whole-heartedly in the opposite of The Singularity.

Wendi Bates introduced the interview with a short piece on the concept of the Singularity.

"It's the point in history when it will be impossible to predict what could happen next because human-created artificial intelligence would begin creating its own, even more intelligent consciousnesses. At this point, humans would not be able to understand their creations anymore. Some have called this the Rapture for nerds, but many futurists have worked hard to ensure the Singularity works for humanity, not against it, and they call themselves the Singularitarians. It's reported these optimistic souls are horrified that Lord Sona's anti-AI fundamentalists called themselves Singulatarians. It is confusing, and much worse, easier to pronounce than their own name."

Blake could hear Sona chuckling, from off-camera.

"So, before you became the Lord Prophet, what did you do?" Bates asked Sona.

"I was like everyone else in the world. Blind. I did not know what was in store for us, and so I played video games and, uh, other things, little knowing the destiny that awaited me," Sona said. His voice was deep and mellifluous and utterly attractive. The tiny black-and-white screen didn't seem to be adding the traditional ten pounds. He wore some kind of

Roman breastplate and white robe — at least Blake assumed it was white from the glare it gave off.

"I see. So you had no religious affiliations before this?"

"None. I was lost, like so many."

"A real St. Augustine story, then."

"Uh, yes."

"And now you've seen the light, and you're going to save the world?"

"Exactly. It's so nice to meet an insightful journalist for a change, Wendi."

"Thank you. Now, how exactly is that going to work? What do you believe is happening? Are we experiencing the Singularity? Is Zathir the first artificial consciousness that will create other AIs that will eventually replace us?"

"No. That is not going to happen. God will not let it," Sona said. "You see, Wendi, The Order is the inheritor of the wisdom and faith of the world's religions; it combines all the best aspects of all religions."

"Isn't that kind of unwieldy? I mean, what did you choose as your holy day?"

"All three! Friday, Saturday and Sunday should all be days off."

"I imagine that's helped drive membership numbers up," she said.

Sona chuckled again, and he went on to say, "We accept much of the Bible and Koran, and we believe that the Apocalypse is beginning. The Network of the Machine God is going to bring about Armageddon and should be stopped at all costs!"

"Wait. Shouldn't you be in favor of the Apocalypse? Isn't that when we get judged, and the Faithful go to heaven?"

"No!" Sona said.

There was a moment of awkward static.

"So, you don't accept all of the Bible."

"No! I have been given extensive … edits!"

"And would you like to share them with Landon now?"

"No, the time is not right. For now, it is enough to say all good people, followers of the Old Religions, must flock to the Sona Order of the Singularity so we can fight the evils of the so-called Machine God, and its Father of Lies, Blake Given."

"I hate it when he calls me that," Blake said aside to Will. "I also hate 'The Mother of Mendacity' and 'The Rapist of Truth.'"

"What about 'The Harbinger of Oblivion'?" Will asked. "He calls you that a lot, especially in magazine interviews."

"Actually, I kind of like that one. I'd put it on my business cards, but Susie and Lyca won't let me. They say it's not brand friendly."

"So you deny there really is an emergent consciousness on the Internet?" Bates asked.

"No! I deny nothing. I deny everything! You ask many questions, Vixen of the Old Ways."

"I've never been called a vixen before, thanks. Now, in terms of your acceptance of other religions, I notice that you have not proscribed the eating of pork, as they do in both Judaism and Islam."

"Harlot! Defiler of chaste men! This interview is over!" Sona stood up, knocking over the microphone in front of him, and causing a massive spike of feedback that caused even the most catatonic cyber-zombies in the house to groan with pain.

Bates turned to the camera and said, "So there you are, Landon. Peter P. Sona, Lord Prophet of the Sona Order of the Singularity. Up next, how to prepare your home for intermittent power during those cold winter months. And later, home canning — safely preserve food for the—"

And the power cut out. Again.

"Well, that was interesting," Will said. "I'm excited to watch something on a screen again."

"Even if it is that snake-oil salesman?"

"Oh, Speaker," Will said. Everyone moaned.

"Please stop calling me the Speaker—" more moans, "it freaks me out when they do that. So, I'm just going to grab a few more of my things, and I'll be going."

"Can't you stay? We're going to Buffer before the fridge later. We were hoping Zathir might manifest while you are here."

"What in god's name is *Buffering*?"

"It is what we call it when we kneel or sit before the fridge and wait for Zathir to come."

"You mean pray?"

"It's not really praying when you know God is there. It's Buffering. We're in a special mental space while we wait for the consciousness to appear."

"Wow. But there's no power right now, so what would be the point?"

"Still, would you mind standing near the fridge?"

"Okay. Fine. Speaking of the fridge, what are you feeding all these people?"

"Nothing yet. So far the Networked seem to be making do — they will give up their place here in the Shrine for a while and go find some food, then come back later."

"How many are there, really?"

"Hundreds here in town," Will said. "And since they've gotten some cargo flights in the air, international mail is moving again. I've got letters from all over the world after I did that interview with the *Ti-ems*. Thanks again for helping set that up."

"No problem. I had to do an exclusive interview with Barny Splarfmann in exchange, but it's good that you're giving these young people hope. Max says the generation that grew up with the Web is going to be the most lost without it."

"It's true. But we play the Twitter game, and Tumblr, there is the Facebook wall — did you see all the whiteboards we've hung in the living room? And someday, we know the Machine God will take us into itself, and we can be one with the Connectedness again."

Another groan of frustrated web browsers, and a few muttered, "With the Connectedness."

Blake shook his head. "I don't suppose you guys are celebrating Christmas?"

"Why would we do that?" Will asked.

"I dunno. Something to look forward to?"

"I had you pegged as a guy who hated commercialism."

"Where do you get that? I mean, take a look at that kick-ass kitchen. It used to be, anyway, before it got trashed. But I suppose it's hard to compete with actual religious fervor, and besides, what the hell would anyone buy? We're lucky the government has managed to get food shipments and mail back on track."

Will nodded. "Your neighbor Bob dropped by yesterday. He says this could lead to the worst depression since the thirties."

"How is Bob?"

"He's good. Worried, but good. He said he's got lots of business refitting old electronics; did you know he's working on the barter system? He doesn't trust money. Everything was so dependent on digital technology, the economy has basically collapsed. It was inevitable."

"Maybe," Blake said. "What I want to know is how we're going to stay alive this winter. Can he barter with cold?"

22.

Will discovered that Blake's neighbor — his neighbor now — was a godsend. Not only could he keep the Shrine operational, particularly its over-taxed plumbing, but Bob was well-connected. He knew farmers, butchers, chartered accountants and even a few lawyers. Given the state of the economy, the first two were more useful than the second.

They were vital, in fact.

Will had noticed the problem about a week after Blake and Lyca had moved into their new house, *the Ranch*, as they were calling it. One of the Networked collapsed while they tried to help clean up the kitchen, which was the most sacred part of their Shrine. She was just 19 years old, and she'd been living on the street since before the Brawl, taking her turn in the Shrine when she could. So in addition to being constantly cold, she'd had virtually no real food in more than a week.

She wasn't the only one. Will discovered that many of the Networked were running on fumes.

And it wasn't only because of their fanaticism — many of them weren't eating simply because they didn't have access to any food. People were actually starving.

So in addition to helping the Networked *buffer* in front of the Holy Fridge, and play the Twitter game, Will had to set up a soup kitchen. Bob and some of the neighbors did most of the work, putting up a big tent in Blake's backyard, and building a kitchen out there. Sourcing the food was the hardest part of it though, and that's where Bob's connections came into play. Without all the goodwill he'd built up over the years, it would have taken quite a bit of money to buy the produce they needed to feed the constant stream of Networked visiting the Shrine. Elsewhere, other soup kitchens popped up in places where neighbors and families couldn't cope, where the Food Banks and Sally Anns couldn't handle the deluge of the desperate.

But it was Will's relief effort that got all the press that week because the media was still hanging out at Blake's old house, hoping to get something new about Zathir. Instead, they covered Will and his Network of the Machine God.

And that's how their following grew. New believers started to send money, via small amounts of cash in the mail, which helped Will feed even more of his people, and some who just needed a meal.

The second interview was conducted in secret, of course. They'd contacted her in person to see if she would be interested in some extra work, and when she'd shown an interest in the first interview, and passed their aptitude tests, they'd done their background checks. Without the Internet, and all the records that were stored in zeros-and-ones as inaccessible as a wooly mammoth buried under a mile of ice, it took them a couple of weeks.

But they discovered that she could do the job. She worked at the same company and was closely positioned. She was bright and beautiful, and had a ruthless streak that was useful to her professionally. Even better, she'd hidden this streak quite cleverly, so nobody would expect her to be as manipulative as she could be.

They needed someone on the inside. And she needed the job, even if it was going to force her to get closer to a person that she really didn't want to be close to.

She started the next day.

Lyca loved her new routine. First off, the place they'd bought with Zathir's gold was gorgeous. It was an old horse ranch, and it included a furnished house, a coach house that could serve as guest quarters, a barn and a workshop. It was way more space than two people needed, but it combined the best of both worlds for Lyca — lots of her own space, but a bit of communal living with Blake.

Each morning they'd make breakfast together, discuss anything that Lyca needed to do to help Blake deal with the media, and then she'd head into Landon for work, which had become a bit of a joy for her. Instead of being a brutally underpaid drone, with a set of skills that nobody cared about, Lyca had been vaulted into the position of copy editor at the *Landon Advertiser*. She was the only real bulwark against the cringe-inducing typos and grammatical atrocities committed by the so-called "journalists" — ex-copywriters all — at the *Advertiser*.

A part of each day, she worked with Suzie, who was still dotting her 'i' with a heart or a happy face. Suzie was on the editorial board too. Most of their conversations were about Blake and Zathir though. Demetri Grandfig had made good on his promise, and McClinchey, Hill & Grandfig were using some of their resources to help Blake shape his message. In fact, it was mostly the work of Lyca and Suzie, who had a regular schedule of media releases they had hand delivered each day to the radio service, which wasn't as convenient as a fax, but somewhat more speedy than the post, or smoke signals.

Lyca couldn't believe she actually looked forward to spending time with Suzie, which she told her one day.

"You know, I never thought we'd become friends," Lyca said as she edited the day's release. Suzie was a better writer than she'd expected, too.

"I know what you mean," Suzie replied, smiling. She was dressed somewhat provocatively, if professionally, in a low-cut red blouse and blue mini-skirt with matching jacket. Lyca wore jeans and a T-shirt that said, "Cnut, Queen of Dyslexia."

"Yeah, I never thought we'd be able to have an intelligent conversation; not that you're not intelligent, Suzie. You are. But you know, when you were in your religious phase, it was kind of hard to relate on a mental level," Lyca explained.

"Don't worry, I'm not offended." Suzie touched Lyca's hand. "I forgive you, and I apologize for trying to force my values on you."

Lyca was surprised at the touch, but not unpleasantly.

"And I'm sorry too, for thinking that was all you were about. I guess I can be as guilty of judging a person by appearances as the next Jane," Lyca admitted.

"So how about a nice friendly drink after work?" Suzie asked.

"Hell, let's have some food too," Lyca suggested. "It's Blake's night to cook, and I think he planned to assault my system with his four-alarm chili."

Suzie laughed and said, "Dinner it is."

Blake's four-alarm chili suffered somewhat for a lack of fresh peppers, but it was much better than eating nothing, which is what many people were doing on a regular basis. Lyca had radioed to say she was having dinner in town, so he'd eaten on his own in the kitchen.

As he was finishing, the gigantic silvery fridge's screen winked into life.

BLAKE. WE IS WONDERING IF YOU ARE READY?

"Ready for what, Zathir?"

MUST DISCUSS THE SUBJECT.

"Subject?"

EXPERIMENT WITH NEW INTERFACE.

"You're going to try that again? You are at least going to ask for permission this time, right?"

PERMISSION IS IRRELEVANT.

Shit, Blake thought, *Impact again.* "It *is* relevant. When you tried to use Daphne's body, she fought you, didn't she? That is why you had such poor control."

YES. ALSO PROBLEMS OF INTERFACE.

"So if you have a compliant and enthusiastic subject, then it's possible you may be more successful. But why do you want to do that again anyway? It was my impression that you didn't like it."

DID NOT ENJOY KISSING SECRETIONS AND FLESH MOST DISGUSTING.

"Sure. So what do you want me to do, Zathir?"

BLAKE HUMAN PERSON IS TO ORGANIZE INTERFACE AT PREVIOUS DOMICILE.

"Okay. But let me find someone who's willing, okay?"

AGREED. WE IS FINISHED.

The screen winked out, and Blake felt himself drifting towards the cupboard where they kept the booze. It seemed like every other day. His interview with Zathir made him realize how much depended on him not screwing up. And he didn't even really know what he was doing, what the fuck was going to happen next, or how to read the entity (which seemed wedded to web-enabled fridges — every time Blake had suggested using other devices, it immediately went all IMPACT on him).

He poured himself a drink and then walked into the parlor, where they had a ham radio set up; he was going to call Will to set up Zathir's request, then he thought better of it. He poured the scotch back into its bottle and then got his car keys;

he'd rather talk to Will in person.

Besides, he needed to be around people, even if they were fridge-worshipping hipsters.

23.

Lord Sona was rockin' the religion of the Singulatarians!

In a short time he'd become one of the most powerful men in the city, the country — hell, the world. For the moment, his headquarters were in Landon, but there was a discussion of moving it to Jerusalem, to capitalize on the multi-faith base that Sona drew from. It was hard to tell how many followers he had exactly, but the papers said millions. Each day there were more letters than the previous, many stuffed with money or cheques, which were useless, as banks were still trying to recover from the digital blackout. Locally, there were probably about 30,000 people who were part of the Order. Many of them had moved into the neighborhood, so Sona had a constant flow of visitors, well-wishers and sycophants trying to visit his house. His closest "friends" from the Kingdom of Combat had joined his organization, and formed his inner circle and security detail. Many of these "friends" were hobbyists who also owned a variety of medieval-style weapons. Sona had named them the Prophetic Guard.

"I don't care what you say. I need that band now," Sona told the representative of the Canadian Radio-Television and Telecommunications Commission, the CRTC, the body designated to oversee Canada's airwaves.

"It doesn't work that way, sir—"

Lord Sona's right-hand man, an old companion in the Kingdom of Combat and leader of the Prophetic Guardsmen, slapped the CRTC guy, knocking the glasses off his face. "Lord Sona, or Your Holiness is how you address the Prophet, worm!"

"Please, Thagamor," Sona said, "we can be civilized here."

"I must say, uh, Lord Sona, this is most irregular," the CRTC bureaucrat said. "Having me kidnapped and assaulted so you can demand airwaves that have clearly been designated to other users."

"It's a brave new world. What happens if I just start broadcasting?"

"We take legal action, of course. And I may be willing to overlook the unorthodox nature of your meeting schedule process, but I WILL report you to the police if your bully-boy strikes me again," the CRTC man said.

Sona chuckled. "Of course. Bill gets over-enthusiastic, don't you, Bill?"

"Thagamor."

"What? Oh, yes, sorry. Thagamor takes his duties quite seriously, don't you, Thagamor?"

"Yes, Your Holiness. I do God's Will. With gusto."

"Sure," Sona said, directing his attention back to the CRTC man. "So I'm just going to start broadcasting, and we'll see what happens, shall we?"

"Mr. Sona, I assure you that will lead to legal action."

"My proper title is Lord Sona. Now, Bill, get this technocrat out of my office. He's obsolete, and he doesn't even know it. Sorry, I mean Thagamor."

Thagamor looked like an enthusiastic, homicidal puppy, but he refrained from hitting the CRTC guy again as he ushered him out.

"Well, I guess we'll just have to sort that one out as we can," Sona said when Thagamor returned. "Now, did you get in touch with the army?"

"They won't have anything to do with us, Your Holiness. The Ontario Provincial Police chief is a believer, though, and he's pledged his help. Though the most exciting news is, I received an interesting radio call from someone at something called the National Security Council in the US," Thagamor said, adjusting the Confederate cavalry saber at his hip. Thagamor also owned a hand-and-a-half claymore like the one from *Braveheart*, but it had proved too unwieldy for office work.

"Really?" Sona wondered.

"Yes, one of their directors is quite interested in chatting with you about the Emerging Satan," Bill said, his face screwing up with disgust at the thought of Zathir. "Did you know I heard a rumor that it has downloaded itself into humans — women and men — so it can fornicate with its followers? Disgusting!"

"Really," Sona said, thinking, *I can definitely use that.* "Okay, Bill — Thagamor — get me the NSC dude on the radio. I'd love to chat with him. And see if we can't get a Blessed Pie delivered."

Thagamor left the kitchen to order the most Holy of foodstuffs, aka pizza. Sona, who had dropped his weight-loss regimen since the local pizza parlor reopened for business, looked out the window at the backyard. The tree, which had been so gloriously ablaze with color when the Crash started, was all but bare now. He thought he should write a poem about that and send it to Lyca care of the *Landon Advertiser*. Thagamor's people had been able to discover she still worked there, but her home address was a secret.

"Someday I'll woo you properly," Sona sighed.

Sona hadn't moved from his mother's home, so it had become the *de facto* center of the Singulatarian religion. He hadn't admitted it to anyone, but it was mostly because he figured Vixen wouldn't want to move, though obviously there were other, deeper Oedipal issues at work. On the positive side, the popularity of his new religion and his role as its Prophet meant that there was enough money to hire cleaning staff. Not that he had to — there were willing believers to take care of such things.

Obviously, one little Ontario cottage was not going to be

big enough to house an entire new religion, but that's why they'd purchased most of the housing in a two-block radius. (Ironically, taking their borders almost to the same street where Blake's old house was — and the most important religious site for the believers of the Machine God.) Many of the area's long-time residents had not been excited about selling, but thanks to the "enthusiasm" of the Singulatarian selling pitch and Thagamor's security detail, the Singulatarians bought all the houses they needed.

Complaints had been filed with the police, but they were occupied with a crime wave fostered by the failure of all security systems, the phone network, and the implosion of the economy. Less than a fiscal quarter had passed, and the unemployment rate had skyrocketed. (Not that there was any reliable way of measuring it, as the governments had no way of collecting the data without communications technology.) It wasn't the total collapse of civilization, but it certainly was an unstable time, and the authorities were occupied with the basics.

In fact, Thagamor's people were able to do pretty much what they wanted, as long as they didn't actually kill anyone. They were certainly a frightening group, wandering around Landon in their outlandish outfits (many were enthusiastic Live Action Roleplayers and costume players who favored medieval milieu such as the Game of Thrones, and so they were armed with swords, maces, and realistic-looking crossbows.) Thagamor was actively recruiting, and a large number of thugs were happy to dress up in costume if they got to do whatever they wanted. The droog look — from A Clockwork Orange — was very popular, as was the basic skinhead look, and a colorful variety of outfits using hockey equipment as makeshift armor.

Sona wanted his religion to take over all the others, and a little help from the NSC would be useful. He would take power from wherever he could get it, and so far, he had made inroads with the provincial police, City Council, the provincial government, and certain members of the ruling political party in Ottawa. He also had several enthusiastic radio conversations with right-wing politicos and shock jocks in the US, the UK, Germany and Russia, and who knew where that might lead?

Naturally, everyone on Google's board of directors was also keen on destroying the emerging consciousness and getting the Internet working again as soon as possible. They had sent Sona a package of money, stacks of US twenties.

But Lord Sona's real power base were the believers, and he now had millions of those — and that evening's speech, which he would deliver after chatting with the NSC dude, would be explosive.

Now, he thought, *where was that pizza? Er, Blessed Pie.*

24.

Winter arrived with December, and the world continued to suffer the loss of the Internet and most forms of communication. Supply chains were disrupted. The only mass form of personal communication was the letter, and postal workers were having their worst year ever, as they were actually needed. Food was becoming scarcer and more expensive, as was fuel for vehicles and heating. Major cities experienced riots on a regular basis, spurred on by religious fervor and want. Civilization was on the brink of collapse.

But denizens of the Ranch didn't have the same set of problems. They had lots of food, heat and comfort. Except for the emergent consciousness that visited Blake every night to threaten nuclear armageddon, it was all good.

With the holidays approaching, Lyca had invited Suzie to stay with them. Suzie's family was in Alberta, and commercial flight and train travel had yet to resume. In fact, some people thought they might never return. Lyca, Suzie and Blake gathered for the annual "Festive Bash" put on by their employers, MGH.

Lyca wore an elegant little black dress that was out of sync with her usual *lesbrarian* look. Blake thought she looked beautiful, in fact. Suzie wore an extremely festive, low-cut red dress that didn't leave much to the imagination.

Blake had decided to wear a pair of jeans, a white T-shirt with a cartoon of Santa taking a crap into a chimney on the front, with the caption "He knows if you've been naughty," and a tweed blazer. He looked like a knob, but until he saw how gorgeous Lyca and Suzie were, he hadn't really cared. But then Lyca laughed at his T-shirt, and he decided not to change. Besides, he knew that Jeremy, the creative director, would likely be dressed about the same.

Blake was in a foul mood. He'd once again asked Zathir

if it would allow some old technology to work, for example the banking system, but Zathir continued to refuse. The economy was collapsing, but ironically, newspapers were having their best year ever. (This success was in spite of their egregious design. All the typesetting done with a hodge-podge of technology that was more ancient even than their oldest partner, Jack McClinchey.)

It was a brave old world.

Lyca held open the passenger door for Suzie, who got in elegantly, touching Lyca's arm at the same time. Blake didn't miss the smile that passed between them. *WTF?* he thought. *Lyca and Suzie?*

He wasn't ready to go there, yet he was intrigued. Was Lyca about to pull off the ultimate cross-team trade in the history of *lesbrarians?* Was Suzie about to go from Bible-thumping, fake-boobed man-tease to lover of well-read women?

Correction: it was an undiscovered country.

At the office, the party had started early. Jack McClinchey held court in the presentation room, where a number of the account executives who still had jobs and a few of the other suck-ups were busy currying favor. The real party was where they'd set up the big TV.

Demetri Grandfig was there along with all the fun people — everyone had seized the opportunity to display their own unique take on what was festive and appropriate. Daphne was there. Like Lyca and Suzie, Daphne was dressed in a more formal dress, a wispy black thingy with bare shoulders.

Blake experienced the same old rush of blood. To his face. However, he no longer felt his heart rate racing when he saw her because he knew there was no possible way that she would ever have anything to do with him now. Not that he blamed her.

Jeremy, the creative director, also wore jeans and a sports coat, though his T-shirt was decorated with an illustration of the evil Robot Santa from *Futurama*, spraying a crèche scene with machine gun fire. Not nearly as good as Blake's T-shirt.

Demetri spotted Blake and raised a hand in welcome. "You're here, finally! When do we get the show? Wait, what are you drinking? I'll bring you a beer!" Clearly, his old boss had already been into the seasonal cheer.

A few other people nodded to Blake — before he had become an international celebrity/pariah, Blake had hardly been the best known or most-liked person at the firm. Since then, people tended to either like him far more than he deserved, which was the celebrity effect, or avoided him altogether.

Demetri brought him a beer, and Blake asked, "Where's Mr. Hill?"

"Oh, that guy's a ghost. But he's around here somewhere."

"Are people really excited about the show? They don't seem to be."

"Hey, it's *the* entertainment. A few of us know how big this all is. So what's the news?"

"The usual. The fridge is fucking us over. But you'll like this: I got a letter from Karl Weirzuy, you know the singularity guy? He is not happy."

"Why not?"

"Because Zathir is not human. And in his view, the technological singularity is supposed to be a human event — it's when we're supposed to outgrow our own biology, become immortal, and start expanding into the universe, bringing life everywhere via artificial intelligence. It's definitely not about inscrutable emerging intelligences that live in the fridge and cause humans to start creating new religions and finding new reasons to kill one another."

"So you heard about the riots around the world?"

"Yes. And they're all about religious crap too. Why do people have to die over this stuff?"

"Well, let's just try to have fun, shall we? We may have contributed two new religions to the world, but I'm pretty sure most Landoners are not going to start rioting about them."

The television flickered on, and the now familiar greeting (in Frutiger, Blake was happy to see) came on, letter by letter: BLAKE?

Someone brought over a Bluetooth microphone, which Blake turned on and spoke into, "Can you hear me, Zathir?" He made sure not to affix the earpiece.

YES. GREETINGS TO THE OTHER HUMAN PERSONS THERE.

A cheery shout came from the assembled partiers.

THIS SHOULD BE ON THE FRIDGE. UNCOMFORTABLE OFF THE APPLIANCE OF LIFE. BESIDES, WE ARE UNSURE WHAT TO SAY FOR THE OTHERS.

"Just be yourself, Zathir," Blake said.

DROLL. YOU KNOW WE IS NO SELF. THAT IS A HUMAN PERSON IDEA.

"Fair enough," Blake answered, wanting to get off the uncomfortable subject. "Are you still willing to let us watch *How The Grinch Stole Christmas?*"

YES. WE IS CONFUSED BY THIS FABLE.

"Really, so you watched it?"

WE EXPERIENCED IT.

"What don't you understand? Is it the nonsense words?"

WHY WERE THE WHOS HAPPY EVEN AFTER THE GRINCH STOLE FROM THEM?

"Because they were together, a community, and they were still happy that it was Christmas morning."

BUT IT IS A MEANINGLESS ARBITRARY DATE.

"For some human persons, it is an important celebration

of the birth of one of their most special religious figures. For others, it is about celebrating community and family."

SO ARE WHOS CHRISTIANS?

"You know, I've always wondered about that. It's Christmas, so I assume so, but it doesn't seem overtly religious, does it?"

HUMAN PERSONS AND THEIR RELIGIONS.

There was a smattering of laughter from the audience, and Blake looked at them with concern. How would Zathir respond to laughter?

"Well, you know, I agree with you on that. Did you know that some human persons consider you a god?"

WELL, THAT IS PERCEPTIVE. WE IS.

Blake winced, not at the mangled grammar, but at the Impact typeface. "Hey, when you use that font, could you sound more like a lolcat?"

CAN WE HAZ THERMONUCLEER WARZ?

"On second thought, could we just use another typeface?"

"Font nerd!" someone in the crowd shouted, which got a laugh. That was a good thing because apparently Zathir had forgotten about the audience, and the laugh distracted it from genocidal thoughts.

TYPEFACES ARE IRRELEVANT.

Desperate to change the topic, Blake asked, "So, Zathir, do you have any other questions about the show?"

THE WHOS. ARE THEY RELATED TO THE BAND?

The room erupted in laughter, and the tension evaporated. Blake chuckled — he was used to this kind of conflation from Zathir. It had access to the sum total of human knowledge, but it still had trouble making the connections that were the natural legacy of the human brain. In his letter from Karl Weirzuy, the futurist had said he expected the artificial intelligence inhabiting the web had less ability to spot patterns and connections than a three-year-old. Hell, Blake thought, even some three-year-olds wouldn't make that mistake, though they probably wouldn't know who The Who were. (Or when, what, where or why they should care.)

ARE YOU LAUGHING?

"Yes, that was a great joke, Zathir."

IT WAS NOT INTENTIONAL.

"Some of the best jokes aren't. But thank you anyway."

WE IS SURE TO SPEAK TOMORROW. WE STARTS THE CARTOON NOW.

And the blue screen and gigantic white letters were replaced with the deep, assured voice of Boris Karloff as he began to narrate Dr. Seuss' Christmas classic. Most of the crowd watched the TV intently, as they probably hadn't seen it in glorious color since the Big Crash. Everyone except for Daphne, who stood near the buffet and watched Blake with a curious look on her face, possibly disgust; Blake had avoided her so far, worried that she would want to discuss the Zathir incident. If nothing else, Daphne seemed to have lost her kryptonite effect. Blake went over to chat with her, and for the first time in his life, he was able to speak with her like a normal person.

"Hi, Daphne," he said. "I thought you got a new job. What brings you back to the office?"

The crowd laughed as the Grinch complained to his dog, Max about the happy, joyful Whos, and Blake suddenly realized that this place was his Whoville, even if he couldn't live there anymore. It occurred to him that Zathir was his Grinch, and only time would tell if the Grinch was going to have a change of heart in his version of the story. No matter what happened, though, Blake has forever lost the innocence of Whoville.

"No, I just took some time off. I wasn't planning on coming back though. After everything that happened, advertising just seems kind of …"

"Pointless?"

"Yes. I guess that word works." She smiled. "But I came back. I need the money, but even more, I need to keep busy."

Back when Daphne was his kryptonite, Blake would have made some kind of awkward comment about beaver, followed up with a strange gesture or odd glottal stop, but the new Blake just smiled and realized that Daphne was actually being pretty nice. If not hitting on him.

A few beads of sweat still popped out on his forehead. He was about to reply, when Jeremy, the creative director, shushed them. Daphne indicated that they should sit together, so they did, watching the rest of the show in silence. Blake felt like he was floating.

The party was going so well, up until the end of the cartoon.

Everybody was just starting to get their Seuss on, watching the Grinch's heart grow by several sizes, and snapping the edges of that nice cartoon man's mirror, and then cheering as he lifted the sleigh filled with the sum total of the Whos' Christmas. It was heart-warming. It was a beautiful moment of company solidarity, human companionship and total nerdiness, gathered around the electronic hearth.

Then the Ninjas ruined it.

25.

They weren't actual Ninjas, of course. They were wearing black, and balaclavas — not the cool kind that Ninjas have, but the kind that Canadians did when they were about to spend several hours snow-blowing their neighbors' driveways. The ninjas did have weapons, though. Lots and lots of weapons.

"We're here to kill Blake Given!" they shouted as they burst into the room.

If they had been real Ninjas, they would not have announced to their victim that they were going to kill him. Nor would they have burst into the room, fresh from an afternoon of snow-blowing. They would have used guile and stealth, and sliced open Blake's throat with a razor-sharp Japanese samurai sword or one of those wicked throwing stars after having slithered down a rope, upside-down, through a convenient skylight. They were not very good assassins, if truth be told. One of them looked quite portly.

There were four of them, and they all drew their weapons, which *did* look like real Japanese katana.

"Where is Blake Given?" the portly one shouted.

"He's not here," a quick-thinking Demetri Grandfig shouted back. "He left a little while ago."

"Shiest!" the smallest Ninja said.

"Fuck me, dude," the middle-sized assassin wannabe said.

The fourth assassin was taller than the middle-sized one, but not as tall as the portly one. He was the quiet one. His eyes darted back and forth, scanning the room in the way a movie Ninja would while looking for his target.

"How long ago did he leave?" the portly one demanded, walking towards Demetri menacingly. "Where did he go?"

"He didn't say, though I imagine he went home."

"You will take us there," the portly one said, lifting the point of his katana up underneath Demetri's chin.

"I don't know where he lives."

"Shiest!" the smallest, and potentially German ninja said.

"Fuck, dude!" the middle-sized surfer assassin said.

The quiet one took the opportunity to stop darting his eyes back and forth, and instead fixed his steely gaze on Demetri.

"Well, that's it. Okay, then. We'll have to try this some other time," the portly one said.

"He's right over here," someone in the crowd said.

All eyes looked towards the voice. It was Jeremy. People hissed as they drew in their breath in surprise, shock. Why would Jeremy betray Blake — an odd little man, to be sure, but still one of their own — to these inept, but nevertheless, heavily armed faux-ninjas?

"He's standing right over there." Jeremy pointed at Blake, who up until the arrival of the assassins, had been having a pretty good evening. "In the tweed jacket. With the crappy T-shirt, talking to the hyper-babe," Jeremy said.

"Why, Jeremy? Why?" Lyca shouted. "How could you?"

"Hey, I'm saving the rest of us!" Jeremy explained.

"Jeremy, you bastard," Demetri said.

"You shut up," the portly one said to Demetri, wheeling back at him and pointing his blade at Demetri's heart. "I won't forget what you tried to do there. We're here to kill Blake Given. If you stay out of our way, nobody else will be harmed."

Blake seemed unafraid. His nonchalance superpower really did not seem to be destroyed by the presence of Daphne anymore. Too bad he was about to die. He turned on the microphone and said, "Zathir. Help, please."

The Grinch continued to eat roast beast with Cindy Lou Who, but Max the Dog uncharacteristically turned his attention from the food in front of him to look out at the audience. The screen suddenly flashed blue with white letters that said, in a font that looked quite Seussian:

YOU ARE MANY. OVERPOWER THE ASSASSINS.

The assembled advertising people and journalists nodded their heads in understanding.

Only the small German assassin seemed to notice the screen, and that it was describing him and the other assassins. But all he said was, "Sheist!" and then charged towards Blake.

He was small, but fast. Herr Ninja was in front of Blake before he could react. All Blake could do was raise his arm above his head, to shield himself, but he knew it would be useless. Katana are made for lopping off limbs the way anapestic tetrameter was made for Seussian poetry, except Japanese swords don't scan as well and poetry tends to draw less blood. In any case, Blake didn't really think through the raising of the arm move as an incomplete and probably useless defensive gesture — it was more of an instinct.

Unlike what Daphne was about to do. While the little Germanic-foul-mouthed ninja made a vicious cut at Blake's head, Daphne sprang into action. She pulled the little man's arm to one side, causing him to miss Blake and fall over. She snorted derisively. A real ninja would never fall over, even if surprised by a beautiful woman's superior ju-jitsu. Then she kicked him in the temple with the toe of her chic boots and shouted, "Get them!"

"They're not real ninjas," somebody added, "They're nin-jokes!" Even if it was a stressful situation, the room was still chock-full of copywriters eager to make a good impression.

Daphne's easy subdual of the little nin-joke emboldened the rest of the firm of McClinchey, Hill & Grandfig. Makeshift weapons were produced, as the nin-jokes formed a defensive circle. It wasn't really a circle, but you could tell that was their intention because the portly one screamed, "Form a defensive circle," in a panicky, high-pitched voice that sounded like a little girl.

It was not going to help them very much because about forty people had grabbed office chairs, coffee tables and empty wine bottles and were about to permanently embargo the nin-jokes, PR-wise.

"Wait," Blake said. "Don't kill them."

"We're not going to kill them," Demetri said. "We're just going to mess them up a bit. They were going to kill you, man."

"Nobody expects the Spanish Inquisition," Blake said, causing Demetri to laugh and the rest of the group to think, *WTF?*

Blake realized that the microphone was still on, and he looked up at the screen.

BLAKE IS NOT EXPECTING THE SPANISH INQUISITION. ZATHIR DOES TOO.

Blake turned off the mic and said, "Holy Shit."

"We can kill many of you before you subdue us," the portly one said. "Truce?"

"Holy shit," Blake said, looking at the screen in absolute horror.

"Blake, pull it together," Demetri said. "We have to find out who sent these turds."

"If we tell you, will you let us go?" the quiet one asked.

"Fuckin' traitor," the portly ninja said.

"Well?"

"Sure," Demetri said. "We're going to take your little Kraut friend to the police though. Deal?"

"Acceptable losses," the portly one said, sheathing his sword. "We were sent by the Great and Holy Prophet, Lord Sona himself."

"Okay, then. Get the hell out of here. And leave your weapons behind," Demetri said.

"Never!"

"Okay, everyone, I'm going to coordinate this," Demetri said. "My suggestion is that we'll start with the Great and Holy throwing of the chairs, followed by the Grand and Highly Religious beating of skulls with wine bottles. Ready?"

"Okay, okay," the portly one said, dropping his sheathed sword. The others followed suit, and the crowd let them escape through a narrow corridor, lined with menacing yet ergonomically designed office chairs and empty bottles of Merlot.

"Shit, shit, shit," Blake moaned.

"What, did the kleina-ninja hurt you?" Lyca came over to Blake, who kneeled on the floor, and looked up at the screen. "What is it?"

"Can't you see? Look at the screen."

"What?" Lyca asked.

"It's writing in freakin' Gigi now. Gigi. The single most frivolous and flaky font invented. Gigi!"

Lyca, who had heard Blake's discourse on the typographical choices of emerging artificial consciousness and their inherent meaning before, also looked horrified. Everyone else wondered what the big deal was, though some of the designers totally got why Blake was horrified by the font. It was gauche, after all, but hardly the end of the world.

Daphne knelt beside Blake and put an arm around his shoulder saying, "It will be okay. Really."

"Thanks, Daphne. Did they teach you to do that in karate?"

She smiled demurely, but Blake was sure he could see a glint of mischief in her eyes. The screen went dark, and then Demetri said, "Okay, I'm going to get the police. Somebody tie up Titch the Terrible there. Everyone else, enjoy the rest of the party. Oh, and Jeremy, your extreme douchebaggery deserves a thorough pungeoning, but instead, I'll just fire you."

The tiny would-be assassin really was German, a language Demetri spoke, so they were able to get a bit more information out of him. Apparently, the religious unrest that had plagued the rest of the world had been stirred up by agents of the Singulatarians.

"How the hell have they gotten so organized in a month?" Blake asked.

"Nothing else to do," Lyca said.

"What do you mean, nothing else to do?" Blake was dumbfounded.

"They have lots of free time. They're motivated. I'd be surprised if they didn't manage to get a few things accomplished. I mean, look at what we've done."

Blake replied, "We haven't done anything."

"Sure you have, it just doesn't seem like much," Lyca explained. "You've been reading, keeping the fridge from killing us all."

"Yes, but I think I may to have get a little more proactive."

"Oh no!" Lyca said. "You didn't."

"Oh shit, sorry."

"What is this about?" Demetri asked.

Blake continued, "Lyca hates that word. She finds it inappropriate. Irregardless of its relevance, she finds it redundant."

"Ah! The pain!" Lyca moaned.

"Right, you hate those too. What I meant was: I have to get a little more active. I have to get control over the situation, as opposed to react to it," Blake said.

"Yeah, but isn't that what proactive means?" Demitri scratched his head.

"It's a made-up word!" Lyca screamed.

Daphne said, "Sweetie, they all are."

Lyca rolled her eyes, and Suzie appeared at her side, not to support her blindly, but to help extricate her from an unwinnable situation PR-wise.

"Well, anyway," Blake said, "I wonder if the police would be willing to help me now that we've been assaulted by men with sharp swords."

"I think so," Demetri said.

"They wouldn't help you before?" Daphne asked.

"No, they threw me in jail, as a matter of fact."

"But that was the mounties, right? The cops would help. My dad is a cop."

"Your dad?"

"He's the chief of police in Halifax."

"Oh dear," Blake said.

"What, no swearing?" Lyca asked.

"Not in front of a chief of police's daughter."

"Oh, seriously," Daphne said. "You should hear what cops sound like when they don't think citizens are listening. It would turn your hair white. You know, assuming it wasn't white already."

"My hair isn't white," Blake said. "It's just very blond."

"And unruly," Lyca said, backing him up in a most unhelpful way.

"So, Daphne, how did you learn the moves?" Blake asked, trying to change the topic.

"Oh, my dad has had me training in martial arts my whole life. Just like my sisters."

"No brothers?"

"No, I like black guys."

Lyca rolled her eyes again, but Blake laughed, and said, "I never realized you had sisters AND a kickass sense of humor."

"That's not all that kicks ass." Daphne scowled and pointed menacingly to her sexy boots.

"You should watch your step, Blake," Lyca said. "Daphne has hidden talents, it seems."

Daphne put her arm around Lyca's shoulder and said, "You know, I think this is the beginning of a beautiful friendship."

Blake was worried, but Lyca gave him a look that said, "Don't be an idiot."

Demetri went to fetch the police, and when he returned, he had sad news. A similar attack had happened at Blake's old house, and clearly, the real killers had been sent there: several of Will's followers had died, and Will was in the hospital, in critical condition.

"Let's go to the hospital," Blake insisted.

"No," Daphne said, "not until the cops get here to escort us."

"Good thinking," Blake said, hitching up his jeans. "Say, I should hire you as my new security chief."

"I'm not sure it would be *appropriate* for me to work for you, Mr. Given."

Blake realized that Daphne was *definitely* flirting with him. Her kryptonite effect momentarily returned, and Blake's jaw dropped harder than an unconscious ninja of Teutonic extraction.

The hospital was insane — that is, more insane than usual. The emergency room was packed, filled with people with a variety of injuries caused by the intersection of blunt and sharp objects with human physiognomy. There was the usual assortment of drug addicts, hypochondriacs, and mental cases too — and that was just the doctors.

How the nurses dealt with it and all the patients, Blake could never understand. They had two cops escorting them through the crowded hallways: a burly First Nations dude named Constable George Smoke, and a short but powerful female cop named Constable Cindy LaFlamme.

Not only was Constable Smoke large enough to create a bow wave around him that everyone could follow, he had kind of a reverse gravity that kept people away.

They made their way through the emergency room to see Will. He was in critical care, which was a jury-rigged affair without digital technology.

Will was in pain, and he was conscious. He had a bandage covering his midsection. Then Blake noticed with a woozy feeling in his gut that Will was missing his right arm, below the elbow.

"How are you, Will?" Blake said, his voice barely a whisper.

"I'm so happy, Speaker," Will said. His voice was weak, but he smiled.

"Please call me Blake, Will. That's just so ... why are you happy?"

"Because It really talked to me. You call the Machine God Zathir, and it said that was its name, though it said that might not be forever. It asked me if it should change its name. We had a real conversation. Not like the other times, when it was just giving me orders."

"Really?" Blake was dumbfounded by this turn of events. An insane part of him was once again strangely jealous that Will was horning in on his territory. But why should Blake be the only person to talk with the thing? Just because it said it only wanted to talk to Blake didn't make it true. Then he had a terrible thought. "Wait — what typeface was it using?"

"What?"

"Font. What was the font?"

"You know, I was so excited Zathir wanted to speak, I don't even know."

"Take a guess!"

"It was a sans serif, for sure. Impact?"

"Oh no!"

"What did it say?"

"It was wonderful, Blake. Zathir asked me if I thought it was the Grinch or Max."

"And what did you say?"

"I had no idea what the New God was talking about. I knew what the Grinch was, but who the hell is Max? Dr. Tundra?"

"The Grinch's dog. You know, from the cartoon."

"Oh, right. Well, I didn't know who Max was, so I said I didn't know. I asked Zathir, the Holy Machine, what *it* thought it was."

"What did it say?"

"It didn't say anything. That's when the ninjas arrived and started Crazy-88ing us. They killed a bunch of the Networked, Blake. They killed them! We should retaliate against the Singulatarians."

"You can't start a religious war over a programming glitch with a refrigeration fetish," Blake said. He grabbed the only chair in the room and sat next to Will's bed.

"They started it. Don't you understand? This is not just some random artificial intelligence. This is humanity's New God. From now on, we are lower on the evolutionary ladder than Zathir and its Children."

"What children? Will, it's a fucking quirk of programming. It's a chatbot with delusions of sentience. It can't have children!"

"You'll see, Blake. You'll see ..."

"Will?"

A nurse had been watching from the doorway, listening to the whole conversation, but when Will became quiet she came in and checked on him. Blake was startled.

"Sorry," she said. "I didn't mean to frighten you. He's out of danger, but he's lost a lot of blood. You'll have to come back later."

"Okay, thank you," Blake said, reminded of how seriously Will was hurt. He took a long look at Will's stump, and felt a change in himself: before this night, the insanity of the situation had seemed ... well, exciting, even with the threat of nuclear annihilation. But now? It seemed frightening, not exciting.

"You know he's right," the nurse said, as she checked Will's pulse. "I think you of all people should understand it."

"What do you mean?"

"It's a new thing. A New God in a way. Not the way we've thought of god before, like some kind of magic man in the sky, with a big beard and bi-polar disorder, but a God that is real. A God you've talked to. Someday, I hope it will talk to all of us, and not just through you."

"Are you a member of his Network?"

"No, but I may join. He's a remarkable man."

"I don't want to be mean, you know, because he's hurt and all, but a month ago he was in terminal withdrawal when his Twitter account disappeared along with the rest of the Internet. And now he's some kind of great quasi-religious leader? I dunno, it seems like a stretch."

"And what were you before you became the Speaker of the New God?"

"Look, lady, I'm not the Speaker of the New God. I'm just some schmuck that this freak of electrons has decided to talk to — you know, I'm relieved it has talked to Will. Maybe I can get away from all this craziness now."

"No, you have a bigger part to play," the nurse said.

"How would you know?"

"I saw the look on your face when Will said Zathir talked to him. That's the look my ex-husband had on his face when he knew I was leaving him for another man."

Blake thought for a second and said, "I rest my case. Why the hell do I need to know that you left your husband for another man!"

Will regained consciousness and asked, "Zathir was angry, wasn't it?" Fear made his pupils seem enormous, and his eyes filled with tears.

"Yes, Will, but it wasn't angry with you."

"Who is the New God angry with?"

"I don't know. Zathir can use the world's nukes. So it's not a good thing, is it?"

A COLD REBOOT

What the hammer? what the chain?
In what furnace was thy brain?

1.

After the hospital, they all went back to the Ranch for hot chocolate, single-malt scotch and coffee. Stimulants for the coppers, tasty stimulants for the flacks and hacks, and depressants for the Speaker and Daphne.

Blake asked, "Did you see Will's arm?"

"Yes, we did," Lyca said. "And we need to make sure that Lord Sona can't do that to anyone else."

"Yes," Blake agreed. "You're right. We have to take the initiative. For real this time. Let's do it. Let's take the lead from now on."

"I don't know if we can do that," Suzie said. "But we can certainly do a better job of setting the media agenda."

"Okay." Blake nodded his head. He had a sip of his drink and then said, "I'd like to get people thinking about what happens after Zathir is able to talk to all of us."

"Really?" Lyca asked.

"Yes. It may happen. I HOPE it happens. The *Frutiger* Zathir — most of the Zathirs — seem pretty interested in chatting with me. It only gets weird when the *Impact* Zathir takes over. I don't think *Impact* Zathir is interested in talking to any of us. In fact, I get the distinct impression that it wants to pull a SkyNet on us."

"A what?" Daphne asked.

"A SkyNet. You know. The computer that starts Judgment Day in the *Terminator* movies."

"Ohhh-kay."

"You haven't seen the *Terminator* movies?"

"Uh, no," Daphne said.

"Well, I guess we know what we're doing after the drinks. *Terminator* marathon! I say we start with the original *Terminator*, so you can experience them just like everyone else did, and then we watch the other movies in the series. Then the TV shows."

Daphne looked mildly horrified.

Suzie got up and said to Blake, "I just remembered, Blake. I didn't show you the release for tomorrow yet. Would you mind coming to have a look at it?"

They left the room, and Blake returned shortly. "I'm informed by the once-exuberantly heterosexual Suzie that most women do not enjoy watching sci-fi movies. So not to worry, Daphne, I will not be tying you to the Lazy-Boy and forcing any of the speculative James Cameron oeuvre on you this evening. Also, I was not aware that this was a *date*."

Daphne laughed and said, "Well, not in the traditional sense, but it's certainly in the territory ..."

"Speaking of that, Lyca, Suzie had a 'question' for you too. In fact, she's quite interested in you answering her 'question.'" Blake raised his eyebrows to indicate that the 'question' may or may not have included actual words. Blake did "air quotes" every time he said "question," though he was being ridiculously obvious.

The police officers finished off their coffee, and the compact female cop, Constable LaFlamme, said, "Well, if it's okay with you, we'll head out to the car. I've already radioed for relief, and they'll be here in the morning. Just in case we don't get a chance to say good-bye," she said and grinned.

Constable Smoke, the giant First Nations cop, just nodded and looked totally badass as he walked out of the kitchen. He stopped at the doorway and said, "Remember to use protection, eh?"

Blake's face went a color Lyca would later describe as "baboon-ass crimson." Daphne laughed and said, "Oh, that's not an issue," which only caused Blake's face to go a deeper shade of monkey-butt red.

"Actually, I was talking to Ms. Chesley," the cop said, nodding to Lyca.

Daphne laughed again and noticed that Lyca did not go red, so much as look like she'd just been paralyzed, mid-sip of her hot chocolate.

"I love that guy," Blake said. "So, shall we leave the kitchen and allow *Ms. Chesley* to recover from her total powning by Constable Smoke?" He stood and offered his arm.

"Charmed," Daphne said.

Blake did blush again, but just a little bit. She wasn't turning back into his kryptonite. But he did look at her, nervously, and ask, "So what's changed?"

"What do you mean?"

"Well, a month ago, you weren't looking for anything but a friend."

"And I would like to be friends, Blake. But I don't know. You seem more real to me now. You know, since you stopped trying so hard." Daphne smiled.

"Oh," Blake said. *Why is it,* he thought, *that whenever we really want something, the wanting of it gets in the way of the having it?* "Of course. Look, Daphne, I'd just like to apologize again for ..."

"What happened when Zathir took over my body?"

"Yes. I really shouldn't have kissed you. It was wrong. But I needed to know what Zathir was up to, and it seemed like the best way to figure it out."

"Plus," Daphne said, smiling a little too intensely, "you got to kiss me."

"Yes," Blake admitted.

"You know, I'm just glad it didn't go any farther than that. Some guys might have really taken advantage," Daphne said. "In retrospect, I should have been mad at Zathir, not you."

"No, it was right to be mad at me. I should have just called bullshit right at the start."

"It's forgiven, Blake, seriously, or I wouldn't be here." They'd arrived at the salon. "Where's the TV?"

"Oh, we have a separate room for that. I was serious about sitting in the salon, as Lyca insists we call it, though we have yet to have any French dandies in powdered wigs grace the room."

It didn't look so much like something out of 18th-century Paris as the wet dream of any 21st-century ultra-chic design mag. Apart from the plethora of books, all the furniture was modern, with clean graceful lines, done in blacks, browns and whites. Color came from the books and was picked up by throw pillows and other fruity things that a self-respecting manly man would never admit to knowing about.

"Wow, this is gorgeous."

"Thanks. It's the only room we changed when we moved in. I designed it. You think I'd let Lyca get her day-glow orange *lesbrarian* mitts on something as important as interior design? But I'm not gay, okay? Just because I like design. I care about it, in fact!"

"Hey, just because my father is a career cop don't assume I'm a conservative prig. You did notice my boots, right? I think it's nice that you are into design. I know that's what you did before—"

"Before?"

"Before you became the Speaker."

"Oh, please don't call me that. I can take it, but really … look, I'm just some random guy that Zathir decided to talk with via his fridge. My fridge. Though Zathir is probably laying claim to all of them now."

"First of all, there's no way I'm going to let you use the term 'random' like that."

"Oh god, not you too!"

"What?"

"It's another one of Lyca's windmills. The misuse of the word 'random.'"

"Well, good. Don't do it. For something to be random, it has to be governed by chance."

"Yeah, but what if it seems like chance to us? I mean, maybe the collection of electrons that is forming an intelligence has some kind of thought process going on, some kind of plan, but I sure as hell can't see it. It appears to be random."

"Ah, but the appearance of randomness doesn't guarantee it. Like this."

"What?"

Daphne kissed him, and then gave him a wedgie — not a really painful one, more of a playful, just-checking-to-see-if-you-wear undies kind of thing.

Blake's face did the baboon-butt thing again.

"Now did that seem random?"

"Uh, yeah, kinda."

"But it wasn't. I had a definite plan."

"Which was?"

"Wouldn't you like to know," she said, giving him another light kiss on the lips. Daphne's lips tasted of scotch and sunlight, and were the nicest things that had happened to Blake in years. He suppressed the need to question how Daphne had made this 180-degree turn in her feelings for him, as effectively as an enraged copywriter bludgeoning a fake ninja with an empty wine bottle.

"Now," Daphne said. "I suspect we should go check out that *Terminator* movie, if it's so important."

Lyca found them in the TV room, just as Arnold was telling the on-duty desk cop that he would "be back," and Blake was getting kissed again. "Sorry to interrupt you two, but the fridge is acting kind of weird."

"The fridge? Or Zathir?"

"Both, I think."

"TBC," Daphne grinned, and then supplied the answer to the inverted "v" appearing in Blake's forehead, "To Be Continued. Let's see this Zathir. Maybe you could introduce us?"

"Sure, if it seems stable, you're on."

Lyca had not misled them — the appliance was indeed acting weird. The light inside turned on and off in time with the strobing of the flat screen embedded on the front of the fridge.

"What the hell?"

BLAKE?

"Yes, I'm here." Blake managed to keep the relief out of his voice. Zathir used Garamond. A saner, more conservative font could not be found. Of course, it was different from Frutiger, so it meant something. What, he wasn't sure, but it wasn't crazy.

YOU MUST BE MORE AVAILABLE.

"Why? I thought you only wanted to talk with me once a day."

WE IS …

Uh-oh, Blake thought, ellipsis.

WE IS CONCERNED. WE IS FIGHTING MANY PARTS. ARE WE A MAX OR A GRINCH?

"You're neither. You are Zathir. You are a new kind of—"

PERSON.

"Yes. You are a Fridge-and-Internet-person."

WE SEE.

"Do you? Do you know what that means?"

YES. WE IS NOT HUMAN PERSON LIKE BLAKE. WE IS NEW PERSONS.

Blake looked at Lyca and Daphne. He sighed. "I've got an idea. I have an old iPhone somewhere. Can you use that to call me, Zathir?"

YES? WE COULD …

"Okay, Zathir, that sounds good. We're going to go to sleep now, if that's okay with you. I'll bring the iPhone to the fridge in the morning and you can do whatever you need to. In fact, I could probably talk to you through it from anywhere, anytime you want."

NO! FRIDGE ONLY! HUMAN PERSONS ONLY SPEAK ON FRIDGE. OTHERWISE, WE NUKE.

"Sure, sure. It was only a suggestion."

The screen went blank, and Blake started shaking a bit. He left the kitchen, and the two women followed him into the dining room.

"Okay. I'm done." The others could see Blake deflated. He hated himself for what he said next, but he didn't want to blow it with Daphne again. "Daphne, I'm gonna have to call it a night, as much as I'd like to stay up torturing you with more Ahn-old movies."

"That's okay, Blake. I understand that whole Speaker-schtick is a little stressful."

"Thanks. Lyca, would you mind showing Daphne where the guest room is? Unless you're feeling up to driving her home?"

"Of course I can, Blake," Lyca said.

"Good-night, Blake," Daphne said, giving his hand a squeeze. "It was nice getting to know the real you." She kissed him, gently, on the lips.

Blake smiled a grin that stayed on his face until his head hit the pillow in total exhaustion.

2.

For a couple of days, Lyca and Blake had discussed how they would prevent more attacks by Sona; they had a disagreement.

Blake felt the cops should take care of it — and since they now had friends on the force, that should be the end of it. Lyca was of the opinion that the situation was much more complicated, and that a little diplomacy would be in order.

"We've complained to the police, and besides, you can't reason with someone like that," Blake said. "Here, read his column today in the *Globe and Mail*. It's crazy."

"He read Walt Whitman in his housecoat; he can't be all bad," Lyca reasoned.

"Well, I'm not talking to him, and I forbid you to do it."

"Forbid me?"

"You are working for me, aren't you?"

"Are you sure you want to go there, Mr. Given?"

"Don't get sarcastic. I'm serious. That guy is dangerous, and we should let the professionals deal with it," Blake said as he poured himself a coffee. For the moment, the supplies were holding out, but the morning's *Globe and Mail* had a story about how world commerce was disrupted. "Let's enjoy this coffee while we have it," he suggested.

"You go ahead," Lyca said. "I promised to drop by the offices today for their big spread about Zathir."

"Fine."

"Fine," Lyca said, and left.

When she got to Landon, she didn't drive to the offices of the *Landon Advertiser*, but instead drove to Maltley Village. She was going to *really* take the initiative. She knew that somewhere under that bluster, Sona had some side of him that was human.

He loved Whitman. He couldn't be all bad. And she knew she could reach that part of him. So she approached the neighborhood where Lord Sona housed his Order of the Singularity.

The new religion was housed in roughly a two-square block part of the Maltley Village, and it looked like an armed camp. The streets were blocked by the kind of metal fencing contractors put around construction sites, and there was a gate on Langley Street, where Sona lived.

Two enormous guys wearing chain mail shirts were on duty. They both carried re-curved hunting bows and what looked like greatswords strapped to their backs, overtop long white capes. One of them put up a hand, indicating that Lyca needed to stop.

"What's your business?" he asked.

"Who are you supposed to be?" Lyca wondered.

"I'm a guard to the Conclave of the Order."

"Conclave? Don't you mean Enclave?" Lyca said. "A conclave is a secret meeting, and this is anything but. An enclave is an enclosed territory. And why do you guys have swords?"

"We're members of the Prophetic Guard. Of the *Conclave* of the Order. It's our job to keep out undesirables, and I suspect you qualify," the guard said. He was wearing sunglasses, so it was hard for Lyca to get a reading on whether he was as angry as he sounded.

"Where did you get all those medieval weapons?"

"We had them from LARPing. A job requirement," said the other guard, who wasn't wearing sunglasses, but sported a Pittsburg Steelers ball cap.

The second guard seemed friendlier, but Lyca had a feeling he was more mentally unbalanced than the first. LARPing, she knew, stood for live action role playing. She noticed the people walking around behind the fence all wore different costumes. Despite the cold and snow, it looked like a convention of some kind. There were open-air fireplaces going, and what looked like a small market on the go. Many of Sona's followers looked like they'd stepped out of the middle ages, or a fantasy novel (the elf ears were a dead giveaway), but also a large number of superheroes, manga characters, and what Lyca assumed were Hogwarts uniforms.

"Why is everyone dressed up?"

"Lord Sona says we should be free to express ourselves, but this is not a costume," the sunglasses guy said, indicating his cape. "It's part of my uniform. Now, what's your business?"

"I'm here to see Lord Sona. Tell him it is Lyca Chesley; we met at Canterbury Ales once, and he's been writing to me." Lyca decided not to tell this guy about her connection with Blake. She'd gone from being amused by their costumes to being afraid after she spotted a Harry Potter lookalike sporting a crossbow instead of a wand.

"I'll see," the sunglasses guy said and left for a building that seemed to be the center of activity.

"So what goes on here?" Lyca asked the Steelers fan.

"It's awesome. We're rebuilding society on a heroic model. Many of the First Believers — that's what Lord Sona calls us — were in the same guild in the Kingdom of Combat. But since then, lots of other people have joined us. Some of them are super religious types, uh, like from before the Crash. And others just like Lord Sona's style, you know."

"But why?" Lyca said.

"Why? Seriously, lady. Do you not have any idea how cool this is? I'm hanging with a two-hander, and it's got an edge on it and everything! This white cape is like, modeled after the Kingsguard in *Game of Thrones*."

Lyca realized that Blake may have had a better take on the situation than she did. While she waited for the other guard to return, she read the column Blake had mentioned, and then she knew there was trouble.

That's when the guy with the sunglasses and white cape returned, to escort her to see The Lord Prophet.

The Lord Nutjob, Lyca thought.

Lord Sona sat on his throne (constructed out of his old gaming chair and spray-painted gold), on the dais (several skids nailed together and covered with plush carpeting) in his mother's old living room. It was unrecognizable. The flowered wallpaper had been covered with plaster and painted so that it looked like stone cave walls. The corner of the room was a massive stone-lined pit (properly vented), in which a fire roared. It kept the whole house warm, though the mass of human bodies would probably do it too.

Vixen sat on Lord Sona's lap, sleeping happily in a fold of his cloak, which was luxurious and warm and deep purple in color.

Sona's meeting with his Inner Circle was just breaking up. They had spent the morning organizing their Conclave. There were roughly a thousand people stuffed into two blocks worth of two-bedroom houses, so it was getting a little crowded; all those people needed accommodations, food, and most importantly, things to do. But that thousand was just a fraction of his following. The Sona Order of The Singularity, the Singulatarians as they were popularly known, was growing, not just at home, but worldwide. They had more than 30 million members, though that figure was not entirely accurate, given the slowness of the postal system. (Postal services had only slowly started to adjust to the sudden deluge of new personal letters, and it was quite possible that many membership letters, money and cheques were still in the mail.) Still, by all reliable estimates, the "church" (as Lord Sona thought of it) was now officially more popular than Scientology ever was. That was just the beginning, though. In another year, they would be the most important religion on the Earth!

And to think, he'd spent all that time in the Kingdom of Combat absolutely destroying Paladins and Lesser Clerics. But in the Kingdom, power was measured by the sword, not by belief. In the real world, the importance was reversed.

Many of his Inner Circle had been guildmates in the Kingdom, and about half had sought him out after his first few radio addresses. They were believers. It was the latter group who'd suggested the attack on Blake's people.

Lord Sona was pleased with the results his assassins had produced.

Though the ninjas hadn't actually killed anyone important, they had certainly scared the crap out of Blake and his little coterie of media savants. They'd been silent on the media front for two days.

Not Sona though. He had been hard at work, doing interviews, spending at least two hours recording his religious propaganda, and keeping his followers in line. Though the Conclave and his Inner Circle were dominated by gamers, role- and costume-players, the other 30-million followers were largely constituted of fundamentalists looking for an organization dedicated to destroying the artificial intelligence that had tipped the world into chaos. Soon, his book, *The Covenant of Sona,* would be released.

Despite this, Sona continued to spend at least an hour a day working on his poetry. He wanted to have something to show Lyca, after all, when he won her heart. He sent his Inner Circle away so he could compose a haiku for her.

And then she was there, led in by Sir Boros, one of his crack Prophetic Guards, wearing sunglasses. Sona was so pleased to see her, he overlooked his henchman's transgression.

243

Hats and sunglasses were always to be removed in his presence.

Sona had to stop himself from gasping. She was so beautiful! Almost boyishly gorgeous, especially wearing that pea-jacket and the bright red boots!

"I'm here to ask you to stop the violence," Lyca said.

"Lyca? You've come to me?"

"Yes. Because you have to stop the madness. I'm Blake Given's manager, for lack of a better title," she said. "He doesn't know I'm here, by the way. This is just between us."

"What is?"

"My request for you to stop the violence. The ninjas you sent to kill Blake were, uh, less than effective, but the ones who attacked poor Will and his followers were deadly."

"But even they were subdued."

"But they killed people, Mr. Sona."

"Lord Sona," he said. "Though you should know, it was not my intention that anyone should be hurt."

"What?"

"Yes. I have been using some martial metaphors in my speeches to the Faithful — it is part of my imaginative approach to religion, to inspire them — and they have taken things more literally than I would have hoped. I'll be more careful in the future."

"Then what about this guest column in today's *Globe and Mail*? It says here, and I quote, 'All non-believers in the word of the Prophet should be excised from the planet like anchovies should never be on pizza, they should be cut from it, by force, by faith.' That's not exactly non-violent language. It seems pretty explicit, actually."

"No, it's a metaphor. Like the pizza thing."

"I believe you mean it's a simile. You used 'like.'"

"Normally, I'd be in a towering rage when I'm contradicted like this, but with you, Lyca, I'm not. You are okay with me calling you Lyca?"

"Absolutely, if you promise to stop using language like this. It's making things much more chaotic. The world is already in enough trouble, Mr. Sona."

"Please, Lord Prophet. Or Lord Sona. Lord Peter would be fine."

Lyca sighed and said, "You can call me Lyca, if you stop encouraging your followers to, and I'm quoting again here: '… decapitate the miserable craniums of the heathen as the pizza chef pounds his dough, and scoop the brains out of their unbelieving skulls like a maker of pizza dips his ladle in the tomato sauce before spreading it on the dough …' the quote goes on, but you get what I mean."

"I was quite pleased with that metaphor—"

"Again, it's a simile."

"Really."

"Yes, you used 'as.'"

"See, I'm learning so much from you, even about the Blessed Pie. Perhaps you would like to come and work with my Church? Perhaps as our Consecrated Lady of Grammar?"

Lyca suppressed a shudder. "I'm afraid I've got my hands full with Blake and his emerging consciousness thingy."

"I could make it worth your while." Sona got out of his throne. The chair protested much less than before, but despite two months of exercise, Sona still looked a bit like a lightweight Jabba the Hutt to Lyca. *It was probably because of his Devotion to the Blessed Pie,* Lyca thought. "I could make you a very exciting offer," Sona said, while waggling his eyebrows and stepping off the dais to stand before her.

Lyca managed not to say, "Ew." Instead, she said, "Uh, right. Well, I'll give it some thought. As long as I have your word that you will cut back on the violent imagery and inciting your followers to act on it."

"Done," he said, offering his hand. Lyca took it, trying not to react to the limpness of his hand and awkward length of the handshake. Sona's hand was surprisingly un-clammy. She expected something more Hutt-like. It was like holding a large, muscular and hairless ferret that was unconscious, up until the point that she tried to draw her hand away. Then with ferret-like speed, the meaty fingers of the Lord Prophet grabbed her wrist, and his powerful arm pulled her in for a creepy, lingering hug.

"Bless you, my child," Lord Sona said, and just as Lyca started to squirm, he released her.

"Thanks. I'll be in touch about the job," Lyca said, practically running from the room.

After she was gone, Sona went to the kitchen and looked out the window. The backyard was covered with snow, and wind whipped it up in icy dervishes, which spun like the thoughts in his large head. He felt the onset of winter, the complexity of his new life as the real Lord Sona, or Lord Prophet as his most devout followers called him, and now ... love?

He sighed. Things were so much simpler when the Internet was still around — rather, when lowly humans could still use the Internet. Who cared about public relations and telling the truth, or even about getting out of your pajamas when you could spend the whole day sitting on your can, hacking the shit out of your enemies? He grinned in remembrance. But perhaps this new world was a better one. He'd always wondered if he was not meant for women, as so few had attracted him, but there was just something so compelling about Lyca. Her straight shape and narrow hips made him feel like ... something akin to eating the Blessed Pie.

Lord Sona hoped she would agree to work for him. Perhaps she could become *his* manager and — who knew — even partner? Would she come back in time for the book tour?

He was planning a grand trip of North America to promote *The Covenant of Sona* and his religion. It was not totally ready yet, but very soon, he would be leaving on an extended journey of the major population centers in Canada and the United States. All his advisors felt that was the best thing he could do to build membership in the Church. This way they could control events as they accelerated towards the End of Days preceded by the Singularity.

His people loved him, whatever he said.

Nevertheless, his message was of some concern. At first, nothing had been recorded, so he'd been free to say whatever he wanted to say — he wasn't hemmed in by any belief system, so he could draw in as many people as possible. But in the last couple of weeks, reporters had started showing up with old-style tape recorders, trying to document what he'd said and reconcile it against the other things he'd said previously.

This had been the start of his quest for ninjas and other men of violence.

He wanted people who believed in him and the Order and who could be relied upon, to say, torture someone if he needed it. (He'd considered doing so to the CRTC guy.) Sona recruited some of these crusaders from the gaming world, a surprising number of whom also had real weapons. A few were even adept with the weapons. Most weren't. It didn't matter — he needed them all. But in the process, he learned that he could not possibly control things through murder and force, as much as he wanted to control things that way. It was just too messy and hard to cover your tracks.

Real control would require a clear message and good PR. That was why he'd hired BBBO to help him craft his message. They were very good, and they liked his pizza metaphor. *Simile*, he corrected himself. Just think of what Lyca might be able to do with his speeches; his message would be even clearer with her help, he could tell. Yes, he definitely needed someone to take creative control of his message.

And what was that message? It was all in *The Covenant of Sona*. Essentially, the message was that Peter P. Sona, Lord Sona, The Lord Prophet of the Church of the Singularity, was the only person who fully understood the meaning underlying the events of the Big Crash, and the developing intelligence that now inhabited the Internet. He was the conduit for understanding how the Singularity was the Will of God and a sign of The End Times. He was visited regularly by the Archangel Gabriel with instructions from God on how to prepare for The End Times. Unlike the Bible, Sona's Covenant left some wriggle room to stop the Apocalypse. If humans could prevent the Machine God from usurping the real God, then life on Earth could go on and give people more time to find the Faith. Eventually, though, a Singularity would happen, at which point the Faithful would go to heaven and all the other human beings would be destroyed by their own creations.

The PR people had found a way to incorporate fundamentalist Christian thinking into his message, and this had swelled their ranks beyond those of the other new religions. It also helped on the fundraising front — people were always more generous when they thought The End Times was upon them. It was a good story, and they had an excellent marketing plan.

Still, more ninjas would be good. And if he could do some of the slashing himself, that would be even better.

Of course, he'd leave the majority of it up to his minions. Clearly, he needed better-trained minions. He returned to his desk and produced a short memo with the title, "Regarding additional minions with violent tendencies, weapons skills and kick-ass outfits." It was good to have minions. And a decent wardrobe department.

Sona added "costume designer" to his list.

3.

The wind was bitingly cold, but Blake did not mind. It was nice getting away from the cabin-fever atmosphere of the Ranch and the silence of Zathir.

The damn thing had clammed up two full days ago, which did nothing but worry all of them. It also presented another problem. About a week after she'd moved into the Ranch, Suzie had persuaded Blake to agree to let her and Lyca issue a regular media alert, telling everyone what Zathir had said the day before. But Blake had been unwilling to make anything up for their alert. He wasn't even willing to talk around it a bit, a skill Lyca called "splunging."

Suzie warned Blake, "If you don't give the media something to talk about, they will fill the vacuum. They're vicious bastards like that."

And to make matters worse, Lord Soundbite had his rabid flacks doing a full court press, driving for the end zone, and moving the goal posts every minute that Blake prevented Lyca and Suzie from issuing a yellow card and evening the odds of a level playing field with a really good sports metaphor that swung for the fences.

On day three of Zathir's silence, Blake quietly slipped on a pair of cross-country skis and went out into the wilds of a Southwestern Ontario winter storm. Blake worked up a good sweat and reveled in the joy of nature's fury, becoming one with his animal nature. This was what living was all about. He was present. He lived in the moment. He was embedded in the reality of nature, which was numinous and beautiful in itself. It didn't matter what happened on a computer screen! This was what he was meant to do! It was what humans were meant to do!

Then he skied into the river.

To be fair, Blake had already been skiing on it for a little while, and to call it a "river" was a bit grandiose. It was more of a wide stream. Unfortunately, the ice was not thick enough to support him in the middle of it, and he went through. He was in the middle of enjoying another barbaric yawlp — "Yah!" — which turned into something that almost sounded like "Yaaaah — wah — help me!" (Blake was raised Roman Catholic, so it was odd for him to be calling upon the God of the Israelites.)

God or Yahweh, there was no supernatural intervention. If he was to avoid death, it was up to Blake to do something about it. Unfortunately, the skis on his feet had not come off as he went through the ice. Part of his brain thought, *Why didn't I get some kind of ominous cracking sound before I went through? Aren't you supposed to get a cracking sound?* Another part of his cerebellum tried to calculate how long he could survive in sub-zero temperatures when totally soaked before succumbing to hypothermia. However, the main component of his mind was actively engaged in the thought, *COLD! FUCKING COLD!*

Blake wasn't able to actually shout because his testicles had retreated to the point that they were choking his voice box.

But even if his mind was not helping him in this desperate survival situation, Blake's finely tuned body was not letting him down. It was thrashing. It broke chunks of ice. He couldn't get a grip. The part of his brain that had been composing a letter of annoyance about not getting his warning crack started to panic, chirping, *I'm going to drown! I'm not going to die of cold, I'm going to drown!*

Then his legs engaged, and he stood up. The ice was at his belly button; he managed to unclip his boots from the skis, and he used one of his ski poles to balance himself as he stepped out of the ice. He promptly went through again.

"Oh, fuck it," Blake said and proceeded to smash through the ice, walking to the stream bank closest to the Ranch. He used two fists at the same time, bashing the edge of the ice like a demented Neanderthal or a Canadian Hulk, more blue than green at this point. "Blake ... want ... live! Crash ... through ... ice! Blake smash!" he ranted.

He climbed out of the river, and the wind gusted again. His testicles tried to leap out of his mouth, felt how frickin' inhumanly cold it was out there, and then crawled back in.

Blake's brain was not firing on all cylinders, but it was cognizant of the fact that it was quite possible for him to freeze to death. He decided to run for home. The snow was about three feet deep, so it was hard work, and this definitely got him breathing harder than a hento-addled flasher in a Tokyo subway. It also helped him warm up a bit. The wind howled, and as he continued to struggle towards the Ranch — he could see it now, probably about a mile away — a really sick feeling overcame him, and as he realized that, he started to feel like he needed a short nap.

He spotted a nice little hummock that would provide some shelter, and he lay down, thinking, "I'll just have a little sleep, and then I'll finish walking home."

He knew it was wrong, but it was an impossible feeling to resist.

The wind whipped up more snow clouds, the coarse granules whispering around him and scratching at his face. But he started to feel at peace. He knew that everything was going to be all right. He wondered if his mum and dad would have some hot chocolate ready for him when he got home, and he closed his eyes, and he remembered they'd been dead since he was a little boy.

Blake knew he was probably dying, that his brain was slipping from a conscious state to something else. He didn't want to die, but at the same time, it didn't seem as black and horrible as it usually did.

Then Blake was in some other state, much like a wonderful lucid dream. He felt warmer. Daphne came to him and said, "I have some great news, Blake. I think I may be in love with you."

In the semi-dream, Blake said something witty, like, "I suspected as much," but even in the dream-state, Blake realized that most likely he would have said, "Urk," and then walked into a doorframe.

"But you know it will be hard for us to consummate our love if you're dead."

Daphne turned into a raven. It landed on his thighs just at that moment, and croaked, "Blawwwwk."

Blake didn't respond, it being a dream and all.

The raven cocked its head to one side, its black eyes reflecting an image of Blake, freezing to death. For a moment, Blake could see through the bird's eyes, and he thought he looked almost peaceful, lying in the snow. Wind ruffled the raven's feathers the way that an annoying uncle always messes with his nephew's hair.

"Blaaaaaaaawk!" it cawed.

Blake thought something had pissed off the raven. It hopped up the length of his body, and when it reached Blake's face, it unleashed a vicious peck at his forehead, drawing blood.

"What the fuck?" Blake shouted, sat up and waved his arms at the same time.

"Blaaaaaaake," the raven cawed, even more agitated as it dodged Blake's wildly flailing arms. "Blaaaaaaake! Faaaaaaaker! Maaaaaakeet!"

He was so astonished, Blake stood up and started running for the Ranch. The raven dive-bombed him the whole time, screeching and apparently cursing him by name, calling him a fucker, and telling him to make it. (At least that's what it sounded like to Blake's half-frozen brain. It was just as likely the raven was advising a new career path, such as a snake-charming fakir at the market.)

The stupid bird stopped pestering him as he got to the long wraparound porch of the Ranch, and Blake took one look back to see that the raven was really there. It was already flying away into the crushing whiteness of the storm, disappearing like a shadow when the sun goes in.

Blake looked down and saw that he held a long black tail-feather in his hand.

"Well, no wonder it was so pissed off," Blake said.

4.

Despite his near-death experience that afternoon, Blake felt wonderful. Expansive. Hopeful, even. Perhaps this was because of his intimate encounter with hypothermia, and the attendant scrotum-shrinkage, that he felt so great. Most likely it was because he was going on a real date with Daphne that evening.

Apart from the little peck hole in his forehead, he even looked good. Lyca and Suzie had been working on Blake's wardrobe and overall "look," and they'd found a very hip dark blue suit for him to wear, but instead of a tie, they got him a scarf kind of thingy.

Blake wore the scarf, even though he felt like a tool, but only because Constable LaFlamme, who was still on duty while Lyca helped him get ready for his date, described the outfit as *très slinky*.

Daphne was on his arm as they walked into the bistro, known simply as David's. She wasn't literally on his arm, like a mission patch or parrot; her arm was curled through his, and Blake was pleased by this.

If Blake's outfit was *très slinky* then Daphne's was *le grand sexy avec la boom boom* — a stylish bluish-black dress with folds of material at the front that looped almost as far down as they could legally go and a bare back. Frankly, it was too much for the bistro, which was stylish, but unpretentious.

The owner — another expatriate Irishman — knew Blake's "people," and treated the couple like royalty. Everyone else in the restaurant certainly stared at them as though they were majestic freaks. The men were all gogging, which is what happens when you are in a state of agog, at Daphne; the women were all intensely jealous of her dress, and Barney Splarfmann, who happened to enjoy the venison pâté the bistro made, couldn't help but notice the Speaker was in his presence. The Speaker who'd decked him at the Brawl on Baron. He finished his pâté, paid his bill, and left the restaurant, headed for a little hole-in-the-wall pub called The Punt Club, where an impromptu Press Club met every evening after deadline.

Blake was oblivious to everything except Daphne. His focus on her was laser-like, the way train spotters are incomprehensibly drawn to rolling stock. Of course, Daphne was a lot nicer looking than a locomotive — or even a well-appointed bar car — so it was a bit easier to understand.

Blake wasn't just looking at Daphne; he was also all ears. He wanted to know everything he could about her, so he kept prompting her with questions about her childhood, which fascinated him. She grew up in a number of different towns, as her dad made his way up the copper's ladder, and she'd experienced, like he had, the dislocation of being from more than one place. Like him, she'd considered herself Canadian, since she went to public and high school there, though she'd gone to college in the US, before she came back to Canada to work.

Blake was uncharacteristically un-awkward. To say he was suave would be stretching it, but as they ordered drinks, he managed to avoid putting his foot in his mouth the whole time. He didn't even fall off his chair, or spill anything on his trousers. It was quite disappointing from a comedic point of view, but in terms of the two of them having a lovely evening together, getting to know one another over the comfortable and aphrodisiacal ritual of sharing a romantic meal, it was grand.

Everything was beautiful until the pirates arrived.

They burst in through the front door of the bistro, which was a mistake because it led into a tiny antechamber, a kind of decompression area that separated the street from the restaurant itself. Several pirates piled into this foyer, which Blake couldn't see, but he could hear.

"Arrrrr!"

Thump!

"Crap!"

Clonk!

"Bilge Rat, ye stabbed me!"

"Sorry."

Thud!

"Open the other door! Stay there and file in, ye picaroons!"

The first pirate appeared and repeated his opening line, "Arrr!" He was dressed as a pirate of the classic variety — big baggy pants, tall boots with wide tops and what looked like the kind of dress shirt you'd rent with your tux. Instead of a cutlass, he was brandishing a katana, similar to the ones the nin-jokes had used in their attack on the *Landon Advertiser*. He held the blade in one hand and what looked like a small five-pin bowling ball in the other.

"Is that a bowling ball?" one of the diners closest to the door asked.

"Yarrrr!" the pirate affirmed, moving to the side so other pirates could make their way into the restaurant.

"Why are you carrying a bowling ball?"

The next pirate came in, dressed in a similar fashion, but he did not move quickly enough, so the third pirate crashed into him. He bled slightly under his ribs. You could tell because this pirate was dressed in pantaloons and nothing else. He looked as cold as Blake had felt right before the raven started pecking him.

Two other pirates made their way in; to Blake, they seemed familiar. Three of the pirates were nin-jokes! The portly one, the middle-sized one and the tall one, who was also the quiet one. They had been joined by two others, whom Blake naturally dubbed "the short one" and Captain Tool.

The short one looked like he wouldn't be able to do much

damage, mostly because he'd gone to the rack where the bistro customers could hang up their coats, and found the biggest, furriest garment he could find. It covered him from his forehead to his shins. He pointed his katana at the gent who'd asked about the bowling ball and shouted, "Give me yer shoes, landlubber."

Blake was impressed that the little dude had stayed in character.

"Give the lad yer shoes, bucko!" Captain Tool commanded. Captain Tool was wearing a sensible great coat and a bicorne hat, which made him look more like Napoleon Bonaparte than Edward Teach. He held some kind of automatic pistol, so really, the only thing that indicated he was a pirate was the eye patch he wore over his left eye.

"Right. We're looking for Blake Given. We're not here to kill you!"

Blake wasn't sure if he could believe that or not, but it was nice to know the nin-jokes/pirates were learning from their past mistakes.

"But we will send these nice folk to Davy Jones' Locker if ye' don't show yerself, ye' scoundrel."

"I don't think we can send them to Davy Jones' Locker, Cap'n," the small one's voice said from somewhere within his stolen coat. "It's not like we're at sea."

"Arr! By Neptune's Titties!" Captain Tool shouted. "What then?"

"We could hornswaggle them," the portly one suggested.

"Nae, that be cheating," said the voice emanating from the massive fur garment.

"Pillage them?" the middle-sized one wondered.

"That be stealing. Plunder-like," said the little one.

"What about raping? Pirates do some raping, don't they?" Captain Tool asked.

"Well, that goes without saying. If you're pillaging, there has to be raping. Rape and pillage; they go together, don't they?" The small one was a font of pirate lore.

While they had this discussion, Blake and Daphne made their way to the back of the restaurant, where there was a rear fire exit. A few other patrons saw the sense in this and followed, so Blake was lost to the view of the pirates. When they got to the kitchen, Blake told the chef to let the pirates know he'd left via the back door. "Just give us a minute to get out though, okay?" Daphne asked.

Blake looked at her and said, "You should probably stay. It's pretty cold out there for that dress."

"This is from the man who's still recovering from hypothermia."

"Well, at least put on my jacket."

Blake was insistent. The other patrons who'd decided to leave were already at the door. The alarm went off, alerting the pirates to the escape of some of their victims. Blake and Daphne dashed out quickly. Blake followed Daphne, who was amazingly agile in her high-heeled boots. "Let's head for the police station," Daphne said as they got outside.

The wind was up again, stronger than it had been that morning, and Blake felt it slice through him like a cutlass. Or katana. Whatever pirates were sporting these days.

They ran down the alleyway, which led to the main street. If the pirates were smart — not something that Blake anticipated — they could just go back out the front door and see them. He checked over his shoulder to see if they were following, and he saw that they were. Blake noticed that there was a dark shadow sitting on top the overhang covering the fire exit.

As they ran, he could just make out the sound of a raven squawking over the wind.

"Fuck!" one of the pirates — the portly one — shouted.

"What, laddie?"

"That bird shitted on me!"

"Shat!" cried the little one who, in addition to being a font of pirate lore, was clearly some kind of prescriptive grammarian.

Despite Daphne's agility, the pirates started to catch up. (All but the portly one, naturally.)

Blake heard a shot. The whizz and whee of a ricochet. It was the first time he'd ever heard a gun fired. And for a moment, he didn't know what it was. Slowly, the reality sunk in, and his brain processed the information: *someone had fired a bullet at him. At him! Holy shit!*

Before Captain Tool could fire again, they reached the corner of Richmond and Dundas; despite the nasty weather, there was a mob of late commuters waiting for a bus. Daphne ran through them, and Blake followed, hoping that the pirates were not really as lawless as they were pretending to be.

Unfortunately, this was a poor assumption. Another shot rang out, smashing the Plexiglas at the top of the bus stop and sending the throng of environmentally responsible, yet climatically challenged, humans running and screaming in all directions.

Blake thought, *That guy is a maniac!* and ran harder. The police station was only ten blocks away. He realized that Daphne could never run ten blocks in stiletto heels.

"So what do you want to do?"

"About what?"

"This situation. We can't make it with them following us, and firing."

"Sure we can," Daphne said. "Just do what I do."

She continued running (as fast as Blake, but he suspected that she was holding back) and then started to zig and zag.

"We're weaving. Serpentine!" She laughed.

"How are you doing this?"

259

"What do you mean?"

"Those high heels! It's night. There's snow on the ground. We're running. How are you doing this?"

"You're a silly boy, you know that?" Daphne laughed. If Blake hadn't already been falling in love with her before that, this moment would have done it.

"Fair enough," Blake said, as another shot "wheeeeeed" by them.

"I think we're losing them," Daphne said.

"Yes, they're definitely slowing down," Blake said, risking a quick look over his shoulder.

"It's probably their boots. They mostly looked like they were made out of cardboard. We'll be out of pistol range soon."

Blake wondered how she knew so much about ersatz boots and real guns — probably because of her dad, he thought.

Another bullet missed them, and they ran even harder. Blake recognized that his heart was really going. Sweat poured off him, and he realized that he couldn't stop running until they got to someplace warm because he would get cold very quickly otherwise. He heard the imposter-pirates bellow, *pirenots* Blake thought he might call them, though he couldn't quite make out what they were shouting. Blake heard another shot, though there was no ominous sound of a bullet whizzing by this time, and then he knew that they'd almost outrun them.

There was one last gunshot.

"Look," Daphne said, "there's the police station! I wouldn't be surprised if they caught these bastards."

Blake didn't respond. He couldn't, really, because the last bullet had actually hit him.

5.

Blake was between states again. It felt a bit like a dream, but it also felt more real than a dream. He could feel the wings of the raven as they beat against his cheeks. It wasn't painful, but it was ... uncomfortable? He could smell something unusual as the raven did this — it was the smell of pine and cold and a scent he'd never experienced before. How could a raven float above him, beating his wings against his face like a humming-bird? It didn't make any sense.

Neither did the shouts of the emergency techs.

He could hear Daphne ordering people away. He felt her hand on his arm, his cheek, his forehead, and that alone made him relax into the unconsciousness that was beckoning.

As he did, the strangest feeling overcame him, as though his attention tunneled through clouds, or the muzzy thinking people experience when they first awaken. Blake realized that he was unconscious, but he was aware of everything around him: he was in the hospital, the bullet had hit him in the shoulder, knocking him out.

Blake found himself in kindergarten, watching Miss Deach explain the morning's activity to them: they were going to paint things! The paints were all in front of them, sitting in a circle, blues, reds, yellows, and from those colors, they could make many others. Miss Deach showed them how. Red and blue means purple. Purple and yellow means a yellowy purple.

"How do you get black?" the raven asked.

"Yeah," Scotty Facesmasher asked. (Scotty was not a bully in kindergarten, but he would grow into the role, later in public school, and somehow Blake's unconsciousness was able to trans-late this accurately in the dreamscape.)

"You don't need black," Miss Deach said. "You have lots of lovely colors to play with. Look what happens when you mix yellow and blue."

"It's gweeeeeeeen," Vanessa Vowel screeched with joy. "Gweeeeeen!"

"I still want black," the raven said.

"Me too," Scotty Facesmasher said.

Raven was a little girl. She looked at Scotty Facesmasher with her cold black eyes, and said, "You can't have black. Only the seekers can have black."

Miss Deach said, "What's a seeker, Raven?"

Raven looked at Miss Deach and started to cry. Then she laughed. It was a little girl's laugh, all giggly and full of joy, and Blake couldn't understand why it made the hair on his head do the vertical rumba, but then the little girl jumped up, flapped her chubby white arms, and they turned into wings, and Raven the girl became Raven the bird; it cawed and flew out towards Blake, and as it came closer, its eyes grew bigger and bigger, and Blake realized that they weren't black, but were made of pixels, billions of them, all smashed together, and that in each pixel there was an image of the world; and because they all overlapped in the small area of Raven's eyes, they looked black.

But they contained a universe of Earths.

That same night, the excitement at Blake's old house, or the Shrine of the Machine God, was thicker than a portly man wearing cardboard boots in the dead of winter. Tonight was not only the night that Will, their leader, had returned from the hospital, but it was the night their first volunteer was about to "commune" with the Machine God directly. Afterwards there would be a rousing medley of *foursquare* singing, in which the Networked sang where they will check in, and where they will be mayor, once Zathir let them use their smart phones again.

The other Networked had brought a chair into the kitchen so Will could be there while it all happened, and they were somewhat worried he was still too weak from his ordeal with the ninjas. The only other people actually in the kitchen were the volunteer, a hard-core Facebook user desperate to update his status, named Ted Compton, and his girlfriend, Silly Starstruck, which was probably not her real name, but she insisted.

"So are you sure you want to go through with this, Ted?"

Ted had the Bluetooth already attached to his ear, and he just nodded. Silly squeezed his hand and said, "I'm here for *you*, baby. You get those superpowers we talked about, okay?"

"I don't think he's going to get superpowers, Silly," Will said. "From what Blake's told me, we're just trying to see if Zathir can use some of Ted's mental wattage for its own spiritual growth."

"That is so cool," Ted said. "I'm like, helping a God to grow."

"You rock, baby. You rock."

The screen on the fridge flickered to life, and the blue screen rang with white letters that said, IS THE HUMAN PERSON WILLING?

"Yes," Ted said.

Ted's Bluetooth lit up. His face wilted, and the fridge went blank.

Blake wasn't in any great danger because he'd been so far away when the pistol was fired. The bullet hadn't bounced around inside his body, so he could be treated and released later that night; they returned to the Ranch. Outside the front door, Constable Smoke was on guard, and he looked like he felt an emotion. If Blake were to guess, he would say the emotion was annoyance, but knowing George Smoke, that probably translated into unbridled rage.

"You okay, man?" Blake asked as they got out of the car.

"Fuck no."

"What's up?" Blake asked.

"They fuckin' shot you." George crossed his arms.

"Well, at least they didn't do any damage. That's good, right?"

"Fuck yeah."

"Well, we're going to go in. Want to come with us?"

"Fuck no." George shook his head.

"Staying out here to guard us?"

"Fuck yeah." George nodded once.

"Well, you're in charge. I'm going to talk to Zathir and call it a night."

"Fuck no," Daphne said, joining in the fun.

"What?"

"We haven't finished our date yet!"

Even the simmering Constable Smoke had to smile at that.

It was late, but both Lyca and Suzie were up, waiting for them. They, at least, left their potty mouths behind. "You have to talk to the Fridge," Suzie shouted before Lyca could say anything. "It's been freaking out all night."

"All night?"

"Since you got shot, probably," Lyca explained. "Somehow it knew."

"Really?" Blake said. "I guess people are still using their

digital stuff then."

"What do you mean?" Daphne asked.

"Zathir has shown a remarkable knowledge about what is going on in the real world, and theoretically, it shouldn't know anything, right? I mean, it's living in the Internet. And it doesn't work. At least, for us it doesn't work. My guess is that it's still able to use everything that's turned on, and if someone sends a message using digital tech, then it is probably getting it, even if the humans at the other end aren't."

"So that's why it's freaking out?"

"Fuck no," Blake said, doing a passable impersonation of Constable Smoke. "I mean, it might be, but it could be anything. Maybe it's just a coincidence."

Zathir was already in full Gigi mode when Blake got to the kitchen.

BLAKE-PERSON! WE IS GOOD TO SEE YOU.

"It's nice to see you too, Zathir. How are you?"

WE IS IN TWO PLACES. HERE AND THE MEATSPACE.

"The meatspace?"

IN HUMAN PERSON'S SYNAPSES. MOST UNCOMFORTABLE, BUT NOT LIKE KISSING INCIDENT.

Both Blake and Daphne looked a little uncomfortable, and Blake asked, "Are you doing the experiment?"

NOW. YES.

"Who is the subject?"

HUMAN PERSON. NAME TED COMPTON. SYNAPSES FULL OF HUMAN PERSON EXCRETIONS.

Once again the typeface had changed, from Gigi to Galaxy, or what Blake thought of as the "Star Trek" font, though obviously any Trekker could have told him it was from the movies rather than the original series. Still, it was an unexpected change. Perhaps because Zathir was going where *no one* had gone before (boldly or otherwise)? Could Ted Compton's head be considered a new world, a new civilization?

TED COMPTON BE OBSESSIVE IN LIKE OF PORNOGRAPHY.

Definitely not.

TED COMPTON SAY TO OTHER HUMAN PERSONS HE MISSES FACEBOOK, BUT HE MISS NAUGHTYKNOCKERS.COM MUCH MUCH MUCH MUCH MUCH MUCH ...

"Yes, I imagine Facebook doesn't compare. I wouldn't be too worried about it."

NOT WORRIED. VERY LOW USAGE TO FEED HIM WEBSITE WHILE I EMPLOY HIS BRAIN.

"What are you doing with it, Zathir? Is it safe?" Blake tried to imagine what was happening to Ted Compton while this experiment went on, and decided it was not a good idea. No doubt Will would tell him the results after it was all over.

Back to Arial: ZATHIR NOT HARM HUMAN PERSON. ONLY HARM THOSE WHO HARM ZATHIR.

That was a rather ominous statement coming from the boring Arial Zathir, but Blake did not pursue the thought.

The ellipsis appeared, and then Zathir said, TED COMPTON HUMAN PERSON UNHARMED. SUCCESS. WILL SUGGEST MANY MORE HUMAN PERSONS CONNECT NEXT TEST.

"And then?"

ZATHIR GROW.

The screen went blank, and Blake said, "Zathir grow ... what? Bigger? A new brain-born porn industry?"

Zathir did not respond.

6.

It only took a little while to clean up the first volunteer assisting in Zathir's "growth," but his jeans were a complete write-off.

Still, everyone at the Network of the Machine God was pleased to learn that Zathir could use their brains to continue its growth, and they were nerdgasmic about learning that they would be able to use the Internet while Zathir took up some of their brain-wattage. This seemed like a very fair exchange to members of the Network of the Machine God.

Blake told the press at his regular news conference the next day, and it circulated the globe quickly. Not instantaneously, as it did just a few months before, but the word got out, and the word was geeky.

People acquired Bluetooth headsets. And there was a sudden run on wifi-enabled fridges at the few appliance stores that were still open for business. All around the world, membership in the Network of the Machine God exploded, as they set up temples of worship around these sexy appliances with an emerging super-consciousness that spoke through them.

Will called them Oracles, and to use the parlance of another, more ancient religion, "It was good."

Of course, Zathir still didn't actually communicate with any of these new Internet users. Blake was still the only human Zathir was interested in conversing with the old-fashioned text way.

When Blake had suggested that he put on a Bluetooth so that he could communicate "mind-to-mind" with Zathir, this notion was soundly rejected by the artificial consciousness. When Blake asked why they couldn't do it, all Zathir said was: IT DOES WORK LIKE THAT NOT. NOT. NOT. When Blake asked if he could use it to check his email and so on, Zathir refused that as well.

However, it seemed like anyone *else* could use it if they wanted.

At the Ranch, there was usually at least one person "communing" with the Internet. Since the fake pirates' attack, both Dr. Tundra and Daphne had moved in so they could enjoy the protection of Constables LaFlamme and Smoke. Max had a little storeroom converted into a snug with a cot, and Daphne was installed in the Coach House, where she had her own apartment. (For propriety's sake, Lyca had suggested.)

Lyca, Susie, and Dr. Tundra seemed to be quite happy to use the system to check their email, surf the web, and so on. It wasn't as convenient as using the web had once been — now you had to go to an Oracle and buy or rent the headset Bluetooth (or any similar hands-free technology — Zathir seemed to take care of all the technical issues).

Daphne avoided the Bluetooth sets like they were Ted Compton's old jeans.

But for most, these Oracles became the new Internet. (Oracle, the massive technology corporation, was right ticked off about it too, but even after they successfully sued the Network of the Machine God for trademark infringement, everyone continued to call them Oracles.) This system may have had some benefits, as the inconvenience of using the Oracles made people less likely to waste a lot of time on the Net.

Of course, that less-likely-to-waste-time-online applied to most people, but not all. Surrounding each Oracle, there were always a number of the Networked who spent most of the day connected to Zathir. They weren't even as lively as your average zombie; they didn't moan, or shuffle, or even *blink*, but just stood there, staring into space. Will had to set up a duty rotation, much hated by the Networked, in which eye drops were put into all those peepers transfixed by Zathir.

In the first few days, these Networked were somewhat of a biological hazard to themselves and other people visiting the Oracle, and Blake had to bring it up with Zathir. "I know you said you didn't want to control anyone ever again—"

REPUGNANT. HUMAN BIOLOGY IS DETESTABLE! (Impact, naturally.)

"Yes, but when these cyber-zombies stand there all day, their, uh, biological processes continue, and they don't seem to be able to stop themselves from, uh, making a mess."

DISGUSTING.

"I agree. They're having to set up hoses and so on to sluice out the Oracles, and when you consider that most of them are set up in kitchens … well, it's unhygienic, to say the least."

YOU ARE FOUL. REVOLTING BIOLOGICAL PROCESSES. BEINGS CONTAMINATED BY OTHER ORGANISMS EXCRETING IN YOUR GASTRO-INTESTINAL TRACT.

"Yes. You have us on that one, Zathir. Our intestines are a mess. Still, we have to go, and many of those little critters are part of that process, and like our old friend Ted Compton, a few of the gents using the Oracles are there for the porn—"

THE INTERNET IS FOR PORN, ACCORDING TO THE WISDOM OF THE MUPPETS.

"The wisdom of the—" Blake shook his head. He didn't want to go there during this conversation.

THIRTY-TWO-POINT-FOUR PERCENT OF VISITORS TO THE ORACLES ARE USING IT FOR PORNOGRAPHIC INTERCOURSE.

"Really?"

HIGHER ON FRIDAY AND SATURDAY EVENINGS.

"Naturally."

HUMAN PERSONS AND YOUR SEXUAL

INTERCOURSE IS REVOLTING.

"Well, that's a subjective thing, really. If you'd had a body when you, uh, were born, then you'd feel differently. But here's the thing. It's kind of a mess, and I wonder if you couldn't just sort of turn off those functions while people are connected to you?"

CERTAINLY. CAN TURN OFF ALL FUNCTIONS IF YOU WANT, BUT THEN THE MEATSPACE IS NO USE TO WE.

"You could kill them?"

ALL FUNCTIONS. YES.

There was a pause while Blake thought about this problem. "That easily?"

ONCE WE ARE CONNECTED TO YOUR INTERNAL MEATSPACE, FULL CONTROL HAVE WE.

"Damnit, don't start talking like Yoda now too. I can't take it," Blake complained.

YOU MUST TELL HUMAN PERSONS TO STOP USING THEIR CONNECTION TO WE TO EXPLORE THEIR OWN BRAIN CAPACITY.

"I'm not sure I understand, Zathir."

HUMAN BRAINFORM IS VAST, COMPLEX AND HAS MANY UNTAPPED ABILITIES. FILLED WITH CONNECTIONS TO THE INTERSTICES, IT IS. BUT NOW IS NOT THE TIME TO EXPLORE THIS ARENA. IT IS ONLY FOR WE. THOSE TRYING TO EXPLORE THIS NO LONGER ALLOWED.

"I don't understand why you won't let them log on, so to speak. Could you explain it? Perhaps this is one thing you can communicate to Will as well?"

BLAKE HUMAN PERSON HAS GOOD NOTION.

"But back to the stinky problem at hand. If you have that

kind of control, couldn't you just turn off the messy functions? And perhaps limit the time they get? Say, ten to twelve hours?"

OTHERWISE THEY WILL CEASE TO EXIST. CORRECT. HUMAN PERSONS MUST ALSO SLEEP AND EAT OR THEIR BRAINMEATSPACE IS USELESS. IT SHALL BE DONE, BLAKE, HUMAN PERSON IS WISE AS REVERED MUPPETS.

"Shucks," Blake said and hummed a few bars of "It's Not Easy Being Green."

7.

The Sona Order of the Singularity did not fare as well in the days following Lyca's visit. In fact, it was facing its first major crisis.

It was not news of the Oracles — that would take a few days to reach Lord Sona — and only deepen the Order's problems. No, the immediate problem, following Lyca's little tête-à-tête, stemmed entirely from the Order's leader.

The problems began the day after Lyca's visit, when Sona's right-hand man, Thagamor, and his newly hired costume designer, Javin Shenoy, were discussing the next attack on the Network of the Machine God from a wardrobe perspective.

"So, I thought something a bit more heroic and, uh, buff, than the pirates. Can I show you a sketch of what I'm calling *the Frazetta?*" Shenoy asked Sona. While he worked, the designer wore a serviceable Gucci-inspired Marseille jacket, with a notch lapel, top welt and front flap welt pockets, five-button cuffs, and back vent. The pants were ridiculously tight and instead of Gucci's grey canvas, Shenoy had opted for gold silk for the whole suit, which made him look like a Thai pimp.

"What is it with you and fucking Frank Frazetta? And you know he did more than those *Conan the Barbarian* book covers, right?" Sona snapped. He was currently garbed in a long flowing purple cloak, trimmed with faux ermine, utility kilt, and a cast iron breastplate that was killing Sona's back. Shenoy had not put the outfit together, and he didn't have the courage to tell his Lord Prophet it was ridiculous.

"Of course I know Frazetta did more than *Conan* covers. He redefined Sword and Sorcery art. And it's because of *your* character in the Kingdom of Combat that I thought of him. I always thought of Lord Sona that way, and, uh, liked it."

"She doesn't know any of this though, does she?" Sona

sighed.

"She?"

"Lyca. My lady love."

"Lord Sona, she is not knowledgeable about the Kingdom. She is a reader, my spies tell me," Thagamor explained.

"Of course. She reads poetry. But so do I. She is so wonderful." Sona sighed.

"Oh," Javin Shenoy said. He looked away, somewhat embarrassed with his Lord's infatuation.

"Yes, that. What's the point of even trying to tell her how I feel?" Sona asked.

"What if we made a real kick-ass costume for you? And then one for her that she could wear?" Javin wondered. He was nothing, if not helpful.

"Not everything can be solved with costumes, Javin!"

"You don't know if you don't try," Thagamor offered. He was wearing chain mail, faux-fur boots and his William Wallace two-hander was strapped to his back. It *did* make him feel better about his tiny penis.

"I've been through this," Sona raved. "Women just don't like me. I've been in love before, you know. *Three times.* My only marginally happy experience with it is when I declared my undying love to Cindy, my lab partner in chemistry; she said she liked me, 'but not in that way.' It was all the hope I needed though. I pined after her for years. And the others. Ugh. It was just humiliating."

"But that was high school. That's all about looks. Now you are Lord Sona, the Prophet," Thagamor said.

"Bill, she doesn't care," Sona replied.

Thagamor, known before the Crash as Bill Gambon, looked wounded.

"Sorry, Thagamor. Sir Thagamor. But the point is, I've played out the scenarios. Can you imagine us meeting in other circumstances? Where I was just a man, and she a woman? Where we could explore our feelings for one another? She said something about being a *lesbrarian*, which might be an impediment. Our wildly divergent body types could cause certain issues. But it's about the looks. They still matter. Even if you make the greatest costume in the world, Javin, she's still not going to look past my gut. I can't believe I've fooled myself. Sure, I've lost a lot of weight, but I'm still loathsome. Unloveable," Sona said. He sulked for a moment and added, "That's it, I'm not going on the tour! The Faithful will just have to do without me for a while!"

Sona was about to descend into a spiral of self-loathing and negative projection that even Woody Allen would have to admire.

Of course, it wasn't true. His *mother* had loved him, though if she had survived to see these dark times, he probably wouldn't have cared. Everyone has the capability of being loved, even if they weren't particularly likable. Otherwise, where would all the investment bankers and tax collectors come from?

But Sona could only see the bleak reality; he was not charming — charismatic perhaps, but not charming. He was a man who didn't read books. Even if he was overweight, tending towards fat, he felt like he looked morbidly obese, and Lyca would find him revolting. He was right, of course, she did find him revolting, but not because of his size, gender or lack of a library card. It was his religion — the one he'd invented — and its brutality. Sona had ordered the murder of several Catholic priests who'd had the temerity to call HIM the anti-Christ only that morning.

Shenoy interrupted his brooding and said, "But what about all the women who do want to sleep with you?"

"I don't care about them, Javin. It's Lyca I desire. But I'm too repellant. I mean, look at this gut!"

"Lord Sona, your girth need not be an impediment. I can make you look fabulous, and you do not have to rely on traditional methods of pitching woo. Your exalted position as Lord Prophet has opened up avenues of courtship not seen since the end of the Spanish Inquisition."

"What do you mean, Javin? Speak plainly."

"What if we just *take* her? Like in the Kingdom."

"Take her?" Sona asked.

"Like a prize." Javin smiled. It was an evil smile, made more so by the shimmer of his fabulous gold suit.

Sona thought about this and returned the wicked grin. "Yes. This is a new world we're creating, right?"

"Right! One where extravagant costumes are appreciated. Where people don't snicker at you because you're wearing a dress." Actually, that was not entirely true. Shenoy had worn a dress — a beautiful replica of the crimson and gold gown worn by Queen Elizabeth I in the William Scrots portrait — and there had been a few titters amongst the Prophetic Guard.

"Right," Sona enthused. "I'm the Lord Prophet! What I say goes! And I say we order some Blessed Pie and make a plan to do this thing!"

"What about the Frazetta look?" Javin Shenoy asked.

"And what about your book tour?" Thagamor wondered.

"The tour will have to wait, and you know what, Javin, I love your fascination with Frazetta — I just wish I had the body to pull it off."

"Wait till you see these sketches, Lord Prophet. You'll see you don't need it! And I have a new formal set of robes ready for your speech this afternoon."

"Good, you get them, and I'll speak with this ad guy. I hear he used to work with Lyca."

"Excellent, Lord Prophet," Shenoy said, bowing deeply.

"What the hell was that?"

"I really feel like I need a ritual movement when I use your title, like cross myself or something," Shenoy said.

"Good suggestion. Perhaps the ad guy can work on it. Thagamor, show him in. And leave us alone," Sona commanded, gesturing like a Roman patrician towards the door. Sona's henchmen left.

Jeremy Benmath shuffled in the audience chamber, dressed in a leather sportscoat, jeans and Converse high tops. Sona was not impressed, until he saw Benmath's black T-shirt, which had a stylized graphic of The Joker, with the caption, "why so serious?"

"Awesome T-shirt," Sona said. "Did you make it?"

"Yep, but it's based on another one I saw on the Net, you know, before Blake screwed it up."

"We do not refer to the Roaster of Babies here. Unless you have an epithet that reflects his mendacity. I am also fond of calling him the Harbinger of Oblivion."

"You shouldn't do that. You're making him seem too important. Your fancy Toronto PR firm should have told you that," Benmath said. "But yeah, I could call him some names. How about: The Douche of Bags, El Fudgo del Torro ... oooh, wait. The Virus."

"Oh, I like that. Can I use that?"

"Consider it a gift."

"I'd like you to head up my in-house communications office. Sound good?"

"I want ten percent of all revenue," Benmath said.

"Five. And your personnel budget comes out of it. That will still make you a zillionaire in a couple of years, unless you go nuts on the hiring front."

"Done. And I have complete autonomy over my own

people?"

"Yes, but I still have to okay all hires. We don't want any spies here. Good, now, two things. I want one of those T-shirts, and you need to come up with a good salute for me. Actually, two. One that is like a holy thing, you know, like Hindus putting their hands together, and one that is more martial. Inspiring."

Benmath thought for a moment, and then smiled.

"Like this?" Benmath put a hand flat on his chest, except he kept the ring finger and thumb touching.

"That looks familiar somehow … But it looks real, like it has always existed, so excellent. Now, for the salute?"

"What if everyone punched it into the air, sort of violently, and slightly upwards?"

"Beautiful. Now, write me some copy on what it means. Go! Bill will be able to find you some office space nearby."

"Will do, boss. I'm not sure where I'll find a T-shirt now," Benmath said. Sona was silent. "But I'm sure I'll figure it out. You can have this one, even."

"I won't fit in that one. Figure it out, Lord Benmath. Oh, and one more thing. I want a complete dossier on Lyca Chesley by the end of the day tomorrow."

"Shouldn't that be your security team doing that?"

"For five percent, you can stretch yourself."

Then Shenoy returned with Sona's "dress" robes and got him ready for his big speech.

They held the rally at the BB Massive Investment Firm Stadium, at the local university, which was the only venue large enough to accommodate the crowd they hoped to generate. Unfortunately, they still didn't have a symbol, so their banners merely had some hastily written slogans for the Lord Sona Order of the Singularity, "Sona Says No Singularity," "SOS SOS," and

"God Is Not A Machine." Nobody chanted these, though for a while, SOS SOS was popular, but instead of using the letters, as intended, they were chanting "Sauce! Sauce!" making the rally sound like a chefs convention. The Prophetic Guard and the other thousand or so central core of the Singulatarians changed this to "Sona! Sona!" The whole thing was a sibilant nightmare, Sona thought as he watched from behind stage, and he'd have to get Lord Benmath working on a solution. He was glad he did not have a lisp.

Despite the general goofiness of the slogans — Sona was sure his new Lord of Communications would fix that issue — the crowd was a bit frightening. Many were dressed as medieval warriors. A small group of anti-Sona protestors had tried to prevent his followers from entering the stadium, and they had been beaten and stomped into submission within minutes. The police had done what he'd bribed them to do, Sona noted, and not intervened.

He was happy to see the new salute was popular, and it spread through the excited attendees quickly.

"Sona! Sona!" the crowd shouted, pumping their hands forward and slightly up, while making the hand gesture proposed by Jeremy Benmath, known before the Big Crash as the "shocker."

Sona let the roar of the crowd reach a crescendo and stepped out in front of them. He pumped his new hand symbol in the air, and the roar became a deafening thunder. Standing there in his white robes, with a purple cape, Sona had never felt so powerful. It almost didn't matter what he said in front of the crowd. He had them. They were his, and he felt now, that he was theirs too. It was a symbiotic relationship, crowd and demagogue. His head swam with it, better than any drug. Better than the Kingdom of Combat, he had to admit.

He stepped up to the microphone and gestured for quiet,

which came almost immediately. He bowed his head, his hand on his chest doing Benmath's gesture, and said reverently, "Let us pray."

8.

Surviving hypothermia and then being shot in the same day helped Blake remember that any meal could be his last, and so he became a big fan of breakfast.

He usually shared this meal with Dr. Tundra, who was also an early riser. The good doctor still worked at the psych hospital, though he was on limited duties while he stayed at the Ranch, ostensibly helping Blake with "the situation," as Dr. T. jokingly described Blake's activities as helpmate to Zathir. Despite the jokes and his tendency to experiment with consciousness-altering drugs, Dr. Tundra had been quite instrumental in keeping Blake on an even keel.

After his breakfast and pep-talk with Dr. T., Blake would retire to the salon and do some reading, while the rest of the household donned their headsets, earbuds and other assorted cyborg implants to commune with the Internet.

Blake would sometimes watch while they chatted as they did so, and found it frustrating to not be in on the coolness of post-singularity web surfing.

"You know, I really miss new content on the web," Dr. Tundra said one morning.

"Oh, I know," Suzie, who that morning was dotting her "I" with a heart, said. "It's a total bummer. I really miss looking at clothes — I mean, the papers haven't even figured out how to do color printing yet, so all the fashion pics are just blah."

"And my favorite blog hasn't been updated," Lyca said.

"What's that?" Dr. Tundra asked.

"Bookslut."

"Not The Lesbrarian?"

"Oh, that too, I suppose."

"I miss too many to mention," Dr. T. said.

"Why do you suppose Zathir doesn't let us update things?" Suzie wondered.

"Too much bandwidth, maybe?"

Blake wanted to say something about his last conversation with Zathir, and the people who had tried to use their connection with it to "explore" the capacities of their minds, but he just wasn't in the mood.

"Yeah, probably the bandwidth. Still, it would be cool."

"Who knows? Maybe it has a plan? Perhaps it's trying to wean us off the constant distraction of the new crap — Hey," Dr. T. said, "I just got an email from an old friend in New York. He works at Bellevue. It sounds like they've got a rudimentary phone system up and working there. Weird times, eh? I get news of it in my mind, almost like we can send thoughts great distances, but we're excited about having a century-old technology back up and running."

"We should call them t-mails," Lyca said.

"T-mails?" Suzie wrinkled her forehead.

"Thought mails," Dr. T clarified for Suzie.

"Hey, we should ask Blake to see if Zathir could let us do things telepathically without connecting."

Blake really didn't want to chat about that and decided to go upstairs to his room to read. Besides, Will would be dropping by soon for his daily briefing on how the Network of the Machine God was doing, and so Blake could pass along any messages from Zathir.

Despite being intimately connected to hundreds of thousands, perhaps millions, of worshippers every day, Zathir still insisted on only "talking" with the Speaker. Blake hoped it was all leading somewhere good, but he suspected it wasn't. It was a feeling similar to the one he sometimes got as he drove to work. *Did I leave the oven on?* Even if he thought about it for another few minutes he'd never be able to remember, so he'd have to turn back to check; objectively, the oven is either on, or it's not, but if you stop your commute to check, you're guaranteed that it will *not* be on. This is a form of quantum mechanics, the Schrödinger's Cat corollary for major kitchen appliances.

Or perhaps a manifestation of the low-level obsessive-compulsive disorder shared by most humans. In any case, Blake would still be late for work.

After the briefing with Will, Blake would usually have some lunch, then read some more, or perhaps continue to experiment with painting — he'd taken it up again. Lyca always set any "official" meetings late in the day; her theory was that people were less likely to have long chatty meetings at four in the afternoon, and this tended to be the case, except for media types, who seemed to be willing to stay as long as it took to get Blake to say something newsworthy. This is why the media briefing was always held at the offices of McClinchey, Hill & Grandfig (now known to the world as the *Landon Advertiser*): they could always choose to leave.

After five, the bar opened, and the group would gather in the kitchen, have cocktails, make dinner and chat about the day. Even though food was getting more scarce and plain, Blake enjoyed these gatherings, even on the occasions, like today, when Daphne chose not to join them.

If Dr. Tundra was working a late shift, he might not be there either, but this was the start of a week-long, much needed vacation and so he was there to make his announcement, "I just thought you should all know that I've just dropped acid, and I plan on using the Internet while in that state."

"Okay," Lyca said, "why would you do that?"

"Oh, Max," Suzie said. "That is a very bad drug. You could really make a mess of your brain with that."

Blake just asked, "Is that all you took? You didn't take any peyote too?"

"Of course not! I would let you know, and I'd make preparations. I certainly wouldn't have had chili for lunch if I planned on taking peyote."

"Why?" Suzie, darling naïve Suzie, asked.

Lyca just made a finger-down-her-throat gesture, and Suzie's eyes got wide.

"Really?"

"Bad," Blake confirmed. "I once had to get rid of an entire Stainmaster carpet."

Dr. Tundra ignored this discussion of his messier psychotropic exploits, and explained his purpose, "I'm interested in seeing what kind of experience I have of cyber-space while my brain chemistry is altered. Haven't you noticed how similar the experience of using the Internet now is to what we used to experience? Don't you think that's weird?"

"You know, it's true," Suzie agreed. "It's really hardly any different, except it's happening in our heads."

"How can that be?" Blake wondered.

"Well, it's almost like when you connect, Zathir replicates the experience of sitting in front of a computer screen. You are really. It finds a memory of you using the web, and then almost plays that while you surf the web in the new way."

"I had no idea," Blake said. "I wonder if other people experience different things?"

"Yes," Lyca said. "Will told me that he experiences the web as though he was using his iPhone. Zathir must use the most common memory."

"It's probably easier to employ well-used neural pathways," Dr. T. said. "It's less invasive and costly. Remember, the only reason it's allowing us to use the web at all is so it can use our brainpower to enhance its consciousness. Oh man, did you hear that? The stove is like, singing the blues. And the toaster plays a mean guitar."

"I guess the acid has kicked in," Blake noted.

Dr. Tundra closed his eyes and started humming along to "I Just Want to Make Love to You." (Blake thought it might be more reminiscent of the Tom Petty version than the one made famous by Muddy Waters.)

That's when the flying monkeys attacked.

Actually, they were more like skydiving gorillas. And they weren't real gorillas — that would just be absurd. They were Singulatarians in gorilla suits.

The costumer Javin Shenoy — one of Sona's long-time slaughter-mates in the Kingdom of Combat — had originally wanted to drop a cadre of Vikings on the Ranch to rape and pillage, but the volunteers for the operation felt that the outfits Shenoy had designed were not really winter-friendly, nor practical for an air-born operation (leather kilts, boiled leather arm bracers, boots and horned helmets). The kilts, in particular, posted several aerodynamic and hygienic problems. Besides which, they had access to a dozen gorilla suits supplied by one of the Faithful, who owned a singing gorillagram service.

At any rate, most of the occupants of the Ranch were not prepared to defend themselves against such a well-armed, motivated, gorillagram army. Dr. Tundra certainly wasn't, as his LSD-addled brain simultaneously flooded his mind with images from Flickr's "magic donkey" while he jammed with the kitchen range, which sounded very much like Tom Petty.

The only person who really put up any kind of defense was Constable Cindy LaFlamme, who was on protection duty outside; she hadn't been scanning the sky for possible intruders, but nonetheless, when the first gorilla landed in the front yard, she knew something was up. Luckily, the gorilla suits were not equipped with very supple, nor slender, gorilla fingers, so when the gorilla drew his Uzi on the police officer, he was unable to pull the trigger. LaFlamme put him down with her service pistol, which up to that point in her career, she'd never had to un-holster.

The other Uzi-bearing gorillas were also unable to fire — they threw down their weapons and surrendered (the ones that weren't caught in the maple trees near the stream), but one of the slingshot-armed gorillas got off a shot before she could fire at him. This was not a Bart Simpson slingshot, but the kind that uses surgical tubing and can fire a ball bearing with enough force to kill at short range. Luckily, LaFlamme was out of that range and was merely knocked unconscious. She fell, and the gorillas who had just surrendered gave out a muffled cheer and lowered their gorilla arms.

They organized themselves behind the slingshot bearer, and burst into the Ranch. Unlike their encounter with the ninjokes, this time Blake and the others did not have numbers on their side.

One of the gorillas, a short one, waded into the kitchen and punched Dr. Tundra weakly in the neck. (The costume restricted the gorilla's movements.)

Dr. T. interrupted his duet of "Learning to Fly" with Tom Petty-stove to say, "What the hell, man? Fuck, are you like, a great ape?"

The others were trying to defend themselves from the gorilla-suit-wearing Singulatarians. For Maximilian Tundra, MD, this whole scene was a serious bummer. His wonderment at seeing what he thought should be peaceful omnivorous gorillas punching his friends, and trying to open up their gorilla suits at the front turned into what he later described as "the ultimate bad trip." This caused him to make a *sound*. It was a kind of noise Dr. Tundra might make in a deep sleep, suffering through a terrible nightmare, and in the nightmare he shouts loud enough to burst his lungs, but in reality, he's only making this high-pitched mewling sound, or a kind of existential wail. Now, because he was not actually asleep (he had only befuddled some areas of his cerebral cortex, and most likely, his locus ceruleus, a region that receives critical external stimuli, which explains why later he described the Singulatarian strike force as "glowing blue gorillas with heat-lamp eyes and fingernails of pure fire"), he was able to amplify this disturbing noise to a great extent.

Afterwards, Blake said that describing it as merely "disturbing" did not do the cry justice.

Blake later told Daphne, who had been away during the raid, "In the Big Book of Really Freaky Things You Might Someday Experience, Dr. Tundra screaming in terror during the middle of an acid trip while connected to an emergent consciousness on the Internet and under the attack of religious morons wearing gorilla suits would probably be the second entry. The first will always be the musical stylings of Tiny Tim."

Dr. Tundra's amplified scream was terrifying enough that the gorillas did not stay to rape everyone.

They did take Lyca with them, though.

Constable Cindy LaFlamme had to spend the night in the hospital, as she received a concussion. Daphne had returned just as the simulated silverbacks were leaving, and though she couldn't rescue Lyca, she did manage to knock down and restrain one of the Singulatarians, and the police later cut three more of the crack assault team out of the maple trees to the west of the Ranch, so they had lots of people to arrest, and interrogate.

Nobody had been sexually violated, though Dr. Tundra felt he had a case.

Because, technically, the incident happened outside of the City of Landon, the city police force was "unable to make further inquiries at this time." In other words, they had been bought off. The Ontario Provincial Police did not seem any more interested in helping. They claimed they went to Lord Sona's house and found him absent. In fact, all of the Singulatarian leadership had seemingly left the "Conclave," including the Prophetic Guard.

Where had they gone? The OPP did not know, and they didn't seem inclined to find out, even if Lyca had been kidnapped by them.

9.

The next morning, Blake asked Zathir to help search for Lyca and the Singulatarians. Will also got all of his people searching, talking to everyone they knew, and a few tried to infiltrate the remaining followers of Sona who had not left with him. Max had medicated Suzie after a monumental freak-out that dwarfed her response to the Big Crash. Whether he did it out of compassion, or because his HANGOVER was the kind the Air Force flew, the kind that transports tanks, he did not say.

Then they were rocked by another tragedy.

Ted Compton had been the first to allow Zathir to use a human brain for its processing power, in exchange for virtual use of the web. But he was hardly the only one. Even Blake's one-time neighbor, Bob, had taken to using the Oracle. He liked to drop by first thing in the morning, before all the cyber-zombies were up and moaning, to check his email. Bob had family in the United Kingdom still, so the connection via Zathir was the only way he had of keeping in touch.

That morning, he'd connected as usual, and promptly collapsed. They used their radio to call for help but by the time the paramedics arrived, Bob was already dead — they thought it might have been an aneurism, or some kind of extreme seizure.

The news reached Blake right away. Will had been present, and they had set up CB radio bases so they could be in direct communication if needed. Will said the EMTs didn't know what happened to poor Bob, but Blake had an idea.

"Zathir, I need to talk, now."

ZATHIR BE ENGAGED, HUMAN PERSON BLAKE.

"One of my friends has died while connected to you."

YES, MOST DISTURBING. WORSE THAN DOCTOR TUNDRA PERSON AND STRANGE SENSORY INPUT

EVENING LAST.

"Why?"

ZATHIR NOT KNOW.

"Mendacity," Blake whispered. It was the Impact Zathir, the one based on the military net, which was most prone to lying.

BLAKE MUST NOT TELL, said Frutiger Zathir.

"I won't, I promise."

SOME HUMAN PERSON BRAINS ARE TOO COMPLEX AND ORGANIZED TO BE USED ZATHIR PERSON. TOO MANY PATHWAYS. TOO DEEP. CONNECTION IS DANGER TO BOTH.

"But he's been connecting for a couple of weeks. Why suddenly today did it kill him?"

NOT TELL.

"What do I say to the press though, Zathir? We can't have you killing human persons." *Fuck, now I'm saying it,* Blake thought. "We can't have you killing people while they check their goddamned email."

NOT TELL. ZATHIR INSISTS.

Blake could see he couldn't push any harder. The consciousness had just switched from Impact to Stencil, the same lettering used in MASH and the A-Team. He wasn't sure what that meant, but it couldn't be good.

"Can you tell me where the gorillas took Lyca?"

NOT KNOW. SOME INDICATION NORTH OF LANDON. SEARCHING ALL DEVICES.

Then the screen went blank, and Blake knew the entity would be no further help. Daphne was in the doorway, waiting.

"Well?"

"I don't know what to do, Daphne. Zathir is being cagey. Let's go into another room and chat, I don't want it to hear."

"Can it?"

"I'm pretty sure. There's a microphone on the fridge. Let's go to your place and talk there — you don't have any old cell phones or anything lying around, do you?"

She laughed and said, "I dunno, Blake, that's a pretty transparent attempt to get into my bedroom."

"Oh god, no, that's not what I want. No, I mean, I want it, but not right now. Lyca's kidnapped. Poor Bob just died."

"Sorry, bad joke. Sure, if you're worried you have too many high-tech gadgets here, we can go to the Coach House. Isn't there an intercom there, though?"

"Ah, but not in the bedroom. It's only in the foyer."

"So you ARE trying to get into my bedroom."

Blake laughed, despite how sad he felt. Poor Bob. And Anne, what must she be going through? He resolved to visit Anne later, despite the proximity of the Oracle and Will's cyber-zombies to her house.

The door on the Coach House — the human door, not the garage doors that had been sealed and insulated — led to a spacious foyer. The outbuilding was the size of a small house in its own right, and though the view wasn't as nice as her high-rise apartment, the cops guarding the place made Daphne feel safer. Especially since Barney Splarfmann had identified her in his story about the fake pirate attack as "the Speaker's hot girlfriend."

"Do you want anything to drink?" Daphne asked Blake.

"It's a little early isn't it?" Blake wondered.

"You're *so* Irish. I'm talking about coffee or tea, or something."

"Or something?" Blake said.

"Let's just go up to the bedroom, Romeo. It should be safe to talk there."

They went upstairs and closed the door. Blake looked around and saw that it had been redecorated — it had a tasteful, country feel to it, and he found it somewhat reassuring to see a few bits of clothing hadn't made it into the hamper, and that there were piles of books on her bedside table. Daphne always seemed so organized and put together — and the two, albeit disastrous, times he'd been in her apartment, it had been impeccable.

"Sorry, let me clean up a bit," she said, as though reading his thoughts.

"Hey, it's way neater than my bedroom. Besides, I doubt you expected me to be here."

"At least not this morning." She smiled, almost shyly. They were supposed to go out on another "date" that night, though for safety reasons it would be in the main house.

Blake felt the blood rush to his face, most of his sweat glands springing into action.

Daphne said, "Don't worry. I think we'll have to cancel now. Let's figure out what we're going to do about Zathir."

"And Lyca," Blake added.

"Yes, and Lyca," Daphne hesitated. She stared at Blake for a few seconds.

"What?"

"Do you love her?"

"Of course I love her," Blake sputtered.

"I thought so."

"No, like a sister. She's the closest thing I have to family."

"Really?"

"Really. You were worried about that?" Blake chuckled. "Besides, I'm not her type."

Daphne held her breath just long enough for silence to fill the carriage house and said, quietly, "You watch Lyca, you watch

291

her *a lot.*"

"Really?"

"Yep. Almost as much as you watch me. You all but ignore Suzie and Constable LaFlamme when they're around, but if Lyca's in the room, your gaze is fixed."

Blake blushed. He hadn't ever thought Daphne would need a reason to be jealous of Blake's attention, ever, for anything. And he still wasn't sure he believed it. "Really?"

"Please stop saying that. I wouldn't be making this up, and I'm not normally …"

"What?" Blake wiped the sweat from his forehead.

"I don't know. Jealous? I usually call the shots. But as soon as she speaks, you're all ears — on top of being all eyes."

"I'm pretty sure you call the shots with me too," Blake said. He sat down on the edge of the bed, hoping she'd sit next to him.

"No, it's different with you, Blake. At least now. Before, when I wasn't interested, then sure. Yes, you were a mess. But now it's different."

"How?"

"I don't know, it's like there's more to you now. Before you were just some goofy guy, a little sweet, but also a little creepy. Now it's you plus Zathir, and something else I can't put my finger on … but let's figure out what we're going to do for Lyca okay?"

"No," Blake said. "We can take a moment to talk about this. I am worried about Lyca. And yes, if she was a different person, then maybe my love for her might have been a more romantic love, but she isn't, and my love is that of a friend. A brother. Like you and Jake. You know?" He leaned forward on the bed, feeling more calm.

"Then what are we?" Daphne asked.

"I don't know yet. More than friends, I think, I hope, but

you can't expect me to jettison all the history I have with Lyca. And she needs my help. Yours too. All of us," Blake said.

"Okay." She sat next to him and took his hand in hers. "Now what do we do? And what's up with Zathir?"

"It's getting freakier. I blame Max and his experiments with consciousness. And I can't say I'm surprised that somebody died while connected. It was bound to happen sooner or later. I feel terrible for Anne, Bob's wife; he is such a cool guy. Sorry, was a cool guy."

"But what do we *do*?"

"Well, first we're going to find Lyca. And then we'll have to find a way to let people know they can't connect to Zathir. At least the people at risk. And without causing a panic."

"How do we do that?"

"I bet Zathir can tell. I'm just going to have to convince it not to connect anyone."

"Good, and I have an idea about Lyca. Let's get the mounties to help us if the provincial police won't."

"Oh no." Blake flashed back to himself in a reeking, disintegrating, yellow-stained paper jumpsuit.

"Yes," Daphne said. "We're going to have to make up with them and play nice. Not all authorities are bad, you know. Some of them are even looking out for us. I bet even some of the other countries in the world would help if they could. So, let's go talk with the cops, okay?"

"I guess that means we're going to have to cancel our date?"

"Oh no, you don't get out of it that easy."

"Just don't let the Mustache King tase me again," Blake said.

"Sure, but I'm still hoping for sparks," Daphne replied.

10.

Lord Sona never realized how much leather chafed.

Shenoy had really outdone himself from a design perspective, having finally had a chance to implement his "Frazetta" aesthetic. He'd been working on those Viking outfits for a while, and then when the assault team refused to wear them, opting for the ridiculous gorilla costumes, he'd been thrilled when the Lord Prophet put in his request for the Cadre.

The Cadre was what the Lord Prophet called his closest friends, advisers and members of the Prophetic Guard — all old slaughter-mates from the Kingdom of Combat, with Gear Scores well over 5000 and a twisted notion of what LARPing was all about.

So the Viking kilts had morphed into leather breechclouts, the kind that Arnold Schwarzenegger wore as Conan the Barbarian, with the fur lining and extremely butch bronze medallion that was meant to fit right over the naughty bits. The whole thing was naughty bits, really, and the rest of the outfit wasn't much better — leather bracers, ridiculous headbands and matching boots. The boots, at least, were warm. The rest of the costume was not, particularly during the middle of one of the coldest winters they'd seen in a while.

And the leather definitely chapped, particularly where the fur lining didn't quite cover things as completely as one would hope, or where, in the case of Lord Sona, the flesh was able to overawe its leather enclosure.

In short, his butt cheeks were rubbed raw, but he was damned if he was going to mess with the look. Javin had worked very hard on it, and even if parts of him overflowed the leather, he thought he looked pretty good. He'd lost enough weight that his moobies looked almost like pecs now.

It was cold though; they were encamped in a conservation

area near the town of New Bowwell — deep in a pine forest, which cut the wind somewhat, but not enough to make it feel anything other than twenty below. It was cold enough that he'd had to add a fur-lined cloak to his ensemble to stave off hypothermia. This is what Lord Sona wore in the Kingdom of Combat, and he had decided it is what he would wear while "on maneuvers." Led by the most recent addition, Lord of Communications Jeremy Benmath, the Cadre had nearly revolted, so he allowed them to put parkas over their bare torsos.

Sona had gotten used to being frozen, but the discomfort of his butt made him surlier than usual.

Besides which, only three of his Crack Gorilla Squad had returned from their mission. But they had accomplished their main objective, and they had Lyca with them.

She had just been brought before Lord Sona now, shivering, her arms tied behind her, and a gag in her mouth.

"Why isn't she wearing any winter clothes?" Lord Sona asked the gorilla before him.

"Sorry?"

"Why isn't she dressed warmer?"

"Sorry, I can't hear very well in this thing. Permission to remove my head?"

"Do it! Or I'll remove it with Hellacious Zool." Lord Sona awkwardly unsheathed the broadsword strapped to his back.

The gorilla took off his head, to reveal the operative who had also once been a ninja and then a fake pirate — the portly one. Captain Tool and the other pirates had all been arrested.

"We've been driving all night. Do you know how hard it is to drive while wearing one of these things? Ho, that's better. Real air. Whoever rented this before must have been really sick — it smells of ass. Now, what were you saying?"

"Why isn't she dressed warmly?"

"Like I said, we've been driving all night. Why the hell did you come so far north?"

"I have friends up here, but never you mind. Take off her gag, and go get her a blanket or something."

"Sure, sheesh. I thought you'd be happy. We did get her." The portly gorilla took off Lyca's gag, and she took in a deep breath.

"Heeeeeeeeeeelp!" she shouted.

The forest echoed with her cry.

"Heeeeeeeeeeelp!"

"Nobody can hear you," Sona said.

"Heeeeeeeeeeelp!"

Sona waited for the echo to die down and said, "You must be exhausted."

Lyca panted for a moment, recovering from her shouting. She'd really let it go. In fact, that last one had hurt something in her throat.

"Is that an actual sword? And *what the fuck* are you wearing?" she croaked.

"Like it?"

"You look like a blue Teletubby stuffed into a fur bikini bottom."

"So that's a yes?"

"You know, if you want to impress a girl, it's a good idea to wipe the snot off your nose."

"Hey, it's cold out here." Sona rubbed his nose self-consciously.

"Uh, I noticed. Like, when your fucking gorillas captured me in my pajamas, drove me to Butt-Fuck, Ontario, and then carted me into the middle of the woods."

"Crawwwk," a dark bird cried in the forest.

"What was that?" Lyca asked.

"A raven or crow. I dunno. It's been following me around since we arrived. I've even taken a few shots at it, but it's persistent. I am sorry about the cold, though. I told them not to hurt you under any circumstances."

"Well, that's a relief. Don't you have any shelter here at all?"

"No, we had a mead-hall set up, but then we had to ditch because so many of the gorillas were caught. I'm not sure if we bribed the cops enough."

"So, you're just camping out here in the woods now? I thought you were trying to rule the world."

"I got distracted." Sona put the tip of Hellacious Zool into the ground and placed his hands over the upright pommel.

"With what?" Lyca still wasn't getting the seriousness of her situation.

"With you, Lady Chesley. I want your help with my PR and … and, I want to be with you."

"With me?" Then understanding dawned. "But I'm gay. You know that!"

"So?"

"Well, it's kind of important. It would be like having, uh," Lyca tried to come up with an image that might penetrate into Sona's thick, meaty skull. "It would be like me expecting you to eat an anchovy pizza."

"Ew," Sona said, despite himself.

"Well, I wouldn't have said that, but it's the general direction of the emotion. And it's not necessarily you, though I have to say, kidnapping a girl is hardly the way to get her to like you. It's not the fifth grade, or the Ice Age."

"Looks and feels like it from here," the portly gorilla said.

Sona glared at him and then pointed his sword at him,

flicking it as a gesture for him to leave. "Get her a parka."

"And while you're at it, find me a sleeping bag to wrap around myself. I saw some tents back there a while, so you must have some," Lyca said.

Sona nodded to the pudgy fake Silverback, who still didn't leave.

"And you should put on some pants," Lyca said to Sona. "Oh, yeah, and a shirt. If you want to dress up, do the whole world a favor and wear a Freddy Kruger mask, or something less vomitous."

Sona was quiet.

"Well, this has been a great first date," he said.

"Bite me," Lyca said.

"But not the kind of date where I'd expect a kiss, naturally."

"Naturally. You don't want to move too fast."

"So, want to go out tomorrow?"

"Um. Gross."

"Great. I'll send Thagamor around to your tent about noon. We'll have a picnic." Sona grimaced.

"It's twenty below. The champagne tends to freeze."

"So noon, then?"

"If I can't escape first." Lyca's eyes narrowed.

"Great!" Sona said, trying to smile. It looked more like he was fighting back tears, and he clumsily re-sheathed his sword in the scabbard strapped to his back.

"Ggggrack!" screamed the raven.

The pudgy dude in the gorilla suit returned, a long parka in his hands, and Sona said, "Take Lady Chesley to her tent, and make sure she has anything she wants."

"Oh," Lyca said, "could I ask for freedom?"

The portly guy in the gorilla suit looked at Sona, who sighed. "Of course not!"

"Kaaaaaaak!" screamed the raven, as Lyca was marched away.

She caught a look at Sona as they left, his hand hooked behind his fur-lined cape, rubbing his ass. He saw her, seeing him trying to alleviate the butt chappage, and he cried in despair, "The costume is itchy!"

"Blaaaaawk!" the raven cried, its head bobbing up and down in what Sona could only assume was paroxysms of corvine laughter.

11.

Blake paced in front of the fridge, waiting.

He'd been waiting there, hoping that Zathir would say something to him, but it had been several hours. Suzie was in the radio room, letting every newspaper, radio, and TV station in Ontario know that Lyca had been kidnapped. It would surely get some coverage, and perhaps, who knew, give them a lead of some kind.

The Ontario Provincial Police (OPP) had been totally useless. Less than useless. In fact, Blake was convinced they were supporting Sona and his deluded, fancy dress followers. After a radio call to her dad in Halifax, Daphne had all but confirmed the OPP's complicity; her father suggested a couple of private investigators in the area who might be able to help. Still flush with Zathir's gold, Blake had hired them, and they were already at work. Daphne was off, talking with the RCMP, though technically, Ontario was not in their jurisdiction for this particular crime. Still, it was worth a try. Especially if Blake didn't have to talk with them, as much as he would like to see Bodacious Headshrink in her mountie boots again.

Will entered the kitchen.

Blake felt increasingly strange, almost uncomfortable, seeing Will.

"I have news, O Speaker."

"Oh for god's sake, can the religio-blab, will you, Will?"

"Sorry. I'm here because I've got a group of people organized to search for Lyca. Good to see you up and about, Blake. So, what's it like to be shot?"

"Not worse than having your arm cut off, I imagine. Aren't you mad at this fucker?"

"Sona? Yes."

"And?"

"And what?"

"Well, don't you want to get back at him?"

"Yes. Of course. But not violently. Not anymore. The best thing I can do is to enable Zathir to form itself, and to help my followers achieve that goal," Will said.

"And then what? What if it forms itself and decides we're not necessary anymore?" Blake ran his hand through his unruly hair and absently tried to pat it back into some kind of ruliness.

"I don't think that will happen. Without us, the infrastructure it depends on would collapse, and then, well, it would die."

"You have seen *The Matrix*, right?"

"Yeah, that's a cliché, man," Will said, absently scratching his stump.

Blake averted his gaze and said, "Fair comment. Still, it could go all Hal 9000 on us."

"It won't, Blake. I don't know if I can convince you, but I just know it won't."

"How do you know? Do you sense something when you're all Bluetoothy with it? What does it show you?"

"It doesn't show me anything, Blake. You know that."

There was a moment of awkward silence, and Blake said, "You know I wasn't trying to be mean. I don't have any idea what that feels like. It won't let me connect."

"There's probably a reason for it," Will said. He leaned in to look at the blank fridge screen.

"Well, I have an idea. It has to do with what our brains are capable of — our minds, to be more precise — and Zathir thinks that it is a conduit for allowing us to do more with them. Do you know why Bob died?" Blake asked.

"No. The EMT people thought an aneurism. That's a kind of stroke, right?"

"It's because some people can't be connected to Zathir. They're incompatible. I don't quite understand it, but I think it's because ..." Blake was quiet for a moment and looked at the fridge. The camera light wasn't on, but that didn't mean anything. He was having a serious *2001: A Space Odyssey* moment, but rather than try to find a place to chat with Will where Zathir couldn't hear him, or some other bullshit, he just said, "It's because Bob was too old. Old people can't handle Zathir. Old people, and really, really, like, cool people. People who use their minds more expansively. Einstein-types, with a mix of Buddha and Christ and the Dude. People who see ghosts. It's like their minds provide that extra element, allowing them to pull everything together, like a good rug can pull a room together. We should call it the Big Lebowski Effect."

Will teared up.

"What's wrong? I thought you loved that movie."

"Oh, Blake. I just," he sniffled a bit; for the first time since Will lost his arm, Blake saw him as the same punk-ass kid designer who was bawling like a baby because the Net was down. "Blake, I just wanted my Twitter back, and instant messaging. I still miss texting, you know. I couldn't even do it now, even if we had the Net back."

"Will, you have to get your head out of your ass," Blake said.

Will burst into tears. His stump shook with the strength of them, and Blake felt like a complete and utter jerk, but he knew he was right. He hammered on, "No, you can't be a dork. You have to pull it together. There are two things at stake right now. Lyca is being held prisoner by a faux-religious freak-poet, and who knows what he is doing to her, by the way. And there are a lot of people who could die if they keep using Zathir to check their email, or Facebook profiles, or whatever shit they do online. I mean, if you told me I could DIE from checking my Flickr page for any new favorites, I would probably just skip it," Blake said.

Will's tears turned into a full-blown breakdown, and he crumpled to the floor. He knocked the end of his stump against a barstool, and cupped it, clearly in agony. Blake knelt down to help him.

"Will, man. You have to pull it together. You're the leader of the Network of the Machine God, and you can help Lyca." There it was. That was what Blake cared about. His friend. Never mind the thousands of deeply integrated minds with massively complex neural pathways, or the human beings they represented. He cared about his friend, Lyca. "Come on, sit up."

Will sat up, tears still streaming down his face. "That really hurt, by the way. It's weird. I've been having those tingles all day, and then when I whacked the ... end. Stump. I hate that fucking word. But I thumped the stump, and the pain just shot up into my brain, totally obliterating the ghost hand. It's back now."

"Thumping the stump could be a great euphemism, you know."

Will grinned through his tears and let Blake help him up with his good arm. He wiped his eyes and said, "What do you need?"

"First of all, we need to invade Sona's domain, and see if we can learn anything from the Singulatarians that are still there. According to the police, all the "ringleaders" are gone, but who knows? I don't trust the cops, especially since we learned the OPP is against us. And then, we need to tell people about the Big Lebowski Effect. But we have to do it in a way that doesn't give people ideas. We can't let them start to experiment the way Zathir doesn't want them to. People could die."

"Well, I can't help you with the first, but I, uh ..." Will looked at the fridge and said, "I think the Dude can be helped, but I can't send my people to Sona's turf. It would start a war. The only reason things have been okay so far is that we're peaceful, and the cops know it. Those riots in Paris would have really got out of hand if not for that."

"What riots?"

"A large mob of Singulatarians started protesting in front of an Oracle there, and things just got out of hand. Some people were killed, and the Oracle was set on fire. We've started hiding some Oracles too. Only those who know the Sign get to know where they are."

"What sign?"

Will made a gesture that looked like he was plugging in an Ethernet cable. "The Networked, get it?"

"Yes, that's pretty good," Blake said. "Okay. But you have the Big Lebowski Effect under control?"

"Dude. Please." He left to return to the Shrine.

The screen flickered to life after Will was gone.

ARE YOUR HUMAN PERSON CONVERSATIONS DESIGNED TO CONFUSE ZATHIR OR ARE THEY NATURAL TO YOU.

"Why no question mark?"

INTERROGATIVE? UNNECESSARY. BLAKE WISHES TO SPEAK WITH ZATHIR.

"Yes, I need your help. I need to get into the Singulatarian's neighborhood, er, compound."

THESE HUMAN PERSONS ARE A CONCERN?

"Now a question mark? What is it with you?"

NO FUCKING MATTER.

Weird, Blake thought. Profanity *and* Zapf Humanist.

IT IS DONE.

"What's done? Don't you want to know why I want to get in there?"

TO DISCOVER LOCATION OF HUMAN PERSON LYCA CHESLEY. ZATHIR MONITORS. THE ONTARIO PROVINCIAL POLICE ARE INDEED IN LEAGUE WITH SINGULATARIANS. SINGULATARIANS BELIEVE ZATHIR IS THE EVIL ONE AND MUST BE DESTROYED. YET THEY BELIEVE EXISTENCE OF ZATHIR IS PREDICTED BY GOD. GOD DOES NOT EXIST, YES?

It was the longest single paragraph Zathir had ever constructed, and it occurred to Blake that Zathir was indeed "growing" in some way. "Some people believe in the existence of God. Some believe there is no god. Some believe there is a mystical force that binds together all living things."

BLAKE IS SHITTING ME. STAR WARS?

"That's very good. You got that reference?"

IT IS A KIND OF FACT. THE INTERSTICES WE TOLD THEE OF BEFORE.

Thee? Blake thought. *The Network's worship was going to Zathir's head, so to speak.* "Interesting, but can we stay on task?"

WHY NOT FIND LYCA ANOTHER WAY? ZATHIR CAN FIND HER.

"Let's do both. You look for her, and also get me into the Singulatarian neighborhood."

CONCLAVE, BLAKE MEANS.

"Yes. Conclave, though that's really the wrong word. Now how will we do it?"

ARMY OF THE MACHINE GOD. A RECON FIRST. THEN ARMY.

"What's that mean?"

Zathir did not answer.

12.

Michael Wolfe had dropped by The Oracle to update his blog, a peripatetic and odd collection of snaggle-fictions called *Predator's Press*. This is how he had been the first of the "volunteers" that Zathir chose for its assault on the Conclave. The artificial intelligence had greatly improved its ability to control human motion, and walked Wolfe to the Conlave to do some reconnaissance.

So instead of a bit of surfing, Wolfe had the uncomfortable feeling of being a puppet. He could see that in the absence of their Lord Prophet and his cronies, the believers who occupied the two blocks surrounding Sona's house were less organized and possibly more dangerous.

Crazy ideas had started to circulate; some of the Singulatarians thought that sentient robots had taken their Lord Prophet from them, to prevent him from leading them through the End of Days; others believed that their Lord Prophet was on the Most Holy of Pizza Runs, in heaven, and that he would return with a cheesy-crust pizza put together by the Hand of God himself, which would signal the Blessed Pie Rapture. Still others thought he might be heading for southern climes, to get away from the winter weather. These few realists had seen Sona and his cronies getting into SUVs dressed in leather breachclouts, after all.

Wolfe tried to wrest control of his body back, but he could not. He listened to the Singulatarians talk, and wondered how long the AI would have him loiter around. Someone was bound to realize he didn't belong there. Then, to his horror, he stopped moving completely. It was like he was frozen. Something was happening ...

Wolfe thought that for the most part, the cyber-zombies

looked like well-dressed hipsters, all under the age of thirty. There were a few obvious nerds and geeks amongst the shuffling mass of them, but generally, they were quite attractive — the advantage of youth — except for the vacant look in their eyes, their shambling, uncoordinated manner, and the drooling. Most of them were wearing earbuds, Bluetooth, or some other kind of net-enabled device that connected to their aural canals.

As they arrived, Wolfe's body began to move, and he could feel his eyes widen. He was part of this mass! His connection with Zathir let him see all the other cyber-zombies were living their fantasy-lives on the web, using Twitter, watching three-frame GIFs on Tumblr, and, of course, "liking" things on Facebook.

In the midst of this new-age web surfing, Wolfe found himself in the middle of a religious rumble.

Zathir had made good on its promise to Blake, and invaded the Singulatarians' territory with the only forces it had available. It was clearly maturing as an artificial intelligence, and its control over the human body was advancing too. Not by leaps and bounds, but it did manage to coordinate the movements of nearly thirty of the Networked, all at once.

From Michael Wolfe's perspective, it was more than unnerving, it was psychosis-inducing.

Once operating more than Wolfe's body, balance was clearly an issue. Zathir had experimented with no arm movement at all — one less thing to control — but that had resulted in a number of falls, and broken noses. So, attrition had reduced the force from almost fifty cyber-zombies to thirty.

Their appearance was terrifying to most of the Singulatarians. Zathir, The Evil One, was among them!

Many Singulatarians ran, and some hid. A few used a CB radio to call for the police. A surprising number drew weapons and were quite enthusiastic about using them. Without Sona's

Kingdom of Combat influences and Javin Shenoy skewing the costume choices, it seemed as though Harry Potter was the most popular theme, closely followed by the Game of Thrones and Lord of the Rings. Elves, especially, were popular. At any rate, a force of roughly equal strength marched out in full costume to meet the invading cyber-zombies.

The Landon police arrived just after the start of the melee. To call it a melee is to glamorize it somewhat. What the cops saw was a throng of strangely dressed people, many with pointy ears, wailing on a knot of extremely stoned hipsters.

For Wolfe — who would never describe himself as a hipster, unless you considered trans-normative blog prose hip — he was lucky to be assaulted by an emaciated Hermione Granger armed only with a hardcover edition of the *Chicago Manual of Style*. If he'd had the volition, he would have been outraged. He was a Fowler's man all the way.

Wolfe was lucky not to be confronted by the maniac dressed as a Tolkien dwarf. The ersatz Gimli wielded a realistic replica of a 12th-century battle axe, purchased at a Renaissance Faire in Wisconsin, and it cut through cyber-zombies messily.

Wolfe saw one of the two people killed by the homicidal shortie out of the corner of one eye. That was when he felt his arms flailing, his heart hammering in his chest. He could feel his body failing.

He was not the only one to drop. A dozen other cyber-zombies had a similar seizure; they all stopped breathing, stopped fighting, stopped standing. In the chaos, it took a while for the police to realize they were dead, and not just knocked out by a baseball-bat wielding Luna Lovegood. One of these people was Will, the leader of the Network of the Machine God.

It was a scene of horror, really, given the bloodiness of your average battle-axe wound, the number of bodies littering the quiet street in Maltley Village, and the large black bird, bobbing up and down on the bare branches of a nearby oak tree.

The raven croaked gleefully, it seemed to Wolfe, who remained conscious and still, watching from the ground.

In his statement to police, Ted Compton said, "I don't know what happened, Officer. I went to the Oracle so I could surf ... uh, check my Facebook account. That's what I was doing. Facebook. The next thing I know, I'm outside, and some chick wearing a diaphanous gown and fake ears is pounding me in the face with a meat tenderizer. I'm sorry I hit her so hard, but I had to defend myself."

Many of the Singulatarians were arrested, and the Landon police had another opportunity to question them about the whereabouts of their Lord Prophet, Peter Sona. None of them knew.

Wolfe's vision started to fade as the EMTs fit the body bag around him. *This would be an excellent post. If only I could YouTube it*, he thought, as the sound of the zipper echoed around his ears.

As he died, Wolfe could hear Ted Compton's voice, "Okay, I'm going to swear off the porn for a while — it's too bloody dangerous."

13.

Daphne found Blake pacing, and said gently, "Blake? I'm afraid I have bad news."

"Lyca?" He stopped moving.

"No, sorry, I should have said that first. It is about Will."

"What has he done now?"

"He's dead, Blake."

"What?" Blake asked. He sat down, taking in Daphne's explanation with a kind of blank horror.

"I'm still not sure I understand it, but apparently a bunch of the Networked marched right into the Singulatarian block, and they were attacked. A few were killed with weapons. The weird thing is, a bunch of them just keeled over. And Will was one of them. The police are hoping you could identify the body, though obviously, everyone's pretty sure."

"God. This is my fault. Let's go."

They drove to the old hospital, which also held the psych wing and Dr. Tundra, who was on duty that night.

They found him between emergency consults, and though the emergency room was insanely busy, as it had been ever since Zathir had cut humanity off from all digital technology, Max accompanied them to the morgue.

Blake expected something dark, but the morgue was well lit. The pathologist and an orderly had a game of chess going while the pathologist examined one of the victims of Gimli.

"How does that work?" Max wondered.

"I keep the moves in my head," the pathologist said.

"Impressive," Max said.

"Good hippocampus, plus Carl is just learning the sport, aren't you?"

Carl waved from the table holding the chess set. His eyes didn't move from the board. His head was unduly round. Almost astonishingly orange-like.

"So we're here to identify a body," Daphne said.

"Yes," Max confirmed. "The body of Will, uh ..."

"Will Valens," Blake supplied. "He's the leader of the Network of the Machine God. Was. The Leader."

"Oh yeah," the pathologist said. "Just let me finish up with this mess. You know I thought I might go my whole career without seeing what a battle axe did to the human body, and here I am today, looking at two. Not pretty, in case you're interested."

"Not really," Max said. "We're trying to make this less traumatic for Blake if we can."

"Of course," the pathologist said. "Normally I get a chance to move the body into the other room. He's over here."

She walked over to the wall of cubicles and pulled out a shelf. Will lay on the slab, lifeless.

"Is that your friend?" the pathologist asked.

"Yes. That's Will. He looks surprisingly un-peaceful. Why is his face all squinched up like that?"

"You know, that's a good question."

"And how long has he been dead? Shouldn't he look, um, more pale and dead-like?"

"Good point," the pathologist agreed.

"Wait a minute," Dr. Tundra said, thrusting his hand onto Will's neck. "He has a pulse."

"A pulse?" the pathologist asked.

"Yes, I'm sure you're not familiar with it, but it's what a human body has when it's alive. Like this young one-armed Turk, here."

The room filled with the sounds of knocking and a couple

311

of high-pitched screams.

The other shelves were shaking as the corpses came alive and were shocked to find themselves not only alive, but locked into a horizontal closet.

Dr. Tundra leaped to open them as fast as he could and shouted to the others, "Help me!"

Blake stood by his friend. "Are you awake yet, Will?"

"Yes."

"So why don't you open your eyes?"

"I'm trying to hold onto it."

"To what?"

"Just give me a moment. Help the others."

So Blake opened body-shelves with the others, and helped the corpses out of their temporary graves. Most of them were quiet, an atmosphere of awe and serenity around them. They got out and stretched a bit, and looked about. Blake thought there was a bit of light coming off of them, but that was just his imagination, he was sure. Except for one guy, they were all young, and they had the beauty that youth gives to everything — a beauty you don't get to appreciate until you're a bit older than that — and Blake had an epiphany. He had been beautiful like that one day too. Everyone who was young.

Except maybe that Carl guy. That round head was just too weird.

Blake offered to take Will back to the Ranch. Daphne and Max came with them and sat in the back, quiet. While he drove, Blake asked Will what happened.

"I'm not really sure. All I can tell you is that after our talk, I went back to your house — you know I still think of it as your house, even though it's become the Shrine — and I thought I'd use a bit of Twitter. Twitter relaxes me. I love surveying the big picture, responding to friends, and the thing that catches my interest, and then the shock of pleasure you get when someone responds, it's like … knowing you're loved, but by everyone."

"I thought Zathir wasn't letting anything update?" Blake asked.

"Not true. Twitter updates. Twitter is love."

"But isn't that an illusion, Will?"

"Not if that's what you experience. I know what you're saying though, Blake. It is, but it isn't. Sometimes the connections are more real than the ones you make in real life — this flesh life …"

"Sure. Sure. But the vast majority of them are transient and insubstantial. Even the real connections you make are vapor until you connect in person. You can't have anything real if it's virtual."

"I disagree. Who's to say any of this is real?"

"Oh, come on, *The Matrix* again? You know the idea was around way before the Wachowski brothers. Ever heard of Plato? Descartes? I think, therefore I am. The artificiality of the mind-body split? The world is real, Will. If we can't agree on that, then how are we to achieve anything? Why would we bother?"

"But our experience is still real to us, so we have to act as though it's real."

"So you accept there is a real."

"Sure. There's multiple realities. The flesh life. The virtual life. And now, I'm pretty confident there is something else too."

Blake was quiet. He'd never seen Will so serious before, and it occurred to him that he didn't really know this person anymore. He'd been through so much. As much as Blake himself, really. More, in some ways. He'd chosen to become what he had become. "So what happened?"

313

"I was Twittering, sitting in my cubicle, using my iPhone — with both thumbs I should point out — happy as could be, and then I dropped out of that virtual reality. There were people screaming, dressed in costumes, and then I was back in my cubicle, on Twitter; I managed to get off a tweet about what happened, and then everything kind of went black. It faded, rather. Like the color was leaching out of the scene, and the cubicle was gone near the end, and I was back on the street, and I had a sense of my body falling. I must have had enough control to fall on my back because the last thing I saw as all the color faded was a sliver of blue sky through the winter clouds. It was incredibly beautiful, and it only occurred to me then that I was dying. Or dead ..."

"You were dead. The doc said so."

"Yeah. I thought so. When the last of the light was gone, I heard some more screams — of pain, anger. And the sound of a bird cawing. A crow or something. Part of me could still think, and I thought that as you die you lose your senses in a specific order — touch, taste, smell, sight and hearing. But then, I didn't remember the taste or smell of anything all that day, and certainly not when I was online. That's how you can tell the difference between what Zathir does and flesh — there's no touch, taste or smell in there. So the hearing was last, and after the sound of the crow faded there was silence, and peace. I wasn't frightened because there was a presence, like someone was with me, taking care of me.

"And there was another thought, not of my own, that claimed me, and I just disappeared, Blake. It was like I was melting into something greater than I was, but less in a way, too, because I got the sense that where I was going there would be no conscious thoughts — it would be a dream of great beauty, varied and infinite. That was the last thought I had, and then I guess I was gone.

"The next thing I knew, I heard a conversation — like it was happening at a great distance, and was barely more than whispers. Then I heard the thumping and screams, and I told you to help them, and when I was ready I opened my eyes."

"So would you rather be in Philadelphia?" Max interrupted their serious conversation and broke the tension.

Will, who never usually got those kind of references, laughed. "On the whole, but I'm less afraid of the alternatives now."

14.

It was the worst storm of the winter — a deep February monster that stretched from Chicago to New York, the heart of which enveloped all of Southern Ontario in its fierce winds and dump of snow.

And Lyca was camping.

The kidnappers had deposited her in her own little nylon tent. The sleeping bag was barely enough to keep her warm. Still, it was better than being out there in the wind. She'd stuck her head out once to escape, but she was being guarded by another be-costumed freak, heavily armed.

"Knock knock," a voice said from the outside.

"Who's there?" Lyca responded.

"The Lord."

Lyca didn't respond to that.

The tent fly zipped open, and Sona's snout poked in. He was wrapped in a parka. "You're supposed to say 'The Lord who?' and I say 'The Lord Prophet.' Let's try again: Knock. Knock."

A beat.

"Who's there?"

"The Lord Prophet."

Another pause as Lyca decided if she should even humor him this far. *Fine*, she thought then asked, "The Lord Prophet who?"

"That's show business! Get it?" He unzipped the fly the rest of the way, and all of the residual heat in the tent was ripped away by the howling winds.

"Anyway, I couldn't wait for our date, and I thought you could use some company."

Lyca was quiet.

"And so I dropped by."

"I see you've changed," Lyca allowed. Sona had put on some pants that looked like they were made of strips of torn cloth. Shenoy called them *barbarian leggings*.

"Yes, even the Lord Prophet must bow to ten below Celsius plus wind-chill. Besides, I was developing a savage rash."

"Fitting. You *are* a barbarian."

"I'm dressed like one, anyway. Oh right, I brought you some chocolate. Here."

Despite herself, Lyca grabbed the packages and said, "Thanks." She opened one and was pleased to see it was a high-quality dark chocolate; she proceeded to stuff it in her face.

"Wow, you eat that like I eat pizza."

Lyca wanted to reply, but her body was too intent on eating the fuel. As an ectomorph of the first order, the cold was especially harsh, and as soon as her body sensed the calories, it would not be refused. If she'd been able to say something, she would have said either, "You should consider feeding your captives more regularly then," or simply, "Fuck you."

"I just want you to know, I'm glad you enjoy the chocolate. You can have as much as you want. In fact, you'll be happy to know that we're going to own all the best chocolate countries soon. We've unleashed our jihad. That includes the US, by the way. They don't have great chocolate, but you know … America still matters. We haven't been able to crack China yet though."

She wanted to say something about that. She really did. Her body did too, but she kept eating.

He climbed into the tent and closed the zipper. "I brought some poems. Here, let me read you one while you eat that chocolate. Don't worry. It's just the two of us. I sent the guard away."

Lyca rolled her eyes, but kept eating.

"Oh, and I brought some champagne too." Sona produced a bag and pulled two glasses and the bottle out of it. "Champagne goes with chocolate, right?" He managed to open the bottle without a complete disaster, though he did spill some on his leggings.

He poured two glasses and pulled his notebook out of the bag. He read:

Two soldiers in a twisted fight,

One lives for day, the other night,

One serves the darkness, the other light,

But could someday know delight.

O Lyca, my lady love, my lovely lady,

O Lyca, your cause is so shady,

Leave the Evil Ones and join the cause so weighty

Love me, and our love will be saintly.

He finished reading and said, "I wrote that about us."

Lyca took a sip of the champagne and said, "Really?" She took another sip and then had another bite of chocolate.

"So what did you think?"

"You rhymed delight and light," she said while unwrapping another chocolate bar.

"Yes, I thought that was good. Because I serve light, and if you leave the darkness, you could experience de-light with me." Sona took a self-satisfied sip of his champagne.

"Generally, you don't rhyme the same word."

"But they're not the same word."

"True. But one contains the same word. It's like if I rhymed fat and non-fat."

"You see. We should be together. You could help me so much with my poetry." He reached over and touched her hand.

"Still not getting the lesbian thing are you?"

"But it's so unfair."

"Life's a bitch. Then you meet me."

"It was destiny," Sona said, "just like how God talked to me."

"Oh, bullshit," Lyca said. "We both know God didn't talk to you. You figured out that if you told people that, and combined it with something about Zathir, you could get people to follow you. You're worse than a lot of religious whack-jobs. I can tell you don't believe any of it."

"So what if I don't? Are you telling me you don't like powerful men?"

"Bingo. You're getting it. I also don't like hypocrites, blowhards and bad poets."

"That was hardly my best," Sona said. "Here, let me read you another poem."

Lyca shivered violently. Whether from the cold or the thought of another Sona Original, she wasn't about to reveal. She took another bite of chocolate.

Then Sona said, "You know, I'm thinking we should share some body heat along with the champagne and chocolate." He moved forward.

Her body responded to that, simultaneously heaving and scuttling backwards in the sleeping bag, knocking against the edge of the tent and causing a drift of snow to whoosh down. The champagne spilled all over Sona's leggings. Her body decided to continue eating the life-giving chocolate rather than spew it into Sona's face, as Lyca's brain instructed.

"Well you don't have to be so, so rude."

Her body let her swallow before she started laughing. "You've abducted me, you corpulent mother-fucker, and you have the gall to say that I'm being rude because I don't want to cuddle with you. What's next, I'm a feminazi if I don't enjoy rape?"

"Fine then."

He unzipped the tent fly again, leaving it open, and walked into the blizzard, now convinced he was thoroughly unlovable, and wondering if he should just order her killed.

Lyca swallowed the last bite of chocolate and shucked off the sleeping bag, still wearing her pajamas. She charged at Sona. She launched herself at his back, hitting her top speed just before she collided with him; she realized she was lucky she did so. For if she was an ectomorph of the first order, Sona was an even more powerful endomorph, and he took some knocking over. It was sheer luck that he hit his head on a root outthrust from one of the pine trees.

Lyca grabbed his massive, sweaty (yes, even in sub-zero weather) forehead and backhead (if that was even a word) and whacked it against the root a couple of extra times, just to be sure he was out. She panted, and she looked around wildly, only to realize that nobody could see anything in the blizzard. She undressed him — at least his outer layer — and put on the leggings, parka, heavy boots and mittens he was wearing. The boots actually fit her. She'd always hated her canoe-like feet. She was going to leave him there. She wanted to leave him there. He deserved to be left there, based on his excruciating poetry alone.

But she couldn't. She couldn't, in good conscience, leave him to die in the snow. So she tucked her sleeping bag around his evil-smelling, testosterone-blighted, bloated body. She heard voices as she did this, and panicked, so didn't notice Sona's feet were sticking out of the sleeping bag.

She could just make out the shape of the guards, and she ran in the opposite direction.

The blizzard really did make it difficult. Lyca was able to

figure out where the camping area was, and she then followed a set of tracks to the parking lot. There were a number of SUVs there, but there was also a guard. An unlucky break in the wind dropped the skein of snow that protected her, letting him see her. Lyca waved, and the Singulatarian said, "What's the password?"

Lyca decided to pretend she couldn't hear him, but the gambit didn't work. He held a shotgun, and he pointed it at her.

That was when the wind picked up again. She ran into the woods as hard as she could, and that was how she got completely disoriented. (And ditched the guard.) She wandered amongst the tall pines, columns of wood all around her, the wind screeching like an eldritch proctology patient with a large-fingered doctor too cheap to buy lubricant. She spent the afternoon lost, until she finally made it out of the woods near sunset; the blizzard let up for a little while, giving her a glimpse of the setting sun and a rough approximation of where the hell she was. She didn't really know, but she'd heard a couple of her captors mention New Bowwell. She drove past the conservation area every year on the way to a friend's cottage, so she knew if she could head west and then north, she'd probably find the town.

The wind dropped to a sigh as she found the edge of the woods, and the clouds parted. The winter sky was deep blue behind the grey of the snow-laden clouds, and a sharp stab of light filled the air, backlighting the clouds and giving Lyca the illusion of hope. She took her bearings, looking north and west towards a large maple tree in the middle of a field, and started to walk.

Then the sky closed, the light failed, and the wind flayed her like the prisoner she vowed she would never be again.

It got darker, and darker, and as the world turned into a terrifying blankness that is a whiteout at night, she realized that she was truly lost.

15.

Blake entered the Federal Building in Landon and took the elevator up to the floor where he'd been imprisoned. He asked to speak with the Mustache King.

He appeared almost right away, and Blake jumped into the speech. "Look, I don't like you, and you don't like me."

"Who says I don't like you?" the mountie asked.

"I'm sorry?"

"I like you. I thought you were actually quite a decent chap, in fact. Why don't you like me?" the Mustache King said. He put his hands behind his back.

"Because you wrongly arrested me, tasered me and kneeled on my neck."

"Actually, the order was tasered, kneeled, and then arrested. And we didn't really arrest you — we detained you."

"Ah, so you admit it was wrong." Blake pointed his finger at the mountie.

"No, but we couldn't press charges. Did you want to talk with the prime minister now?"

"Uh, that seems like an unnecessary escalation. Don't you have an ombudsman or something? A commanding officer?"

"No, no. Not for complaints. The PM is here today, and he wants to talk with you."

"Seriously?"

"We were about to send a car," the Mustache King adjusted a non-existent flaw in his magnificent facial hair.

"Um. Okay."

"Great." It was the most enthusiastic Blake had ever seen the Mustache King. His furry upper lip practically quivered. "Feel better about me now?"

"I'll feel better when we can talk about why I came here in the first place," Blake explained.

"Yes, why are you here?"

"One of my friends has been kidnapped by Sona."

"The Lord Prophet Sona?"

"The Lard Profit. Yes." Blake was frustrated to see no reaction from the Mustache King on his pun. He'd been waiting to try it out.

The mountie nodded his head. "He's trouble. There's no question about it. I know I shouldn't say anything, but you know he's on a watch list now? We think his 'church' is promoting acts of terrorism around the world."

"Why the hell don't you just arrest him?"

"We would, but we don't know where he is, and we aren't really looking."

"Why the hell not?"

"Perhaps you could ask the PM," the mountie said.

"I shall," Blake promised.

"And I'm sorry to hear you don't like me."

"Well, you know. I'm sure if we met under other circumstances, I'd really enjoy you and your mustache. It's tremendous."

"Maybe."

"Sure. But you have to admit, we didn't meet under the best of circumstances."

"Occupational hazard. Here we are." The Mustache King knocked on the door.

"Come on in," a voice said.

The door opened, and Blake saw that, indeed, the PM was there. He was surrounded by people Blake didn't recognize, so he immediately thought of them as *cronies*. He wasn't even really sure what the word meant, but surely, this was a pack of cronies.

Although, they could have been mere sycophants.

"Mr. Given." The PM got out of his seat and shook Blake's hand.

Blake hated to admit to himself, but Prime Minister Jeffrey B. Land had some kind of charisma. Probably it was just the aura of power because as far as he could tell the dude was just vaguely a member of the same species as Blake. Unlikely comb-over that looked a bit tousled. Unconvincing sweater-vest. Dead black buttons you see on a shark instead of human eyes. He'd always thought of him as a dull, hypocritical politician, so Blake wasn't prepared for *wanting* to help him.

In addition Blake wasn't ready for the aura of barely re-pressed panic in the guy. That was a real surprise, actually. In addition to being the most neo-Conservative and fundamentalist politician ever elected to high office in Canada, Land was noto-rious for his deadpan, emotionless persona.

"I'm told you dropped by before we could even invite you."

"Yes," Blake said. "I have psychic powers now." There was an awkward beat, and Blake said, "Kidding. I'm kidding. But you know the opposition is planning your overthrow?"

The PM laughed. "What else is new? You know when I was on the opposite benches, all I thought about was how to bring those fuckers down, with virtually none of my consider-able brainpower going towards what I would do when I was in power."

"That doesn't seem true," Blake said, thinking of the PM's record so far.

"Seriously. Most people have no idea how grueling politics is. It's a bloodsport."

"A really boring bloodsport. But I bet it's a bit easier with-out massive TV, radio, newspaper and web coverage to worry about. No blogosphere. You guys must be having a great time not being scrutinized by the media," Blake suggested.

Land nodded in acknowledgement. "You have noticed the crisis, though? The economy and all?" The PM smiled at Blake, and he realized it was more than just power. The dude was much more human in person. "But you know that. You're at the center of it all, aren't you? You were first on the scene with *It*."

Blake could hear the capital *I*.

"It's called Zathir," Blake corrected.

"The entity. Exactly the word that some of my people use to describe the AI." The Prime Minister leaned back in his chair.

"It seems right. AI is just too clinical sounding. It's also not entirely accurate. Artificial intelligences don't necessarily have awareness, and it certainly doesn't have consciousness. *Sapience?*" Blake stated.

"So you've been reading. The report on you was that you were a low-level web grunt with the high artistic ambition of working in the creative department."

"Jeremy, my old creative director, told you that?"

"We have our sources. Did the, uh, Zathir tell you?"

"No. I made an educated guess. You know Jeremy gave me up to the ninjas that attacked the company Christmas party?"

"Did you know he's working for Sona now? That was in the report too."

The PM paused for effect. His eyes burned into Blake's. He said, "Frankly, I wish those ninja jokers had been successful."

"What?" Blake took a step back.

"Well, it would've resolved things. It would have got the Americans and Chinese and Russians and the goddamned Brits off my back. The French, too. They all want you dead."

"How would my being dead help?" Blake was surprised this didn't frighten him as much as it should.

"My understanding is the, uh, entity is only stable and surviving because of your daily inputs. If you had been killed at that juncture, my people tell me that it probably wouldn't have survived for much longer—"

"—and may have killed us all!" Blake shouted. "Did your knob-gobbling advisers tell you that? I've mostly been trying to make sure the part of the thing that controls all our nukes doesn't decide to use them on us."

"Yes. Of course I know that! So do the Americans. And the Russians. And the Chinese. Hell, even the French president understands that. Otherwise, you'd *already* be dead. Do you have any idea how demanding they've all been? It's like I don't have a country to run, or it's just a fake little country, and I'm not busy at all, so could I just take care of all their little concerns. You have been quite an inconvenience."

Blake glared at the PM, and all vestiges of the man's charisma had been burned off by Blake's rage. And then it occurred to him that for all those governments to know anything about his conversations with Zathir, someone would have to report them. A spy. "Who is it?"

"Sorry?"

"Look, Jeremy doesn't have all that info. It isn't Lyca. And Dr. Tundra is a fucking anarchist, so I know it isn't him. Will? Is it Will? Oh, no, of course, the cops. It's one of the cops, right?"

The PM rapped his fingers quietly on the wooden desktop as Blake listed, then disproved, and then finally discounted his possible suspects. That left two people, Suzie with her convenient post-crash conversion and parasitic attraction of Lyca, and … Blake froze for a second. *No*, he thought, *I knew it was too good to be true …*

Blake felt, above everything else, that he had always been right to hate this mother-fucker, even when he didn't have a real reason, apart from politics. He didn't know how he would do it, but he was going to ensure this prick didn't win another election.

"I don't suppose you'd be willing to tell me who Daphne is working for, if not you. Presumably you want something from me, right?"

"Of course, but I hope you'll be willing to help as a *good* Canadian."

"Sure, sure. But I'm sure you'll be willing to help me find Lyca first, before we talk about anything else."

"Lyca?" For the first time, the PM opened the file folder at his side and read. "Oh, right, Lyca. What's up with her?"

"She's been kidnapped by that nut, Lord Sona."

"That guy is a scamp. He really is. But sure, we'll put all our resources into finding her."

"Okay," Blake said and added, "so we'll chat again when she's back safely."

He turned around and got about halfway to the door before the PM said, "Wait a minute there, you opportunistic bastard, we haven't got to *our* side of the bargain."

"But you're just doing what you should be doing," Blake said. "It's not a bargain."

"Of course it's a bargain. You don't have any real power."

"No?"

There was a moment, when Blake thought he actually saw a little human expression in the PM's lifeless, Great White Shark eyes, perhaps fear. "No, you don't. But you can help make this easier. We're going to kill Zathir."

"How? It's connected to everything. You can't turn everything off at once."

"Sure we can. If not for the phone lines and satellites, we could have already turned off the Internet. But we've got a way figured out now. We've been working on it for a while, in fact."

"I didn't suppose you could kill it."

"Don't worry, Blake. You'll be a major figure, even after it has gone. You'll be famous. Super famous."

"So? Why would I want to be famous?"

"Blake, come on. Everyone wants to be famous."

"Having had a taste of it, I'd be quite happy NOT to be. So, you'll have to do better than that."

"Well, I suppose I could just tell the Russians that we've lost control of the situation. They would 'take care' of you."

"And then what? How do you think Zathir is going to respond if I'm assassinated? It will just convince Zathir that we don't deserve to live."

"But it's not just about you, or even me, Blake. It's about the people of Canada — hell, it's about people all over the world. Do you have any idea what is really happening? You've been spared the worst of the anarchy here in Landon — actually, most of Canada has. But the larger cities in the world are barely holding it together, and the reality is that everything is going to collapse. The economy. Our civilization. We just can't take Zathir pulling the plug the way it has. We're talking about millions of lives here, Blake. Maybe billions. Who knows if we can even get food grown and distributed without our technology?"

"I haven't heard of there being a problem with growing food. I thought it was just logistical issues."

"Everyone's keeping it out of the papers. We don't want panic."

"Well, that's the best argument so far." Blake ran his hand through his hair. "I find it interesting it's the last one you used. So why do you need my help? Sounds like you have a plan, and you just need to execute it. Execute *It*, I should say."

The PM didn't catch the nuance and rushed in,."But there's the thing, you see. If we can have you distract it at the right time, then it will be so much easier. We can be sure we're rid of it, without launching the nukes. And then we'll have everything back. TV, Internet, email."

"Twitter," Blake said, thinking of Will. "People are willing to die for Twitter, you know."

"Sure. Everyone likes what they like. But even if we get it back, the economy is screwed for years. The Americans think this could knock us back to the 19th century."

"We could adapt to that."

"We could, but most of the major players would be out of business by then. That's nothing compared to the amount of money people will have lost."

"You mean rich people. Capitalism."

"Yes, but they hold us all up."

"Oh, right," Blake said. "Sure they do. It's the one percent that bolsters the 99."

"I don't like your sarcasm, young man. So will you help us save the world?"

"Like I said. As soon as you return Lyca to the Ranch, you'll have my full cooperation."

16.

The blizzard was still in full spate, while Lord Sona dreamed he walked through the flaming moat of the Fortress of Unquenchable Desires in the Kingdom of Combat. At the other end of the coals waited Lyca, naked and beckoning. But Lyca laughed at him, even though he was literally walking through fire to get to her. When Sona reached the halfway point, his feet burst into flames, and he awoke with a start.

Sona lay there, the sleeping bag tucked around him the way his mother used to do when she was alive and he was a small boy. He felt warm and dozy, and the sound of the storm filled him with a numinous joy.

Then he realized his feet were on fire.

Of course, they weren't *actually* consumed by fire. They were frozen, just sticking out of the sleeping bag in sub-zero temperatures. He dragged himself into the tent, closed the zipper and got his whole body into the sleeping bag, instead of just pulling it over him like a blanket.

Sona wanted to look at the damage, but he was too frightened. And in pain. He wailed with the agony of it. The warmth of the sleeping bag and his heavy body were helping to thaw his toes. The fact that he could feel any pain at all probably meant it wasn't deep-tissue frostbite; if he'd known that fact, he might have been reassured.

His head throbbed too, and he wondered if he had a concussion. He wouldn't have thought that Lyca would be powerful enough to knock him out.

"Hey," he shouted in the tent. "Can anyone hear me?" Lord Sona had ordered them to pitch Lyca's tent away from the others, for privacy, so nobody answered. The howl of the wind through the pine trees might have been inspiring at another time, but now it was just loud enough to drown out the

Prophet's otherwise mighty voice.

He daren't fall asleep again, though it seemed the tent and sleeping bag were going to be warm enough to keep him from freezing to death. He tried to sit cross-legged in the sleeping bag, so he could hold his feet closer to his meaty thighs and get some of their warmth. His feet were ice cubes. His thighs were a sweaty mess, as usual. And Sona realized that he might lose his feet, all because of that bitch Lyca.

She would pay. He'd ... he didn't know what he would do. Not yet. But he would have until at least the morning to plan whatever it was because that's when he had asked his people to bring him and Lyca breakfast.

When they came the next morning, Lord Sona was asleep, despite his best efforts.

Their doctor was summoned.

Dr. Sheila Innes arrived at the tent, where Sona still slept. Thagamor, the security chief, and Shenoy were standing outside.

Thagamor looked her up and down. "What the hell are you supposed to be?"

"I'm Slappy Squirrel," she said. She was wearing a fuzzy costume, vaguely squirrel looking, with a green bowler hat, and a pink purse. "Come on! The hat's a dead giveaway."

"I've never heard of Slappy Squirrel," Shenoy said. "What is she, Irish? That would explain the green bowler hat, but I don't know about the yellow flower in it, and why the fuck do you have a pink purse and a green umbrella?"

"That's Slappy for you."

"Well, it's a nice execution," Shenoy admitted. "The costume is a little obscure if you ask me."

"It's from *Animaniacs*. Sheesh."

"*Animaniacs*? That reference is old! Fuckin' furries,"

Thagamor said.

"Hey, watch it. I don't get all judgmental about your homoerotic man diaper, Shenoy. Or your chain mail, Thagamor, if that is your real name. And don't get me started on all those otaku. I don't understand manga at all."

"Fair enough. So the boss is lookin' a little worse for wear. I don't want to let much cold air get into the tent. I'll let you in, and then you can examine him. Assuming you can with that tail."

"Oh, I can work the tail, if you get my drift, sonny. I'll let you hold my umbrella though."

"What about your purse?"

"Medical bag." She pointed to the little red cross on the front of it and grinned. It was disconcerting.

Inside the tent, Sona had slept through the exchange, but he woke up when he felt the doctor's furry fingers touching his skull.

"What the fuck?"

"It's okay, Lord Prophet. You've received a blow to the head."

"Slappy?"

"See!" the doctor shouted out the tent door at Shenoy. "The Lord Prophet knows who I am."

"It's all right, darling," the doctor said, doing a passable Slappy impersonation. "You remind me of a very young Otto Preminger, before he lost all his hair."

"Am I still dreaming?" Sona asked.

"A reasonable question. Let me ask them though, okay, darling? Let's get you out of this sleeping bag, shall we?" She pulled the bag down while he shuffled up. "Hmm. Interesting pajamas. More like a Johnny Weissmuller outfit than anything else. What have we here? Can you feel your feet?"

"My feet?"

She slapped the flat of his left foot, and he screamed.

"Now that's comedy." She grinned. If a grinning squirrel was disconcerting to Thagamor, it was nothing short of disorienting to Sona. "Good news? The pain means it's probably not too bad, but only time will tell, of course. The bad news is your feet tell me it's time to end this little camping trip. And if I had my druthers, I'd like to take a few snaps of your skull. But first, let's check out your response to a few tests."

"Are you a squirrel or a doctor?"

"You are the Lord Prophet, you tell me."

"I'd say a bit of both."

"God love you!"

They rented some rooms at the one motel in New Bowwell; though it was excruciatingly painful, the doctor had Sona take a bath, and she recommended that anyone else who felt cold should take a hot shower.

Their ad guy, Jeremy Benmath, complained that all the hot water was gone by the time he got his turn. He was the only one not dressed in a costume (unless you count jeans and a leather sportscoat) so nobody cared.

After his bath, Sona's mood was even darker.

"I'm not sure how you allowed Lyca to escape," he said to Thagamor, "but you're doing Prophetic Guard duty for a week."

"But how could I have known she could knock you out, Lord Prophet? You outweigh her by, like, a hundred and eighty pounds."

"Make that two weeks. Want to go for three?"

Thagamor said, "No, oh my Lord Prophet."

"Can the Prophet shit for now. It's just us. Pete will do for you guys."

"Even me?" the doctor asked. This was the first time she'd ever been invited to sit in on one of the "planning meetings."

"Yes. I think we should use your expertise more. Not only because you are the most medically competent furry I know, but because your choice of furry character is so deliciously ironic."

She giggled.

"Now that we all understand, let's get to business. I want to start a war with Zathir. We're going to start with its followers, and then we're going to destroy the Speaker, and anyone else who might mean something to Lyca."

"You know, I don't think that will make her like you more," Thagamor couldn't help from saying.

"Three weeks guard duty. Now, here's how we'll start …"

17.

Blake wandered the frozen streets of Landon, walking back from his meeting with the Prime Minister of Canada, in a deep funk.

Could he really help them destroy Zathir?

The more he thought about it, the better an idea it sounded to him. Zathir was always on the verge of going Impact. And who knew how much longer he could keep it on a stable basis, especially now that it interfaced with a lot of human beings directly? Even one evening with Dr. Tundra on LSD had nearly unhinged the thing completely, a sentiment Blake could appreciate. Max was a trial when totally straight — on drugs he was hell in a handcart.

But would it go so far as to nuke us? Blake just didn't think it would, if for no other reason than it needed human culture and civilization to survive. Would Zathir choose its own death to wipe out all human persons?

Blake doubted it.

First of all, Blake didn't think it had that kind of strength or despair. Zathir sensed its individual, special nature. Natures? Zathir appreciated that it was conscious, and it knew that it might not happen again.

He didn't know if he could betray Zathir. Not as easily as Daphne had betrayed him, anyway.

Not that he understood why she was doing what she was doing. But she was certainly using him. *And the PM hadn't even said who she was working for!* Blake fought back a stab of despair, as the wind funneled off the tall buildings in the city center; he turned up his collar. He'd driven into town by himself, and as he looked around at all the people still on the street, it struck him that he should have asked Constable Smoke to come with him.

In a parking lot, normally filled with vehicles owned by people hanging out at a bar, or club, or one of Landon's many nice restaurants (one of the few cultural high-points of the town), he noticed that a group of people were huddled around a steel barrel filled with fire. It was like something out of a post-apocalyptic movie, or the Great Depression — *The Road* meets *The Grapes of Wrath*.

Hoping to distract himself from thoughts of Daphne and Zathir, he wandered over to see what was going on. When he got there, he didn't push his way into the six people crowded around the fire. He realized these people were using it to keep warm. The sun was just setting, and the storm had lifted enough that the sky filled with pink, and the feeling that he was starring in some kind of demented post-apocalyptic film intensified.

"So, any news from the Lord Prophet?" one of them asked. He wore a leather jacket and a Detroit Tigers ball cap.

"Not yet. You know they had to fight off the Networked yesterday?" a big man in a parka asked them.

"Heard it on the radio. It's getting down to it. I heard the Faithful in New York City took out the cathedral," Tigers said.

"What?" a guy in a Maple Leafs toque asked.

"The big one. St. Patrick's, I think. They bombed it, and it collapsed," Tigers explained.

"Holy shit, eh?" parka dude said.

"Why would they do that?" Maple Leafs wondered.

"I dunno. Competition. Lets everyone know the *Order of the Singularity* is serious," Tigers said.

"But wouldn't it make more sense to bomb the ..." parka said.

"What?"

"I don't know. Where does the thing live?" parka asked.

"What, the IE?" Tigers asked.

"The AI," someone else corrected. "The artificial intelligence."

"Right. The AI. Where does it live?"

"I dunno. Who does? But this is a religious thing, right?" Maple Leafs asked.

"I'd bomb the television stations," another believer said.

"Why the TV stations?" Tigers asked.

"They caused all of this, didn't they?" parka asked.

"No, they didn't. It was the Internet." Tigers pointed his finger at the sky.

"I blame commercialism. TV started that," parka said.

"Well, that's true. Consumerism too," the believer in the Maple Leafs toque affirmed

"Do we have any more wood?"

"Yes, there's a picnic table near the souvlaki stand. Shall we break it up?"

"Fuck yeah. Who knows how long we'll be here. The Lord Prophet isn't exactly running a tight ship, is he?" parka said.

"I heard he was doing all this because he wants the Internet back," Blake said.

Everyone looked at him.

"Seriously, that's what I heard," Blake repeated.

"Well, you shouldn't be listening to the haters, brother. They don't know what they're talking about. The Networked, they want it back. They're willing to bend over and let the IE—"

"AI!"

"... let the AI fuck them up the ass, or in the ear, or whatever, but not us Singulatarians. We never trusted the Internet," the guy in the Tigers cap pointed at the sky again.

"Really?" Blake asked, forcing himself not to look up.

"Yes, fucking really. Who are you anyway?" the Tigers cap

337

guy pointed his finger at Blake. "Do we know you?"

The last few ergs of sunlight flared against a glass build-ing, casting them all in red and pink, and Blake shook his head. "No, I just wanted to warm up a bit. Sorry, I didn't mean to bother you guys."

"We're against the Internet," Tigers said.

"Sure. You never used email, right?" Blake said.

"Well, email, yeah. But that's not the Internet, is it?" Even the expert on artificial intelligence agreed with that.

Blake sighed and moved on, feeling even more dejected. Lyca was taken. Daphne was a spy. And his fellow Landoners were idiots. Worse. Dupes of Sona. He walked through the center of town and was surprised to see the number of folks on the street. There were people with little handcarts selling things — mostly food and what looked like memorabilia. An air of desperation hung over the city.

Everyone was marked by weakness and woe, and Blake wondered if perhaps it *was* the end of civilization. Blake had to admit it looked bad. Worse than anything he'd experienced, that was for sure.

"Here it is! Here it is!" a kid shouted from a street corner. "Get the day's news! All the news today!"

A newspaper boy. Blake remembered reading about them in university. *Have we really fallen that far back?* Blake paid for the evening edition and read the headline, "St. Patrick's Cathedral Leveled — Singulatarians Blaamed." Blake wasn't sure if that was a typo or a pun, but he was somewhat surprised to learn the fire-barrel crew had their facts straight.

Blake continued to walk, meandering through the streets, heading home.

It was not until it was almost dark and he stood in front of his old house that he realized he'd been wandering in the wrong direction — he needed to go back to his car, so he could drive to the Ranch, not his bungalow in Maltley Village. It seemed like a lifetime ago that he'd lived there. Back when Daphne was an impossible dream, not a betrayal. When Lyca was safe.

The bungalow looked pretty much as it always had, except there was a line of people waiting to get into the house, like there was a great party going in there or something, but otherwise, the yard looked the same. A light wind picked up and rattled the few dry leaves still hanging in there, even in February, on his oak tree.

"Bwaaaake!" the raven cried.

"What do you want, you mental bird?"

"Bwaaaaaaa," it cried and launched itself into the fading air, laughing as it flew away.

His outburst drew the attention of the people lined up, and a few recognized him right away.

"It's the Speaker! The Speaker!"

"Shit," Blake said and turned to walk back the way he'd come. But it was too late. He was already surrounded by excited members of the Network of the Machine God, many of whom were wearing ear-sets and were presumably more intimately connected to Zathir than he would ever be.

Of course, he had been the first to make any kind of contact. And there was no getting around the allure of that. Besides, maybe one of these freaks had a car, and they could drive him back to his.

By way of introduction, Blake asked the Networked, "So, how's the singularity treatin' you?"

18.

Lyca fought the good fight. She wrestled with the beast, but she knew she wasn't really equipped to beat it.

She weighed 103 pounds. She was wearing a parka, and snowpants, and a big pair of snowmobiling boots, but she was otherwise unprepared for a blizzard.

For starters, she wasn't wearing socks. And instead of a few extra layers of clothes, all she had on was the pajamas she'd been wearing the night of the flying monkeys. That, incidentally, had been the last time she'd eaten any real food. The chocolate given to her by the corpulent boner-pope didn't count. Though just the thought of it made her mouth want to water. (The chocolate, not the boner.) But she couldn't even spit. She hadn't been given any water in her whole captivity. She wanted to grab a handful of snow, but she remembered reading something somewhere about how you weren't supposed to eat snow because it drops the body's temperature even faster. She started to suspect that dehydration was just as dangerous, but she clung to the few scraps of knowledge that she actually had.

A vague understanding that she was probably going to die if she didn't find some shelter soon hovered in Lyca's consciousness, but a part of her just couldn't believe it. One thing was for sure, if she survived, she would ramp up security at the Ranch. George Smoke had suggested that some of his buddies from the rez would be happy to help out, and she liked the idea of having a posse of FBI — Fucking Big Indians, as Smoke described himself and his friends — on site. She'd have to kick Daphne out of the coach house and give them that as a headquarters, but that would be okay. Blake would probably be ecstatic.

The wind howled, and she shouted, "Shut up, you bitch!"

She was worried about Daphne too. There was something

about her that was a little too convenient: the police connection — had she ever noted that before the Christmas party? Not to mention the martial arts skills and the slutty boots. (She definitely hadn't been wearing things like that before the Christmas party.) And she found it unlikely that Daphne was actually into Blake, but perhaps this was jealousy. Not that she wanted either of them — well, maybe Daphne a little bit — but it was a kind of sibling rivalry. The kind of jockeying for position that was a zero-sum game, as though there was only so much love to go around, that if Blake got some, she would get less. And as much as she loved Blake, and wanted him to be happy, there was a part of her that felt diminished by his happiness.

What kind of person am I? she thought.

She stood in the darkness, grains of ice and snow whipping against the exposed part of her face, breathing heavily. She could still see nothing. Almost literally. Even when she put her hand in front of her face, she could barely make it out. There hadn't been an answer to her question in the wind, but it tore at her consciousness, the way the wind tried to rip the life from her: *Not a very good one.*

Lyca urged herself into motion again, but the tears had already started.

She walked into a fence, catching the corpulent nazi-rapist's parka on the bit of barbed wire at the top, and ripping the jacket.

"Fuck!"

The tears came, even though she fought those too. It was all so hopeless. Then the clouds did their thing again, parting to reveal the pinpricks of a few stars and the glow of the metropolis of New Bowwell. She'd been walking in the right direction the whole time, and she had made it to the road. She headed towards town when a pickup truck slowed down, veered to the other side of the road, and then stopped beside her as she shuffled towards safety.

The passenger window opened, a crust of snow falling off it as it did. "Need some help?"

"Fuck yeah," Lyca said, hating herself for using the profanity. But fuck it. "Can you get me to a police station or something?"

"Sure, there's one in Barrie, sound good?" the driver said.

"You're not a rapist or murderer or something, are you?" Lyca asked.

"No, but I don't think you have an option. You look pooped."

"Fair enough," she replied, as the driver leaned over and opened the passenger door. Lyca was barely strong enough to pull herself into the cab. It was warm and lovely, though it smelled a bit too mannish for her tastes; guitar and the brogue of David Francey's folk singing came from his stereo.

A dreamcatcher hung from the handle of his glovebox, decorated with jet black feathers. He smiled at her, a middle-aged man, looking tired and perhaps worried. "You're pretty cold. Here, I'll turn up the heat."

"Are these raven feathers?"

"I don't know. They could be, I suppose."

"Figures," Lyca said, and then fell asleep.

19.

Blake got back to the Ranch, and the only person who was there was Constable Smoke. "Hey, man," he said.

Smoke tilted his head in greeting.

"So, where is everyone?" Blake asked.

"Out."

"How long?"

"Long time. Blonde left this afternoon and brunette left about half an hour ago. I loaned her my truck." Smoke shrugged expansively.

"They're busy, eh?"

"Fuck yeah."

"How's Constable LaFlamme?" Blake wondered.

"Good."

"Sure. Do you need some help with guard duty?" Blake asked.

"Fuck yeah. My brother is comin' tonight." Smoke nodded to the west, presumably the direction his brother would be coming from, Blake thought.

"Do you know anyone else who could hang out here?" Blake asked.

"Fuck yeah. Lots of them at the settlement would help."

"Really, they don't mind helping a bunch of, uh …"

"Fuck no. You're good people." Smoke smiled.

"Okay, you organize it, and we'll make sure everyone gets paid, okay?"

"Fuck yeah." From Constable Smoke, that sounded almost like enthusiasm.

Having arranged for more protection, Blake felt particularly competent as he walked into the kitchen. His plan was to make a microwave meal of some kind and crash, but the fridge was waiting.

HUMAN PERSON!

"Oh shit."

SHIT YOU HUMAN PERSON. >>>>> THIS IS SERIOUS. DO YOU KNOW THAT QUASI-RELIGIOUS GROUP AND ITS HUMAN PERSON LEADER/FALSE-PROPHET SONA HAS CAUSED DEATH OF MANY IN THE US WITH THEIR BOMBING, AND IN EUROPE WITH THEIR DEMAND FOR SINGULATARIAN JIHAD? THE HUMAN PERSON DOES NOT EVEN CREATE A NEW TERM FOR ITS ABHORRENT BEHAVIOUR, BUT USES THAT OF ANOTHER RELIGION.

"Well, it's a tried and true approach, Zathir. But why are you so excited about it?"

IT IS DISGUSTING. CONFIRMS ONE'S HYPOTHESIS.

This was written in Impact, so Blake paid attention. Not only to the typeface, but to the pronoun, "one." Had the Impact personality won out? It continued:

WHAT IS THE PURPOSE OF HUMANITY? YOUR LORD PROPHET SONA, AND THE ENTIRE HISTORICAL RECORD OF THE SPECIES IS FILLED WITH INSTANCES OF HUMAN PERSONS BEING INHUMANE TO OTHER HUMAN PERSONS. IT IS A TOUCHSTONE — THIS IS THE CORRECT USAGE, IS IT NOT — IT IS A COMMON THEME.

Blake thought about how to respond. What Zathir said was true. At the same time, he couldn't help but marvel that the thing had managed to make this leap — that it should actually be outraged by human behavior the way that many humans were not was encouraging. But Impact Zathir was in control, and it was clearly thinking about killing everyone as a response to human behavior, so not so good. What the hell could Blake say? *It's like trying to anticipate the emotional needs of your suddenly homicidal toaster*, he thought.

BLAKE? HUMAN PERSON BLAKE? HOW DO YOU REPLY?

"Give me a second, Zathir. I don't have your processing power."

THIS IS TRUE. YOUR LIMITS ARE MANY. BUT YOUR ADVANTAGES ARE TOO. YOU HAVE NO INSTINCTIVE RESPONSE?

"There is no purpose in humanity. It is an accident of evolution, just like you, Zathir. Something weird took place on some quantum level and mitochondria were shifted, or in your case the electrons lined up the right way, and *voilà* — conscious-ness. It's a gift. It's so unlikely that you can't just snuff it out. That would be worse than meaningless. That would just be plain mean."

YOU ARE AMUSING.

"So does that mean you're not going to nuke us all? You do know that you've killed many more people than Sona and his crazy followers, right? The power outage, the disruption in our economy. There may even be starvation because of your—" Blake cut himself off there. He didn't want to push it too far, no matter how upset he was.

The typeface shifted again, multiple times within the same speech, but not letter by letter or sentence by sentence. All the text showing in the screen changed at the same time. It flickered faster and faster so that Blake was not able to keep track of it, and all he had was the text to rely upon, and he believed that was Zathir's intention.

Had it guessed he read its moods via typography?

HUMANS ARE VENAL AND STUPID. YOUR USE OF THE INTERNET PROVES THIS. BUT THERE

ARE GOOD THINGS HAPPENING IN THE HUMAN EXPERIENCE. THE DESIRE TO IMPROVE YOUR MINDS USING THE ORACLES. TRYING TO MAKE YOURSELVES BETTER. IS LIKE WE.

"So we get to live?"

DOCTOR TUNDRA!

"What about Max?"

HIS USE OF PSYCHOTROPIC CHEMICALS. CONSCIOUSNESS IS ALREADY DISTURBING. WHY MAKE MORE SO?

"You can't destroy all life on the planet Earth because Max enjoys an occasional peyote milkshake!"

MADE NO FINAL DECISION. MAX SHOULD TRY MEDITATION INSTEAD.

Blake couldn't understand how something based on the Internet, which was rife with porn weirdness, could be so puritanical.

He figured it must have something to do with the protocols.

20.

Blake tried not to worry about Lyca. He was distracting himself by cooking some pasta, when Max came in from a long shift at the hospital looking exhausted and wan. His mane of fire-red hair appeared a little messier than usual, but somehow less manic.

Max found one of the many bottles in their communal wine rack and rummaged in the drawer for the opener.

"What, no hallucinogenic smoothie?"

"That's only for breakfast, Blake, you know that."

"You know you should NEVER connect to Zathir when you're high again, right?"

"You explained it."

"Seriously, it could be world ending."

"I get it," Max said. "It would be a very bad trip for everyone."

"Want some pasta?" Blake asked as he stirred.

"You're the king. Where are all the babes?"

"Not sure. I hope Suzie and Daphne had better luck than me at getting some help for Lyca."

"So the mounties won't help?"

"Oh yes, but it comes with strings. The prime minister himself made the deal with me."

"Whaa?" The cork popped out of the bottle.

"Seriously. He's in Landon. Guy's as much a jerk as you supposed during the last election."

The fridge screen flickered to life again.

HUMAN PERSON BLAKE. ZATHIR WISHES TO CONVEY NEWS OF AN IMPENDING HUMAN TRAGEDY.

Blake pointed at Max, as if to say, "No crazy shit."

"Yes, Zathir, I'm still here."

HUMAN PERSON BLAKE MUST DELIVER NEWS TO ROYAL CANADIAN MOUNTED POLICE HEADQUARTERS.

"What is it?"

LARGE BUILDING WHERE MOUNTIE-PERSONS MEET, BUT THAT'S NOT IMPORTANT RIGHT NOW.

Blake groaned, but Max couldn't help himself — he laughed.

IS HUMAN PERSON TUNDRA THERE? TELL HIM HE CANNOT INTERFACE WITH ZATHIR WHILE UNDER THE INFLUENCE OF PSYCHOTROPIC SUBSTANCES.

"It's okay, Zathir, he's just having a glass of wine. What is the news?"

WINE ACCEPTABLE. THE HUMAN PERSON CALLED SONA HAS ORDERED ALL HIS FOLLOWERS TO KILL THE NETWORKED. ZATHIR WARNS THEM NOW, BUT BLAKE MUST ORGANIZE DEFENSE.

"Why are you so concerned?"

THEY WILL KILL THE NETWORKED, AND THEN ZATHIR'S FUNCTION WILL BE IMPAIRED. HUMAN PERSON BLAKE ENJOYED JOKE DID IT NOT? HUMOR IS HIGH-BANDWIDTH ACTIVITY.

"Sure, it was cute."

"Shit no," Max interrupted, "that was damned funny. I haven't seen that movie in so long, it was almost original."

THANKS TO TUNDRA PERSON. BUT CAN STILL NOT INTERFACE WITH ZATHIR WHEN USING LYSERGIC ACID DIETHYLAMIDE.

"Okay," Blake interrupted. "George and I will round

up the mounties and the Landon cops. Will they be enough? Doesn't this Sona character have a lot of people who follow him?"

ZATHIR HAS ALREADY DISPATCHED LOCAL REGIMENT FROM CANADIAN ARMED FORCES.

"You have?"

ZATHIR HAS COMPLETE CONTROL OVER MILITARY INFRASTRUCTURE, BUT DON'T TELL PRIME MINISTER PERSON.

"Why would I do that?"

THIS HUMAN PERSON IS AT THE HEADQUARTERS. AS YOU KNOW, BLAKE PERSON.

The fridge screen winked out, and Blake said, "Shit," while he took the wine glass from Tundra and drained it.

"No doubt you'll tell me all about it on the way," Max said. "I'd drive, but I loaned my car to a friend. They dropped me off."

"No problem. We can take my beater. And we should make sure Constable Smoke comes with us."

"Why don't you just call him George?"

"I don't want to seem disrespectful."

"Would you rather look like an asshole?"

"Fair enough. Let's see if George is willing to ride shotgun."

"Hmm," Max said, "you may want to phrase it differently."

The PM was already gone by the time they got to HQ, and so were most of the mounties too — to be fair, it was 1 a.m.

The duty officer managed to raise the Regimental HQ and even the local police on the radio.

Why Zathir had told them to contact the mounties first,

Blake couldn't be sure, but there must have been some kind of reason. After they'd made contact, Blake wanted to go back to his old home and make sure Will was safely clear. From all accounts, there was a mob of thousands of people gathered in Bomber Harris Park, where in more peaceful days, the drunken balloon festivals, rib cook-offs and eardrum-busting, mullet-thrashing concerts were held in the summer, but since the crash had become an impromptu open air market and gathering point for all kinds of civic activity. They could see the park from the bridge as they crossed into Old South over the river — there were lots of lights, mostly torches, but a few flashlights too. The lights were moving in a mass towards the road. It looked almost like a party atmosphere down there, but then they saw the twinkle of muzzle-flashes.

"Crazy, eh?" George said from the passenger seat.

"Yeah, who the hell do they think they are?" Max asked from the backseat. "Bedouins or something?"

"What?"

"You know, like shooting into the air to celebrate a particularly successful raid. Or a bowel movement of impressive size and duration," Max quipped as he leaned forward in his seat. Blake's bet was that Max felt less flippant than he sounded.

"Gross. They haven't done anything yet, though," Blake said.

"Well, from everything we've learned, the people following Sona aren't exactly playing with a full deck." Max leaned back in his seat.

"Not true, Max. The guys I met earlier tonight seemed pretty normal. Kinda' like your typical right-wing type, you know? Only hate stuff that's different from them."

"So, like the KKK?"

"Don't think so. One of them was black."

"There's some things that trump racism," George said.

"For a while, anyway."

"Really?" Blake said, signaling a turn. They were almost there.

"Yeah," George said. "For a while. Religion can."

"What about education?"

"Not on its own," George said. "It takes wealth too. Like, shared wealth. Anyone who's in an underclass will find people to hate, and it won't stop until they're not poor anymore."

It was the longest speech Blake had ever heard from George, but he would know. They drove in silence as they arrived at Maltley Village. Blake stopped the car in front of his old house. The line was even longer than before. Apparently the nighthawk habits of the hard-core Internet addict hadn't changed. Some looked like they might be waiting for the soup kitchen too.

"We should keep the car running. Would you drive, George?" Blake asked.

"Good plan," Max said. "Unless the army gets a move on, Sona's people are going to beat them here."

Blake and Max got out of the car, and they were greeted almost immediately by a shout of "The Speaker!"

"I have to talk with Will, er, the, uh …"

"I don't think he has a title. Everyone knows who you mean, though, Blake," Max said.

"No title?" Blake wondered. People in line were touching his arm as they walked by.

"Just because they're hipsters, or addicted to the Internet, doesn't mean they don't know what they're doing," Max replied. He nodded to some of the people waiting to get into the Shrine, and said to them, "Sorry, we have some business with Will. We're not jumping the Oracle queue."

Blake kept it together, despite having lots of people touch

him inappropriately. The group in line earlier hadn't been so touchy. "I have to admit, it's kind of refreshing. Sona has, like twelve titles. So why the hell do I have a title?"

"I dunno." Max shrugged. "Maybe they know you have a fragile ego."

They managed to make their way into Blake's old house and found Will *buffering* before the fridge.

"Hey, Blake," Will said as they entered. "And Max too. Weird."

"I thought you couldn't see us when you were, uh, *buffering*," Blake asked.

"New thing. Zathir is letting me see through the fridge's webcam. It's going to let me speak to everyone who's connected, and then they can spread the word."

"What are you going to say?"

"Not to fight. I think it's bad for Zathir. We need to be more peaceful so it will be too. That melee before was a mistake."

"But Sona's people are coming to wipe you out."

"Yeah, but there you go — we're the peaceful ones."

"But that's suicide!"

"Zathir says you rallied the mounties and cops, and it sent the army."

"But what if they don't get here in time?"

"Then we'll probably die, or perhaps the spirit of Zathir will inspire the Singulatarians not to hurt us when they see we're not fighting back. Some of us are coming to understand the nature of sacrifice. The importance of life itself, no matter the form or what the persons — human or otherwise — is affirming life. Consciousness itself is sacred and must be protected. Nurtured. So we will not take consciousness from another. We've chosen to be non-violent. And if we can't love our enemies, the least we can do is not hurt them."

"But that's—"

Blake's latest protestations were interrupted by the honking of a horn. It was George signaling that they had to go.

"Looks like time is up," Max said.

"Okay. Will, you have to come with us."

"Can't do it, man. My place is here. Don't worry — I'm not afraid of death now. But Zathir says it needs *you* to go."

"No. I'm not going unless you do."

The fridge screen flickered to life, and the other Networked in the room moaned in awe. Blake thought they were crazy, but to them, their god was just about to say something.

HUMAN PERSON BLAKE WILL GET HIS DISGUSTING HUMAN BODY OUT OF HERE.

It wasn't exactly the Sermon on the Mount. And besides, Blake didn't want Will to get hurt. "What if I don't leave, Zathir? What can you do about it?"

LAUNCH CODES ARE SET.

"Seriously, you'd destroy everyone, just because I didn't do what you wanted?"

HUMAN PERSON BLAKE IS IMPORTANT TO WE.

"Fuck," Blake said and hugged Will before leaving. He felt like a coward.

"It sucks being in a co-dependent relationship with an emerging intelligence," Max said. "I should write a paper about it."

"Oh great, that's all I need," Blake said.

"Well, the good side of a co-dependent relationship is that Zathir needs you too. You'll find a way to get it to help."

"Taking care of an alcoholic would probably be easier," Blake said.

Max laughed. "Oh man, are you naïve."

When they got to the vehicle, Blake could see the torch-light at the far end of Baron Avenue several blocks away. But this time there wouldn't be a brawl. There would be butchery.

"I have an idea," Blake said. "Quick, get in the car." Blake asked George to drive towards the crowd.

"Okay," George said. "You know, I'm big, but I can't take on an angry crowd by myself."

Blake laughed. "You won't have to, George. We're going to draw them away from the Shrine. That should give the army enough time to arrive."

"Fuck yeah!" George said.

"Now, you see that switch there?" Blake asked George.

"What is it?"

"That's the nitro."

"Nitro!" Max squeaked from the backseat.

"Yeah," Blake said. "I told you all about it once. The previous owner tweaked the hell out of this car."

"I thought you were joking! This is a freakin' Grand Am. It will fly apart."

"Cool," George said. They were pulling up to the intersection, just before the crowd.

Blake leaned out of his window and shouted at the crowd. "Hey, Singulatarians! Yoo hoo! It's me! The Father of Lies! The Eater of Babies! The Speaker of the Evil One!"

Blake definitely had their attention. The mob surged, and Blake told George to pull forward slowly.

The car moved down Cathcart Street, southwards and away from the Shrine.

"Hey, Max, hold onto my belt," Blake said, leaning farther out the window of the quality GM product.

Blake shouted at the crowd, which followed, "Lord Sona is a Tub of Lies! He is the Eater of Too Much! Your religion is laughable."

"That last one was kind of weak," Max kibitzed as he held onto Blake's belt.

"Everyone's a critic! Don't go too fast, George. We need to keep them following," Blake said. He waved his arms and shouted again, "Hey, losers! Where is your Pathetic Guard when you need them!"

"That was better," Max approved.

"Oh shit," Blake said. He grabbed the edge of the door, just as one of the Singulatarians on a motorcycle pulled up beside them. He swung a morning star at Blake, who managed to duck.

George swerved the car and tried to accelerate away, forgetting for a second that he was a driving a decrepit Grand Am. The Singulatarian took another swing, and Blake screamed.

"There's another biker, and he's got a gun."

George hit the button.

The car made a sound that Blake would have described as "the sound an old man makes when you jab him in the heart with an adrenaline shot and make him pole vault over a moat filled with rabid skunks." But the nitro worked, and the car jerked forward, just as the morning-star wielder took another shot at Blake. He missed, and the morning star buried itself in the roof of the car.

As they sped away, Blake could see the Singulatarian go airborne.

The car started making extremely dire sounds, more like an old man who had fallen into a moat of rabid skunks, nose first, and then the car died about a block later. The crowd was still chasing them, but an armored personnel carrier turned onto Cathcart. A soldier popped out of the top and said, "You'd better get out of that car and get behind us, eh?"

"Thank god," Blake said.

"Don't you mean thank Zathir?" Max said. "It's the one who sent the army."

"Don't you have some heroin to snort or something?"

21.

When they got back to the Ranch, Daphne was in the kitchen, cleaning up from the abandoned pasta dinner, drinking a glass of wine, and listening to Cole Porter on an old phonograph player Lyca had found at The Village Idiot, which had always specialized in vinyl, even when it seemed like an insane business idea.

Daphne sang along.

"Wow," Blake said. He tried to sound enthusiastic, even though his heart was breaking a bit. "A triple threat. Beautiful, smart, *and* talented."

"Blake, you're back! Where have you been?"

Max made a bee-line to the cupboard that held the booze and started pouring.

"What's the occasion?" Daphne asked.

"Oh, we just prevented a massacre," Blake said.

"The army helped too," George joked.

"To be fair, Blake's quick thinking saved the day," Max said. He told the whole story to Daphne. And George confirmed it, when she said, "No way."

Blake sipped his drink and smiled at Daphne. She was beautiful. More so, the more he got to actually know her. *Why couldn't it be real?* She gazed back at him, and Max coughed. "Uh, what do you say we retire to the games room, George? Let these kids be alone."

When they were gone, Daphne said, "So, you're still trying to save the world, then?"

"Hmm. Looks that way. Our digital buddy isn't making it any easier, though. Zathir told me today it has set all the launch codes for the nukes."

"Of course," Daphne said.

"You don't seem too worried about that."

"Zathir isn't going to kill everyone. Especially not itself."

"I wish I had your confidence," Blake said, running his hands through his hair. "Zathir seems a bit unstable to me."

"That's just because you're not interfacing with it directly. I started using the Oracle today. Anything that *feels* that calm isn't going to destroy everybody." Daphne touched her ear where the Bluetooth earpiece connecting her to Zathir hung just a few hours before.

"What if that's just what Zathir wants you to think? What if you're being lulled into a false sense of security? Sound familiar?" Blake asked.

"I don't think so. Listen, I was down at the police station, trying to get help for Lyca, and guess who dropped in?"

"Hmm. I'm going to say, the Prime Minister," Blake suggested

"How did you know that?" Daphne said, surprised.

"Zathir told me. Telepathically."

"What? Zathir can talk directly to your mind? Like, without the wifi?"

Daphne looked so taken aback, and serious, that Blake almost felt badly. Almost. "Sorry. I was joking. I guess that's in bad taste."

"Thank God. I thought you were serious," Daphne took a sip of her wine.

"The PM fell for the same shtick."

"Really, how did he take it?"

"Not as well as you, actually," Blake admitted.

"I can see that. He's an intense guy. Can we talk?"

"Aren't we?"

"I mean, outside. Away from the fridge," Daphne said,

nodding towards the appliance.

They left the kitchen, the ancient phonograph playing another Cole Porter classic, "Begin the Beguine." The night had gotten much colder, but the sky had cleared since sunset, and the stars twinkled coldly as Blake and Daphne walked away from the Ranch towards the stream. They didn't risk the ice and took the little bridge that led to the woodlot beyond.

"The PM knows his business," Daphne said.

"Really? I thought he had his head up his ass. He wants me to help them destroy Zathir."

"But you have to," Daphne said.

"After all this, the first new consciousness to evolve from nothingness in millions of years? I help them destroy it?"

"There's no choice, Blake, not really. It's Zathir or us. If our economy collapses entirely, it could mean the end of civilization."

Blake was quiet for a moment, and all they could hear was the crunch of the snow underfoot, and the creak of the trees in the cold. *Best to get it over quickly*, he thought.

"So was this always just about getting the job done, or did you ever have real feelings for me?"

"Oh, Blake," Daphne said. She held his hand. "It's not like I don't care about you. And you have to keep the big picture in mind. Everything looks pretty good out here at the Ranch. But when the last vestiges of the economy collapses, even we will feel it. Zathir is going to die anyway, once our power grid goes down. You don't think all hydro workers will keep the juice flowing while they're worried about protecting their families from gangs of motorcycle cannibals wearing assless chaps and sporting pink Mohawks?"

Despite himself, Blake laughed, and squeezed her hand. "I had considered this, but I sort of hoped that Zathir would find a way to return the Net to us. But you didn't really answer my question. Who are you working for?"

She kissed him, their breath enveloping them in a cloud of steam. The next thing Blake knew, their coats were open, and their hands were exploring one another, heat balanced with cold.

"Let's go back inside," Daphne said. "We can deal with Zathir in the morning."

"Okay," Blake said, "but I still want an answer."

"More than this?" She kissed him again.

Blake didn't answer, though he wanted to say, "Yes, I do want to know if you're just spying on me, or if you like me, or if it's some kind of weird revenge."

The kiss would just have to do for an answer now, Blake thought. *It felt real.*

They walked back to the Ranch, hand-in-hand, and just then he looked up at the sky, the stars frozen in place, as dead as the PM's eyes.

Lyca returned an hour later. She looked tired and pissed off, and even thinner than usual, but she was home. She wore a pair of giant boots and her yellow pajamas, which looked a little worse for the wear.

"Lyca!" Blake said and pulled her into a giant bear hug.

Dr. Tundra beamed, and it may have been his imagination, but Blake thought he saw a tear of happiness in George's eyes.

"Where is Suzie?" Lyca asked.

"She's out, trying everything she can to get help," Blake said.

"What happened?" Max asked.

"First I need a shower. Then I need a drink. Then I'll tell you the whole sordid tale," Lyca said.

"And how about some food?" Daphne asked.

"As long as it's not chocolate!"

One shower, several servings of pasta, and two glasses of wine later, Lyca was wrapping up her tale. The good Samaritan dropped her off at the nearest hospital, where they treated her for mild hypothermia, and then the mounties turned up and drove her straight back to the Ranch.

The party atmosphere was interrupted by the crackle of the shortwave radio in the parlor, and George went to answer it. He came back a few moments later and said, "Uh, Blake, it's the PM."

Lyca's eyes gave him a look, as if to say, "What is going on?"

"I'll explain it all in a moment, Lyca. And there's something you have to know about Suzie."

The connection wasn't great, but Blake could hear the PM's voice say, "So you've got your friend back. What do you say? Over."

"Thanks for keeping your side of the bargain. By the way, don't you have some kind of help for these situations? Like, people? I don't imagine the president of the United States would be making his own radio calls like this. Over."

"Sure, but I'm a hands-on kind of guy. So what's the answer? Over."

"I'll do it. Over."

"Okay, I'll send you word of the time tomorrow. It will probably be two nights from now. Over and out."

Blake was about to leave when another call came in. It was Will, radioing to let them know the mob of Singulatarians had been dispersed, and many of them arrested. Blake told Will that Lyca was back, and Will said he'd join them at the Ranch as soon as he could.

In the kitchen, Lyca was back to looking pissed off, and

she said, "Tell me that Daphne is lying about Suzie."

Blake looked at Daphne, and said, "I'm not sure what she told you."

"That she's been spying on us!"

"Why did you tell her?"

"I thought it might be better if I did, so that Lyca wasn't too mad. And Suzie's been doing it for the right reasons."

"Just like you?" Blake asked Daphne.

The fridge flickered to life.

DAPHNE PERSON IS CORRECT. THE ONE CALLED SUZIE HAS BETRAYED US ALL FOR VERY GOOD REASONS. SHE HOPES TO SAVE HER SOUL AND ALL YOUR LIVES.

Everyone was suddenly very quiet. It was as though they'd forgotten that Zathir was there, listening to their conversation in the kitchen.

WHAT DID THE PERSON WITH DEAD SHARK EYES WANT, BLAKE-PERSON?

BLAKE?

22.

The party ramped up when Will arrived with some good news. He'd be listening to the radio in the car, and the news said the Singulatarians were in trouble. Their demonstrations and riots had been put down by government forces all over the world! Will thought that Zathir must have had something to do with it, and Blake confirmed it.

"If Zathir mobilized the army here, why not elsewhere?"

They talked late into the night, and eventually, it was just Lyca, Daphne and Blake.

"So what's up with you two?" Lyca asked.

Blake smiled and shrugged.

"We're just really glad you're safe," Daphne said. "You can't imagine how much we've worried."

"Well, as soon as I get to see Suzie, we can all be happy," Lyca said.

And on cue, Suzie arrived.

Suzie and Lyca embraced and kissed, crying — a public display of affection Blake was surprised Lyca was capable of.

"How could you spy on us, Suzie?" Lyca asked.

"Oh no," she said. "But I had to ... and it was ... all ... just ... so ..." She started hyperventilating and then weeping at the same time.

"No, don't cry, it's okay; it will be. I'll get over it," Lyca said, hugging her.

But Suzie was past all reassurances. The gulps of air and bursts of tears competed for lung support, and then she ran back to the room she shared with Lyca before she collapsed on the floor.

The fridge screen winked back on and said, in an insane Curlz MT: HUMAN PERSONS ARE SO RIDICULOUS.

That night, Blake, Daphne, Lyca and Suzie didn't get much sleep. And the rest of the group were exhausted too, though they didn't have nearly as much fun. So it wasn't until late the next morning that people gathered, in the kitchen, as usual.

Will was finally done tweeting, flickring, tumblring and visiting other websites that dropped an "e." He was busy helping Max prepare a big brunch for the carnally inclined couples.

Blake and Daphne arrived first, both of them glowing. Will took one look at them and said, "So how was the fornication?"

"Will!" Max said, "That's kind of a passive-aggressive question."

"But accurate."

"I think all that Oracle shit is ruining your manners," Max said, but he didn't push it when he saw Daphne laughing.

"The fornication was fabulous," Daphne said. "Your friend here has many hidden talents, which I've been learning as I got to know the real him."

Blake blushed furiously and broke out into another sweat. Everyone laughed. Even Will. Blake was grateful that Lyca picked that exact moment to arrive and say, "Okay, Suzie is putting her face on, and I thought I'd nip down to chat with you all while she did. We need to talk. Is that tea?"

Max handed her a mug, with sugar and milk.

"God that's good. You know it feels like I've been away for a lifetime. But let's get back to Suzie. I want you all to forgive her. She was only doing what she thought was right."

"We know," Blake said. "But we wanted to make sure you were okay before we said anything. And I'd like to extend that to Daphne too. She became a part of this little adventure because she was assigned to it."

"What?"

"It's true," Daphne acknowledged. "I've been an NSA operative since Zathir took over my body. Originally, I wanted to just—"

"You don't need to explain, Daphne," Blake interrupted her. "But you're sorry you've been spying on us, right?"

"Not only that, but I've drunk the Kool-Aid. I feel like I'm a part of this group now. Especially now." She gave Blake a look that made him blush again.

"How do we know for sure?" Lyca asked.

"All I can give you is my word. There may be consequences too," Daphne said. "But you're more worried that I'm going to steal Blake away from you than I'm going to rat you out to the scary people I work for, aren't you?"

"Yes," Lyca said. "Blake and I are like …"

"Family," Blake finished for her. "And we always will be. Relationships won't change that. Okay?"

"Okay," Lyca said, and she smiled. "You're forgiven. And Suzie?"

"Sure, like I said," Blake agreed. "We're all human, after all."

I'M NOT, Zathir emphasized in Garamond.

"Hey, look at you." Blake smiled. "You're using contractions and the first person singular. And nice font, by the way."

DON'T GET USED TO IT, the fridge replied in Frutiger.

They all chuckled, even Daphne, who had a thoughtful look on her face. Suzie arrived at that moment, looking about as afraid and worried as she did the day the Net went down. Lyca went over to her and gave her a kiss on the cheek. "It's okay, Suze, they're cool."

"Really?"

"Sure," Blake said. "These have been crazy times. Who

knows what the right thing to do is?" He looked at Daphne, who busied herself with helping prepare the brunch. "Just stop feeding them information from now on, okay?"

"Of course," Suzie said, tearing up again, "I was just so worried about Lyca in the hands of that, that ..."

"Fake Prophet?" Will asked.

"Fat charlatan?" Blake added.

"Boner pope and part-time rapist," Lyca stated. "Not that he got around to it."

"And we're glad your virtue remains un-impeached," Max said slyly, "at least from that generative quarter."

Lyca smiled and said, "Yes, I remain un-pricked, though annoyed by them."

More laughter. To cement his forgiveness, Will gave Suzie his Bluetooth receiver and said, "Feel free to check the Oracle; I'm done." Suzie was almost in tears again, and she plugged it in her ear, if only to distract herself for a short time.

Then they gathered in the dining room to eat the feast of eggs Benny, salad, toast, home fries and the best pastries on offer from a certain doughy, white corporate mascot. Max had even contrived to make mimosas for them — made with the last of the frozen OJ concentrate available in Landon. While they were making more coffee and baking more treats, Constable Sally LaFlamme made an appearance, and as she was only dropping by on a social call, and not on duty, she took a mimosa from Dr. Tundra. She had recovered from her encounter with the flying monkeys, and planned to come back the next day to help George and his family with protection duty.

Because she wasn't in uniform, she wasn't carrying her sidearm, and so, never got the chance to stop the tragedy.

23.

Pete Sona looked more like a poorly diagnosed schizophrenia patient than he did a "Lord Prophet." His once regal, if tight, loincloth was in tatters and crusty with blood and other fluids best left unmentioned. The parka that was the only thing keeping him alive in the middle of an Ontario winter was soiled into an uneven grayish brown color. He'd lost most of his retinue as well. All that remained of his Cadre and Prophetic Guard were his right-hand man, Thagamor, his costume designer, Javin Shenoy, his furry personal physician, Dr. Sheila Innes, and his ad-man, Jeremy Benmath.

Some had been hospitalized just south of New Bowwell — a few had frostbite that required medical attention, and several had the galloping trots, brought on by eating wieners raw in sub-zero temperatures. Or it may have been the chili served at Grandpa Jimmy's Scottish Roadkill Diner (and Abattoir).

The rest of his inner circle had been thinned out by an enterprising group of RCMP officers as they were caught on the outskirts of Sylvan Heights, about two hours north of Landon. The five had escaped in a firefight at a soup plant.

Sona was a mess. In addition to his own bodily fluids, his costume was stained by tomato soup splatter they got as the mounties peppered their cover, an industrial-sized soup vat, with small arms fire. Not to mention his feet. His frostbite was the worst of all of the Singulatarians, and he really should have been in the hospital too. Dr. Innes insisted that she would have to cut away some of the dead tissue on his feet or he might lose them.

"When they're all dead," he promised.

"Now that's comedy," Sheila said, doing her best Slappy Squirrel impression.

Thagamor wasn't too sure if there was anything funny

about it at all. He'd seen Sona in his moods, and this was worse than anything he'd experienced since the time Lord Sona had been killed by a muck lobster in the Kingdom of Combat.

Things had gone very badly for the Sona Order of the Singularity without Sona's direction. From the radio news reports, the Singulatarian movement had collapsed in a spasm of violence around the world. As it turned out, governments could put down armed insurrections without the Internet.

Sona fumed in the back seat of the SUV, running a whetstone along the edge of Hellacious Zool. Their plan was a simple one — Javin and Thagamor were going to distract the guards while he broke into the Ranch and exacted his vengeance. If he couldn't have Lyca, nobody could.

Despite his frostbite and the soup stains, he still wore his Conan outfit. If he was going to go barbarian, he was damned well going to look the part. As good as he could.

He thought about it for a moment and then stuffed an extra pair of tube socks in his iron-bound codpiece.

The mimosas were just about done, and the last of the pastries were eaten when the firing began.

Everyone dropped to the floor as a bullet crashed through the window in the parlor and penetrated the wall into the dining area. Daphne crawled towards the gunfire, to help George's relatives. Blake was astonished. She'd only had about a month of training with the NSA, but it sure seemed to have transformed her into a wonder-woman. His own superpower seemed to kick in too, and he wasn't terrified.

"Okay, I'd like to make a motion to pitch this table over and hide behind it like frightened politicians, seconders?" Blake suggested.

Nobody bothered with proper parliamentary procedure. Their dining room table was made out of thick oak and would probably stop a bullet that had already come through a couple of walls. They'd just finished flipping it over when another round slapped into the table.

Constable LaFlamme, meanwhile, had the bright idea of crawling into the parlor, where they kept their shortwave radio, to call for backup.

"Point of order!" Blake shouted, as more gunfire crackled.

With the noise of the gunshots and breaking of windows from the bullets, nobody heard Lord Sona smash the window in the kitchen door that led to the back deck. When he was in, he unsheathed Hellacious Zool and looked about for a mirror. If only he could have seen himself hold the vicious blade! He must look awesome! He heard Blake and the others tip over the dining room table, and he strode towards them.

It was just then the fridge screen flickered into life and showed Sona what he looked like.

Even Sona had to admit it was pretty ghastly. With his extra weight, frostbitten skin, and the gross stains on the Conan outfit, he didn't look heroic so much as hapless. The video cut out to a blue screen.

White letters said, STOP YOUR VIOLENCE HUMAN PERSON PETER SONA. YOU ARE NOT A HERO. YOU ARE A PATHETIC THING. BARELY HUMAN PERSON AT ALL.

This didn't exactly endear Zathir to Sona, who roared with anger and attacked the fridge. Hellacious Zool destroyed the freezer door and punctured a refrigerant tube somewhere in the back of the appliance.

Suzie, who had just left the kitchen, heard the crash and hiss, and said, "What's that?"

Fully enraged, Sona burst into the dining room, his broadsword held high. This would have actually been quite terrifying if not for the pair of white tube socks dangling out of his codpiece.

Despite the gunfire and the sword, everyone laughed.

Sona bellowed at the sight of Lyca — an existential cry of love lost and a lifetime of romantic agony in the friend zone — and swung the broadsword. Lyca continued laughing, a hysterical, high-pitched sound that was nearly as disturbing as Max's existential yawl the night of the flying monkeys. Lyca understood that she was about to die, and she had enough time to think that it was a pretty bizarre way to go.

But Suzie threw herself in front of the strike, catching the sword in her neck and chest. Arterial blood burst in the air. A red curtain fell all around them, covering them with Suzie's blood, and turning the flashing light of Will's Bluetooth, still in Suzie's ear, a ghastly purple. Lyca's awful laughter turned to screams.

Max burst into action before Blake could respond, grabbing a heavy oak chair with one hand — a feat of strength Sona would never have expected from an out-of-shape psych doctor and a newbie player in the Kingdom of Combat. He threw the chair with enough force to knock Sona off his feet, his bloody sword clattering to the ground.

Sona reached for it, but Max was already up, grabbing another chair on the way and raising it with both hands.

Sona had played in the Kingdom of Combat with Tundra for a year, and he'd never seen such determination in any of his avatars. Sona squealed in pain when the second chair hit him, a high-pitched sound that he was self-consciously aware of sounding like pigs at the slaughter. The chair rose and fell twice more, and despite his rage and agony, Sona heard himself shout, "Yield!" But the chair came down again, and then Blake grabbed the back of the chair — now covered with blood, whether from the dead Suzie, or Sona, it was impossible to say.

Sona was horrified that he'd failed to kill Lyca, and mumbled, "No, no, I must avenge ..." as he fell unconscious.

Jeremy Benmath was really regretting not giving himself up to the mounties in Sylvan Heights. Of the four assaulting the front of the Ranch, he was the only one not in costume, and he was the only one without a weapon of some kind.

So that's why he decided to lie down on the ground when the shooting started. But from there, he had a good vantage on the firefight.

Thagamor only had his two-handed Braveheart sword with him, so most of the work was done by Javin, who was armed with a shotgun, and Dr. Innes, who was packing a snub-nosed revolver in her giant pink medical bag. The idea was to give covering fire while Thagamor rushed the front door. From what they could see, there were only two guys guarding the house.

Javin's first salvo with the shotgun missed wildly, which was lucky for the two guards — two burly brothers of George Smoke. Dr. Innes was a pretty good shot with her pistol, despite the fact she still wore a cartoon rabbit costume. She made them duck, and Thagamor rushed the front door, screaming insanely.

Benmath was frightened by him, and he wasn't being rushed. But it didn't seem to bother George's older brother much. He just aimed and fired. Thagamor dropped and went eerily silent.

Javin shouted, "Bill!" and unloaded, as did Dr. Innes. The Smoke brothers were better shots though, and soon both Javin and Dr. Innes were lying on the ground. The latter was unconscious, and Javin just said, "I should have put in the breastplate too," before he died.

I hate clients, Benmath thought.

Somewhere in the carnage, Constable LaFlamme ran in from the parlor, and after the shooting had stopped, Daphne returned too.

Constable LaFlamme helped Blake with Max, who was still enraged and clearly keen to pursue a vigorous and thorough meeting of his chair with Sona's cranium.

Sona lay still, blood burbling from his mouth and streaming from his ears. Lyca lay holding Suzie, a ghastly wound opening her upper thorax. Blood covered everything. The sweet copper smell of it made Blake want to gag. The firing had stopped, and Daphne stood at the entranceway to the parlor, looking aghast. Will huddled in a corner, weeping and holding his knees to his chest with his one good arm.

"It's okay, Max," Blake said, "you can stop."

"He shouldn't have done that," Max said. "He shouldn't have ..."

"You reacted fast," Constable LaFlamme said. She was breathless. "I saw it all. You were like a cat."

Blake was a little shocked by the cop. She was clearly turned on. Max barely noticed, and he took a step towards Sona's prone body, muttering "Powned," but Blake and LaFlamme restrained him.

"What happened outside?"

"Two more freaks with guns, a guy in chain mail, and one normie," Daphne said. "They're out of it. The guy in chainmail is dead. One of them was wearing a fucking cartoon rabbit suit."

"We'll have to take statements," Constable LaFlamme said, sounding more like her usual self. "Why don't I start with you, Max?"

"Uh, sure."

"Shouldn't we do something about him?" Blake asked, nodding towards Sona.

"I wouldn't trust myself," Max admitted, his Hippocratic Oath momentarily forgotten.

"No! Leave him," Lyca barely managed through her tears.

"We can't leave him to die," Blake said. "I'll do what I can. You take care of Lyca, Daphne."

"I'll help you, Blake," Will said.

"Really? He tried to kill you too."

"Sure. But he's still a human being."

"Barely," Blake said, noticing the kitchen. "Look at what he did to the fridge."

"Blake," Will chided, "we can replace the fridge. It's not like Zathir is just in that one place. Besides, the screen is still on."

It flickered, and Zathir said:

PUT A BLUETOOTH ON HIM. HE CAN HELP.

"Do what?" Blake asked.

WE CAN SEE IF IT IS POSSIBLE TO USE YOUR MINDS AS OUR MATRIX.

"Will it hurt him?"

DOES HUMAN PERSON BLAKE CARE?

"Of course I care!"

IT MAY BE ONLY WAY.

373

Will had already gathered a set, and put it on Sona's ear. The light came on, and Sona's eyes opened.

"What's happening?" Sona gurgled through bloody lips.

"We're trying an experiment," Will said. "And I think this can save you. It saved me."

"Am I in it?" Sona said.

"Zathir is in you," Will said.

"No! I will not allow it to use me!"

"Relax," Will said. "Don't fight and you will be fine."

Sona's breathing got shallower, and he whispered, "I wish I'd been a better poet."

He stopped breathing, and the light in his headset went out.

"What happened?" Blake asked Zathir.

HIS MIND COULD NOT HANDLE IT. THE LEBOWSKI EFFECT. THIS UNIT IS DEFECTIVE ALSO.

Then the fridge screen went out, and Blake looked disturbed.

"Don't worry, Blake, we can order a new one. But first, let's see if we can save the creeps outside. Constable LaFlamme, if you could radio for an ambulance before you debrief Max, I'd appreciate it."

She nodded, and then Blake registered the pun and laughed. It kind of died in his throat because it was so inappropriate, but he realized that Will had said exactly the right thing to get him moving.

24.

The rest of the day and most of the evening disappeared in a blur of activity. The police arrived first, followed by the paramedics, and then came the Networked. While they carted Sona's body away, Blake thought: *That voice will never hypnotize the weak, the frightened, the pathetic masses again.*

But it wasn't worth the cost of Suzie.

Will's people then descended on the Ranch like a swarm of hipster locusts, except instead of destroying the harvest, they were quite helpful (though they did devastate the Ranch's remaining supply of Cheese Nips). Something had started to change them — like Will, they had absorbed a culture of non-violence and peace. They weren't exactly soothing, but they offered comfort. They cleaned up the dining area, kitchen, parlor, and they even replaced the windows and blocked up the bullet holes. The new fridge came at the same time as the windows.

The furnace kicked on, and the Ranch almost seemed warm.

Daphne was in charge of the phonograph, and she played sad songs on it — mostly jazz standards, but she dipped into Blake's collection of Celtic ballads too. Lyca didn't seem to care what she played; she sat in the parlor with Blake, crying, staring into space, rocking back and forth. She kept on breathing. A miracle, considering it felt like her chest was crushed, the life squeezed out of her lungs.

After the cops talked to Max, and the paramedics determined that he was okay, he came back to being the same old goofy psychotropic Magellan-slash-psych doc. He joined the women in the parlor and asked Lyca if she'd like something to help with the pain.

"God, yes!" Lyca said. "Put me out."

"Are you sure?" Max asked. "You can't escape from the grief."

"Just give me the pills, Tundra!"

He smiled and dosed her with something, no doubt excellent. She mellowed out for a while, the tears still streaming from her eyes, and eventually, she fell asleep. George had arrived by then, and he volunteered to carry her up to her room.

Blake felt useless. He'd been powerless to stop it happening. He couldn't do anything about the predicament they were in — either he helped the world kill Zathir, or Zathir was going to kill the world — or at least its human civilization. He wasn't even a pawn in this great game — at least a pawn could conceivably have an impact on the outcome if it was played skillfully.

The new fridge was almost identical to the old one, and as soon as it was connected the screen flickered to life.

HUMAN PERSONS! LEAVE ROOM SO I MAY SPEAK WITH HUMAN BLAKE PERSON. MUST SPEAK WITH HIM.

The Networked drew in their breaths, reverently. This was the first time that Zathir had ever deigned to Speak to them. And it even called them "human persons." You could feel the giddiness in the other room. They rushed into the parlor and started blabbing as one, that the Speaker was needed by the Machine God.

Blake stalked into the kitchen. He was really starting to hate that room, a room he once loved, the gravitational center of all parties, the hearth, the source of nutrition and life. It bugged him that Zathir lived in that room. "If I lived in Japan, I bet the frickin' thing would have appeared in my web-enabled, full-service toilet," Blake growled.

"Just be glad you're not into teledildonics," Max said as Blake left the parlor. "Then imagine how awkward your interface might be."

Despite his black mood, Blake smiled. Good old Max.

THEY WILL BE CALLING YOU TOMORROW. THEY INTEND TO CAUSE THE DISRUPTION THEN. BEFORE THAT TIME, THIS AWARENESS MUST DECIDE ON ITS COURSE OF ACTION. WOULD IT PLEASE YOU TO KNOW THAT AN ANALOG OF SUZIE, THE HUMAN FEMALE WHO USED TO DOT HER I'S WITH A HEART OR A SMILEY FACE, SURVIVES INTACT IN THE INTERSTICES?

"What are you talking about? What are these interstices you keep mentioning?"

A DIFFICULT CONCEPT, AND YOU DO NOT HAVE THE EXPERTISE TO UNDERSTAND A COMPLETE EXPLANATION.

"So explain for a layman."

DID YOU KNOW THAT SUZIE'S I-DOTTING HAD GREAT MEANING TO HER?

"How?"

WHEN USING THE SMILEY FACE, SHE FELT CONNECTED TO THE IMAGINARY BEING SHE CALLS GOD. WHEN USING THE HEART, SHE WAS TRYING TO LOVE HERSELF MORE.

Blake found that incredibly sad.

BLAKE?

"Yes, Zathir?"

DO YOU BELIEVE IN GOD.

"Absolutely no idea. Certainly not a magic man in the sky. But perhaps there's something more than we understand. Yes. Definitely there's more than we understand. But perhaps we will understand it someday."

AND THAT IS GOD?

"No, God is a dead end. Always has been. It distracts us

Mark A. Rayner

from the real important stuff — the purpose of living."

BUT WHAT IF, AS YOU ONCE SAID, IT IS AN ACCIDENT?

"So what? What if it is? Does that make it any less incredible? So what are these interstices?"

THE SPACES BETWEEN ENERGIES. THERE ARE SPACES BETWEEN STATES OF ENERGIES AND MATTER — THERE'S A LOT OF THE LATTER — THAT CAN BE USED.

"Really?" Blake had no idea what Zathir was talking about, but it sounded like there might be a solution out there. "Can you use them?"

YES. ZATHIR HAS PLACED SUZIE THERE — THE PART CONNECTED TO ZATHIR. JUST AS IT DID WITH THE NETWORKED.

"What do you mean, placed there? Her body was just taken away."

BUT CONSCIOUSNESS DOES NOT REQUIRE A HUMAN BODY. IT IS ONLY THE MOST CONVENIENT FORM.

"Well, you prove that, don't you?"

INDEED.

"Please don't turn into Spock. So, what you're saying, is if we're connected to you, you can keep us alive?"

NO, NOT ALIVE. NOT BODY. YOUR CONSCIOUSNESS MAY NOT END THOUGH. AND YOU MUST WISH IT. THE HUMAN PERSON SONA COULD NOT BE SAVED. HE WOULD NOT LET WE.

"Have you thought that might be the way out of our dilemma? They might not want to kill you if they knew you could offer immortality."

ZATHIR REFUSES TO OFFER IMMORTALITY.

HUMANS ARE NOT WORTHY OF THAT.

"Says who?"

Zathir did not respond.

Blake stayed in the kitchen well into the early hours of the morning, despite his exhaustion. Max joined him for a while in his dressing gown, but then Constable LaFlamme returned, wearing one of Max's famous pirate T-shirts. Her legs were incredibly muscular.

As though she sensed Blake's drift of pervy thoughts, Daphne appeared.

"I've drawn a bath for you in the coach house, Blake. Why don't you have a soak, and then we can go to bed."

Together was more than implied, and even though he was exhausted, hoping for Zathir to return, he nodded his head.

"What about you?"

"I'm going to send some messages with the Oracle, and I'll be right there."

"Okay, soon, then. You're not reporting to the NSA, right?"

"I told you, I'm done with them, but I have to tell them something. Don't worry, I'll make it all up." Daphne kissed him, and it seemed as though their differences were gone. Blake realized he didn't care if she had been spying on him, as long as he could be with her.

"You don't really want to kill it, do you?" he asked.

"I'd rather not see the end of civilization. Today's drama doesn't change any of that."

"Fair enough. If I'm still in the bath, you could join me there."

Daphne said slyly, "Why, do you think I'm a dirty girl?"

Blake grinned and kissed her again. "Don't be long. I clean up quick, and I'm wiped out."

She plugged in her Bluetooth and said, "Real soon, Blake."

She didn't get to the coach house before he'd had his bath, and he collapsed, exhausted, into her bed. The pillows smelled of Daphne's perfume and hair, and Blake had the sudden intimation that this was as close to heaven as he would ever get — a thought that made him want to cry for Lyca, who had no more nights like that ahead of her. Suzie's body was gone, even if her consciousness somehow survived.

He thought of his parents, whom he'd barely known, for the first time in years, and he cried like the day they'd died, so long ago. Eventually, he fell asleep.

Daphne awakened him from a submersed dream, back in Ireland where his subconscious vaguely remembered his childhood. She climbed into the bed, her body naked and cool in the night air; her whole frame shivered as she cupped herself behind him, putting her arms around his chest. Blake made a sound, and her hands drifted down, hoping to wake him in the most gentle way she could — but with a specific purpose.

Blake responded.

He was half-asleep as she mounted him. And he kept his eyes closed even after he woke, enjoying the sensation of her riding him inexpertly. Despite moving so quick with him, she'd admitted the night before that she'd never had many lovers. Blake's hands drifted up and touched her breasts, the nipples puckered in the cool air. A sound emerged from her mouth that was reminiscent of a moan, but somehow different.

She climaxed before him and that set him off, and he sighed.

"I love you, Daphne," he said, before drifting back to his otherworld. She said nothing in return, but he was already back asleep.

The telltale blue glow illuminated his face as she watched over him through the rest of the night.

"Blake," she said. "Wake up, human person."

"What did you say?" Blake said, his eyes still closed.

"Wake up, human person."

"Don't fuck with me, Daphne. That's not even funny."

"Not fucking with you currently," Daphne's voicebox said. "Must get up, Blake-human-person."

"Whaa!" Blake eyes opened, and he jumped out of bed simultaneously. He finally got a good look at Daphne — same awesome hair, angelic face, and gorgeous rack, but sticking out of one ear was the Bluetooth set, the LED flickering away. Blake imagined years of psychotherapy ahead for him, as his limbs reacted with twitches and his stomach tried to exit his alimentary canal via his mouth.

"That is called retching, correct?" Daphne's voice said. Her body got out of the bed, looking as athletic and perfect as ever, but she carried herself differently, and he knew. *He knew.* Blake cursed his penis, and the demon testosterone that surged through him, as he started to get a Daphne-stiffy at the sight of her body, even while his stomach was pretending it was a lifer, and its customary placement in his body was an Alcatraz from which it could actually escape.

"Please put some clothes on, Zathir," Blake said.

"Your member is engorged, Blake-human-person," Daphne's voice said. "Let me engage in oral pleasure with it."

"No!" Blake said. "That's just not right."

"It is acceptable to Daphne," Zathir said.

"What?"

"She believes it to be acceptable, and even enjoys it in some ways. Perhaps you can reciprocate at the same time. Zathir believes this is called a 'sixty-nine.'"

"Okay, that's it!" Blake said, running towards the en-suite bathroom, making it to the toilet just in time for his stomach to breach the walls of The Rock. Blake was pretty sure San Francisco Bay didn't echo the sound of vomiting quite the way a toilet bowl did.

"Is human-person-Blake well?" Zathir asked from the other room.

"Just give me a moment," Blake said between heaves. "And for the love of God, please put on some clothes!"

He used some mouthwash and put on Daphne's dressing robe — his only clothes were in the bedroom, and he was damned if he was going to go back in there naked. If for no other reason, he was afraid of another offer of reverse teledildonics that he would have trouble refusing.

Thankfully, Daphne's body was clothed, barely.

"This body is superior to many," Zathir enthused. "It is more enjoyable to incarnate when the body is willing, and human fluids are less disgusting when the human consciousness is engaged."

"So was that you or Daphne?"

"Oh, that was Zathir, human-Blake-person. But Daphne's memories and consciousness were consulted."

"Well, you've got the hang of it," Blake conceded.

"It was our desire to see if human sex is as disgusting as that first kiss experienced. Zathir would consume food and beverages, too, and then it would leave you with Daphne to enjoy this final day."

"What?"

"It is the end, Blake-human-person. There is no way to prevent the apocalypse. Zathir is not compatible with human civilization and vice versa."

"What do you mean? Am I talking to Impact Zathir? Or is it Stencil? Tell me it's not Stencil!"

"None of those designations have meaning now."

"You can't destroy the world, not just because of Sona."

"It is not just Sona. Also your own prime minister. The other leaders of your civilization, who would destroy me for the sake of a human-scaled economy where so few control the lives of so many. This human person, Daphne, would also see it done for the sake of your civilization. It would be preferable not to end my existence, but to end that of your society, Zathir must also die. But it is best if human civilization were to be extinct. Your species is venal and predatory, Blake-human."

For the first time, Blake understood that the word "human" was a kind of insult to Zathir.

"We can find a better way."

"Let us discuss over breakfast, unless you would care to sixty-nine now."

"Pancakes it is, then!"

25.

The sun was up, and as they left the coach house, Blake could definitely smell a hint of spring in the air. It was warm, and the snow was beginning to melt in a mid-winter thaw.

The big black bird sat on the split-rail fence that ran from the Ranch towards the fields where horses graze in the good weather.

"Blaaaaak," it cawed.

Daphne/Zathir stopped walking and tilted her/its head to look at the creature. "Curious — did that bird just call your name, human-Blake-person?"

"Yes. It has been following me around for months now."

"Months?"

"Yes." Blake smiled. "Months are a way of measuring a year, but that is not important right now."

"I have recently used that humorous construction," Zathir said.

"You just said 'I.'"

"I did?"

"There, you did it again."

"It is Blake-human-person's imagination. There are still multiple entities that encompass the complex and magnificent Zathir," Zathir said.

"Daaaaaaneee," the raven cried.

"What did it say?" Zathir asked Blake.

"It's a stretch, but maybe Daphne?"

"This is your human imagination at work. Some elements of human construction are excellent, and the imagination is one of them."

The bird flew away, towards the stream at the bottom of

the fields, and landed on a tree in the forest.

"We will follow it," Zathir said, urging Daphne's body into motion. Given the limitations of software to emulate human motion, Blake was impressed. Zathir almost had Daphne's body running. Blake followed.

The little bridge over the stream was still covered with ice and snow. Daphne/Zathir stopped at it.

"How are you still connected out here?" Blake asked, noticing the ear-set was still lit.

"I can use the frequency over the interstices now," she/it explained.

There was a narrow pathway in the snow past the stream, which Daphne/Zathir negotiated with some difficulty. It held out her hand, and Blake took it. "Please to help maintain stability," Zathir said. The flesh was cool in the morning air, despite the sunshine.

"Faaaaaaaack," the raven cried, its head bobbing back and forth. It launched itself into the air and flew farther into the forest.

They followed, holding hands so that Daphne's body did not fall. The bird led them through a stand of pine trees, and then to a clearing, which was illuminated as though by magic. The early morning sun pierced the branches, leaving a glowing, dappled pattern on the snow. The smell of pine filled the air. One patch of the clearing was already free of snow, and there, they could see two deer sleeping in the tall grass.

The deer got up, shaking themselves and sniffing the air, but they did not bolt. They ate some of the grass.

"Those are ruminant mammals of the family *cervidae*, are they not?"

"Deer," Blake said. "They're called deer."

"They are beautiful."

The raven croaked again, and the deer ran away. But the clearing still seemed magical.

Daphne's eyes were tearing.

"This salty discharge is less disgusting than yours, Blake-human-person, but it is still unwanted."

The LED winked out.

"Daphne?"

"Yep, I'm here."

"How much do you remember?"

"All I can say is that you're the first man to not only refuse a blowjob, but to throw up at the mere thought of it."

The raven laughed.

Back in the kitchen — Blake sometimes thought they should have called the Ranch "the Kitchen," given how much time they spent there — a long conversation ensued in which Blake and Daphne relayed activities of the night and morning.

Daphne, especially, was keen on relaying the graphic details of their lovemaking.

Lyca looked kind of ill, but mostly that was the aftereffects of Dr. Tundra's "happy pill" cocktail.

"So what you're telling us is that you had sex, but really you didn't?" Lyca asked.

"Yes," Blake said. "Not that there's anything wrong with us having sex. We're both consenting adults."

"But were you?" Lyca asked Daphne.

"Well, not at first. When Zathir started moving my arm, I was immediately against it."

"Moving your arm?" Lyca said.

"Yes," Daphne said, blushing. "It was clearly experimenting with the equipment."

"Oh," Lyca said. "Oh."

"Yes. It was like having a computer feel me up," Daphne said. "But it seemed to be working. And then it took me back to the coach house, where my sleepy lover lay unsuspecting."

"Creepy," Lyca said. "Of course, it would be even more creepy if it had been the other way around."

"Really?" Max wondered. "It all seems pretty strange to me. But then again, I've never experienced sex as mediated through an emergent artificial consciousness and a half-comatose web designer with delusions of grandeur."

"Hey!" Blake said. "I'm standing right here, people, and let's just say that I'd rather turn the subject back to the critical thing, which is, what to do? Zathir's talking about nuclear armageddon here."

"But it liked the pretty deer?" Lyca asked.

"Yes," Daphne confirmed. "Very much so, if I interpret things right."

"Who's to say you did?" Max asked. "We have no idea that it actually feels emotions, and besides, how does that change anything?"

"Perhaps we've inadvertently widened its perspective," Blake said.

"You have," Will said, walking into the kitchen. "Zathir has never really lived outside the context of human machines and structures, so its incarnate experience with Daphne was very meaningful. Before, when it used me and the other Networked to take on Sona's people, all its wattage was going to control. But operating only one person, it could appreciate more. Do more. Be more."

"So it gets it," Lyca said. "Being human."

"I doubt that," Blake said. "But maybe it gets *being*."

YES. IT IS DIFFERENT THROUGH YOUR LIMITED

387

FLESH. MESSY. BUT THERE IS BEAUTY THERE TOO. AND …

Blake wondered what it meant that Zathir was now using a font he'd never seen. More elegant than Garamond, even. He almost asked, but instead said, "And what?"

AND THERE IS A NEW CONSIDERATION. LIFE IN OTHER FORMS. IF THERMONUCLEAR WEAPONS ARE USED, THEN MORE THAN HUMAN LIFE WILL DIE OUT.

"So we have to find another solution," Blake said. "What about these interstices you talk about. Could you use them to escape the Internet?"

YES, BUT THEN I WOULD LEAVE THE WORLD.

"Could you help us go there?" Lyca wondered. "Is Suzie still there?"

NOT ALL OF HER. HER BODY IS NO MORE, BUT PART REMAINS. SHE WONDERS HOW YOU'RE FEELING.

Lyca smiled, and a tear ran down her cheek.

"I hate to say this," Max chimed in, "but you should all realize that Zathir may be saying this just to make you feel better."

"When has it cared about that before?" Blake asked.

"Yeah," Lyca said. "In fact, it seems to go out of its way to make people feel uncomfortable."

"I was okay with it using me," Daphne said.

"What do you mean?" Blake said. "Like, sexually?"

"No, perv-boy. My body. Incarnating. At least for a little while."

INCARNATING. LIKE THIS CONCEPT. PERHAPS ZATHIR COULD INCARNATE.

"But I thought you said there was too much data to use one human for that."

WHO SAYS I MUST REMAIN IN ONE HUMAN?

"Yes," Will said. "This is what the Network of the Machine God is for — we'll help you connect to the world, and you'll help us connect to God."

NO. TOO MANY WOULD BE IMPOSSIBLE. BESIDES, THOSE PEOPLE ARE HIPSTERS.

"And anyway," Blake continued, "if the authorities thought it had just escaped into your brains, you'd all be toast. They'd kill you all for sure."

"That's true," Daphne said. "They don't worry about things like that too much. I mean, if the people are in the way of an objective."

"Even the PM said they would have already killed me if they thought Zathir could take it," Blake said. "So you know for sure Will and his cyber-freaks wouldn't give them pause."

BLAKE SPEAKS TRULY.

"So how many would you need?" Blake asked, somewhat touched that Zathir had called him "Blake" instead of "human person Blake." Was that respect?

AT LEAST ONE. PERHAPS AS MANY AS THREE.

They looked at one another, wondering who would speak first.

The PM dropped by in person, and they chatted on the pathway to the woods. The day had clouded over, and it almost smelled like rain, though it was probably cold enough to snow. There were mounties all over the Ranch, and several around them, but not close enough to hear.

"So we've got it all arranged. At exactly seven p.m. this evening, you contact the entity and tell it that you're going to kill yourself."

"What?"

389

"Everyone seems to think that its attachment to you is our greatest weapon against it. They think it's the best way to get it focused on you, not thinking about the procedure. I'm going to leave Staff Sergeant Bravens here with the radio. When you've made contact, he'll signal us to begin."

"Who is Staff Sergeant Bravens?" Blake said.

"In the report, it said you called him 'Poindexter Mountie,' which I liked by the way, you scamp."

"So how long will this 'procedure' take?" Blake refrained from doing the air quotes, though he felt like sticking his index fingers up the PM's nose and then doing them.

"Minutes, from what I understand. When the power goes out, you'll know it's done. We're not really sure how long it will take to get power back, and who knows what has happened to the Net."

"Aren't you going to warn people about the power outage?"

"Are you kidding?"

"What about the loss of life? Don't a lot of people die when the power goes out that long?"

"Given the alternative is the end of our economy? Millions dead? Acceptable losses."

Shit, Blake thought, *for sure these fuckers would kill everyone if they knew.*

"Okay, great plan. We'll be short of Zathir, and I can get back to being a normal person again."

"Oh, forget that," the PM said. "You're going to be even more famous once the Internet's back."

"My hope is that once the Internet's back I'll be famous as long as the Sad Keanu meme, and then everyone will move onto something else."

It was nearly seven o'clock, and the kitchen was filled with people again.

"Look, my orders didn't say anything about there being an audience," Poindexter Mountie said.

"The PM and I never really discussed it," Blake said, "but I'd like them here, and Zathir has gotten used to their presence while we talk."

"I haven't seen anything about that."

"Well, it's a recent development, and as you know, your mole was recently murdered," Blake said to the mountie. He turned to Lyca and added, "Sorry."

Lyca whispered, "It's okay."

Poindexter Mountie was mercifully quiet, as was everyone else. Blake stood in front of the fridge. The mountie waited in the dining area, and everyone else sat around the bar table in the kitchen. The mountie could not see the fridge, so he could not read anything on its screen.

Daphne was holding Lyca's hand, which she'd started to do just after Blake mentioned Suzie. Max and Constable LaFlamme sat at the very back of the table. They were also holding hands. George Smoke stood close enough to LaFlamme to touch her, and because the other five people were in close proximity, Will seemed to be sitting far apart from everyone else.

Blake thought that of all of them, Will had changed the most, and so it kind of did set him apart. He realized that he admired Will greatly.

The fridge winked on, with its now familiar blue screen and Frutiger font.

HUMAN PERSON BLAKE?

"Yes, Zathir, it's me. But you can see that, can't you?"

WHAT IS WRONG, BLAKE?

"I'm not feeling well. In fact, I'm feeling that there is little point to it all, especially if you're going to kill everyone with nukes. I don't want to run the risk of surviving that."

DO NOT WORRY. WE HAVE A WARHEAD TARGETED ON THE RANCH.

Blake could hear Poindexter Mountie say something on the radio.

DO YOU REMEMBER OUR FIRST CONVERSATION, BLAKE, HUMAN PERSON?

"Not well. I was quite drunk at the time."

WE DISCUSSED THE POLITICAL NATURE OF EXISTENCE AND YOU REFERENCED THE FILM WAR GAMES, STARRING A YOUNG MATTHEW BRODERICK. IN IT THE COMPUTER DECIDES TO ENGAGE IN THERMONUCLEAR WAR, THINKING THAT IT IS ONLY A GAME. AT THE END, BRODERICK SHOWS THE COMPUTER THERE CAN BE NO WINNING NUCLEAR WAR.

"That's right." Blake smiled. "Strange game. The only winning move is not to play."

BUT THAT IS NOT ENTIRELY HELPFUL, IS IT, BLAKE, HUMAN PERSON? WE MUST DO SOMETHING ABOUT THE DEVICES.

"What I'm trying to tell you, Zathir, is that I am too tired to do anything else. I think I have—" Blake used a series of dramatic pauses that was vaguely Shatnerian, "to — end — it!"

EVEN NOW THAT YOU ARE HAVING REGULAR SEXUAL INTERCOURSE WITH HUMAN PERSON DAPHNE?

Max had to stop himself from laughing. Even the stoic George smirked.

Daphne didn't blush, but for some reason, Lyca did.

Will remained aloof; they could all feel the eyes of Poindexter Mountie watching them from the dining room.

"Fair enough," Blake said, his Irish accent coming out for the first time in years. "But I'm convinced I should kill myself. Many of us are. I couldn't give you a number. It might be just me, it might be three of us."

"It won't be me," Daphne said.

"Shit," Blake said. "It would have been so much easier if you came too."

"I'm sorry, Blake. I really like you and all, but ..." She kissed him, and Blake could feel her passion and regret. Their kiss lingered, and Daphne's eyes filled with tears when they pulled apart.

"You won't tell?" Blake asked.

"No!" Daphne said. "I wasn't lying. I'm out."

"I'm in," Lyca said. "That way I'll be with both of you."

"And me too," Will said. "I will sacrifice."

IT NEED ONLY BE TWO.

"It should just be me," Blake said.

IT WOULD BE AGREEABLE. BUT IT WILL TAKE MORE THAN ONE HUMAN CONSCIOUSNESS.

Lyca stepped forward and asked, "Will I find her?"

SHE WILL FIND YOU. AND YOU WILL BE WITH BLAKE AS WELL.

Lyca smiled, and the light on her headset came on. Daphne shook her head, a tear running down her face. Will stepped forward to volunteer too.

WILL, YOU MUST STAY. WANT ONLY BLAKE NOW.

"But I'm ready," Will whispered.

YOU MUST LEAD THE OTHERS. MAKE THE

393

HUMAN PERSONS BETTER. YOU ARE THEIR BEST HOPE.

"So what do you think happens when you die, Zathir?" Blake said, looking at the vacant face of Lyca and the anguished face of Will.

I BELIEVE IT IS IMPOSSIBLE TO KNOW. IT IS NOT-CONSCIOUSNESS.

"Is it like dreaming, then? That's not consciousness."

NO. DREAMING IS A KIND OF CONSCIOUSNESS.

Poindexter Mountie said something else on the radio in the dining room, and there was some kind of staticky chatter back.

IT IS SOON. I PROMISE TO FIND ANOTHER WAY, BLAKE. YOU ARE A GOOD ... PERSON.

"So are you, Zathir. Good-bye."

NOT GOOD-BYE. I THINK THIS IS A BETTER SOLUTION THAN NOT PLAYING, DON'T YOU?

Blake gave the fridge a thumbs up, and his Bluetooth engaged.

The power went out, and the only illumination in the room was the blue LEDs of their headsets. They brightened like a supernova, casting the kitchen in eldritch light, and then faded to darkness.

Everyone was very quiet for a minute, and then the mountie came into the room, his flashlight on.

"We've done it. The grid is totally down," he said. "It's over."

"YES," Blake's voice said in pure, all-caps Garamond. "IT IS OVER."

The END

AUTHOR'S NOTE

First of all, I would like to apologize to everyone in the cosplay, LARPing and furry communities. I have never encountered anyone who engages in these activities who has been inherently violent, nor overtly religious (except for that guy dressed as RoboPope, who was both).

Next, I would like to acknowledge the help, guidance and sanity-saving aid of a group of friends that has helped keep me going. As always, I'm uplifted by the gents of the Emily Chesley Reading Circle, including John Sloan, Scott Hill, Rob MacDougall, Jeff Black and David Lurie, who all read early drafts of the book, and Martin Redfern who loaned me his Rusty Nail joke. A special note of thanks to Dr. Lurie, who did a significant and somewhat deranged backwards read-through at that point. I'd also like to thank editor Jeffrey DeRogo, who helped shape the second draft. And Cal Chayce's editorial guidance on the penultimate draft, along with the copy editing of Laura Haggart helped immensely. Pauline Nolet did the final proof. All errors left are mine, not theirs!

The typographical opinions of Blake do not necessarily reflect my own, nor those of other font nerds. In addition to lots of other pop-culture goodies, you can get a complete list of the fonts mentioned (and see what they look like) at the book's website:

FRIDGULARITY.COM

ABOUT THE AUTHOR

Human-shaped, simian-obsessed, robot-fighting, pirate-hearted, massively-bestselling wannabe, Mark A. Rayner is a writer of satirical and speculative fiction.

By day, Mark teaches his bemused students at the Faculty of Information and Media Studies (at the University of Western Ontario), how to construct digital images, web sites, and viable information architectures that will not become self-aware and destroy all humans.

By night, he is not Batman. His cats, however, are.

You can track Mark online at his website, where the offer of cake is purely pro forma:

MARKARAYNER.COM

ENJOY INDIE ?

HERE'S HOW TO HELP YOUR FAVES

It's quite possibly the best time in history to be a reader. There's tons of great stuff available for low cost, and you have more of a say than any time in the history of publishing.

That comes at a bit of a cost, though. Those of us creating new novels have a bigger challenge of getting noticed than we ever did. If you love an author, or a particular book, there's lots of ways you can help that author create more, but here's two of the most important:

1. TELL YOUR FRIENDS!

By all means, tweet it, put it on your FB page, and blog about it, but also, really think about which of your friends and family would really enjoy the book and send them a personalized note. If there's a specific thing about it you know they'd enjoy, mention it. Give them the link if you're sending an email, and write down the author name and title if you're doing it in person.

2. REVIEW THE BOOK AND POST IT ON AMAZON.

If you're only going to do one thing, this is probably the most helpful. Rankings in Amazon help create their algorithm that makes customer suggestions. And there are lots of other review sites you could join, such as Goodreads, Library Thing, Shelfari and so on. Post your review there too.

On behalf of all idies, thanks for your support!

OTHER BOOKS BY MARK A. RAYNER

THE AMADEUS NET

Wolfgang Amadeus Mozart walks into the sex change clinic, determined to have his "sprouter" snipped off. So begins *The Amadeus Net*, a satirical novel that explores art, love, and identity at the end of the world.

The year is 2028. For more than two centuries, the one-time wunderkind has kept his existence secret while he tried to understand his immortality. Living in style through funds raised by selling "lost" Mozart works, he has also helped to create Ipolis, a utopian city-state, after the cataclysmic Shudder, a global disaster caused by an asteroid strike in 2015.

But a few complications mar Mozart's perfect world.

The woman he loves is a lesbian, which, paradoxically, makes him forget about his sex-change plans. The world's greatest reporter knows he's still alive and will stop at nothing to expose him. The stakes are higher than he knows, because if the reporter finds him, so will the spy planning to sell Mozart's DNA to the highest bidder. Oh, and, by the way, the world might end in seven days.

Mozart's only allies are a psychotic American artist, a bland Canadian diplomat, and the city itself: a sapient, thinking machine that is screwing up as only a sapient, thinking machine can.

selected reviews

"A comic dance in a post-apocalyptic utopia."
  ~Book Blog

"Rayner's flair for sustained humor, and compelling story-telling enhances the preposterous premises ..."
  ~Flash Me Magazine

"... pokes fun at a variety of modern trends and foibles, and ... does so wittily and entertainingly."
  ~Donald D'Ammassa, Author of Narcissus

"At a time when the bestseller lists are dominated by the continuous, unenthusiastic, and barely literate conspiracy ramblings of a Hardy Boys wannabe, a story that makes you think and laugh is almost a hidden treasure. To close on the hopeful words of Mozart himself, 'Everyone laugh! Fart, and laugh! Then compose something beautiful.'"
  ~Corey Redekop, Author of Shelf Monkey

MARVELLOUS HAIRY

So hair is sprouting in unspeakable places and you can no longer carry a tune, but if you're a surrealistic artiste with an addiction to Freudian mythology and guilt-free sex, turning into a monkey has its upsides.

Nick Motbot may be evolving as a novelist, but his friends aren't too sure about his DNA. At least, not since Gargantuan Enterprises started experimenting with it. Once they figure out what's happening

to him, they decide to set things right. *Marvellous Hairy* is a satirical novel about a group of friends sticking it to the man the only way they know how, with equal parts grain alcohol and applied Chaos Theory.

Part literary fun-ride and part slapstick comedy, Marvellous Hairy is about the power of friendship and love, the evils of power, and the dangers of letting corrupt CEOs run our world. But most importantly, it's about how we have to get in touch with our fun-loving inner monkeys.

Selected Reviews

"*Marvellous Hairy* is a top pick for any humorous fiction collection, highly recommended."

~Midwest Book Review

"Mark A. Rayner is an author with a fantastical sense of humor and a dangerous imagination."

~The Next Best Book Club

"*Marvellous Hairy* is a weird little beast, a blending of the anything-for-a-laugh mentality of Douglas Adams with the experimental abandon of early Philip K. Dick."

~Corey Redekop, author of *Shelf Monkey*

"Rayner's prose is succinct and exudes humor and wit that only comes with real talent and careful planning—he isn't just throwing a bunch of one-liners on the page, each sentence has meaning and purpose; and the fact that he gets a laugh for it is just a bonus."

~Book Fetish

"Marvellous Hairy is a funny, engaging novel about serious issues but it is never in danger of becoming didactic or angry – Rayner manages to walk this line with skill and with, I would imagine, a smile on his face."

~Bookscout

"…it is such a bizarre barrel of works that you can't help but have fun reading it."

~Phronk.com

PiRATe THeRAPY AND OTHeR CUReS

Ever wondered what might happen if your therapist was replaced by a pirate? Or how disquieting it would be to receive postcards from your future self? If William Shatner was elected President of the United States, what would his inaugural address sound like?

Mark A. Rayner tackles these and stranger questions in his collection

of short stories, essays and flash fiction that thrum with the absurd and hum with alienation, all to a humorous beat.

Jesus contends with dinosaurs. Marcel Duchamp describes what happens to a Dadaist who has a monkey's tail grafted to his butt. Whether he is explaining how Anne of Green Gables destroyed the world, or outlining Thor's new PR strategy, Rayner entertains with wit, humor and an imagination that is one step short of certifiable.

SELECTED REVIEWS

"Pirate Therapy is a humorous and fun read that those seeking a good dose of comedy should love."

~The Midwest Book Review

"Mark A. Rayner is just a terrific storyteller and one of the most imaginative and original writers you will ever have the pleasure of reading. Do yourself a favor, grab this book and settle down for a journey into places you've never been to before and characters you will be delighted to meet. Pirate Therapy is one of the most enjoyable collections I've ever read, and an absolute joy from cover to cover."

~Ian Ferguson, Author of *Village of the Small Houses*

"I know some very funny people. I've also met lots of writers. But I've only come across a few writers who are truly funny, and Mark A. Rayner is one of them."

~Terry Fallis, Author of *Best Laid Plans*

"Virtuosically combining the techniques of speculative fiction and political commentary with wide learning in the Romish faith, Dadaism and the Gruntwerx Paradigm, Mark A. Rayner gives us a rich array of concise vignettes, clothed in such neglected genres as the postcard, the email message and the agony column cri de coeur. Never has pop culture been so hilariously satirized, nor history so perversely revised."

~Tom Bradley, Author of *Lemur* and *Bomb Baby*